WOLF SPRINGS CHRONICLES

UNLEASHED

WOLF SPRINGS CHRONICLES

UNLEASHED

NANCY HOLDER

&

DEBBIE VIGUIÉ

DELACORTE PRESS

Visit us on the Web! randomhouse.com/teens

Educators and librarians, for a variety of teaching tools, visit us at randomhouse.com/teachers

Library of Congress Cataloging-in-Publication Data
Holder, Nancy.
Unleashed / Nancy Holder and Debbie Viguié. — 1st ed.
p. cm. — (Wolf springs chronicles)
Summary: Orphaned Kat McBride, nearly seventeen, must leave California to live with her grandfather in small-town Arkansas, where she is drawn into a paranormal world of feuding werewolf clans.
ISBN 978-0-385-74098-2 (hc) —ISBN 978-0-375-98979-7 (lib. bdg.) —
ISBN 978-0-375-98346-7 (ebook)
[1. Supernatural—Fiction.   2. High schools—Fiction.   3. Schools—Fiction.
4. Werewolves—Fiction.   5. Moving, Household—Fiction.   6. Orphans—Fiction.
7. Grandfathers—Fiction.   8. Arkansas—Fiction.]   I. Viguié, Debbie.   II. Title.
PZ7.H70326Unl 2011
[Fic]—dc23   20011023301

The text of this book is set in 12-point Tibere TF.
Book design by Angela Carlino

Printed in the United States of America

10 9 8 7 6 5 4 3 2 1

First Edition

❧ ❧

To our readers, bloggers, reviewers, librarians, and booksellers—
thanks so much for running with us.
—Nancy

To my beloved wolf-hybrid, Wolfie—I miss you every day and I
hope you're playing your heart out in puppy heaven.
—Debbie

❧ ❧

Things that love night

Love not such nights as these . . .

—KING LEAR, 3.2.42–43

1

I can fly.

Katelyn Claire McBride was the girl on the flying trapeze. Her sun-streaked blond hair streamed behind her as she soared above the crowd on the Mexican cloud swing. Thick stage makeup concealed her freckles, scarlet smudging her mouth, which she had always thought was too cupid-cutesy. Smoky ash-gray kohl ringed her light blue eyes. The soaring melody of "Alegría" moved through her like blood. Music gave her life. Movement gave her a soul.

She had made it. After years of sweat, blisters, pulled muscles, and sprains, she was finally performing in the Cirque du

Soleil. Far below, in the massive audience, her mother looked on with her dad, their fingers entwined. Their faces shone with pride and maybe just a few hundred watts of suppressed parental fear.

Like all performers, Katelyn was a chameleon. Away from the spotlight, she was a tanned California girl who preferred Indian-print camisoles, jeweled flip-flops, and big sunglasses decorated with flowers. But now she looked like a dramatic flamenco dancer . . . and much older than sixteen. She wore a black beaded leotard trimmed with stiff silver lace. A black lace choker encircled her neck, and in the center, a large red stone carved to look like a rose nestled in silver filigree.

The Mexican cloud swing was Katelyn's specialty, and she pumped her legs back and forth as she sat in the V created by the two long pieces of white braided cotton fibers. A kind of crazy mania worked its way through her as she breathed deeply, preparing herself for her last trick—her death-defying escape from gravity.

I'm the only one here who can fly!

She swung higher, then grabbed the rope dangling from the complicated overhead rigging and, with practiced circular motions of her foot, looped it around her right ankle. The familiar texture of the cotton rubbed against the toughened skin. She looked delicate, but like all dancers and gymnasts, she was made of muscle.

Cool air expanded her lungs as she leaped, arching like a swimmer and grabbing the V as it went taut. Gracefully she held the pose as applause washed over her. Scarlet rose petals showered her from overhead, high in the rigging, and at the crescendo, she defiantly let go. Thrusting back her arms, she raised her chin, ignoring the forbidden camera flashes. Fearless. Of course she was.

Yet gasps changed to screams as she plummeted down, down, headfirst, air rushing past. In that split second, her joy flashed into panic.

The net's gone!

The ground rushed up and she flailed wildly.

I'm going to die!

Then the floor split open. From the deep, jagged fissure, flames shot up, straight at her. The heat slapped her face as she kept falling, straight into hell—

"Katie, Katie, oh, my God, wake up!" her mother shouted into her ear.

Katelyn's eyes flew open and just as quickly squeezed shut. Coughing, she opened them again. Half-smothered in smoke, she was lying on the sofa in the TV room, and her right arm was slung over her mom's wiry shoulder. The Art Deco floor lamp behind the sofa tumbled light over the rolling layers of smoke. The feet of the sofa rattled like a machine gun against the hardwood floor; the plaster ceiling was breaking off in chunks. Her mom was wearing her old Japanese bathrobe— nothing else.

"Earthquake," Katelyn slurred. Her gymnastics coach had given her something to take for the swelling and pain after she had twisted her ankle in practice, and it had knocked her out.

"*Alors, vite!*" Her mom was losing it, screaming at her in French to hurry. She yanked on Katelyn's arm, then draped her across her back like a firefighter and began to straighten her legs. Katelyn slid off, grabbing her mother's wrist, trying to fan the smoke away as she doubled over, coughing.

Clinging to each other, the two staggered through the acrid haze. Katelyn knew she was holding her mother back. She was slow—still not entirely awake because of the painkiller—and incredibly dizzy. She stepped on something hot, searing her instep, one of the few places on her feet not protected by calluses. The room shook and swayed. The lamp fell over, throwing light against the portraits of her mother, the famed ballerina Giselle Chevalier, as they jittered against the cracking walls and crashed to the floor.

"Get under the doorjamb!" her mom yelled.

Katelyn was so disoriented that she couldn't remember the layout of the living room. For a moment she froze, foggy and confused. Her knees buckled and her mother clung to her, keeping her from collapsing completely.

The room was exploding around them. Katelyn fought hard to make herself move, to wake up. Her lungs were burning.

The lights went out. Then her mother moaned and let go of Katelyn's hand.

"Mom?"

Katelyn swayed, reaching out into the darkness for her mother and stumbling forward. Her toes collided with something soft. Her mother's face. Then something hard: a huge chunk of plaster, on top of her mother's head.

Katelyn dropped to the floor and threw herself over her mother's still form.

"Mom!"

Her mother groaned. "My darling, run," she managed to say.

Then the floor opened up.

And Giselle Chevalier was gone.

- ⊷ ⊷ -

Two weeks later Katelyn was on a very small jet and swathed in black. Black leotard top, black wrap sweater, jeans, and riding boots that were a little too snug around the calves. She wasn't wearing makeup and the black washed her out. She looked how she felt—drained and half dead. It was better than shrieking with grief—or having another nightmare. She counted off the last three: a repeat of falling to her death in the Cirque du Soleil; dancing the Black Swan in *Swan Lake* as the roof of the theater crashed down on top of her; and bursting into flames as she carried the Olympic torch for the USA gymnastics team. Her best friend, Kimi Brandao, told her it was survivor's guilt and to get over it—Giselle Chevalier would have been glad her daughter survived . . . even if she herself had not.

Blinking back tears, Katelyn hunched her aching shoulders. She was trapped up against the window. Unfortunately, the purple overnight bag containing her iPhone, which Kimi had helped her load with music for the journey, was stuffed into the overhead compartment three rows away.

She had figured she could get it once they were airborne, but then the guy on the aisle had made the woman next to her straddle him in an effort to escape the row and use the restroom. Katelyn had decided to stay put. She wasn't about to

⊰ 5 ⊱

straddle anyone. So she sat and tried very hard to ignore the man and woman sitting next to her.

"Jack Bronson is a genius," the man was saying to the woman, who grimaced politely at him as she clutched her e-reader with her French-manicured nails. Everything about her body language screamed that she wanted him to shut up. "I'm going to his seminar. Actually, it's more like a retreat. For executives."

The man puffed up a little. He had thin, mousy brown hair and he was a bit on the jowly side. He didn't look like he was from Los Angeles. In L.A. executives worked out. A lot of them even got plastic surgery. Image was more than half the battle.

"You need to embrace the wolf side of your nature." He flushed slightly, as if he just realized he'd said something risqué. "I mean, to achieve your goals."

A pause. "What is the wolf side?" the woman asked with a slight Southern accent, and Katelyn couldn't tell if she was curious or just trying to humor a stranger.

"It's the side that knows no fear, that sees what it wants and goes after it." He leaned toward her with a lecherous smile. Blech. "Committing completely to the goal."

Blech to the nth degree.

Maybe that was why Katelyn was stuck on the airplane. She hadn't fully committed to the goal of emancipation. Ultimately her grandfather had refused to let her stay in Los Angeles—to try to live her life on her own. She had just started her senior year and would be seventeen in one day shy of six weeks, but that hadn't mattered to him. He said sixteen was too young. Blindsided with grief, she had caved without protest, even though Kimi had begged her to stay. Kimi's mom, an attorney, had offered to help her petition the court for emancipation—or at the very least, let her spend senior year living with them.

Her grandfather had refused to consider it and Kimi had been supremely frustrated when Katelyn had "gone robot." Hadn't fought, hadn't argued, had simply surrendered. Mordecai McBride had ordered her to pack and arranged a one-way ticket from Los Angeles International Airport to Northwest Arkansas Regional Airport, a teeny tiny airstrip located in the bustling burb of Bentonville, home to maybe twenty-five thousand people. He lived about ninety minutes away from the airport, alone, in the woods. The closest town was Wolf Springs, and at Wolf Springs High, there were 549 students. Soon there would be 550, even.

"You'll shrivel up there, you will," Kimi had moaned. "You *have* to speak up! Tell him you are *not not not* coming."

But how could Katelyn speak up for herself when she spontaneously broke into tears over the smallest things?

In fourteen months she would be eighteen. Then her grandfather couldn't say anything if she moved back to Los Angeles to resume her life, her *real* life. And if she got accepted to a California college? He wouldn't dare stop her from going. So maybe she'd have to stay only eleven months. Some colleges started in August.

But if I have to go a year without serious training, I'll never do anything great. And I want to have a big, amazing life.

The thought flooded her with anger and even deeper grief. It wasn't enough that both her parents were dead. Her dreams—the good ones—were dying, too.

Reflexively, she gripped the stuffed bear Kimi had shoved

into her hands at the security checkpoint at LAX. Soft and white, the bear was dressed like a gymnast in a sparkly aqua leotard and matching leg warmers. When she pressed the embroidered heart on its chest, it said, "Kimi misses Katie," in her friend's voice. She'd tried plugging her earbuds into it so she could listen on the plane without embarrassing herself, but no luck.

"And so all y'all are going into the forest, to show y'all's wolf side," the woman was saying to the man. For a few blessed seconds, Katelyn had managed to tune them out.

"Just outside Wolf Springs, at the old hot springs resort? That's where it's happening," the man affirmed. "It starts tomorrow. Tonight . . . I'm free."

Katelyn rolled her eyes and leaned her head against the Plexiglas window. She didn't want to watch the *so*-not-a-wolf making goo-goo eyes at an uninterested woman. Then she remembered that she'd been dreaming that her dad was alive on the night of the earthquake. He used to flutter his lashes at her mom to tease-flirt with her. Her mother had always laughed hard. Now they were both gone.

And if I hadn't taken that pill, none of this would be happening.

The tears welled up and flowed and she bit her lower lip to keep herself from sobbing. She pushed the bear under her chin and thought of Kimi.

"Oh, the black gums are startin' to change," someone said in the row behind her. "Look at all the red leaves."

"How pretty," another voice replied. "Fall's comin' early."

Katelyn shut her eyes. She didn't want to see anything

pretty, least of all in Arkansas. Kimi had started calling it Banjo Land.

"Football tomorrow night. Tigers have already got it sewed up."

"That's right."

She wondered if the Tigers were playing the Timberwolves. Despite being small, Wolf Springs managed to field a football team. She'd lived her entire life in Santa Monica. High school football wasn't on most people's radar there. Certainly not hers.

Actually, there wasn't much about high school that held her interest. Her mind had been on other things—gymnastics, dance. The last thing she and her mother had done together was attend a Cirque du Soleil performance—*Alegría*. Katelyn had been enchanted, telling her mom that she could combine her dance and gymnastics skills if she joined a troupe like Cirque du Soleil—or even Cirque itself.

"Maybe," her mom had replied before changing the subject.

Katelyn had never had a chance to ask her if "maybe" meant she thought it was a bad idea. Or if she thought Katelyn wouldn't make it. Or if, as Kimi insisted, her mom couldn't bear the idea of Katelyn leaving home to do anything at all.

During her career as a reigning prima ballerina, Giselle Chevalier had been called the Iron Butterfly, because both her will and her stamina were unmatched. But after Sean, Katelyn's dad, had been murdered, her mother had become fragile and frightened. Katelyn had tried to make her mom's life as easy as possible, teaching the little kids' classes at the studio, making dinner . . . and trying to convince herself she was okay with becoming a classical ballet dancer, too. Katelyn thought the ballet world was old-fashioned and confining, but she'd never told Giselle that. It had been hard enough to get her mom to let her take gymnastics classes.

"What if you hurt yourself?" Giselle had asked her over and over. "What would happen to your dance career?"

Katelyn didn't know how to respond. She only knew gymnastics did something for her that ballet didn't. She'd been dreading the day she would have to "declare a major," as Kimi used to put it. Just *say* what she wanted to do with her life. Giselle had told Katelyn professional dancers had no time for college. But Katelyn and Kimi had spent hours poring over course catalogs. Lots of colleges and universities had dance departments.

"Those are not for *real* dancers," her mother had retorted. "Don't you care about your career?"

Katelyn didn't know. She did know that she cared about her mom. And she cared about being friends with Kimi, who had her own dreams. And yes, maybe Alec, who had agreed to help her learn the flying trapeze at their gym. To be her catcher as she let go and flew. *No Alec for you*, she thought. So there was no point in rehearsing inviting him to prom anymore, though it was hard to stop. It had become a habit.

Hey, so, Tarzan, how'd you like to catch me on the dance floor?

A week and a half before the earthquake, Katelyn had started senior year at "Samohi"—Santa Monica High School. Tons of stars and film people had gone there; Zac Efron had filmed a movie there. Kids there dreamed big, and "big" could really happen. Kimi had no doubt that they would catch the wave of magical lives. " 'Cuz we've got the mojo," Kimi would crow as they strolled down the street in their sparkly flip-flops and shades.

On the plane, sighing, Katelyn tried to smile at the memories, but her heart filled with fresh sorrow. Kimi would need someone new to hang out with, go shopping for her prom dress with, all that. Katelyn wanted that for her, even though the thought of being replaced made her free-fall inside. Kimi was her last link to home, and family.

Turbulence made the plane stutter and she sucked in her breath. Clinging to the armrests, she struggled not to see the ground thousands of feet below her. Fall here, and no net on earth could save her. The pilot announced their descent; she was so afraid she couldn't keep her eyes open. She wanted to scream. Her heart thundered.

When the tires finally bumped on the tarmac, she opened her eyes and stared out at . . . very little. A tiny airport. Minuscule. Beyond, an open field. Banjo Land.

There had been an equipment failure of their aircraft, and their departure from LAX had been delayed by three hours. Instead of arriving in Arkansas around two-thirty, the plane got there at five-thirty, and shadows were beginning to lengthen. Back home, the sun would still be blazing against the brilliant blue Pacific Ocean for hours and hours.

Everyone got up. The Wolf Man was still going on about his retreat and the ebook lady was nodding. Inching along, Katelyn reached up toward the compartment where she'd stowed her bag. Since she was only five three, it was a stretch. A tall guy wearing a University of Arkansas T-shirt hoisted it down to her and she thanked him. He gave her a look—her face was probably swollen from crying—and she ducked her head.

She dug into the bag and found her iPhone. She turned it on. A text had come in from Kimi: *CM WHEN U LAND. CM* meant "call me." She flipped over to her phone function. No service. She tried to text anyway. It wouldn't go through.

"Are you kidding me?" she murmured.

Then she walked down a metal gangway pushed up to the airplane door. The air was boiling hot and muggy, and her ponytail drooped like a wet paintbrush. She followed the other passengers across the tarmac, eventually making her way into the terminal, and looked around for her grandfather. But no familiar face greeted her.

He knew she was coming that day, right? Did he realize that her flight hadn't been canceled, only delayed?

She went with the others to the baggage claim. There was one carousel. Just one. A dozen black bags circled like crows, decorated with bows and colorful pieces of duct tape so their owners could tell them apart. A woman in a Tinker Bell T-shirt grabbed a suitcase tagged with a smiling Mickey Mouse. Most of these people had likely gone to California on vacation. They'd gone to see the ocean, Hollywood, and the theme parks.

Still no grandfather.

So where was he? Had he given up and gone back to the mountains?

I don't want to be here.

Her vision blurred as she stood holding her purple overnight bag. She tightly squeezed the bear, damp and stained dark with fresh tears.

Then she saw the Wolf Man with his prey, the polite Southern lady with the e-reader. They were standing strangely close together while they scanned the conveyer belt for their stuff, and the woman was laughing at something he was saying. Were they hooking up? Katelyn was incredulous.

Her father's weathered leather suitcase appeared on the carousel. The light caught the little brass rectangle with his initials—SKM—Sean Kevin McBride. She adjusted her overnight bag on her shoulder and tucked the bear under her arm, preparing to make her move. When the suitcase circled within reach, she grabbed it, grunting as she heaved with all her strength to swing it free.

Once she had it clear, she turned around, and jerked, hard.

She hadn't seen him in almost five years, but Mordecai McBride hadn't changed at all. He was over six feet tall, with pale green eyes, close-cut gray hair, and deep frown lines that made his mouth sag. Inside a leather jacket, his shoulders looked broad and a blue chambray shirt stretched across a barrel chest. He was sixty, but he didn't look it.

Her throat tightened. She was mad at him. He was her only living relative—or at least, the only one she knew—and he hadn't even come to her mother's funeral.

Their eyes met. Something began to show in his face; then it hardened and became expressionless. He nodded and took the suitcase from her hand, swinging it easily from two fingers as he turned and walked away.

She hurried to keep up with him as he strode through the

crowd. Around her she could see relatives and friends greeting each other, smiling and hugging. Her grandfather hadn't even spoken to her. She clutched the bear even tighter.

The McBride airport limo service was a battered old truck. Parts of it were still red, but the elements had worn the paint away, revealing sections of gunmetal gray and rust. There wasn't room in the cab for her large suitcase, so her grandfather heaved it into the truck bed and began covering it with a tarp. Katelyn climbed into the passenger seat and, pressing the bear against her chest, arranged the overnight bag on her lap and then tried to text Kimi again.

No service.

When her grandfather got behind the wheel, he glanced at the bear, then at her. He probably thought she was too old to have stuffed animals, but she couldn't care less what he thought.

He started the engine. Then he sat there for a moment. She tensed, waiting.

"Things go okay with your mama's . . . arrangements?"

They were the first words he had spoken to her, and they stunned her. She wanted him to ask her how she was, how the flight had been, tell her what the weather had been like that day. Something to ease them both into a conversation. But she also wanted him to care about her mother and acknowledge that he hadn't come to her funeral.

"Yes. She was buried six days ago," she managed to reply. Then, without thinking, she added, "You should have been there."

There was a beat. He backed out of the parking space and turned on the windshield wipers as drizzle dotted the glass.

Clouds rushed across the darkening sky. Treetops bent over the truck, red painting the leaves like flames.

"Couldn't get away."

"You're retired," she said accusingly before she could stop herself.

He glanced at her, then back at the road. "Just 'cuz I'm retired doesn't mean I don't have responsibilities."

It hurt. *But I'm your responsibility,* she wanted to say.

He turned his head again. "I had to get things ready for you."

Things? What things? Was he implying that she was inconveniencing him? If he hadn't wanted her to come, she could have stayed in L.A. If he didn't care about her, why had he made her come live with him? Just to make her life miserable?

They drove past a huge warehouse, brown weedy fields, and some apartments and houses that didn't look much different from sections of L.A. She spotted a fast-food place called Las Fajitas and thought about asking him to stop. She hadn't been able to eat anything on the plane, and she was lightheaded with hunger, if not actually hungry. But to make the request, she would have to speak to him again, and she wasn't sure she could force herself to do it. *How* was she going to make it through an entire school year?

She turned back to look at him. His jaw was clenched and his hands gripped the steering wheel so hard his knuckles looked like they were going to pop through the skin.

He said tersely, "I want to be home before dark."

Why? she wanted to ask him. *What does it matter?* Maybe the headlights on his old truck didn't work.

She looked back through the passenger-side window and

caught a flash of lightning; then the sky opened up and rain poured down. The sky shrank into a thick layer of gray clouds, and the truck scuttled beneath it like an insect, scooting past open fields bordered by batches of leafy trees and ferns. She saw a broken-down mobile home, several huge piles of split logs, and a run-down shack with a hand-lettered sign in the window that read LIQUOR BAIT. Pools of water sparkled with lightning.

She debated asking him if it would be all right if she listened to her music. But since they weren't speaking, it didn't seem to matter. She popped in her earbuds and was soon listening to an old Lady Gaga song Kimi had insisted on adding to her mix. It was too happy and catchy, but she let it play anyway.

They reached a metal bridge. Churning water rushed beneath it, as gray as the clouds. A river. She remembered that Arkansas was landlocked, and for a moment a deep panic shuddered through her as she imagined herself on a map of the United States, trapped inside the box of land. She had always lived near the ocean and she had always found comfort in staring out to sea, meditating on her future. Many times her thoughts would turn to her father's murder. Gunned down, no witnesses, nothing from forensics. The homicide of Sean McBride was an ice-cold case, but he had worked for the district attorney's office, and everybody took his death personally.

The first thing she saw on the other side of the bridge after they crossed it was a white wooden sign with DANGER written on it in black letters. There was something else she couldn't make out; the writing was cracked, peeling with age. A red splotch in the lower right looked a little like a bear paw, but it was hard to tell in the rain.

She pulled out one of her earbuds and turned to her grandfather. She was going to ask if there were any bears in the area, but before she could, a strange, low moan made her jump. It came from outside the truck—or so she guessed—and maybe it was a cow; only it wasn't so much a moan as an echo of a moan. Or maybe a howl. It sounded . . . sad. For a weird moment she thought maybe she'd made the sound herself.

"What was that?" she asked. "A bear?"

"I didn't hear anything."

The moan sounded again, low and sad and maybe desperate. *Like how I feel.*

"There," she said. "You must have heard that. What is it?"

The windshield wipers kept time in the silence. Finally he said, "The wind."

There were no more moans, but just the same, Katelyn was unnerved by her grandfather's response. There was no way that was just the wind. She put her earbuds back in and turned to stare out the window again.

Waving in the storm, the trees *were* pretty, their scarlet branches flickering like flames. Raindrops on the windshield acted like magnifying glasses, creating dollops of color. As they drove, the trees began to press in thick and close on either side of the road, branches arching overhead. The road was steep, and her head began to bob as she dozed.

Suddenly she felt eyes on her. She shifted in her seat to find her grandfather staring straight at her. He said something, but she couldn't make it out.

She took out her left earbud. "I'm sorry," she said. "I didn't understand that."

He frowned. "And I don't understand you at all."

Startled, she took out the other earbud but let the music keep playing.

"Me? What's there to understand?"

"Miz Brandao said you wanted me to find a gym for you."

"And?" she asked quickly, brightening at the ray of hope. "Did you find one?"

"There's a Y. You'd have to drive."

She didn't know why driving would be a problem. She was from Southern California. Everyone drove everywhere.

"And they have gymnastics?" she asked carefully, trying to figure out what he was saying.

He nodded slowly. "Mostly for little kids. Your mama said that you'd given up ballet for the monkey bars."

Her stomach contracted, as if he had punched her in the gut. When had he spoken to her mother? And was he making fun of her? *Monkey bars?*

"I still take ballet classes," she said. "Didn't Ms. Brandao also mention I'll need a dance studio to go to?"

"Found a yoga place," he said. "And the Y's got tai chi."

Katelyn suddenly realized he had no idea what her life in California was like. *Had been* like. Ballet was not yoga or tai chi. What *had* she been thinking, agreeing to come live with this old man and his beat-up truck and his *cabin*? Was she insane?

Kimi was right. She shouldn't have caved so fast. She should have made some demands, set some conditions.

"Look," she said, "I know this isn't the big city. I—I *know* . . ."

But what did she know? This man was a stranger. He didn't

know what she was like. How could he? He'd never come to visit. Never called except at Christmas, and now her mother was *dead* and he hadn't even bothered to fly out for her funeral.

"I need ballet," she said fiercely. "And gymnastics, but not for little kids. I'm in training for—for a life as a performer. And if I don't have a place to work out, I might as well give up now."

He just looked at her. She could nearly hear his thoughts: *Okay. Give up.*

She stared back at him, speechless. She wanted to cry or scream or throw herself from the car. But of course none of those things would prove to anyone that she was old enough to take care of herself.

She remembered the last time they had come to visit her grandfather, how hard she had giggled at thinking of her dad growing up in the middle of nowhere. He had still been alive and it had been their last family trip.

Hot tears stung her eyes as lightning flashed overhead, illuminating the gloom of the woods. She clenched her hands, reliving how hard it had been after her dad had died. She'd gotten through because she'd had her mom and they'd held each other as they cried and kept each other strong each time the police told them there was nothing new.

"You're a senior this year, right?"

Without looking back at him, Katelyn brushed away her tears. "Yeah. School started four weeks ago. I'm going to miss everything. Prom. Graduation. Everything."

"We've got those things here."

Was he actually trying to make her feel better?

"It's not the same," she said, stricken.

"Sure it is. I figure high school, graduating, all that, are the same anywhere you go. Lots of kids scared of their own shadows struggling to survive. It's just like the mountains. Just like life."

She had forgotten that side of him. Blunt and practical, a hunter who lived like Daniel Boone. It was hard to believe that for years he'd been a philosophy professor. Her dad had never had much use for philosophy, and said philosophers were all people with too much time on their hands if they could waste it debating the existence of good and evil or the meaning of life.

Sean McBride had faced good and evil every day. He had spent his life prosecuting criminals until the day one of them killed him. She didn't care what anyone said; evil was real. She knew what it could do.

Did her grandfather really know how scared she was?

"Lots of . . . professional kids in L.A. don't even go to school," she said. "They don't have time. Because they have to focus."

He went silent again. Then he said slowly, "That's the most idiotic thing I've ever heard in my entire life."

"No, it's not." She could hear the desperation in her voice. She felt like she was losing everything. It had been a mistake to come. "It's the life of an artist. Mom—"

"Got married," he interjected. "To a man with a *real* job. How long do ballerinas last? Midthirties?"

"She opened the dance studio," Katelyn shot back.

"And *that* was a big success." He blinked and pulled in his chin, as if he'd surprised himself, and turned his attention back to the road.

She frowned. What did he mean by that? The studio had done okay. Or so her mom had always told her. Did her grandfather know otherwise?

"Mom loved being a dancer," she insisted.

"It's from living out there in La-La Land," he went on, as if he hadn't heard what she'd said. "Kids thinking they're going to become movie stars. Like winning the lottery. The average person has a better chance of being struck by lightning—"

"I'm *from* L.A." Her voice was icy. "And I have friends who *are* making it." That wasn't exactly true, but he didn't need to know that. "Kids *do* become movie stars."

"One in a million, and the rest park cars. You need some normalcy." He frowned, sighed, and said again, "Normalcy."

She realized she'd miscalculated how to approach him. Rather than impress on him how vital it was for her to stick to her game plan, she had convinced him that she needed to give it up. "You have to let me go home," she begged.

Thunder rumbled, and he stopped the truck abruptly. The rain hit the windshield like pellets. The tinny music from her earbuds squawked merrily away.

"Katelyn," he said, "you *are* home."

2

This can't be happening, Katelyn thought. Her grandfather handed her the keys to his front door, then went to retrieve her suitcase. The sun had begun to set, and she barely took notice of the illuminated exterior of the rustic two-story log cabin as she dashed from the truck up a staircase made of planks, to a door with an oval of frosted glass. Her hands were shaking too badly to insert the key into the lock. She was blind with tears.

His footfalls echoed on the wood as he came up behind her, took the key ring from her, and opened the door. He stepped back to let her in first. Her throat was so tight she was afraid she was going to choke.

She crossed the threshold, and her lips parted in shock. Interspersed with oil paintings of mountain landscapes, animal heads hung on the varnished wood walls. Deer, elk. Stuffed ducks with green-and-chocolate-brown plumage, creatures that had been beautiful in life, were displayed as trophies along the top of a polished wooden cabinet. Katelyn thought she might throw up. She was a vegetarian and she and Kimi had been active in animal rights causes. To her, her grandfather's living room was a chamber of horrors. Why hadn't she remembered it from when she was little?

"Let me show you around," he said.

"My room," she managed to say. "I just want to lie down."

He shrugged. "Okay. Follow me."

On the right side of the modest-sized living area, a steep wooden staircase passed more heads, a rifle on a rack, and what appeared to be a stained-glass window. Her grandfather carried her suitcase while she wrapped her arms around her stuffed bear and eased the purple overnight bag onto her shoulder again. She hated climbing the stairs so close to the blank, staring glass eyes and averted her gaze to the window. The stained-glass window was a red-and-white shield with a yellow rose in the center of a trio of fish. Beneath it in black letters was their name, MCBRIDE. Lightning flashed behind it, giving the red the appearance of blood.

He reached the landing and turned right, moving down a short corridor featuring one more deer head and small wall sconces that looked like old-fashioned gas lights. A wooden door to her left was ajar, and the light from the hall revealed a bathroom sink. Then he pushed on the door at the end of the hall, and it opened.

The wall sloped, and there was a small skylight positioned above a double bed covered with a burgundy-and-gray plaid blanket. A carved square headboard held two brass pots of ivy. On a nightstand was an antique lamp of cranberry-colored glass. There was a dresser with a circular mirror. On it was a bottle of furniture polish and a rag. She smelled the lemony odor of the polish and, beneath that, dust. Maybe he'd spent the past several days cleaning, instead of coming to her mother's funeral, to make her feel at home. But it wasn't like her old room at all. The room that had been destroyed by fire.

"Thanks," she said stiffly.

He set down her suitcase and crossed to the bottle of wood polish and the rag. He picked them up. "You must be hungry."

"I'm not. Really. I'm just tired." She didn't look at him but kept her gaze firmly trained on a braided rag rug on the wooden floor.

When the door clicked shut, she realized he'd left the room. Wearily she sank onto the bed, stretching herself forward on her stomach. She brought her fists underneath her chin and burst into sobs. Then she bit down on her knuckle to force herself to stop. The last thing she wanted was for him to come back in and investigate.

Thunder rumbled; rain fell on her skylight, then stopped. Finally she quieted. She pulled out her phone to call Kimi. No service. Then there must be a landline somewhere. Most people had a phone in their kitchen.

She got back up and went into the hall. As she reached the top of the stairs, she smelled smoke. She gasped and took the steps at a run. She was just about to scream when she spotted a stone fireplace on the opposite side of the room, a fire blazing away in the hearth. Instead of looking cozy, though, it sent a wave of fear crashing over her, as strong and real as the ocean. She almost ran back up the stairs.

It's okay. It's normal.

"Normal" was her new most hated word.

She edged along the wall, trying not to see the animal heads, and found the entrance to the kitchen. She flicked on the overhead light, revealing a run-down, but clean-looking, kitchen. The dark green paint on a row of cabinets was peeling away, and the countertops were an ugly-white speckled Formica. The front of his ancient white refrigerator was bare except for a calendar with a wildlife scene and writing in just one square. That day. *Katelyn* was all it said.

She was thirsty and opened the fridge, looking for a water pitcher or water bottles. There was very little inside except for a six-pack of beer, an open loaf of white bread, and a small bundle wrapped in butcher paper. Blood was seeping through the paper.

"Gross," she muttered, and slammed the door. She took a few steps backward, then ran her hand through her hair and looked around for a wall phone. Finding nothing, she started opening drawers. Notepads and pens from realtors, a package of rubber bands, utensils. A dog leash.

She picked up the leash and vaguely remembered a dog from her visit there as a kid. Then she heard a light scratching on the back door, which was made of wood. Maybe it was the dog.

With the leash in her hand, she cracked open the door. The kitchen light spilled onto a wide wooden porch that wrapped around the back of the house. Moonlight cast silver spangles on huge maples with dripping branches. The smells of wet earth and wood smoke, so different from the ocean, filled the air as she walked three steps off the porch, onto flat rocks arranged in a path—stepping stones.

The broad green limbs of the tree directly in front of her rustled. Cocking her head, she toyed with the leash but stayed where she was.

"Doggie?" she called softly.

The back door slammed open against the wall, and she nearly leaped out of her skin. Whirling around, she saw her grandfather, a rifle at his side. Her eyes widened and she stumbled backward, toward the tree.

"Katelyn!" he shouted. "Get in here *now*!"

She lifted her chin and showed him the leash. "I was just looking for your dog—"

"I don't have a dog." He looked past her to the trees. "Anymore."

"Hello?" a male voice called from the front of the house. "Is this a bad time?"

Katelyn jumped, startled. Then she heaved a sigh of frustration. She didn't want to have to be social. All she wanted was a drink of water and a working phone.

"We have company," he said. Then, more softly, "Please. Come inside. It's not safe out here."

Not safe? Two feet from the house, and him with a gun? It frightened her to know there were loaded weapons in his house.

"Grandfather, Grandpa," she said, trying out names to call him. "I don't want company. I want to call my best friend. Do you have a phone?"

"Hello?" the voice called again. "Dr. McBride?"

"Be right there," her grandfather replied in a loud voice.

She stepped up onto the porch and he relaxed slightly.

"When you were little, you called me Extra Daddy." Her grandfather smiled very faintly. "You didn't understand what a grandfather was. So you thought I was an extra daddy. Actually, you pronounced it 'Eee-di-di.' "

She didn't remember that. "I'll call you Ed," she announced, deciding that the abbreviation for Extra Daddy was about what she could handle.

"Yes, ma'am." He tugged on an imaginary hat. "Now, Arkansas is the South, and we got a thing called Southern hospitality. And we have a guest."

She huffed. "So if I say hi, then can I call Kimi?"

"Then you can call Kimi."

They walked back into the kitchen, where she wiped the soles of her boots on a faded blue mat that had seen better days. She quickly shut and locked the door. Then she walked with her grandfather into the living room. The front door was open, but the porch light was off, and someone tall was standing on the porch, silhouetted by the moonlight.

Katelyn's grandfather flicked a switch by the door and the porch light came on. The figure beneath its bluish glare was a guy. A cute guy, actually, with closely trimmed dark brown hair and strangely colored eyes, maybe green—it was hard to say—but they were very light against his cocoa-colored skin. They were almond-shaped, and his cheekbones were high, giving him hollows in his cheeks. He had a square jaw and a nice, wide mouth. The best word for him was "exotic."

He was wearing a long-sleeved black T-shirt with the sleeves pushed up to his forearms, jeans, and scuffed cowboy boots caked with mud. A leather braid encircled his left wrist, and words were stamped on it. She couldn't make out the letters. She didn't want to stare, so she didn't look very hard.

But it was difficult not to.

He slung his thumbs in the pockets of his jeans and smiled at her. It was riveting. There was something about him that made her tingle. Warmth. Charm.

"Hey, Katelyn." His accent was softer than Ed's. She found herself smiling back, even though a minute earlier nothing on earth would have made her smile.

"Trick," Ed said in greeting. Was his name Trick, or was he playing a trick?

"You know the rules, Dr. M.," he said. "You have to invite me in."

"You have to be invited *in?*" Katelyn asked. "So, what? Are you a vampire?" Her question sounded more sarcastic than she meant it to, and she reddened.

The guy chuckled—and remained where he was.

"Don't be a fool, son," Ed said, gesturing for the guy to come into the house. But the guy shook his head.

"Make it official."

"Come in, *now*." Though his words were similar to the ones he'd used with Katelyn, his tone was anything but. Teasing, a bit arch. Clearly, these two were friends. Was this some weird game they played? She didn't know what to make of it.

"Thank you, sir." The guy reached down and pulled off his cowboy boots, revealing fresh white socks. Katelyn didn't know why, but the sight of his stockinged feet embarrassed her a little, like seeing him in his boxers or something.

The guy crossed the threshold, and she saw that his eyes were indeed very green, like the shallows of a lagoon. *Come on in*, they seemed to say. *The water is fine.*

There was dark stubble on his cheeks and around his mouth. A quick glance at his leather wristband revealed a few letters: *R.I.P.* She was intrigued. Had someone close to him died?

"You missed supper," Ed told him as he led the way toward the fireplace. Two overstuffed leather chairs sat in front of a coffee table littered with hunting magazines. As the heat from the fire penetrated her bones, Katelyn stiffened, feeling ridiculous, but unable to stop the alarm bells from clanging in her head. "Because we didn't have any."

"Didn't cook the bird?" the guy asked. "It'll spoil."

"Wait," Katelyn said. "Is your name really Trick?"

The guy paused as they reached the chairs, gesturing for her to sit. Katelyn remained standing. "Actually, it's Vladimir, but no one has called me that in forever." He grinned at her. "Very few people around here have a death wish."

Ed snorted. "Tough guy. That's the sort of talk landed you in hot water."

Trick shook his head, looking suddenly serious. "*Lies* landed me in hot water."

"If you had a lick of sense, you'd stick with your own kind and leave them boys alone."

Katelyn's eyes widened. *His own kind?* It was obvious Trick wasn't completely Caucasian. Could that be what her grandfather was referring to? Was Ed a racist?

"I've got a six-pack of . . . soda," Ed announced. "Might have a box of crackers."

He left the room before anyone could answer. Trick remained, though he didn't sit. Katelyn kept standing as well. They were way too close to the fire for her comfort, and she was dying of embarrassment from what Ed had just said to Trick. Or *possibly* said. Maybe Ed meant something else entirely. Trick seemed unfazed. She wanted to say something, apologize for Ed if need be, but she was the newcomer here, and she really didn't know what was going on.

A log in the fireplace snapped and sparks showered down. It was the first fire she'd encountered since the quake, and she could feel her anxiety building into what might become a panic attack. She'd never had one, but her mom had after Katelyn's dad had been killed. Katelyn wanted to race out of the room. Yet if she did anything like that, it would serve as more "proof" that she needed her grandfather's version of normal.

Trying to look casual, she wrapped her arms around herself and sauntered away from the fire—and from him. Her nerves and the wood smoke were making her sick.

"So, you're the granddaughter," Trick said, giving her a slow, lazy once-over that made her flush to the roots of her hair. Kimi had been a huge flirt, which made Katelyn a flirt by association. So she was used to appraising looks. But this guy made it seem too intimate, like it meant more than it was supposed to.

"I guess," she said reluctantly. She didn't want to be related to Ed.

"Paternity test results not back yet?" He grinned lopsidedly. Then he grew very serious, lowering his head. "I'm sorry about your mother."

It was more than Ed had offered. Sympathy from a complete stranger, and none from her grandfather. She'd almost forgotten about that.

"Thanks." Her throat tightened. Afraid she was going to cry, she turned her back, pretending to stare at an oil painting, this one of mountains, trees, and a waterfall. Her gaze fell on the artist's signature. *M.M.* Mordecai McBride?

"Do you and my grandfather usually drink beer together?" she asked.

"I'm underage," he said, dodging. "Soda sounds ducky."

Ducky?

He came up beside her. She felt his body heat and smelled rainwater and soap. Droplets of rain clung to his long eyelashes. Part of her was planning her conversation with Kimi, looking for words to describe him. Interesting? Weird? Hot?

"My last name's Sokolov," he said. "Russian."

To go with the Vladimir. She was mildly surprised that he wasn't Native American or something. "Are you from Russia?"

"Nope." He sounded amused. "I'm from Wolf Springs."

Now she was afraid she sounded as close-minded as Ed. "What year are you in?" Maybe he didn't even go to high school. He looked older than seventeen or eighteen.

"Senior, like you. This year's gonna take forever. I cannot wait to graduate."

"Same here," she said, feeling herself thaw a little. He had a great smile.

He touched his forehead, and it took her a second to realize he was reflexively pushing back phantom tendrils of hair. The buzz cut was new, then.

"I'd probably better warn you," he went on. "Everyone knows you're coming and there's been a thousand theories about why. Aside from the real one."

She thought about Samohi. Over thirty-five hundred students went to her school, and still the new kids got noticed. She supposed that when there was one-seventh the number of kids, it made sense that you got noticed more, especially on a late transfer.

He held up a finger. "News travels faster than you can text. And gossip travels faster. Except you can't really text here, because we have crappy cell coverage."

He pushed back more ghost hair again. He caught her looking, and he shrugged. "Sorry. I had to have my head shaved for the surgery."

"Oh." She was mildly shocked, but she was too polite to show it.

Unsure what else to do, she studied the next oil painting. It was of a tree, with a deer peering from behind it. In the foreground was a big rock shaped vaguely like a heart. And behind the deer, a shadow, also somewhat heart-shaped. The signature on this one wasn't M.M., but she couldn't make it out.

"I was messing with you," he said suddenly.

"What?" she asked, confused.

"The surgery. That was a joke. Do you always take everything literally?"

She colored. It was true that she'd lost her sense of humor over the past weeks, but he was a stranger. How was she supposed to know when he was full of it?

"What rules were you talking about?" she asked, quickly changing the topic.

"Rules?" He looked from the painting to her.

"Getting invited in."

"Oh, it's a court thing," he said, waving it away. "Some guys at school . . ." He suddenly looked uncomfortable. "Anyway."

"Oh," Katelyn murmured. But a *court* thing? What did that mean? Before Katelyn could prod for any more information, Ed came back with two cans of Diet Coke and one can of beer cradled against his chest, and the discussion was bookmarked. He handed one of the soda cans to Katelyn and the other to Trick and popped the top of the beer for himself.

"No crackers?" Trick asked.

Ed shook his head. "All's I got in the pantry is spaghetti sauce and rat turds." He slid a glance toward her. "We got rats, by the way."

Was that the source of the scratching? She shuddered and decided she wasn't thirsty anymore. Rats couldn't get into soda cans, but they could climb all over them.

"Anyone's a vampire, it's your pappy," Trick said. "He lives on air. You cook?"

It took her a minute to track that Trick meant her. "He wouldn't like what I make," Katelyn said. "I'm a vegetarian."

Ed looked at her as though she had informed him that *she* was a vampire. "Hunting's natural, you know. We're predators."

"I'm not," she insisted, feeling fresh anger. She had never understood hunting. "How can anyone feel good about killing an animal?"

"What you eat from the supermarket . . . ," Ed began.

"Vegetarian," Trick cut in. "In search of the wild tofu beast."

Her temper flared again. "I need to call Kimi," she told her grandfather. "She hasn't heard from me and she'll be worried."

Neither of them said anything in response and she stared while Trick guzzled down the soda and gave the empty can a little squeeze. Katelyn wondered if they recycled up in the Ozarks. She doubted it.

"Much obliged for the soda, Dr. M.," Trick said. "I'll be by bright and early Monday morning." He smiled apologetically. "Don't know if Doc's told you, but we need to leave by six-thirty on account of him living so far away from Wolf Springs."

"Leave? Six-thirty?" she said. Had she missed something?

"I'm your ride to school," Trick said. "Didn't the doc tell you?"

"We ain't had much time to talk," Ed offered.

Trick turned to Katelyn. "I paid him fifty bucks. You're going to class me up." He headed for the kitchen. He was still in his stockinged feet, and now that she knew they had rats, she winced every time he took a step. She was never going anywhere in that house without wearing shoes. Forget about her bedroom slippers.

Trick reappeared and crossed to the front door. When he opened it, she was surprised to see that it had begun to rain again. He bent over to put on his boots, giving her a great view of his butt—a nice butt—and her grandfather glanced at her just in time to catch her gaze. She turned her head, flushing.

Suddenly the same low moan she'd heard in the truck echoed through the *plink-plink-plink* of the raindrops on the porch stairs. Low, eerie, mournful. It was followed by a hollow thud, and then another, in a pulsing rhythm. A chorus of moans joined in, and then they rose in pitch and intensity and the hair on Katelyn's neck stood up. They weren't moans. They were howls.

"Ah, de children of de night," Trick said in a thick Count Dracula accent. "Vat music dey make!"

"I thought they were starting tomorrow," Ed muttered. "Dang fools."

The wolf seminar. Katelyn brightened. She was willing to bet that those howls were the attendees.

"Is that drumming?" she asked Ed.

He rolled his eyes. "Supposed to go on for days and days."

"It's a self-improvement seminar," Trick said. "A guy named Jack Bronson—"

Ed growled and gave his head a shake, then drank his beer.

"I heard about it on the plane." Katelyn cut in before he could say anything more. " 'We all have a wolf side.' "

"Except for me. I'm just a big kitty cat," Trick said, winking. He stood, pressing his feet into the boots, and she was disappointed that the porch light bleached the green from his eyes. Then he stepped out of the glare, becoming a silhouette once more.

"Keep your powder dry," he tossed back, then loped into the rain. She was going to see him Monday. An unbelievably cute guy was her ride to school. Her stomach did a little flip at the thought.

"Let's have dinner," Ed said, coming up beside her.

"I thought you didn't have any food," she replied.

He raised a brow. "*You* didn't want company. I got an eggplant Parmigiana ready to microwave. Tomorrow we'll go to the farmers' market for fresh vegetables."

"You knew I was a vegetarian?" she asked him, surprised not only by his "empty cupboard" performance, but also by the fact that maybe he knew something about her.

"Gimme some credit, gal."

He headed for the kitchen. She thought about the rats and tried to swallow down the acid that flooded her mouth.

"I'll pass."

"I might have exaggerated about the rats," he said over his shoulder. "Trick tends to eat me out of house and home."

So he hung out with her grandfather? She wondered why. Didn't he have a family of his own? Maybe it would have been all right if he'd stayed for dinner. He could have been a buffer between Ed and her. She was a little sorry now that she'd acted so put out by his unexpected visit.

"What did he mean by 'court thing'?" she asked, trailing after Ed.

"A few of the local inbreds tried to pin some break-ins on him. Suspicion was cast, so the judge said for him to make sure he's invited into any houses he enters. She meant it as a joke but Trick's made it his mission to follow her orders to the letter."

"Because . . . of his kind?" she asked uncomfortably. With the exotic combination of his dark brown skin, green eyes, and striking Asian bone structure, he'd have a modeling contract in five minutes in L.A. But out here . . .

"Sure. Same as in your school, I'm guessing."

She was abashed. "Um, California . . ."

"Right. *Everybody* there is a drama nerd."

"Drama," she said slowly. "His kind is drama nerds?"

He walked into the kitchen. "Yeah. Writes poetry, too. No wonder he gets beat up all the time."

"Is he gay?" she asked. She knew it was lame to ask, but . . .

He guffawed. "Trick? No. Definitely not. But I've ordered him to be a gentleman around you. If he takes one step out of line, you tell me. I'll set him straight."

She smiled faintly, amused and relieved by his assessment of Trick, and appreciative of his thoughtfulness. Maybe he wasn't so bad.

"There's your connection with civilization," he said, reaching underneath a cabinet and pulling out a telephone. She stretched out her hand for it just as another howl filtered through the room. He shook his head. "Idiots. Probably all from the city."

Yeah. From a beautiful city full of cell phone coverage, Katelyn thought.

She dialed Kimi's number and Kimi picked up on the first ring.

"Katie!" Kimi shrieked. "Finally. *God!*"

"That's me," Katelyn said, smiling at the sound of Kimi's voice.

"Is it as bad as we thought?"

Katelyn cast a furtive glance at her grandfather, who was bustling around the kitchen. She wished he would just leave so she could have some privacy. She felt weird with him in the room. "You could say that."

"No upside?"

An image of Trick passed through her mind, but she dropped it. "What's going on back home?"

"You're not here."

"I miss you, too," Katelyn murmured, swallowing hard. She was afraid she might start crying again.

The microwave dinged and her grandfather made a point of moving around her to get to it. She clenched her teeth. "Well, I've got to go—dinner's ready. I'll call again later."

"You can't go!" Kimi protested. "How was the flight, what's it like there, and—"

"I do have to go." Katelyn's voice trembled as she tried to hold back the tears. "It's time for dinner." She was suddenly not hungry in the least. All she wanted in the world was to be home with Kimi and her family.

"You're probably eating squirrels," Kimi said. "Oh, my poor baby."

"Eggplant Parmigiana." Katelyn had to dig deep to add lightness to her tone. "But the microwave is powered by squirrels."

A smile flickered over her grandfather's face. She refused to acknowledge it.

"I miss you so much already," Kimi whined.

"Same," Katelyn replied, her stomach twisting into knots. Her friend could never imagine how badly she missed her.

"Okay, go eat with the enemy."

"Bye," Katelyn said softly. With all the resolve at her command, she hung up and faced her jailer.

"Want a glass for your soda?" he asked her.

He would never understand her, not anything about her. He didn't even know what he had done to her by dragging her to this godforsaken place.

He was waiting for her answer. The best she could manage was a nod.

When she finally crawled into bed, she was exhausted. She stared up at the ceiling and listened to all the sounds of the night in this new place. Everything was different than it was back home. Even the smells. She thought she might never be able to sleep, but her exhaustion was so absolute, so complete, that she was out within minutes.

She startled awake hours later and lay still in the dark, heart pounding, as she tried to decide what had woken her. The rain was still coming down hard and she listened to it for a moment, trying to calm herself down. Her mouth felt dry and chalky and she desperately wanted something to drink.

After a minute, she got up and tiptoed into the hall. Her grandfather's door was closed and she hurried down the stairs as quickly and quietly as she could, wincing when the floorboards creaked beneath her. A bolt of lightning outside threw everything into sudden relief and she jerked as the eyes of the animal heads flashed, staring at her. She squeezed her eyes shut tight and made it to the bottom.

Coals glowed in the fireplace. Suddenly she was back in her house, with her mom. She remembered how soft her mother's hair was, the lilt of her French accent. How she had fallen apart after Daddy died. . . .

It's happening to me, too, she realized. Then she took a deep breath. *No. I'm okay.*

She stumbled into the kitchen. Moonlight filtered in through the half-open drapes above the sink and illuminated the heavy rains reflected on the peeled counters. She fumbled for the light switch, but it wasn't where she thought it would be. Feeling along the wall, she still couldn't find it. Remembering all the dead animal heads, she jerked back her hand, afraid she might run into one she hadn't noticed during dinner.

Lightning crackled, making her jump. She thought of the mudslides that happened in L.A. when it rained this hard. The road to the cabin was unpaved, little more than a trail. Would she even be able to get to school on Monday? It was Friday now. Would she be stuck in this cabin, eventually running out of food?

Maybe he'll just go shoot us some.

She tried to tell herself she was making a joke, but it wasn't funny. None of this was funny. She hated it here.

Shoulders tight, arms crossed, she walked to the drainer in the semidarkness. She retrieved a glass, went to the sink, and turned on the faucet with a shaking hand.

Then she froze. The hair on the back of her neck stood up and her face prickled.

Someone is watching me, she thought.

But all she saw in the space between the curtains was the occasional strobe of raindrops falling in the moonlight, almost like blinking eyes.

Shadows shifted; something *was* moving out there.

Trees, she told herself. *Squirrels.*

Katelyn couldn't remember if her grandfather had locked the back door. She stepped forward, and then . . . that same scratching. She took a step backward. Then she heard something low and rumbling. Thunder, or a growl? Scared, she flew across the kitchen, smacking against the edge of the dining table. Wincing at the pain, she turned to flee.

She ran all the way up the stairs and into her room. She got her stuffed bear and held it to her chest and stared up at her skylight. The rain pounded down, hard, almost like someone knocking to come in.

"I'm not inviting you," she said aloud.

But there *was* knocking—on her door.

"Katie?" her grandfather called. "Everything okay?"

Her face went hot. Now, with the light on, and having awakened him, she felt silly. "I went to get some water. I thought I saw something moving." She hesitated. "And a noise. Maybe like something growling. Out back."

"I'll check."

She grimaced, embarrassed, but she couldn't deny the soothing feeling of relief that coursed through her—followed by a prickle of alarm, in case there *was* something out there.

"I'll go with you," she announced as she got out of bed, crossed the room, and cracked open the door.

He was already halfway down the stairs, carrying a rifle tucked under his arm. He turned and said, "No, Katie, you go on back to bed. I'm sure it's nothing."

"Then why do you have a rifle?" she asked.

"*Stay in your room,*" he ordered, and she flinched, stunned by the harshness of his voice. There was no way on earth he thought it was nothing.

Still, she did as she was told, crossing her arms and standing in the center of her room, certain something was about to happen. She shifted her weight, braced for another catastrophe. She could feel panic circling her. The walls of the room seemed to press in.

It felt as if she stood there for hours, tense, frightened, waiting. Finally she decided she'd had enough. She strode to the door, yanking it open—

And found her grandfather on the other side, with his hand raised to knock on it.

"Oh," she said, startled. She took a step backward.

His clothes and hair were wet. The rifle was gone; he was wiping his face with a towel. He looked grim, and her heart stuttered. Had he found something?

"Here's the thing," he said. Then he cleared his throat. "May I come in?"

She nodded, moving away from the door. There was one chair; assuming that he'd sit in it, she perched on the edge of her bed. But he remained standing. He folded the towel as if taking a few moments to consider his words. He was scaring her, and the suspense was leaving her breathless.

"About two weeks ago, a girl was killed," he began.

"Oh, I'm sorry," she said, alarmed. "Was it someone you knew?"

"She was mauled. In the forest." He gave her a long look. "She was out alone."

Katelyn waited. And then she got it. *They* lived in the forest. His house was surrounded by trees.

"I'll stay out of there." She nodded at him as the reality hit her. "I promise." Then she added, "I'm not a hiker. Or a mountain person. I'm a beach person."

"I'm not kidding about this." He regarded her sternly. "She is *dead*."

"I don't mean to sound like I don't care," she said. She did care. In fact, she was terrified. "I swear to you. I promise you, I won't go out alone."

He opened his mouth as if he was going to say something else. Then he sighed, nodded, and said, "All right. Good night, Katie."

"Good night, Ed." Her stomach churned. She was sorry for the girl who had died, but furious with her grandfather for dragging her to live where she couldn't even go for a walk for fear of being ripped apart by a wild animal. She grabbed a pillow and almost threw it at the door. Instead, she hugged it against her chest, bowed her head, and whispered, "I want to leave. Please, let me leave."

—◦—✦—◦—

Katelyn's grandfather's news scared her, but more than that, she began to worry that they were never going to leave the cabin again, even in the daylight. It drizzled and thundered all weekend, and rain, lightning, and mud were all she saw of her supposed new hometown. Because of the weather—or so he said—there was no trip to the farmers' market, no sightseeing in town, but Katelyn realized she was fine with that. She wasn't ready to face the world. She missed her old one way more than she could stand.

The fireplace burned night and day, and Katelyn's phobia—and all the animal heads—kept her out of the living room. She found a picture of her parents and her hanging on the wall next to the staircase and sat for a while and stared at them, all happy and laughing together, until she couldn't handle it anymore. She was exhausted, and aside from talking to Kimi, mostly she slept.

She and Ed seemed to get along better, smirking at the howls and the drums beating away in the bad weather. Katelyn thought of the Wolf Man from the plane and pictured him sitting in a gray rain poncho, urging his inner executive wolf to emerge.

Though she slept a lot, she didn't sleep well. Whenever she closed her eyes and began to drift, she was back in her house as it collapsed around her. She dreamed of her mother, falling, falling forever into blackness, arms stretched to Katelyn, who dove after her, plummeting and never catching her.

She jerked awake a dozen times, shaking, pulling the covers up around her chin and staring up at her skylight. Leaves plunked onto the wet glass, obscuring the view, which was fine with her. She couldn't shake the feeling that someone was watching her. Though in the light of day she was sure that was just nerves.

On Monday, it was barely dawn when she got up. Her

grandfather made her some oatmeal for breakfast; also, coffee. She was surprised again when he handed her lunch. He'd packed her a peanut butter and jelly sandwich and an apple. Despite herself, she found that completely sweet.

Trick showed promptly at six-thirty, in a creased brown leather bomber jacket, a white T-shirt, jeans, and his cowboy boots. Yawning, he asked for and received some oatmeal and coffee, too.

"You look good," he told her. She was wearing an embroidered indigo jacket, a long-sleeved gauze blouse, jeans, white socks, and Mary Janes. She and Kimi had snagged all of it except for the socks at various vintage shops and thrift stores in West Hollywood. Underneath the blouse, she was wearing a blue silk camisole.

"Thanks." She didn't know what people wore at Wolf Springs High School. Her mind filled with images of girls in cutoff denim shorts and guys in overalls, twirling pieces of straw in their mouths. She knew that was snarky but she couldn't shake it.

She expected his car to be a beat-up truck like her grandfather's and was surprised when he led her toward a lovingly restored vintage light green Mustang with black leather interior. He grinned at her and held open the door while she climbed in, settling her backpack on her lap.

"Sweet ride, right?" he asked proudly, slipping behind the wheel.

He turned on the engine, which purred like a tiger, and they began to roll. From the porch, her grandfather waved. She gave him a little wave back. It began to rain.

They blazed away, into the rain and the greenery. The Mustang held the curves and Trick punched on an iPod. "Smoke on the Water" poured through car speakers.

"Cheery," she drawled, then cocked her head casually. "So . . . my grandfather told me you get beaten up for writing poetry."

"Oh, shit." He laughed. "Maybe when I was four. He's just trying to make me sound like a loser to lessen your attraction to me." He shot her a grin and pressed down on the gas. "He wants me to be your androgynous best friend." The car shot through the trees and flew around the corner. "Just FYI, Kat, I'm not androgynous."

"My name's not Kat," she replied, hiding her own smile.

"It is now. Okay, you can get cell coverage here. Go for it."

Even though she knew it was rude, Katelyn texted Kimi for the rest of the ride. Kimi had been waiting to hear from her, so she was texting back at what was an ungodly hour in California. Katelyn glanced up every now and then to steal a glance at Trick. He didn't seem to mind being ignored. He just kept driving like a maniac through the dense woods and heavy rain; she half expected to wind up in a ditch. Then as they began to climb upward, Trick gave the car more gas. Trees bowed above them, creating a tunnel of total darkness. Still the rain came down. The beams of the Mustang's headlights cast blurs of yellow on thick trunks, which Trick dodged with ease, and strobed against the raindrops.

"Brace for impact," he said.

Katelyn turned to ask what he was talking about right as they shot out of the tree tunnel. Then, pressing through the rain, they crested a plateau and Katelyn caught her breath. Below them, a Victorian village spread out like a miniature Charles Dickens town beneath a Christmas tree. Intricate brick-and-wood structures were topped with gables and chimneys. Baskets decorated with orange and red flowers hung from curved lampposts. The streets were narrow and cobbled. Rain fell in buckets.

It was nothing like she'd thought it would be. No tractors parked on the street or broken-down trailers. "Is this a theme park?" she asked, only half joking.

"There's the school."

She followed his hand as he slowed and joined a parade of cars and trucks—lots of trucks—feeding from another road down a steep hill. There was honking and waving. Two yellow buses pulled up beside a large wooden building with wraparound porches on both floors. A pitched roof folded in angles among overhanging turrets and dormer windows. On top of the building an LED sign spelled out W-O-L-F-C-O-U-N-T-R-Y.

"Crap, I forgot my hoopskirt," she moaned, mostly to make his smile bigger.

Score.

"Does this bustle make my butt look big?" he said, playing along.

The parade wound down the side of the village. The overabundance of cute was cut by a low gray self-storage building and a ramshackle convenience store. She couldn't wait to tell Kimi that they had been 90 percent wrong about Banjo Land—which was a relief.

"We'll park in the senior lot and then I'll walk you to the

admin office," he said. "But then I've got to leave you. I'm keeping my head down around the principal."

"Because of the court thing."

He nodded. "Completely unjust, but it's adding to my aura of mystery. Hey," he said, his voice suddenly urgent and somber. "I have to talk to you about something."

She waited. His green eyes seemed to grow darker, the planes and hollows of his face to accentuate. She held her breath, waiting to hear what he had to say, mesmerized by his good looks.

"Just before you got here, a friend of mine was killed."

The girl in the forest. Of course he would have known her. Everyone knew everyone else here. "My grandfather told me," she said. "I'm so sorry." She meant it.

His expression didn't change. "What, exactly, did he say?"

"That she was killed. She was in the forest alone."

He glanced back at the road as he maneuvered into the parking lot. The space between them seemed to fill with tension. She wondered if he had been close to the girl. If she'd been his girlfriend.

"There are a lot of urban legends in a small place like this." He grimaced, revealing deep dimples on either side of his mouth. "Not urban, sorry. I guess they'd be called *country* legends. In any case, us country folks talk about haints and all like that. Her name was Haley, and her death was the hot topic until everyone heard that a movie star from Hollywood was moving here."

"Oh, my God, you mean me?" She burst out with a shocked guffaw, but he didn't crack a smile. Then she realized that he was not only upset, but angry.

"People brought teddy bears and candles, pictures, all that stuff, to school. Everyone hugging, crying. We all went to her funeral. Now it's almost as if she never existed." His voice lowered as he added quietly, "But I'll never forget."

"I'm really sorry, Trick," she said sincerely.

He gave his head a shake. "I don't mean to sound like I'm blaming you for showing up." He slid his glance at her again, and he studied her for a second. "I just want . . ." And then he forced a smile onto his perfect mouth. "You just be careful, ya hear? And not just in the forest."

"Thanks," she said softly. She figured he was warning her about making her way as the new girl in school. She was pretty nervous about it, too.

He parked, came around, and before she'd been able to gather all her things, opened the door for her. The rain hadn't let up, so they dashed along with everyone else toward the arched stone entrance.

Steamy warmth hit her as they entered the main hall. Here they were, her schoolmates, for the time being, at least. Looking around, Katelyn started picking out the jocks and geeks, guessing at who was popular or unpopular. The clothes weren't as upscale as in Santa Monica, nor as funky. But they weren't wearing overalls and cutoffs, either. Mostly jeans and jackets. And she coveted the shiny purple rain boots one girl had on.

She took a deep breath. *Okay, new school, new rules. Who are you going to be, Katelyn? You have a chance to be whoever you want to be here, since nobody knows you.*

Except Trick, she realized. Her chauffer bobbed along, waving at her to hurry. As she tried to keep up, kids did double takes, realizing she was the new girl.

Trick led her to an open office door and pointed inside. "Here," he said. "And watch your back."

"I can't watch my back. That's physically impossible," she replied, and he raised his brows and grinned in response.

Then he hung a U and disappeared into the mob.

And just like that, in a sea of people, she was all alone.

3

Katelyn took a deep breath. She looked slowly around the hall one more time before going into the office. Behind a wooden counter sat a middle-aged woman at a desk. The woman—her nameplate read MRS. WALKER—smiled when she saw her.

"You must be Katelyn."

For one wild moment she wanted to say no, that Katelyn was a girl who had a mother and went to school in Santa Monica. *I'm not her anymore.* The woman kept smiling and Katelyn forced herself to answer. "Yes."

"I've got your schedule printed out for you and I drew you a map. It's crude, but it will get you where you're going." Mrs. Walker slid a packet to her across the counter.

"Thanks," Katelyn said, fighting the urge to ask if it showed the way back home.

"You've got enough time to make it to your first class before the bell if you scoot. It's out the door to the right, down the hall, fourth door on the left."

"Thanks," Katelyn said again before turning to leave. Nervousness and fear washed over her as she headed out the door and down the hallway. Nothing was familiar and it wasn't fair that she had to be starting all over again.

She glanced down at her schedule. Her first class was history. Mr. Henderson. As soon as she walked in, the clamor died down, and all eyes focused on her. The room was almost full and she slid into a vacant seat at the back. A sea of new faces; her stomach tightened further. This was not how her life was supposed to go.

"Hi," a blond guy wearing a gray-and-white letter jacket said as he sat down beside her. "You must be Katelyn McBride."

She nodded tightly. First impressions were everything. She didn't want to come off as a standoffish bitch, but the full realization of what was happening to her was crashing down on her. Her mother was *dead*. And Katelyn was thousands of miles away from her grave, and everything else she cared about.

"Class, we have a new student who just transferred from California," said a man at the front of the room. He had wheat-colored hair shot through with silver, and blue-gray eyes beneath heavy brows. He was wearing khaki trousers and a white button-down shirt. "Katelyn, why don't you stand up and tell us a little bit about yourself."

She stood up slowly, trying to hide the fact that her hands were shaking. *I don't belong here*, she wanted to tell him. *There's been a terrible mistake.*

She took a deep breath. "I'm Kate—" She hesitated. Then she raised her chin and said, "Kat McBride, from L.A. I came to live with my grandfather; my mother . . ."

Her voice gave out. It didn't matter. They all knew anyway. That was what Trick had told her.

"Kat. Okay," Mr. Henderson said mildly, making a note on a piece of paper.

She wasn't sure why, but somehow it seemed like it would be easier to go by the nickname Trick had given her than to hear one more stranger call her by her real name.

"We'll get you a book," Mr. Henderson said.

She nodded and he turned to address the rest of the class. "Okay. Today we're going to start a new project. I want you all to become investigative historians, and to that end, I'm going to pair you up. Now that Kat's here, we have an even number." He smiled at her as if she'd done him a personal favor by moving to Wolf Springs.

Katelyn winced. A project partner on her first day.

Mr. Henderson began running through the list of names, and chairs squealed as everyone started to move around the room, reorganizing themselves. Some surreptitious texting went on. A few got down to business. Katelyn tried to remember names but it was too much to ask. Just sitting there was too much to ask. She tried not to fall apart.

Finally he said, "Cordelia, how about you partner with Kat?"

Kat, that's me, she thought, blinking. *Cordelia. Which one's Cordelia?*

A tall, slender girl with shoulder-length auburn hair, dark blue eyes, and perfect movie-star looks stood, organized her belongings, and flashed her a kind smile. Katelyn had often been told she was pretty, but next to this girl she felt like a dog.

The girl grabbed her bag and made her way over to Katelyn, holding out her hand. "Hi, Kat. I'm Cordelia Fenner," she said.

Katelyn ground out a strangled "hi" and took her hand. She wasn't used to shaking hands with people her own age—maybe it was an Arkansas thing—and she grimaced slightly at the strong grip of the other girl. She wasn't sure if Cordelia noticed her awkwardness, but the other girl broke away quickly.

"So, welcome to Wolf Springs," Cordelia said brightly, sitting down. She flicked her glance over Katelyn, checking out her clothes, hair, and shoes. Normally when girls did that, there was an underlying layer of cattiness, of competition. Not so with Cordelia. It felt more like the other girl was taking her measure, trying to understand her instead of judge her. The really beautiful girls back home were never that way. Staring at the other girl, Katelyn couldn't decide whether Cordelia was just that confident in her own beauty or completely oblivious to it. Either way it was a nice change from what she was used to.

"Thanks," Katelyn said, warming quickly.

Cordelia cocked her head, silky wisps of red hair brushing a flawless porcelain complexion. "Who do you run with?"

"Excuse me?"

"Sorry." Cordelia rolled her eyes at herself. "I mean, who do you hang out with? You know—popular crowd, drama class, chess club, dropouts?"

The question was so direct it caught her off guard. "I—I haven't decided yet."

A smile flitted across Cordelia's face. "It's nice to have a choice. Not everyone does. Okay. Let's make Mr. Henderson happy."

Katelyn nodded, wishing she had thought to ask Cordelia what group *she* ran with, though it was easy to guess that whichever it was, she was popular.

"Mr. Henderson used to be an archeologist. He moved here a couple of years ago," Cordelia added. "So that makes him just about as new as you."

Katelyn let her confusion show. "Two *years*? I've only been here four days."

"It's different here. We've had two newcomers in less than a century—it's a lot of change for folks around here."

"Plus there's that Inner Wolf guy," Katelyn said.

Cordelia grimaced. "Don't even get me started on *him*. Anyway, Mr. Henderson is this big-city guy who thinks outside the box, and you are lucky to be in here, because Mrs. Herbold reads aloud from the textbook. People have been known to jump out the window to end their torment."

"All right, people," Mr. Henderson said, handing a stack of papers to a girl in the front row. "What I want you to do is take some aspect of local history and dig a little deeper. A legend like the ones you-all are so fond of out here, a story that's been passed down in your family, a mystery, something *cool*."

Cordelia grinned at Katelyn, and Katelyn returned an answering smile. Apparently they had both had "cool" teachers before.

"Put on your detective hat and find out where your tall tale or your family story came from." He mimicked pulling on a hat and kept talking. "You have until October twenty-eighth to work on this. A lot of time. Here's the breakdown."

The blond guy who'd first identified her as the new girl passed a stack of papers to Katelyn over his shoulder. She took one before handing them to Cordelia and skimmed it. Historical sites. Haunts. Legends. Ballads. The class started buzzing as the newly paired investigative historians got down to the business of picking a topic.

"Legends sounds *cool*," Katelyn said.

"Oh. Uh-huh," Cordelia said, obviously forcing enthusiasm. "There's all kinds of backwoods stories. About haints. Ghosts, I mean." Cordelia tapped the paper with her pencil. "I know lots of them. My family's been here for generations."

Katelyn was amazed. She couldn't imagine anyone living in Wolf Springs for generations. It was so isolated.

"Ghosts would be interesting," Katelyn said.

The blond guy raised his hand. Mr. Henderson acknowledged him with a nod.

"What about Haley?" he asked.

The room fell silent. Mr. Henderson's expression went carefully neutral.

"What *about* Haley, Beau?" the teacher asked.

"Well, no one's sure about how she died," the guy—Beau—said. "So we could investigate that."

"Dude, that is not cool." A tall guy in Katelyn and Cordelia's row half stood. "Haley's not a *project*."

"Yeah," a girl in a white sweater said, glaring in Beau's direction.

"Haley went here," Cordelia whispered to Katelyn. She had gone deathly pale. "She . . . died a couple of weeks ago."

"Trick told me," Katelyn whispered back.

Cordelia looked startled. "You know Trick Sokolov?"

Katelyn tried to decipher Cordelia's tone of voice. It didn't sound as if she liked Trick much, but Katelyn couldn't tell for sure. Maybe because of the "court" thing?

The girl in the white sweater spoke again. "And besides, we already *know* how she . . ." Her voice faltered. ". . . what happened."

Beau shook his head. "But my grandma said—"

Mr. Henderson cleared his throat. "I think we'll leave Haley out of this," he declared; then he surveyed the class thoughtfully before he spoke again. "I know you miss Haley. Her passing was a shock to all of us. And let me remind you all to be very careful in and around the woods."

"Right. Like *he* knows anything about it," Beau muttered under his breath.

Mr. Henderson didn't appear to have heard him. "Now, I'd like you to choose a subject within a day or two. By the end of the week at the latest."

The students began to murmur among themselves again. Katelyn glanced at Beau, who stared angrily down at his desk. Suddenly he looked up through his lashes, straight at her. She couldn't read his expression, but he seemed as if he wanted to say something. Then the girl beside him nudged his shoulder, and he picked up his handout.

"We were talking about Trick." Cordelia prompted Katelyn in a low voice.

"He's my ride to school," Katelyn explained. She didn't want to be too quick to link herself to Trick if no one liked him. "We live out in the woods. I mean, my grandfather and I. Not Trick and I." She gave a small smile at that.

"Oh." Cordelia nodded cautiously. "Well, Trick's kind of . . . unpredictable," she said. "Maybe you could find someone else. . . ."

Alarmed, Katelyn raised her brows. "Unpredictable how?"

The other girl shifted uncomfortably in her chair. "He just *provokes* people, sometimes. He's so odd—"

"How's everybody doing?" Mr. Henderson said loudly, interrupting Cordelia.

Cordelia's cheeks went pink and she cleared her throat. "Be careful. Okay, Kat?"

Katelyn nodded. It seemed like everyone in Wolf Springs was telling her to be careful. And Trick was wrong. Haley's death was still on a lot of people's minds. More than ever, Katelyn wished she could go home. This place was creepy. She wanted the sunshine back—and everything else she'd been forced to leave behind.

"I don't mean to sound, y'know, *bossy*," Cordelia said uneasily. "I'm just trying to help you out."

"I know," Katelyn replied, trying to reassure her. Cordelia somehow seemed fragile. And was something really wrong with Trick? Maybe he *had* broken into houses.

"It's nice of you to show me the ropes," Katelyn added to change the subject. She made herself smile, and Cordelia relaxed.

"Okay. That's settled. So," Cordelia said, "what do you have next?"

"P.E.," Katelyn replied after consulting her schedule.

"Me too." Cordelia wrinkled her nose. "Since it's raining, we'll be doing indoor stuff. It might be a little on the draggy side."

Katelyn didn't say anything but privately figured draggy was about all she could handle for the moment.

"Kat," Cordelia blurted, "if Trick's your friend—"

"He's just my ride," Katelyn said again, more firmly this time. "Really. And I'll keep an eye on him," she added, hoping to emphasize to Cordelia that she was interpreting her warning as friendly advice.

Cordelia nodded, looping her hair around her ear. Everything about her was polished and put together—except for her attitude. Cordelia seemed to be very worried about offending her. Though it could be that Cordelia just didn't know how to treat a stranger. From what Katelyn could tell, they weren't that common.

The rest of the class time was taken up by discussing the requirements for the project, and it ended without Katelyn and Cordelia's settling on a topic. It was hard for Katelyn to focus, and she kept forgetting to answer to her new name. When the bell rang, she and Cordelia headed for the gym together. Guys flirted openly with Cordelia and just as blatantly checked Katelyn out. She didn't see Trick anywhere.

"Our school used to be a church," Cordelia told her. "Sacred ground."

There was a pause, and Katelyn realized Cordelia was waiting for her response. "It's very pretty," Katelyn offered, glancing up at an old stained-glass window of a man with a halo. A large gray dog stood beside him. No, not a dog. A wolf.

"And it's haunted," Cordelia added.

Katelyn smiled. She couldn't tell if Cordelia was being serious. "Why don't we investigate the history of the school?" Katelyn suggested, then pointed to the window. "Who's this holy man in the middle? A saint?"

"I'm not really sure." Cordelia shrugged. "He's just always been there."

"We could find out," Katelyn said, prodding. "Do that for our project."

"That could be 'cool.'" Grinning, Cordelia made air quotes.

By then they had reached the entrance to the gym. Cordelia pointed to a small door next to it.

"Coach Ambrose is in there. You should check in with him. I'm going to the locker room. See you in a few."

Cordelia disappeared inside the gym and Katelyn stuck her head into the coach's office, which looked out onto the gym floor.

"Coach Ambrose?"

A broad-shouldered bald man wearing a gray sweatshirt and a whistle on a lanyard around his neck looked up from his desk. "New kid, right?"

She nodded.

"You buy a set of gym clothes from the office yet?"

"No." She was kind of glad Mrs. Walker had forgotten to sell them to her. She really wanted just to be by herself for a bit. After only one class period, she was feeling overwhelmed. She wasn't ready to undress with a bunch of girls she didn't know yet.

"Then you can sit in the bleachers and watch today. Get some gear for tomorrow."

"Okay, thank you." She offered the man a small smile, then headed into the gym, relieved to be excused from participation.

It was still raining. She could hear it beating down hard as she sat on the bleachers and took in her surroundings. It looked a lot like the gym back in Santa Monica—though, she supposed, all gyms probably looked alike. Basketball hoops towered above the shiny varnished floor. Banners were draped on the walls. YOU'RE IN TIMBERWOLF COUNTRY. GO, TIMBER-WOLVES! She thought about the saint and his pet in the window. Banjo Land certainly had a theme—wolves, wolves, and more wolves. She'd have to tell Kimi.

Gradually, boys and girls started trickling out of the locker rooms, a handful stretching out, doing sit-ups. The uniform was simple—white shorts, gray T-shirt with a wolf's head silk-screened on it.

Cordelia appeared, plopping down on the floor, extending her legs, and making a halfhearted effort to touch her running shoes. Her fingertips only grazed her shins. She glanced up at Katelyn and made a little face, then stopped trying altogether and yawned.

"I'm too tired to do this today," she said.

"Wonder why?" a nearby boy said, snickering. Katelyn looked at him. He had brilliant red hair, redder than Cordelia's, but his blond eyelashes and upturned nose gave him a piggish look. He was a hulk. The king of the banjo men.

"Mike, honey, I'd appreciate it if you would keep your snorts to yourself," Cordelia said sweetly.

"Ooh, touchy." Mike gestured to Cordelia. "C'mon over here and make me, *honey*."

Face darkening, Cordelia made a show of ignoring him. Mike rolled his shoulders and grinned.

"C'mon, Fenner."

Something flashed across Cordelia's features and she balled her hands into fists. Katelyn blinked, a little startled. Cordelia's entire demeanor had changed.

But before the confrontation could escalate, Coach Ambrose appeared with a clipboard, pen, and stack of handouts. He blew a sharp blast on his whistle and looked down at the clipboard. "Okay, today we're starting our section on strength training and balance. You'll do a series of exercises and record your numbers for comparison against your numbers three weeks from now. Here are your forms."

He set the handouts on the ground, along with a few pencils. "Let's start with sit-ups. Everyone grab a partner."

"I'd like to grab *you*," Mike whispered loudly at Cordelia. The coach didn't hear him, but some of the other students did. Three or four boys snickered, and Katelyn heaved a sigh. Jackholes.

Cordelia's jaw was clenched as she paired off with another

girl, dark-skinned with gold fingernail polish. They took turns being the one to do the sit-ups and the one who anchored the other's feet. They had to do as many as possible in the time allotted and Katelyn noticed that Cordelia seemed to be one of the fastest in the group.

"Grab your knees, Cordy," Mike whispered at her. Again, Coach Ambrose seemed oblivious.

A number of other exercises followed, including push-ups and jumping jacks. Students began to drop off, but Cordelia kept going, face grim. She was clearly the most athletic girl in the room. Banjo Boy Mike was the winner among the guys.

"Okay, we'll finish with chin-ups," the coach said.

The students each took a position beneath a long horizontal bar and then jumped up to it, hung for a moment, and began to lift themselves until their chins cleared it. Then they would lower themselves and repeat. A couple of girls couldn't do even one and most of them dropped out after four. The guys began to quit, too.

Katelyn looked on, feeling detached, then glanced down. Her cell phone was vibrating. She'd forgotten to turn it off, but no one but her could hear the telltale buzz.

A text from Kimi had come in. It was a picture of her and Jane, one of the girls they knew, in bikinis at the beach. They were wearing feather boas and had blacked out some of their teeth. They were holding a sign that read BEVERLY HILL-BILLIES!

The message attached read *OK, we r Santa Monica hill-billies but u get the idea. Good luck first day! XO K/J.*

It was incredibly sweet but it tore her apart inside. Kimi and Jane. Kimi had told her that she and Jane had hung out most of the weekend. As much as she wanted to be happy for her best friend that she was having fun and making the most of things, it still hurt to see Kimi having fun without her.

She forced herself to text an LOL and then turned off her phone.

Cordelia and Mike were the only two left on the chin-up bars. As they kept going, the rest of the class started chanting for their favorites, and Katelyn was quick to notice that no one seemed to be crossing gender boundaries. All the guys rooted for Mike, while all the girls called encouragement to Cordelia.

"C'mon, Mike, kill 'er!" one of the guys shouted. "Timber-wolves!"

Half the guys in the room erupted into wolf howls, throwing back their heads. The girls followed suit, and the room shook with the noise. School spirit at its finest.

Sweat drenched the front of Mike's T-shirt. Cordelia's face was shiny, but the rest of her wasn't even damp. Then suddenly she blinked as if she'd just woken up, and looked first at Mike and then at the rest of the class. She scowled, hard, as if she was angry about something, and dropped to the ground in a squat. The girls cheered and applauded, racing to Cordelia and helping her up. Katelyn got up off the bleacher and trotted over to congratulate her, impressed at how strong Cordelia was.

The guys began to howl again. Mike did one more chin-up, glancing down at Cordelia, then pulled another. Then he, too, let go, plopping onto the mat with a wobble. Though he was shaking from exertion, he let loose with a howl of his own.

"Okay, good job, guys. Now hit the showers," the coach said.

The students began to swarm toward the locker room doors, but Cordelia stayed where she was, catching her breath. Katelyn gave her a little fist bump, and Cordelia wiped her forehead with the back of her hand.

"Whoa," Katelyn said.

"Yeah, I guess I got a little carried away," Cordelia murmured sheepishly.

"Carried away?" Katelyn echoed. "You were kicking his—"

"Shhh." Cordelia stopped her as Mike and some of the guys sauntered over.

He adjusted his gym shorts suggestively, his smile fierce and mean. "See, Fenner, men are stronger than women."

"Yeah, well, odor isn't everything," Katelyn said before she could stop herself.

The guys around Mike started cracking up, and Katelyn realized the mistake she'd made. A guy like Mike would not enjoy being laughed at. Face reddening, Mike took a threatening step forward, and she felt the blood drain from her own face. Before Mike could do anything else, though, Cordelia was between them, a hand on Katelyn's arm.

"Let's *go*," Coach Ambrose said to the group at large.

Mike hesitated, and Katelyn's pulse quickened. He wouldn't really try to hurt her, would he? Over *that*?

"Mike, c'mon," one of the other guys said, this one with startling dark black eyebrows.

"New girl," Mike said. "New *bi*—"

"Shut up, Mike," Eyebrows said before he could finish.

Mike glared at Katelyn. Then he turned and loped away. Katelyn didn't realize she was trembling until Cordelia let go of her.

"Don't mind him," Cordelia said, her voice a little shaky. "Don't mind any of them. You know how they are. Jocks."

"*Brain-dead* jocks. We didn't have any of those back in Santa Monica," Katelyn deadpanned, and Cordelia smiled at her. Katelyn hoped Cordelia hadn't realized that he'd really scared her.

"Be right back," Cordelia promised, heading for the locker room.

Katelyn looked around for the teacher and saw that he was still watching. *He would have stepped in and done something if things got out of control, wouldn't he?* She shuddered, wishing she was convinced he would have. She tried to shrug it off, telling herself that it was just her imagination.

True to her word, Cordelia returned to the gym in what seemed record time. Even more incredible was that she still looked perfect, right down to her hair and makeup.

"You barely broke a sweat," Katelyn said accusingly, surprised. "You let Mike beat you, didn't you?"

Cordelia turned red and looked away. "No."

"Yeah."

Smoothing back her hair, Cordelia smiled, but it didn't reach her eyes. "Well, I don't know what it's like in California but out here men have fragile egos. It's best not to shatter them or they get all kinds of crazy."

Katelyn shook her head. "You don't strike me as the type to be cowed by zombies. And how are you so *strong*?"

There was a beat. "I used to be a cheerleader," Cordelia said. "Last year." Her voice grew breathy, a little wistful. Katelyn knew that tone. Her mom had spoken like that whenever she'd talked about performing on the stage.

Katelyn wanted to ask Cordelia why she'd quit, but the other girl seemed to pull into herself. Her shoulders were hunched, and she cast her eyes downward. Her body language was screaming that she wanted the topic left alone.

Cordelia pushed open the gym door and they joined the bustle in the main hall. Thunder rumbled outside and lit up the stained-glass window of the saint and the wolf.

"I'll try to introduce you around," Cordelia said suddenly. "But . . . the girls are still pretty mad at me for quitting the team. We didn't make it to nationals this summer. Because of me . . ." Her voice trailed off again.

"Please, don't do anything that puts you in a bad spot," Katelyn replied, both touched and intrigued by Cordelia's confession.

"It's okay. Friends will help you . . . blend in," Cordelia said.

As nice as Cordelia was being, Katelyn still couldn't imagine blending in. Wolf Springs wasn't exactly what she'd expected, but Santa Monica it was not. *I'm not staying. I'm not, I'm not, I'm not.*

"Anyway," Cordelia said, clearing her throat as she

changed the subject, "we should work on picking out a history topic. I'm free tomorrow afternoon." A flush crawled up her neck. "I could come over to your place."

Katelyn didn't like being at her grandfather's cabin and didn't relish the idea of inviting someone over, especially not when she had an excuse to go somewhere else.

Cordelia picked up on her hesitation. "Oh," she murmured, fretful again. "Um, I'm sorry—"

"It's just . . . I'm not sure of the house rules yet. And we live a million miles away from here," Katelyn explained gently.

"You do? Where?" Cordelia asked, cocking her head to the side.

Katelyn was surprised she didn't know. Didn't everyone know everyone around here? And from what Trick had said, she'd gathered that the town loved their gossip.

"I don't even know. I live with my grandfather. Mordecai McBride."

"Oh, yeah, he's way out in the sticks," Cordelia said. "I didn't put you together with him." She smiled weakly. "Should have with the last name and all."

Thunder boomed above their heads as they strolled down the hall together. Katelyn smelled food. Lunch was being prepared. The school day was both dragging and racing by, the same as the days after her mother's death.

"We should get together, though," Katelyn assured her. She didn't want Cordelia to think she didn't want to hang out with her. Just not at the cabin.

Cordelia caught her lower lip between her teeth and got quiet. Then she nodded. "You'll come to us, okay? My place."

Katelyn hoped it would be all right with her grandfather. But before she could say anything, Cordelia rushed on.

"Yeah, it'll be okay," Cordelia said, more to herself than to Katelyn. "Just ignore my sisters if they're over. They're both crazy. And Justin's still gone. So the coast is clear."

Cordelia's demeanor had intensified. She was tense to the point of edgy. The invitation wasn't a straightforward one, that was for sure.

"I'll need to check," Katelyn said. "We could go to a coffee shop or something." That would be nice. She hadn't seen anything of downtown except on the ride in, and it would be neutral territory.

"Oh, no, my house will be fine," Cordelia insisted. And before Katelyn could argue, Cordelia gave a little wave and darted down the hall. Katelyn watched her go and smiled as the dark-skinned girl with the gold fingernails caught up with her. Katelyn was feeling protective of her. Cordelia seemed sad, almost frightened.

But what does she have against Trick?

Katelyn spent her lunch buying her gym clothes and getting some more of her textbooks. After lunch was art.

She walked into a small room crammed with wooden tables coated with splashes of paint and was hit by the smell of turpentine and newsprint. Paintings and collages hung all over the walls, and framed prints of famous pieces by Monet, Picasso, and Chagall sat on wooden stools against a chalkboard. Rain spattered a large picture window, where a girl wearing a gray Timberwolf sweatshirt stood facing Katelyn. The girl smiled at her and walked away, giving Katelyn a clear view of the senior parking lot.

Trick was outside, standing with a man who was wearing a suit and holding an umbrella. Or rather, the man was standing and Trick was pacing, bareheaded, flailing his arms. He was too far away for her to see his face, but it was obvious that he was angry.

"Oh, my God," a girl with chestnut curls cried as she sailed into the room. "Someone slashed Trick's tires!"

"What?" the girl in the sweatshirt squeaked. *"Again?"*

By the time she was heading home that afternoon, the sun was setting. It had taken a while to straighten everything out with Trick's car and to get replacement tires. He tried to joke about it, but she knew if it had happened to her, she'd be pissed and scared. And she'd seen him in the parking lot and seen how angry he was. She tried to ask him about it—who'd done it, and whether it had anything to do with the court trouble—but like Cordelia, he deflected her questions.

"So this is life on the wild side," she said, feeling bad for him.

"Oh, yeah. It doesn't get much wilder." He rolled his eyes, but it was clear by his clenched jaw that the lightheartedness was a front.

"I'm sorry about your car and everything."

He shook his head and glanced toward the sky. "I'm more worried about getting you home before dark."

She knew now why that was. Haley—Trick's . . . what? his girlfriend?—had been wandering around in the forest by herself when she'd been killed. Katelyn had assumed it had been an animal, but what had Beau been implying in history class? With a shiver, Katelyn thought of the scratching at the door.

She followed Trick's gaze. "I hate to tell you this, but we're not going to make it."

He gripped the wheel tight. "I know."

"It's cool, though. You called my grandfather and told him we were going to be late." It was true; she had heard Trick make the phone call. She was grateful, because she'd realized she hadn't bothered putting Ed's number in her iPhone.

"Unfortunately, it's not cool," she heard him mumble.

"I'm sure he understands," Katelyn said. "I mean, you didn't *plan* to have your tires slashed."

"Oh, yeah, he understands," Trick said, biting the words off.

The road twisted and wound and she watched as trees streaked by, the last light of the sun making them glow. Then it was gone and the trees became shadows, leaning toward the car, branches occasionally illuminated by Trick's headlights. They didn't look nearly as friendly as during the day. She felt like she was in the Snow White ride at Disneyland and at any moment the trees would come to life and try to grab her. Kimi always said Katelyn went for drama.

The road narrowed to one lane and she wondered what cars did when they arrived at those stretches from opposite directions. Then again, there probably weren't enough cars that came this way for it to be a real problem.

She continued to stare outside as she waited for her eyes to adjust. But even after a couple of minutes, she still couldn't see anything not directly illuminated by the headlights. The darkness was complete, impenetrable. *We're all alone,* she realized. There were no other cars, no house lights, nothing. There were just the road, the tree branches that stretched for them as they went by, and them.

She shivered. *What if something happens to the new tires? What if the car breaks down?* Fear began to creep into her mind as she strained even harder to penetrate the darkness around her. Maybe it made sense to be so cautious. She glanced at Trick and wrapped her arms around herself, wishing she could laugh off how silly she was being.

Suddenly, as they rounded a tight turn, she saw Trick's face change. She caught a glimpse of something in the middle of the road; then he was shouting and swerving. The car fishtailed and Katelyn screamed and braced herself against the dashboard.

And as soon as it had started, it was over. They came to a skidding halt.

"Don't look, Kat," Trick ordered.

Of course she looked; just inches from the front bumper, a deer was sprawled across the road, its eyes frozen, blank, dead, and wide in terror. *Dead!* She looked away, her stomach tightening, and thought of the heads on her grandfather's wall. *Someone must have hit it.*

Still, she heard herself ask, "What happened to it?"

Trick didn't say anything.

The deer's body blocked the road; the closely spaced trees on either side made it impossible to go around. Exhaling raggedly, she turned to Trick and saw the muscles in his jaw working. He glanced up at the pitch-black sky and muttered under his breath.

"What?" she asked.

"Stay here."

"Why, where are you going?" she asked. Panic flooded her. What if he disappeared into the woods and didn't come back? What if he left her?

He didn't look at her as he pulled the emergency brake and put the Mustang in neutral. "I'm going to drag the deer off the road. Stay in the car and don't come out for anything. The woods aren't safe at night. Lots of animals and crazies running around."

"*Crazies?*" she echoed. What was *that* supposed to mean?

In the distance, she could hear the sound of drums beginning to beat. Was that what he meant? The wolf retreat? The executive on the plane had been a lot of things—crazy maybe, but homicidal seemed like a leap. She dug her fingernails into her palms, trying to focus on the sensation, trying to make herself calm down.

Trick turned to look at her and there was fear in his eyes. Her heartbeat picked up. "Okay, I'll stay in the car."

"Good." He nodded as if to himself. "This will just take a minute."

Trick slammed the door as he got out, and she watched, on edge, as he crossed into the beams from the headlights. He grabbed two of the deer's legs and began pulling for all he was worth. She was actually glad he'd told her to stay in the car, because there was no way she wanted to help him.

Slowly the deer inched off the road and Katelyn turned her head, not wanting to see the lifeless eyes again. But then she was staring into the blackness that pressed up against the sides of the car, and that was worse.

She looked back and the deer was gone. And so was Trick.

She sat, blinking for a moment, scanning the trees for his shape. The drumming began to pick up, and her heart thumped faster. Every horror movie she'd seen started like this. She'd get killed by an ax-wielding wolfman executive, and Trick would come back and find her body right before he was chopped down, too.

"Haley was out *alone*," she whispered, desperate to hear the sound of a voice in the quiet and the dark, even if it was her own. Another thought flashed through her mind. What if whoever had slashed Trick's tires had dumped the deer on the road to get him out of the car? So that *he* was alone? What if out there in the dark he was being beaten . . . or worse? *He* was being killed by the murderer first. And when that was done, she'd be next.

Stop being an idiot. The deer wasn't left there to stop us.

Finally she couldn't stand it and rolled the window down. "Trick?" she called.

Only the sounds of the woods and the incessant drumming reached her.

"Trick, this isn't funny!" she shouted.

Nothing.

Chills shot down her spine.

Maybe he was hurt or lost and needed help. Yet even if she could find her way back to the school or to her grandfather's through the darkness without crashing the car on one of the hairpin turns, she'd never be able to say on what part of the road she'd left him.

He had told her to stay in the car, but for how long? What was she supposed to do? The engine was still running and she tried to crane her neck over to see how much gas there was, suddenly worried that they would run out. The gauge showed more than half a tank left, and she sighed in relief.

This is ridiculous!

She took a deep breath and then opened her car door and climbed out.

"Trick! Don't make me come after you!"

She scanned the area, but aside from the stand of menacing trees illuminated by Trick's high beams, she still couldn't see anything. The light pouring from inside the Mustang wasn't helping, and after a moment's hesitation, she closed the door, turned away from the wash of the headlights, and took a step forward. Cold crept into her bones and she felt as though someone were whispering to her. She couldn't hear it, exactly; she could only sense it. Her earlier fear that the scary-looking Snow White trees would come alive returned in full force and this time she couldn't shake it off.

The wind moaned through the branches and they began to creak. Something reached out and plucked at her shirt and she screamed and jumped backward, slamming her elbow into the car door. Katelyn hissed sharply at the pain even as she reached for the door handle, yanked it open, and threw herself inside, slamming the door behind her. She twisted around and examined her arm by the light of the instrument panel. Her sleeve was ripped and a jagged scratch was already oozing blood onto it. A tree branch tapped at the glass next to her and she forced herself to take several deep breaths.

The trees are not coming alive. They're just really close to the car.

She tried to still herself so she could listen. *Those stupid drums; if they'd just shut up—*

Crash! Something landed on the hood of the car and she screamed. Two piercing blue eyes were staring at her through the windshield. There was a growl, deep and low and menacing.

The creature shifted and its entire face came into view— silvery gray, enormous. It was a huge wolf with blood dripping from its fangs. It growled again.

It began to scratch at the glass, trying to get at her, and she screamed louder than she'd ever screamed in her life. The creature bounded onto the roof of the car and began to paw at it hard enough to make the car shake while it growled.

The window!

She reached to roll up the open window before the wolf got to it, but before she could, a hand shot through it and grabbed her shirt.

She beat at the hand, but it only tightened its grip on her. Then she heard three words whispered low and fierce: "Gun under seat."

She gasped—realizing it was Trick—and flailed beneath her seat until her fingers closed against cold metal. Then she heard a second growl rumbling beneath the first.

"Trick, Trick," she rasped, trying to warn him that there were two wolves. She couldn't make herself speak loudly enough for him to hear. *"Trick."*

Shaking, she pulled the handgun out and shoved it

through the window toward him, horrified at the very way it felt in her hand.

Trick fired a shot into the air and her ears rang. The wolf jumped off the hood and she heard more growling. It turned to look at her, illuminated in the high beams, foam mixing with the blood around its muzzle. Then the beast leaped toward where Trick was crouched next to her door. He yelled and fired off another shot.

The wolf let out a high-pitched yip. Then it turned and disappeared into the woods. Seconds later Trick was in the car, out of breath and looking every bit as terrified as she felt. He grabbed her head and turned her face to look into her eyes.

"Are you all right?"

She managed to nod, still stunned from what had just happened.

"Did it hurt you?"

"N-no. But there was another one. There were two," she said.

"Okay," he said. He let go of her and then looked down at her arm. He swore.

"What is it?" she asked, panic flaring through her again.

"You're bleeding. I thought you said it didn't hurt you!"

"It didn't. I got scratched by a branch."

He slumped into his seat and closed his eyes for a moment. He took a deep breath and then asked, "You got out of the car, didn't you?"

"Yes," she admitted, wincing. She didn't want him to yell anymore.

"Then you got lucky." He stared hard at her, reaching out

his fingers, almost touching the back of her hand but pulling away at the last instant. "Kat, please, please, don't ever do that again."

She licked her lips. "What was that thing?"

"Wolf."

She could still hear the drumming in the distance. She had seen wolves at the zoo before, but none of them had been that huge or vicious-acting.

"It looked like a monster." Katelyn searched for the words to express what she was thinking. "I . . . I thought wolves didn't attack people in real life. Maybe it thought I was stealing its dinner."

"I'd already moved the deer," he pointed out. "Those idiots with their drumming and howling are upsetting the animals. It was probably scared and confused."

She thought about Haley. Maybe that was what had happened: she'd been out alone and the drumming had frightened a wolf, maybe even the same wolf. The images that rushed through her mind made her feel ill. To die like that . . . it would be hideous.

"The forest isn't safe, Kat," he said, putting his hands back on the wheel. "There's a lot of animals and it's easy to get lost. Besides, you wouldn't want to come across one of those Inner Wolf guys in the dark. They've got to be off their rocker to go to the program, and who knows what that Bronson guy's telling them to do?"

Katelyn thought of the way the wolf had looked at her, its bloody mouth, the light in its brilliant blue eyes. It hadn't looked scared to her. It had looked . . . angry and cruel and amused all at the same time. She could feel herself beginning to shake as what she had seen set in. The drums persisted. Somewhere a little ways off she heard a howl and it sent a new wave of chills through her body.

The tires squealed as Trick floored it. She looked down at her arm and was relieved to see that the bleeding was slowing. She closed her eyes and slumped down into her seat as the tears came.

When Trick and Katelyn pulled up to the cabin, her grandfather was standing on the front porch, rifle in hand. The sight
unnerved her and the fear in the pit of her stomach was joined
by something new—anger. As soon as Trick stopped the car,
she jumped out and ran up the steps past Ed into the house.
She headed for the stairs but the sight of the glassy-eyed animal
heads sent her running instead for the kitchen.

On the porch she heard her grandfather's voice: "What in
the Sam Hill happened?"

She didn't hear Trick's reply, but her grandfather swore
loudly. She cringed as she splashed cold water from the sink
onto her face. She tried to pretend that the rivulets of water

would wash away the past few weeks, but when she had dried off her face and turned around, Mordecai was leaning in the doorway, one thumb hooked in a belt loop, the rifle still gripped in the other hand. He watched her with a fierce, steady gaze.

"You okay?" he asked, and there was concern in his eyes.

She dropped her hands to her sides. "No, I'm really not," she said. "Did Trick tell you what happened?"

He nodded.

"That wolf . . . it was a monster," she said, hating the way her voice shook.

"That's what lives in the forest," he said. Then he put down the rifle and crossed to her. He joined her at the sink.

"Do you know how to shoot a rifle?" he asked her.

"Of course not," she replied without thinking, revulsion thick in her voice.

"Then it's about time you learned."

"A gun?" she said. Before that day, she had never touched a gun in her entire life. And she never planned to again. A gun had killed her father. They were scarier than earthquakes or fires.

"This here's a Marlin," he said, indicating the rifle. "Can't be beat for hunting."

"I-I'm not going to be hunting anything."

He gave her a stern look. "I get that. But it's my job to make sure you don't become prey."

Prey. The word conjured up terrifying images in her mind—blood, and teeth, and death. She remembered the blood on the wolf's fangs. From the deer or something else?

"Okay," she said finally, "but I can't shoot anything. Not even that wolf."

There was a beat. A dark shadow seemed to pass over his face, and his eyes hardened. "There's more than one kind of wild animal out there."

———※———

"Oh, my God." Kimi's voice was distant on the phone but Katelyn was grateful to hear it at any volume. "You have got to get out of there."

Katelyn was in the kitchen with the handset cradled tightly between her ear and her shoulder. She and her grandfather had finished dinner, and she had offered to wash the dishes so she could talk to Kimi at the same time. He didn't have a dishwasher, and she was up to her wrists in Palmolive. She had eaten vegetable lasagna for dinner, while he had apparently fried "the bird" for himself. All through dinner, Katelyn had done her best to avoid looking at his plate, but now she had to wash it. She was afraid she would find uncooked pieces of rotting fowl in the trash—the head, or the claws.

"It jumped right on the hood," Katelyn said. "And it was drooling blood."

"*What?*" Kimi asked, sounding both shocked and excited.

"Yeah, no kidding. It came after me while Trick was dragging a dead deer off the road. We were late coming home because his tires got slashed." As she spoke, she heard how crazy it all sounded.

"*What the hell?*"

"Lucky thing Trick had a gun," Katelyn added, enjoying the chance to goose Kimi a little and get everything off her chest at the same time.

"Mom!" Kimi shouted. "File the emancipation papers stat!"

"Don't joke," Katelyn said, losing her bravado.

"Joke? Who's joking? What could he do if we got a judge to spring you? Shoot you? Like that poor deer and—and that chicken?"

"He didn't shoot the deer," Katelyn said, glancing down queasily at the trash can. She wasn't so sure about the chicken.

"Come home."

"I want to." Waves of homesickness rolled over her as the silverware jangled in her soapy hands. Then she imagined her house the way she'd last seen it—the stucco walls charred and fallen in and sutured with yellow plastic caution tape like a massive broken heart. The interior nothing but ash and a few intact odds and ends—her boots beside the front door, an old doll head, two yellow raincoats on melted plastic clothes hangers, and the picture frames that had once held her mother's portraits. The photos had burned.

"So why not fight him?" Kimi said.

"Because . . . maybe he'll just give up and let me leave," she said. "If I'm nice. But if I, like, sue him, and I lose . . . it would suck."

"Which is why you're there instead of here. If you *had* fought . . . Okay, okay," she said, sounding as if she had turned her head away from the phone. "Mom said to back off. She says unless you're scared he's going to shoot you, the fact that you willingly moved to Arkansas will make it harder, because you're with your legal guardian."

Great. Katelyn felt herself collapsing inside and panic began to set in. "I wish I had—"

And then she stopped speaking, because her grandfather stepped into the kitchen.

"Hey, Ed," she said.

"Can you not talk?" Kimi asked.

"I need to make a couple calls," her grandfather informed her. "Can you call your friend back later?"

"Sure," she said. "Kimi, I need to call you back later, okay?"

"Can you *please* speak to him about getting hooked up?" Kimi asked. "Even on dial-up? So we could at least Skype? And I can see for myself that you haven't morphed into Daisy Mae yet?"

"Sure," Katelyn said.

"Tell him you need it for school."

It was obvious Kimi hadn't grasped how isolated the cabin was. Or that there was no way anyone would need the Internet for Wolf Springs High.

They hung up, and Katelyn looked at her grandfather with free-floating anxiety.

"You okay?" he asked her.

"Just . . . homesick."

He nodded. "That's to be expected." No words of comfort, nothing.

"I got invited over to Cordelia's after school tomorrow," she said as she unplugged the drain in the sink. "To work on a history project." She hadn't brought it up at dinner because she'd been nervous about asking him. If he said no, there would be no escaping the fact that she was basically a prisoner, and she didn't know how she'd deal with that along with everything else. Maybe then she *would* fight him.

He looked puzzled as he picked up the phone handset. "Cordelia . . ."

"Fenner."

His eyes flickered. "The Fenners keep to themselves these days."

"Yeah, I guess. She told me she can bring me back here before dark, though."

He looked at her. Really looked. His forehead creased. His eyes narrowed. Something in his expression sent an uncertain skitter up her spine.

"Ed?" she asked. How weird could this be?

Another beat. Then he seemed to relax. "Sure. Call me tomorrow and give me their home phone number. And let me know before you two leave her place."

"Okay." Despite the victory, it bothered her how happy and relieved she was. So she wasn't a prisoner, but she still didn't want to make connections here, put down roots. She'd get out of the house and do her homework with Cordelia, but that was it.

Conflicted, she went to her room and sat on her bed with her textbooks spread around her in a semicircle and her little talking bear in her lap. She pressed its heart.

"Kimi misses Katie."

It was raining again. She could almost smell the wet leaves through the skylight above her head. Her mind wandered to Trick pacing in the rain in the senior lot, then dragging the deer carcass off the road. He carried a *gun* in his Mustang.

He's weird, she thought, *but he's hot.* She smiled wryly. And there was no denying that there was attraction. But he had a lot of backstory she didn't know—court, enemies. Unpredictability. Cordelia didn't like him and didn't like Katelyn being around him.

Before she knew it, her head was drooping forward; thoughts of Trick and of all the little factoids that together composed the mighty mass of knowledge she was trying to compress into her mind drifted away from each other like stars in the Milky Way. She saw Trick's eyes and then the eyes of the wolf. Cunning, intelligent. Sinister.

It wanted to get at me, she thought as she scooted down and rested her cheek on the sharp edge of her plastic binder. She pushed it away, found the pillow, and nestled in. Above her, the rain tapped on the skylight. She listened as she drowsed. It had rained more in the past three days than it rained in a year in Santa Monica.

Plink . . . plink . . .

She tensed. Was that a growl?

Just the wind, she told herself.

⊷ ▤◈▤ ⊷

The wind. And the drums.

The wind.

And the drums.

And her heartbeat.

The wind.

And the plink . . . plink . . . plink . . .

The click . . . click . . . click . . .

. . . of nails . . . click . . . click . . .

She was asleep, and she wasn't. She knew she was asleep. But it was coming. She could hear it panting.

Click, click.

Coming closer.

Click, click.

She couldn't move. Terror enveloped her, heavy, warm.

It had stopped beside her bed. Her eyes were closed—because
she was asleep—but she knew it was looking at her with its blue . . .

No, not its blue

Leaf-green

Tree-brown

Silvery-moonbeam

Golden-yellow

Her eyes were closed, but its eyes were wide open.

She couldn't move. Couldn't whimper.

Click.

Click.

Click.

Wake up, wake up, *she begged herself.* Save yourself.

If you go into the woods tonight, you'd better go in disguise.

But she wasn't in the woods. She was in her bed.

And It *was here . . . leaning over her. Saliva dripped on her*
cheek.

Wake up, wake up.

Just the wind.

And the drums.

--- ·━◆━· ---

"Hey there, Katalicious," Trick said when he picked her up
in the morning. Katelyn was tired from being awake half the
night, jerking out of sleep, replaying the images of the wolf attack over and over in her mind, hearing things.

The sun was just beginning to rise, and he stood on the
porch wearing a black T-shirt and black jeans, cowboy boots,

and a black cowboy hat. Also his leather bracelet. He smelled like freshly washed cotton, soap, and coffee.

She herself felt gross, having fallen asleep without brushing her teeth or washing her face. Then she'd rushed around to get ready. A hot shower and her electric toothbrush had power-washed away the grime, but still. She wore a black gauze baby doll top embroidered with gold thread over ripped, faded jeans and her Mary Janes. Her blond hair was coiled into a pinwheel-like messy bun with two black-and-gold chopsticks.

" 'Katalicious'? You really didn't just say that." She looked at him askance as she handed him a coffee mug and a piece of toast.

He dipped the toast in his coffee and took a bite. Balancing her toast on top of her coffee mug, she moved onto the porch and shut the door behind her. The air outside was hot and muggy, as if it had been conjured from the steam in their cups.

"Katalicious," she grumbled again. "That's so lame, Trick."

Trick raised his brows as they headed for his car. "Heavens to Betsy, just how shallow *are* they out there in Hollywood?"

"What is it with you and my grandfather and the corny sayings?" she asked, glancing up at the cloudy sky, wondering if she should bring an umbrella.

He tapped his head. "Brain transplant. I share the thoughts of the grandfather. That was what the surgery was for. You look good," he added. He smiled, really smiled as he held the Mustang door open for her.

"Thanks." She dipped her head and climbed inside, drinking down her coffee so it wouldn't spill when they drove over the bumps and dips in the dirt road. Anxiety fluttered in her stomach. She was trying not to admit to herself that she'd been waiting for him to show up that morning and her mood had lifted when she'd heard his car.

"It *is* a joke, right? The brain surgery."

His triumphant smile made her feel foolish for asking.

"I never asked you what you did last weekend," she said, to change the subject.

"Volunteered at a homeless shelter, helped my cat give birth to kittens, wrote poetry." He grinned at her as he shifted into drive and peeled out onto the road. Her head whipped backward. "Drove like an ass."

They raced toward the trees with the finesse of a roller coaster. She gripped the armrest and clenched her teeth. "Twenty-five percent of what you just told me is true."

"Fifty."

They careered into near darkness. He punched on his car stereo. That day it was Bon Jovi's "Blaze of Glory." She felt the bass rumble through her bones and loved the beat, the energy, the "take no prisoners" sense of possibility that rose inside her. A smile cracked her mood. She'd get back to L.A. She'd get back into dance and gymnastics and maybe even acting, and she'd figure out what to do with her life.

And she *hadn't* heard anything growling or felt anything staring in at her from the skylight the night before. It was just nerves.

"You do drive like an ass," she said.

"Just outrunning 'em, Kat." He grinned at her, then growled playfully.

With pleasure, she suspected.

"Hey, I had a nightmare," she said without thinking.

"I'm not surprised, after the day you had. Care to share?"

She paused, realizing she didn't want to. Sharing might make it seem more real and she'd rather forget it. "I don't really remember it. At least, not enough to explain."

"And they call *me* crazy," he said, smiling at her to take the sting out of the barb.

"You're mean," she said, pouting.

"I'm smart," he retorted. "*You* try being smart among the ignorant masses. It would make you snarly, too."

"As far as I can tell, it just gets your tires slashed." She realized what she'd said after it had already come out of her mouth. "Oh, God, Trick, I'm so sorry. I didn't mean to say that."

He sighed. "Don't you have some texting to do?"

"It's too early."

"If she's your best friend, she won't care."

She pulled out her phone, glad to have somewhere else to focus her attention. She was embarrassed. She'd been trying to joke around but knew she'd gone too far.

"Tell her hi."

"Sure will," she said, flushing.

But Kimi didn't reply.

⋯⋯⋯⋯

They got to school early and parted ways. Trick said he had something to take care of. She wondered if it had anything to do with slashed tires.

In hopes of having some topic suggestions for her project with Cordelia, she headed for the library. It was a small dusty room inside the main building, and it smelled of mold. Dim light filtered over wooden bookshelves, books crammed in them every which way. There was a desk with a sign that read LIBRARIAN but no actual librarian sitting at it, and no evidence one sat there regularly. It was as dusty as the shelves. Maybe no one used the library at this school. Katelyn hunted for a computer, hoping for a digital database of the library's holdings, but there was nothing that twenty-first century. She didn't know why she was surprised.

There was, however, an old-fashioned oak card catalog, complete with little white cards and smudged typed titles, authors, and subject headings. She flipped through the cards until she found WOLF SPRINGS: HISTORY. According to the catalog, there were two books in the library on the subject.

She jotted down their call numbers and wandered over to the stacks. One of the books was missing. The other, a thin volume with a tattered gray cloth cover, nearly came apart as she pulled it free. Carefully opening it, she glanced at the table of contents. *Spanish Settlers. Outlaws. The Hot Springs. Lost Dreams. The Wolves of Wolf Springs.* Bingo. She flipped to the indicated page and began to read the section about the wolves.

Hated and feared by settlers, the red wolves native to the Ozarks were thought to have been eradicated throughout Arkansas by the early 1900s. However, Wolf Springs locals have reported seeing packs ever since the first Spanish settlers arrived. The priests who founded the Catholic Church of Our Lady of Mercy wrote of the local wolves: "They remained aloof until winter, when lack of food compelled them to raid our barns for chickens and lambs. For ourselves, we had no fear of them, and they never attacked us."

She grunted. Maybe the nice wolves had died out along with the Spanish priests.

Aware that the hallway outside the library was filling up with students, she read the last two lines on the page:

"However, another creature dwelled in the forest. This one, we feared with all our souls."

And the next page was missing. Tattered, jagged edges were held by unraveling stitching, but the page itself was gone. She kept reading, in hopes that the mystery creature would be revealed.

"And thus it remains that our good company shuns the wooded hills."

"Crap," she said out loud.

The bell rang, and she quickly paged ahead. Apparently that was it for the wolves and the scary thing in the forest, but she still wanted to check out the book. There had to be something useful in it.

"Hello?" she called.

When no librarian appeared, she looked around to make sure she was alone and semi-guiltily dropped the fragile book into her backpack, then slipped out into the hall to join the rest of the student body.

In history class, Cordelia told Katelyn that she'd checked out a ton of books from the public library. She approved of Katelyn's find and explained, with a laugh, that all she had to do to officially check out books from the school library was show them to Mrs. Walker, who kept a list in the office. After the last librarian had moved, they hadn't replaced her. It seemed that Mrs. Walker was the go-to person for everything you needed at school.

Katelyn was relieved to see that Mike was absent from gym. Maybe a day away was all it would take for him to forget that she'd embarrassed him. She suited up and stretched out. She enjoyed the strength and elasticity of her muscles as she went through her routines. And she knew that without regular workouts she'd lose it. The familiar dizzying anxiety hit her in the chest as she remembered that all her costumes, all the videos she'd saved on her laptop of her performances, were gone. *I got out with nothing but me. And there are times when I'm not even sure I got out with that.*

At lunch, Cordelia introduced her to a few girls, including those Wolf Springs High cheerleaders who were still speaking to the girl who had made them lose their big competition— versus the ones who were pretending Cordelia Fenner no longer existed. Boys circled their table, some of them really cute, and Katelyn had to answer a lot of questions about L.A. It was clear that Dondi—the girl with the gold fingernails—and Maria, at least, still wanted to be friends with Cordelia. And Cordelia had plenty of guys swooning over her. But Cordelia herself was sending out vibes that she wanted—or needed—to be left alone.

Trick stayed away, watching from a table of gothy kids dressed in black. But there was something about him that kept drawing Katelyn's attention, and she felt a warmth in the pit of her stomach every time their eyes met. Maybe it was the green of his eyes, or the arty, interesting company he kept. His friends obviously doted on him. He was the center of their attention.

Or maybe she liked it that *she* was the object of *Trick's* attention. Each time she tried to dart a discreet glance his way, he was looking at her. He intercepted every one of her looks, each time, and his smile got bigger and bigger. At first she was mortified, and then she just laughed.

"What's so funny?" Cordelia asked her, and Katelyn shifted her focus back to Cordelia and her friends.

"Nothing," she assured her.

Trick was good with the afternoon off. On the morning drive in, Katelyn had announced that she had plans after school and wouldn't need a ride.

But now she was a little sorry that they wouldn't be riding home together.

Then it was time for art, and the girl in the sweatshirt smiled at Katelyn again. When Katelyn smiled back, the girl picked up her sketch pad and a piece of charcoal and moved to the empty chair beside Katelyn, directly beneath the ticking school clock.

"I'm Paulette," she said by way of greeting. "How're you doing?"

"Pretty well," Katelyn replied.

"For someone who had to move from L.A. to *here*," Paulette said with an eye roll.

"It's not so bad," Katelyn replied, but her voice cracked, and they both smiled.

"Look, *I* know how bad it is." Paulette offered her another friendly smile, then looked down at her sketch pad and drew a long, curving line.

Katelyn let her shoulders sag. "It is kind of . . . um . . ."

"Rustic? Quaint?"

"Wolf Springs *is* quaint." Katelyn decided to try to draw a wolf. How to start? A triangle for the head? She thought about the little town, with its old-fashioned streets. "It would make a great tourist attraction."

"Too hard to get here," Paulette said. "Too far from civilization, and bad roads. So." She glanced at the parking lot. "You're driving in every day with Trick."

Katelyn wasn't surprised by the comment. She figured people were speculating about her. "Yes."

Katelyn looked up to see her reaction and was jolted to see that Paulette had gone all blushy.

"Lucky," she said shyly.

Katelyn was caught off guard. It was the opposite of the reaction Cordelia had had. And if Paulette was crushing on Trick, that meant he wasn't a *total* outcast. She felt a flare of jealousy, then was surprised at herself.

I hardly know him.

"Do you know who slashed his tires?" Katelyn asked.

"No. Do you? Did he tell you?" Paulette stopped drawing as she waited for Katelyn's answer.

"No idea," Katelyn confessed. "But I don't know who anyone is around here anyway."

Paulette nodded. "It was probably Mike Wright. Trick

had a run-in with him and his friends a while back. They're such jerks."

Katelyn shivered. She was right about Mike. She wished she'd stayed off his radar.

"Not Trick, I mean. Trick's not a jerk." Paulette sighed wistfully and went back to sketching. "You eat lunch with Cordelia Fenner."

Katelyn nodded, feeling a little creeped out. Yes, she was the new girl, and yes, people were curious about her, but she was beginning to feel a little stalked.

"Never liked her," Paulette said, biting off the words. "You should be careful."

Katelyn's brows rose in surprise. She hadn't expected her to say anything like that about Cordelia.

"She acts so sweetsy-sweetsy. And I stress the *acts*," Paulette went on. Then she gave Katelyn a slow, measured look. "She and Trick can't stand each other."

"Why not?" Katelyn was struggling to make sense of everything she was hearing.

"It might be something that happened in kindergarten, for all I know. People around here hold grudges. Maybe it's because there's not much else to do." Her eyes went unfocused then, as if she were gazing at a faraway place. "I'd give anything to live in L.A. It must be so . . . *different*."

"Well, after you graduate, you can move there," Katelyn offered.

"Maybe. Most of the kids here will wind up living here. Some of us get out." She shrugged. "Anyway, take it slow. Sometimes it's hard to separate out the phonies, you know what I mean?"

"Okay. Thanks for the advice."

"I just don't want to see anyone else get hurt," Paulette said. She looked hard at Katelyn. "Because Cordelia Fenner *will* hurt you, if she feels like it."

———❧———

Katelyn had no clue what to think about what Paulette had told her, but it weighed on her for the rest of the day. As soon as the final bell rang, she headed for the senior parking lot. Cordelia had beaten her there, and stood waving to her from beside a black pickup truck. Katelyn hadn't pictured Cordelia as the truck type, although she shouldn't have been surprised, given the large ratio of trucks to cars in the parking lot. As Katelyn climbed inside the cab, she noticed that it was sparkling clean and smelled like cinnamon.

"Nice truck," she managed to make herself say.

"Thanks!" Cordelia said. Her voice was upbeat, as usual, but her expression was strange—tense, almost—her smile fake. Katelyn thought about what Paulette had said about her. She couldn't agree with it. Cordelia seemed genuinely nice. And now she was genuinely upset about something—and trying to hide it.

She'd thought about telling Cordelia about the wolf attack. But Cordelia didn't seem to want to chat. Maybe she was sorry she'd invited Katelyn over.

"This is okay, my coming home with you, right?" Katelyn asked.

"Oh, yes, sure," Cordelia blurted, too quickly and too brightly.

She pulled out of the parking lot and in silence they drove through the town and turned onto the narrow road that climbed into the mountains. Like Ed, Cordelia's family lived far outside town. When they turned off the main artery into Wolf Springs, there were no paved roads, and Katelyn couldn't distinguish one twisted Snow White tree from another. Cordelia focused on her driving so intently that Katelyn remained silent, suppressing the urge to fill the space with chatter. Her mind wandered and she found herself thinking about Trick. She thought about asking Cordelia to tell her more about him, partly to see if it was true that she didn't like him. But Katelyn didn't want to seem too curious about a guy Cordelia clearly didn't approve of. Or maybe it was that she didn't want to admit she liked him to anyone—including herself—just yet.

They turned down a winding trail and Cordelia sighed softly. Katelyn glanced at her just as Cordelia's eyes widened like she'd seen something in the rearview mirror, but all Katelyn saw when she glanced at it was Cordelia. Shadows slid over the truck hood, then across the windshield. The trees seemed closer, denser. They slowed down.

"We're he-ere," Cordelia announced in a singsong voice, mimicking an old horror movie. Katelyn couldn't remember which one.

It took a moment for Katelyn to take the structure in completely. She had seen a program on television once where wealthy people into "living green" had built a house around a tree. Cordelia's house reminded her of this, but at the same time it was nothing like it. A rambling structure of redwood, stone, and stained glass seemed to rise naturally from the earth, twisting and sprouting with turrets and bay windows like the limbs and trunks that grew around it and even through it. Leaves the color of flames swirled in eddies in what appeared to be open-air patios. Set at the top of a large stone staircase, situated on a massive stone porch, the front door was a double arch of redwood interspersed with panes of frosted glass. There were window boxes containing pretty purple flowers. Katelyn had seen plenty of mansions before but nothing near the majesty of this place.

Cordelia continued past the front of the house, driving the length of the curving structure, then pulled around to the back and parked next to a couple of other cars—a Mercedes and a Volvo SUV. As she turned the engine off, she heaved a sigh. Her hands dropped to her lap, and Katelyn froze in the middle of opening her door.

"What's wrong?" Katelyn asked.

"It looks like my sisters are visiting." Cordelia's voice was low, hushed as she studied the two cars.

"Is that a problem?"

"Yeah. I'd give anything to be an only child."

"I guess the grass is always greener," Katelyn said, suppressing a nervous laugh. "I always wanted a sister."

"You can have both of mine," Cordelia said with a weak smile. She climbed out of the cab and headed for the back door, which was solid wood.

Katelyn jumped down and shut the truck door, then hastily followed her friend into the house. Inside, she found herself in a sort of courtyard with a trickling fountain and a skylight overhead. She looked around admiringly as Cordelia nervously scanned left and right. There were more of the pretty purple flowers in pots.

Katelyn heard trilling laughter and the sound of high heels clicking on the floor.

"Oh, crap," Cordelia muttered.

Two older girls approached, one blond and the other brunette, and their resemblance to Cordelia was startling.

The blonde was wearing tight bronze leather pants and a sleeveless black blouse that showed off her curves. On her feet were super-high metallic heels with leather straps that wrapped up around her ankles, and chains laden with chunks of amber hung around her neck. Her makeup was perfectly applied, all smoky eyes and shimmering lips.

The brunette had on a black pencil mini, which looked like it was made of raw silk, and a sleeveless red mock turtleneck knit top. But unlike her sister, she was as hip-free and flat as a model. Her makeup was heavy and elaborate, her lips deep scarlet.

Cordelia crossed her arms in a defensive posture as the two approached. Something about how they walked over made Katelyn wonder if it had been a mistake not asking her grandfather if Cordelia could come to their house instead. The two were eyeing her in a way that made Katelyn even more uncomfortable than the staring animal heads at home did. What her grandfather had said the night before about predators and prey came back to her. These women definitely made her feel like prey.

They walked up and, instead of introducing themselves, continued moving around, taking in Katelyn from head to toe.

"Well, well, look what our little sister dragged home," the brunette drawled.

"It looks like a stranger," the blonde said.

It?

They moved gracefully. Katelyn fought down an instinctive reaction to turn in a circle, too, tracking them the way they seemed to be tracking her.

"Smells like a stranger," the brunette confirmed.

"Kat, these are my sisters, Arial and Regan." Cordelia sounded unhappy, which Katelyn understood, because she was feeling the same way.

"Um, o-kay," Katelyn said.

"Hear that voice, Regan? It *sounds* like a stranger, too," the blonde—Arial—said.

What kind of freaks are they? Katelyn thought as they continued to circle her. *Is this some result of banjo inbreeding?*

Before Katelyn could say anything, Arial and Regan burst into laughter.

"Now, dear, don't scare the children," a tall, thin guy with tired gray eyes said as he walked into the room. He looked to be midtwenties, but maybe older. It was hard to say.

"Albert, what are you doing here?" Cordelia asked with a short relieved laugh. She clearly liked him more than her sisters.

"I've come to collect my wife," he said.

Arial sauntered over to him. "Killjoy," she said, pouting.

He gave her a weak smile. "You should be happy if I kill anything, pet." He turned to Katelyn and stuck out a hand. "I'm Al Fontaine. You must be a friend of Cordelia's from school." His smile was strained but his manner was pleasant.

Bemused, Katelyn shook hands with him. "Nice to meet

you," she said, hearing her emphasis after the fact. His tired face lit up one or two watts, and he chuckled.

"Come on, Kat, let's go to my room," Cordelia said, grabbing her by the arm and pulling her quickly away.

Katelyn was relieved to get out of there, and as soon as they were out of earshot, she blurted, "What the hell was that?"

"They like to scare people, manipulate them," Cordelia muttered as they entered a paneled corridor. "Don't let them get to you. I try not to."

Katelyn was embarrassed for her. Her sisters were freaks. "I can see why you said you wished you were an only child. I don't blame you. For the first time in my life, I'm glad I'm sibling-free."

Cordelia glanced back. "Well, then, they were good for something. That's a switch."

"Sorry," Katelyn said, "that was mean of me."

"Not even close, trust me," Cordelia said. "Here's my room."

The room was about three times the size of Katelyn's room at her grandfather's. It was paneled in silvery wallpaper with lavender accents, very light and airy when compared to the dark, heavy furniture. The central focus was a carved canopy bed and, beside it, a full-length oval mirror on wooden clawed feet etched with a moon and a star. Cheerleading trophies covered the top of a chest of drawers. Pictures of Cordelia in her uniform and other girls in Wolf Springs Cheer regalia were everywhere.

Beyond the bureau, a sliding glass door led to a small patio and from there straight into the woods. Katelyn stared into the thick, shadowy blurs of pine needles and fiery autumn leaves.

She wondered if Cordelia was forbidden to go into the woods as well. Given what had happened the night before, it seemed like a pretty good rule.

She turned to Cordelia, who was watching her expectantly. "Nice," Katelyn said. "You've got a lot of space."

Cordelia smiled, but she was still tense. "Yeah. It's a luxury, but I like my privacy." She shrugged as if to apologize. "I'm weird that way."

"Who doesn't?" Katelyn asked. "I would kill to have this much space to myself."

Cordelia plopped down on the bed and stretched out on her stomach, propping her chin up on her fists. "Tell me about L.A."

Katelyn sat down on a wooden chair upholstered with gray tapestry fabric. It was nubby and rough but comfortable. What could she say: *It's so much better than here?*

"Big. Busy. Plus, the ocean." She hoped she kept the longing out of her voice. She didn't want to insult Cordelia by dissing her hometown. Although, Katelyn's impulse to make a friend of her had been dampened a bit by Paulette's remarks in class.

"We have a lot of ponds. Okay, swampy bogs." Cordelia wrinkled her nose. "And the river. When the snow starts melting, it practically *is* like an ocean."

"Hmm," Katelyn said neutrally, but inwardly quaked at the thought of living in snow. In Southern California, you had to make a deliberate effort to find snow.

"So what are your friends like?" Cordelia pressed, obviously eager for details.

"My best friend, Kimi, we did everything together. We

were—are—like sisters," she said, flinching at the use of the past tense. Kimi was still her best friend, and when she got back to L.A., things would be just the same as they used to be. Her eyes started tearing and her vision blurred. She needed to get the attention off herself before full-on tears came. "So who do *you* hang out with?"

Cordelia gestured to all the pictures and trophies. "Well, you know I used to be a cheerleader." She slumped back on her bed, still watching Katelyn curiously. "Lately, though, I've just been spending a lot of time with my family."

"Oh . . . that's . . . cool," Katelyn said, hoping for Cordelia's sake that the rest of the family wasn't like her sisters.

Cordelia grimaced. "My two cousins moved in a few months ago when their father died. It's been an adjustment for everyone—but you know, family."

"Yeah." She knew only too well. The only family she had left was a trigger-happy grandfather she couldn't relate to. But Cordelia had obviously had a life here—one she'd put on hold. So they had that in common.

"So shall we get started?" Cordelia said, sitting up.

"Sure." Katelyn was grateful for the topic change.

Cordelia dug some books out from underneath her bed while Katelyn fished in her backpack for the library book, which she still hadn't told Mrs. Walker she'd taken.

"My trip to the library was a preemptive strike," Cordelia announced. "I checked out a bunch of books before anyone else got to them. Most of the really good local stuff hasn't made it onto the Internet yet." She dropped the books on the bed and spread them around so that all the covers were visible.

Katelyn glanced at the titles of some books. *"Arkansas and the Civil War. The People Rule: A History of Arkansas.* This is the really good stuff?"

Cordelia grimaced. "Kind of boring, huh?"

"I thought we were going to do the school. Because it's haunted?" Katelyn said, prompting her.

"Can't. I saw Maria at the library and she and Jackson called dibs. Her aunt has some old yearbooks or something. I don't think there'd be much left for us."

"Well, what about some other ghost story? Tri—I heard there are all kinds of stories about scary stuff up here in the mountains." She was determined not to mention Trick's name around Cordelia again.

Making a face, Cordelia resolutely picked up a book. Katelyn read the title on the cover: *A History of Arkansas: From Spanish Settlement to Prohibition.* "I'm not really big on supernatural stuff," she said apologetically. "I scare easily. My dad says I'm the biggest baby on the planet."

"Oh. Well, what about your family? Do you have a big mystery? Where your granny's special pumpkin pie recipe came from? Or when you came over from the Old Country, something like that?"

"Oh, gosh, we're boring as heck," Cordelia said with a smile, but her voice sounded a little strained. Katelyn picked up on it and wondered if maybe the Fenners had a scandalous past of some kind. Kimi's mother had told Katelyn that people in the South took a lot of pride in their families—who "their people" were. Californians tended to be a lot more rootless.

"Maybe you can find something in this," Cordelia said,

handing the book over to Katelyn. "I guess I'm just not feeling like an investigative historian today."

Clearly the unexpected appearance of Cordelia's sisters had upset her. She seemed much more subdued than she had been at school. Glancing at the pictures of a laughing Cordelia with her cheer squad, Katelyn thought the Cordelia who sat across from her on the bed looked almost like a different person.

"I'll give it a shot," Katelyn said as Cordelia idly pulled out the handout for their project and read it. Katelyn flipped to the table of contents of the book and skimmed it. Her eyes widened with excitement when she came to "Buried Treasure."

"Cordelia," she said, "what about this?" She tapped her finger on the words. "Spanish treasure, outlaw booty, hidden mines."

"Shake your booty," Cordelia sang softly.

Katelyn thumbed her way to the chapter. She began to scan the text. "Spanish settlements . . . Let's see. . . . Whoa, look at this. Did you know Hot Springs was run by the mob in the thirties? Hidden mines . . . gold mines. Oooh, a hidden gold mine."

"That might be good," Cordelia said. "There's gold in these thar hills."

Katelyn smiled and kept reading. Suddenly the words "Wolf Springs" popped out at her. She followed along and then read aloud. " 'The tiny Victorian village of Wolf Springs, a miniature jewel in the crown of the nearly untouched towns dotting the Ozarks, is well known by treasure-seekers for the lost silver mine called the Madre Vena.' " With a grin, she looked up at Cordelia. "Score!"

To her surprise, Cordelia looked a little pale, drawing up the left side of her mouth in an expression of distaste. "Silver? Gold's . . . *cooler*." She imitated Mr. Henderson's un-Southern accent as she said the word.

"Yeah, but the Madre Vena mine is right here," Katelyn pointed out, surprised Cordelia hadn't made the connection. "It's in Wolf Springs."

"So they say," Cordelia replied, sounding dubious. "How old is that book? It's probably been found by now."

"But if it hasn't been, we should totally do it," Katelyn insisted. "Didn't you say Mr. Henderson was an archaeologist? He would love us." She went back to the first couple of pages of the book. "This book's only a year old," she announced. "Oh, come on, let's do it."

"Well . . . ," Cordelia said, sounding reluctant. Then she swiveled her head suddenly, as though she'd heard something. "We should be going before it gets any later. We can talk about this in the truck. It's a long drive."

Katelyn frowned, puzzled. They'd just gotten there. What was the point in getting together if it was only for ten minutes?

"If we have extra time, we can hang at your place, right?" Cordelia said. Her voice rose a little at the end. She was even tenser than she'd been when she'd seen her sisters' cars.

"Sure." At least, Katelyn hoped it would be okay with her grandfather.

They packed up their bags and headed back toward the courtyard. As they crossed it, Katelyn heard the roar of a motorcycle pulling up outside.

They were almost to the door when it crashed open,

making her jump. Framed in the doorway in front of a blaze of sunlight, a tall guy in aviator sunglasses froze. His face was sharply angled, his jaw square, and cheeks and chin stubbly with a five o'clock shadow. His wavy chestnut hair was flecked with gold. A black leather jacket stretched across broad shoulders; powerful thighs were encased in tight black jeans.

He raised a black-gloved hand, pulled off his sunglasses, and looked Katelyn over, eyes lingering. They were deep, deep blue, the color of a California summer. Katelyn's heart began to pound. He was gorgeous, so sexy it almost hurt to look at him. He unzipped his jacket to reveal a simple black T-shirt pulled across his chest.

As though in slow motion he walked forward, pulling off his gloves, one finger at a time. Katelyn had to tilt back her head to look up at him when he stopped in front of her; he had her beat by at least a foot. Without taking his gaze off her, he stuffed the gloves in the pocket of his jacket.

"Kat, this is my cousin Justin. Justin, this is Kat. She's new here."

Katelyn held out her hand, willing him to take it just so she could feel his skin touching hers. His mouth twitched. He slid his hand around hers, consuming it, and gripped tight. Her skin tingled where it touched his and she parted her lips slightly. He was bending down toward her, his lips nearly touching her cheek. Then he inhaled sharply, as if he were catching his breath, and she jerked, but he kept tight hold of her hand.

What the heck? She blinked as he pulled away just enough to meet her eyes.

"Hello, Kat." His voice was low and a little hoarse.

What did he just do? Was he going to kiss me?

He still held her hand in his, and as he continued to stare into her eyes, she felt an aching sensation in the pit of her stomach. She wanted with everything that was in her to throw her arms around his neck, press her body against his, and kiss his lips.

No, she didn't just want to; she was *going* to. Her free hand was already moving up around his neck when she heard footsteps and a voice suddenly shouting, "Stranger!"

5

"Stranger!" the voice shouted again.

Justin pulled away and Katelyn sagged slightly even as she turned to identify the speaker. A guy with a thick neck that met his chin was standing just inside the door, dressed also in jeans and a leather jacket, a motorcycle helmet dangling from his left hand. His mouth was wide, and his eyes were like Ping-Pong balls. With his right hand he was jabbing his fingers at Katelyn. He began to make a soft whining noise of distress.

Cordelia moved swiftly to the newcomer's side and gently took his arm. "I'm sorry, Jesse. I wasn't expecting you home or

I would have told you she was coming." Her cheeks were red. "I *thought* you two were coming back tomorrow."

Katelyn blinked, still slightly dazed, and forced herself to focus on Jesse. He looked a lot like Justin, although a bit shorter, and with fuller lips.

"Pretty stranger," Jesse said, now grinning at her.

"Yes, Jesse," Justin said without turning to look at him. "She is very pretty."

Cordelia looked over at Katelyn. It was obvious that Cordelia hadn't caught Katelyn's reaction to Justin. And Katelyn was still so bewildered that she turned her back to him. Had *Justin* known she'd been on the verge of throwing herself at him? Her heart was thundering, and she was sweaty. And still very, very confused.

Okay, what just happened? she thought.

"Kat, I want you to meet my other cousin, Jesse," Cordelia said. "Jesse, this is my friend Kat. She's new here and needs friends."

"Hello, Jesse," Katelyn said softly, focusing her attention on him.

He didn't appear to hear her. Katelyn took a step forward and repeated herself.

"The lady said hello," Justin said. "She's a nice lady. It's okay."

Finally Jesse lifted his eyes, took a couple of quick steps forward, and kissed her cheek, then retreated.

Startled, Katelyn looked at Cordelia. Cordelia made a grimace of apology, and Katelyn smiled to let her know she hadn't minded. Then her glance flicked over to Justin. He was staring at her, the left side of his mouth quirked upward, a thumb looped in his front pocket.

"I'm taking her home now," Cordelia went on. "So we'll be out of your hair."

"We can manage dinner," Justin said to her. He turned back to Katelyn and gave her a slow smile. His teeth were very white. "Welcome, Kat."

Katelyn searched for words, but Cordelia had already grabbed her by the hand and was dragging her out the door before she could respond. As she climbed into the truck, Katelyn couldn't help looking back. Justin stood in the doorway, watching them go. A trail of heat flashed up her back and spread across her shoulder blades. And before she knew it, Cordelia had eased the truck out and they were shooting up the driveway.

As the truck rattled along the dirt path, the spell slowly dissipated.

Cordelia was saying, "I'm sorry. Jesse is . . . special."

Katelyn nodded. She was embarrassed that Cordelia thought she cared about that. But it was a good cover to explain how flustered she was by Justin. Just replaying the last minute or two gave her goose bumps. Good ones.

"He seems like a sweetie," Katelyn assured her.

"Yeah. Jesse is great, but he's never going to be able to be on his own. That's okay, though. Family takes care of each other."

Cordelia downshifted as they started up the steep grade. She flicked on an iPod, which Katelyn hadn't noticed, and it began to play through the speakers.

Her brain hit an instant replay of what had just happened

between her and Justin, and this time the memory of his scent penetrated her brain. He smelled like the *ocean*. Salty, plus that indefinable whatever-it-was she inhaled when she stood barefoot in the sand, closed her eyes, and lifted her face to the sun.

"Is the cheek kissing a family thing?" Katelyn asked, trying to sound casual. Now that she'd had a chance to process everything, she'd realized that Justin had been millimeters away from kissing her cheek, too. He'd stopped himself just in time.

Cordelia made a face. "I know it's weird. We can be a bit touchy-feely sometimes. Sorry about that."

So it is a family thing, Katelyn thought, disappointed. But it hadn't felt like it. It had been too charged, too intimate.

"Please. I come from the land of the air kiss," Katelyn said, struggling to mask her confusion. "And my mom was French."

Cordelia clenched her teeth and smiled. "Again, sorry. I thought we'd have the place to ourselves this afternoon and you met half the family instead."

"Your sisters are freakishly weird," Katelyn admitted, wrinkling her nose. "Jesse is sweet and Justin's . . . intense."

Cordelia's face darkened. "He's always been that way, ever since we were kids. Since his dad died, though, he's letting that side show more."

So Justin had lost his father, too. . . .

"What about his mom?"

"Died when Justin was a baby," Cordelia said, squinting through the windshield. "My mom's dead, too."

"Oh, I'm so sorry," Katelyn said, surprised. She hadn't met many other people who had lost parents, like she had.

"I don't even remember her," Cordelia said quietly.

"At least you have your dad still," Katelyn said, faltering.

"Yeah. Gotta love Daddy." She cocked her head at something she saw. Katelyn tried to follow her line of vision, but the sun was in her way.

Katelyn's mind wondered. She wondered how Justin had been coping with losing both of his parents and if he resented living with Cordelia's family the same way she resented living with her grandfather. He was old enough to be on his own. Then she thought of Jesse and realized that he was probably doing it for him.

It gave her a tiny, momentary thrill that there might be someone else out here in the middle of nowhere who understood what she was going through.

"What happened to their dad?" she asked, then realized maybe asking was rude.

"It was a hunting accident," Cordelia said simply, but she suddenly looked pale and she wrapped her hands tightly around the steering wheel.

Katelyn wondered how close Cordelia and her uncle had been and decided not to push any further. "Sorry, I didn't mean to pry."

"No, it's okay. I guess I haven't really had anyone I could talk about it with." Cordelia flashed her a shy smile, and Paulette's warning came to mind.

Was she acting right now for Katelyn's benefit?

"Funny how you can think you have a lot of friends, but when times are hard or you can't really hang out, they just seem to evaporate like smoke," Cordelia added, an edge to her voice.

Katelyn thought of Kimi. She didn't want that to happen with them, but if she was honest with herself, she could admit already feeling the strain of the distance. Kimi was moving on, making new friends to do things with. Paulette's dire warnings aside, Cordelia seemed like she could be a friend. But ever having the kind of closeness she had had with Kimi again was hard to imagine.

Tears stung the corners of her eyes but she was sick of crying, sick of giving in to panic and despair. It was time to stand on her own two feet. What would her dad say? *Don't be a victim.* Although he himself eventually had been one.

"Oh, crap," Katelyn said suddenly. "I was supposed to call my grandfather to tell him we're on our way."

"Use my cell," Cordelia offered. She held it out. The cover was psychedelic-looking, with swirls of color.

"Cool cover," Katelyn said.

"Don't you love it? It glows in the dark."

"Is there a signal here?"

"Yup," Cordelia replied.

"Then I'll use my phone. Thanks, though."

"No problem," Cordelia said.

Katelyn whipped her own phone out. Her grandfather's number was programmed in now. She scrolled through her address book until she came to it, and pressed send, but instead of a "hello" on the other end, she got the answering machine. She told him they'd left the Fenners' and would be home soon.

The sun was beginning to dip when they pulled up outside her grandfather's cabin. The light was already fading, and it irritated her; it was a symbol of the boundaries of her new world.

"It gets dark quick around here," she said, staring at the cabin.

"It doesn't in L.A.?" Cordelia sounded amused.

Katelyn shrugged. "With all the lights it seems like it never gets dark."

"I don't remember that. I was really young when we took a trip out there." Cordelia's voice trailed off wistfully.

"After I move back, you should come visit," Katelyn said, warming to the thought. It would be fun to show her around.

"I'd love to, but . . ."

"What?" Katelyn asked.

The other girl went very quiet. Something seemed to settle around her shoulders like a heavy burden, as if night was literally falling on her.

"Life's just too complicated, you know?" she said.

"Have you met my grandfather?" Katelyn said archly.

The door to the cabin opened suddenly, startling her, and Ed appeared on the porch, staring right at them.

Katelyn sighed. "I guess that's my cue." She gave Cordelia a weak smile and grabbed her schoolbag.

Her grandfather stepped off the porch right as she opened the car door. She hoped that she wasn't in trouble for not calling sooner. But he wasn't headed toward her; he was walking toward the driver's side.

Katelyn got out and shut the door. Ed gave her a brief wave as he bent down toward Cordelia's window, and Katelyn stopped to watch. Cordelia rolled down her window and he shoved his hand through and they shook.

"Stay for dinner?" he asked.

"Um, sure," Cordelia said, glancing over at Katelyn for approval.

She nodded, pleased and surprised that he had made the offer.

"Good." He turned and walked back into the cabin, leaving the door open.

Cordelia got out and joined her, and they headed up the steps together.

"I didn't see that one coming," Katelyn admitted in a whisper.

"I'd rather eat with you guys than see what my cousins decide to call dinner."

"Do you need to call and check?" Katelyn asked.

Cordelia shook her head. "I'll be all right."

Katelyn wondered if she was the only person not allowed out after dark. Cordelia had grown up there, so maybe that accounted for her greater freedom. And the Fenners didn't live in town, but her house wasn't as remote as the cabin—not deep in the middle of the woods. *Must be nice. And normal.*

As Cordelia came into her grandfather's house, Katelyn wondered what she thought of it. The cabin was tiny compared to Cordelia's house.

"Homey," Cordelia said, smiling at both of them. She walked down the row of heads and paintings. "Very nice. Did you bag all these?" she asked Katelyn's grandfather, who was standing at the entrance to the kitchen.

"I did," he replied proudly.

"Wow." She sounded genuinely impressed, and Katelyn had to suppress an eye roll. She just didn't get the hunting thing.

"Want to see my room?" Katelyn asked, feeling a little shy. "Unless you need help with dinner?" she asked Ed.

"Go ahead." He looked pleased as he disappeared into the kitchen.

The two girls went up the stairs. Cordelia paused to glance at the stained-glass window with the McBride coat of arms, then trailed Katelyn into her bedroom.

"It's a lot smaller than yours," Katelyn said as she dropped her backpack on the floor. Cordelia followed her lead while glancing up at the skylight. Then she bent over and dug out the library books.

"Now, before we were so rudely interrupted," she went on, flushing to her roots at the memory of Cordelia's cousin's arrival, "I think we decided on the Madre What's-it Mine as our subject."

Cordelia sighed heavily, and Katelyn raised her brows. "Or . . . something else?" She couldn't figure out why Cordelia was so unenthusiastic. It was a perfect choice.

There was a knock on the door. Then it cracked open. "Cordelia?" Katelyn's grandfather said around the edge. "Carnivore or herbivore?"

"Carnivore," Cordelia said.

"Check," he replied, shutting the door.

Cordelia smiled at Katelyn. "Your grandfather's a honey," she whispered.

"Oh, my God, you didn't just say that," Katelyn moaned, grinning at her. She picked up another book, this one titled *Legends of the Mountains*. "Maybe we can find something else."

"I'll look, too," Cordelia said, reaching for the legends book.

They began to root through a few of the books. As Katelyn ran her eyes along the pages, she couldn't help slowing down whenever she came across a backwoods legend. There was one about the Banshee Lady, a woman who had drowned her children in the swamp in a fit of rage, and who wandered through the pines in the dead of night, shrieking with grief, searching for her lost little ones. There was another one about Tío Oso—Uncle Bear—an old mountain man who had gone off to live with the bears and actually transformed into one and could be heard roaring late at night.

She got engrossed in a really freaky story about Hangman Hank, a backwoods thief who would lean down from trees, dangling nooses made out of vines, to hang unsuspecting passers-by, then go through their belongings. She thought of the trees looming over the cabin and gave a quick glance up at the skylight. Cordelia had a point about not doing something supernatural; given that a girl had died in the vicinity of Wolf Springs, lurid tales of grisly deaths might not be the best thing to read about in a cabin cut off from civilization. Which made her return to the idea of the . . . What was it called? The Madre Vena mine. It was perfect.

"Girls?" Ed called. "Set the table?"

"Free at last," Cordelia said, shutting the book she'd been looking through with a satisfied smack.

They found Ed at work in the kitchen. There was a pot of pasta bubbling and he had a jar of marinara sauce on the counter. He glanced at Cordelia over his shoulder.

"I cook on the rare side," he said.

"You'll get no complaints from me, sir," Cordelia said with another grin.

Fifteen minutes later they were at the table, and Kate-lyn, sitting in front of a bowl of cheese tortellini, watched the other two dig into steaks. She mostly listened as they talked about the weather and local issues. It seemed that while not everyone in the area knew everyone else, they all knew of each other. So though it was the first time the two had met, they already seemed to share a familiarity that she found enviable.

"Do you want to do more work?" Katelyn asked when dinner was over.

Cordelia hesitated, pulling her phone out of her pocket and glancing at it. "I should probably get back home," she said.

Katelyn was disappointed. Having her there had made things more bearable—more normal. She and Cordelia divvied up the library books, and Cordelia put her half into her backpack.

"We can look through them and see what else catches our fancy," Katelyn suggested.

"I'm sorry I'm not more into the mine," Cordelia said, smoothing back her hair.

"It's no big deal," Katelyn assured her, although in truth she was a little frustrated. She had some catching up to do in her other classes and she didn't want to waste a bunch of time spinning her wheels on picking their topic. She couldn't understand why Cordelia was being so particular.

When they walked to the front door, Katelyn saw that it was pitch black outside. She was about to walk down the stairs with Cordelia when Ed put a hand on her shoulder, restraining her just inside the door. She hunched her shoulders as anger bubbled up within her, and she looked apologetically at Cordelia.

"Sorry, he won't let me step outside the house after dark," she said, biting off each word, not bothering to hide her frustration.

"That's smart," Cordelia replied earnestly. "At least, until you get to know the woods better."

"I see your father lets *you* go out."

Her grandfather's grip on her shoulder tightened. Then he moved past her and joined Cordelia on the porch.

"I was raised here," Cordelia said. "Besides, I have a gun in the glove compartment."

Katelyn opened her mouth to ask if *everyone* drove around with guns in their cars, but before she could, Cordelia added, "You should think about learning to shoot."

"I'm going to be teaching her," Katelyn's grandfather said.

"Good." Cordelia looked serious, but her expression passed almost too soon to notice and a bright smile replaced it. "Thanks again for dinner, Dr. McBride. See you tomorrow, Kat."

Katelyn's grandfather walked Cordelia down the steps, then lingered as she climbed into the truck. She waved as she got behind the wheel, and as soon as she had pulled away, Katelyn's grandfather came back inside and closed the door.

"You could have at least let me walk her to her car with you," Katelyn spat as soon as the door clicked shut. "It was ten steps away and you were right there. What on earth could possibly have happened?" She could hear her voice rising. She wasn't used to living like this. It was crazy.

He stared at her for a long moment, eyes boring into her. "A lot," he whispered.

Her heart stuttered. He believed what he was saying. "Like what?"

He just shook his head and returned to the kitchen to clean up. Katelyn looked at the door to her prison and wondered uneasily if it was meant to keep her in or something else out.

—◦—◦—◦—

The next day at school, Katelyn walked from history to the gym with Cordelia and apologized for her grandfather's medieval behavior.

"No need," Cordelia said with a smile. "He's just trying to protect you."

Katelyn thought about the wolf and what had happened in Trick's car. It just didn't make sense. "I'd always heard that wild animals are more frightened of us than we are of them."

Cordelia cleared her throat. "There's a lot of other dangerous things out there in the woods besides animals."

Katelyn raised her brows. She didn't mean Tío Oso or Hangman Jack, did she?

"That crazy wolf guy and all the executives," Cordelia went on. She pounded her chest. "I swear, they could drum you into a frenzy."

Katelyn sighed. She just couldn't believe those guys would really hurt anyone.

The girls changed into their gym clothes and headed out to the gym proper to begin stretching out. Katelyn extended her legs in front of her and then easily grabbed her feet with her hands, bending until her forehead touched her knees. It felt so good. God, she needed a class.

"Wow," Cordelia said. "You are all kinds of bendy."

"The more you do it, the better you get at it."

Cordelia snickered, and Katelyn mock-grimaced and rolled her eyes.

"You're snorting like Mike," Katelyn said.

Cordelia shivered theatrically. "I'd rather die than snort like Mike."

As if they'd summoned him, a shadow was thrown over Cordelia's face. She meaningfully cleared her throat. "Well, hello, Mike, honey," she said in a singsong voice as she gazed at a place above Katelyn's head. Katelyn froze, staring at Cordelia, as it registered that Mike was standing behind her.

"Are you talking about me?" Mike snapped.

"Well, of course," Cordelia said, a purple flush crawling up her cheeks.."We always talk about the good boys."

"Shut up."

Katelyn remained silent and still, watching Cordelia until her friend relaxed, indicating that Mike had moved on. "I'm serious," she whispered to Katelyn. "If I *ever* do anything remotely Mike-like, just shoot me."

"Don't know how," Katelyn replied cheerfully.

Cordelia wrinkled her small, perfect nose. "You will."

⋯ ⋈ ⋯

That afternoon, in the woods behind the cabin, Katelyn found out how serious Ed was about teaching her to shoot. He had set up a target on a tree fifty feet away and was standing next to her, expectantly holding out his wicked-looking rifle.

"It's a gun," she heard herself say. She wanted to be able to defend herself. Just not by shooting anything with bullets.

"It's a gun," he affirmed. "Which you will learn to shoot."

"I don't want to," she said in a rush.

"It's not about want. It's about need. And you may not want to, but you absolutely need to."

He balanced the rifle in both hands and positioned it so she could better see it. "This is a .22," he explained. "It's used mostly on squirrels, rabbits, and small game."

She bit her lip at the thought of shooting a rabbit.

Chicken guts, she thought anxiously.

"This isn't the weapon you'll be using to protect yourself from anything dangerous, but it's the best rifle to start learning on. Now, you're right-handed?"

Katelyn nodded.

"Good."

He moved in close and stood next to her right shoulder, facing her. "Take your left hand and hold the stock under the barrel here," he said, showing her where.

She hesitated. There had to be some other way to protect herself without having to touch a gun.

"Hold it," he said.

"I don't like guns. They freak me out," she said heatedly.

"That's 'cause you don't understand how to handle 'em proper."

No, it was because people used them to kill things. Like he did. He killed things with guns. She shuddered as he took her hand and wrapped her fingers around it.

"Now put your right hand just like this so your finger can touch the trigger," he said, positioning her arms. "Keep the butt of the rifle against your shoulder. When you fire, it's going to kick but it will just feel like someone shoving it back at you so long as you keep it in your shoulder. Now, sight down the barrel toward your target. See it?"

Reluctantly she bent her head and did as he said. "Yes."

"When you pull the trigger, be gentle, squeezing, not jerking. Breathe in."

She did as she was told.

"Notice how the barrel of the gun lifted when you did that?"

She nodded.

"Okay, breathe out. You see how the barrel tilts downward?"

"Yes."

"That's why when you actually fire, you want to be holding your breath, so that it's steady. Let's give it a try. Breathe out. In. Out. In. Hold it. Squeeze the trigger."

She forced herself to do it, closing her eyes and gasping. The butt of the rifle slammed her hard in the shoulder, spinning her around as thunder roared. She dropped the gun, shrieking. Her grandfather caught it just before the muzzle dug into the ground.

"You moved. The rifle wasn't in your shoulder. That's why it bit you. Don't close your eyes. You won't hit anything that way. Don't breathe. And don't drop your rifle. If this barrel digs into the ground, you risk it getting plugged with dirt or debris. That happens and the next time it's fired, it will explode, killing whoever's holdin' it."

Her shoulder throbbed and she was more freaked out than she had been before she fired. His words echoed in her head and she could picture the rifle exploding in her hands, killing her before anyone or anything else got a chance to.

Guns don't kill people. People *kill people.* She'd heard her father say that.

Before he was killed by a person with a gun when she was twelve.

But if the rifle fell in the dirt, it could kill her.

So guns do *kill people.*

By the time her grandfather helped her heft the rifle back to her shoulder, she was having a hard time breathing. As she sighted down the barrel, she began hyperventilating.

She fired and a branch fifty feet above her target fell with a snap. She fired again and it kicked dirt up halfway between her and the target. But she didn't drop the weapon.

Finally her grandfather took the rifle away from her. "I don't think we're going to be able to make any more progress today," he said, face inscrutable.

Relief flooded her. He was probably disappointed, but what had he expected?

Once they got into the house, she headed straight upstairs and took a shower. She let the hot water stream over her face and body and forced herself to let it all go, to stop clinging to how it had felt. Her shoulder was bruised and she winced as she touched it.

After she dressed, she headed back downstairs, refusing to look at the animal heads and their accusing eyes. Her grandfather was in the kitchen, making dinner.

"Do you have any ice packs?" she asked, sounding as miserable as she felt.

"Grab yourself a baggy and some ice from the freezer. It will do the trick."

She grimaced. It meant dealing with melting ice leaking all over. She had to get something on her shoulder, though. She didn't ask if he had any kind of painkillers. She'd never let herself be drugged again. If it hadn't been for those, her mom would still be alive. She was exhausted, emotionally spent, and still freaked-out.

When dinner was ready, she dumped out her ice and gingerly picked up her fork.

"You'll get the hang of it," he said.

She didn't want to get the hang of it, but she also didn't want to fight about it. She just wanted to get through dinner so she could go to her room and be by herself.

"Next week I have to go pick up some supplies in Little Rock," he told her. "To get ready for winter. I'll be leaving next Friday morning and I won't make it back until Saturday morning. Will you be okay here by yourself?"

She could hear the nervousness in his voice. Excitement flooded her until she realized she'd be completely isolated and alone with her nightmares and the strange noises, but she couldn't let that stand in the way of a little freedom, the chance to prove to him she could be on her own. "I'll be fine. I've spent the night alone before."

It was a lie, but the last thing she wanted was for him to find a babysitter for her.

"If you wanted, you could have Cordelia over," he suggested.

Katelyn's spirits lifted at the possibility. It would keep

her from being alone with her fears without jeopardizing the chance to show him she could take care of herself. She wondered why he didn't just wait and go to Little Rock on the weekend and take her with him. She was about to bring it up but then realized she'd much rather take the opportunity he'd given her and spend the time with Cordelia instead of him.

"Thank you. I'll ask her."

She finished her meal, got herself another bag of ice, and headed upstairs.

To the creaking skylight.

6

"What's with you?" Trick asked when he showed up on the front porch in the morning. His long-sleeved black T-shirt was pushed up to his elbows, and his forearms were muscled and heavily veined, like an athlete's. Trick was not some malnourished romantic poet. A solid guy stood before her, with great shoulders and a killer smile.

Katelyn winced at him as she moved the bag of ice cubes to a different part of her shoulder. "My grandfather tried to teach me how to shoot yesterday."

"Looks like that went well," Trick said, raising a dark eyebrow.

Katelyn walked back to the kitchen and dumped the melting ice cubes into the sink. She returned to the door, grabbed her backpack, which was beside it, and headed outside.

"Yeah, it was genius," she said bitterly.

He took the pack from her. "Are you good to go to school?"

"According to Ed. I told him I was hurt and his response was to tell me to put more ice on it and try harder next time."

"You'll get the hang of it," Trick said as they got in his car and pulled away.

She stretched the seat belt off her shoulder, imagining the repercussions if Trick had to slam on his brakes, which seemed likely, given the speed he was going.

"I don't want to get the hang of it."

"You know, living out here in the middle of nowhere, it *is* a good idea that you know how to defend yourself."

"I got this book out of the school library. It says there's some kind of monster in the woods. A priest wrote about it, but it was torn out of the book."

He shrugged. "Kat, this is the Ozarks. There are *tons* of legends."

"Like what?" she asked him, even though she'd finished the entire book about legends before he'd shown up. She wanted to see what he'd say.

"Take your pick. Haints, demon bears, we got 'em all." He glanced at her again. "I'm sorry to burst your bubble, but the woods are dangerous because they're dangerous." Her gaze shifted to the leather bracelet he wore. "And now that those guys are out there at the old hot springs, spooking the wildlife . . ." He smiled grimly. "The old resort's supposed to be haunted. Lord knows it *looks* haunted. It's very 'Victorian in-sane asylum,' lots of narrow brick corridors and stuff. You guys could do a project on that."

"I think we're doing a lost silver mine," she told him. "At least, I hope."

He waggled his brows. "I'll help you cart out the silver."

"How thoughtful," she said sarcastically.

"I'm your man. And not like your BFF, but your *man* man. 'Cuz, you know, I'm not guy friend material. I'm on a horse."

She laughed. It was weird how someone she'd just met could make her feel so at ease. Especially someone so hot.

"So in that capacity I've got a question for you," he said, voice more serious.

"The capacity of . . . ?"

"Me being a man."

"What?" she asked, heart skipping a beat.

"There's a party two weeks from tomorrow. Friday the seventeenth. I was thinking we could go together."

"You mean like a date?" she asked, feeling a grin spreading across her face.

"Well, if you put it that way . . . exactly," he said, his voice suddenly intense.

"In that case . . . yes," she said, a thrill running through her. She felt giddy and a bit light-headed. She thought of the couple of guys she'd liked back in Santa Monica who had never asked her out. There had been plenty of flirting, but never anything else.

"Houston, we are go for launch," he said, and then floored it.

"Just don't kill me first," she said, laughing.

"I won't. Or after. I promise." His grin grew. "But this *is* going to be killer."

⁕ ⁕

When she got to history, Cordelia smiled brightly at her, and as soon as Katelyn sat down, she said, "I changed my mind, Kat. I'm on board with the Madre Vena."

"Oh? Well, great," Katelyn replied. Cordelia's eagerness seemed forced. Katelyn figured it was another instance of Cordelia's trying not to rock the boat, and while she'd rather just move on and get to work, she didn't want to cause problems with her first and thus far only friend in Wolf Springs—not counting Trick, as he didn't want her to think of him like that. The thought made her cheeks go warm as she studied Cordelia's face. "But are you sure?"

"Uh-huh." Cordelia nodded. "My dad said he remembers there was talk that it had been found back when he was younger. But it turned out not to be true."

"Oh, that's so cool." So Cordelia had discussed it with her dad. Maybe knowing there was a family connection was what had changed her mind. "Maybe we can interview him."

Cordelia's face fell. Then, just as abruptly, she smiled her fake smile again. "Yeah, maybe," she said. Katelyn took note of her hesitation. Maybe her dad was as weird as her sisters. If that was the case, Katelyn felt sorry for her.

The rest of the week and most of the next passed in a blur. Cordelia agreed to spend the night Friday. Trick kept flirting with her, and she flirted back. She legally checked out her book from Mrs. Walker, who informed her that the other book about Wolf Springs history was missing or mis-shelved. That, combined with the missing page, piqued Katelyn's curiosity and she started to search for it for a few minutes each day before first period. As she combed the shelves, she dusted and organized the books, bit by bit putting the library back in order.

No one ever came into the library while she was there, until Friday morning. She was bent over a low shelf of books, running a feather duster over the neglected volumes, when she was startled by a voice.

"Hey."

She spun around, feather duster in hand. It was Beau from history. He held up his hands. "Don't shoot. I'm unarmed."

She smiled and lowered the duster. "Hi. You're the first person I've seen in here since I started coming."

"Are you doing some kind of extra credit?" He walked in and looked around at the progress she had made in her tidying project. "Cleaning up?"

"I was looking for a book about the history of Wolf Springs, but it's missing. Then I kind of got into straightening up." She remembered his insistence that the cause of Haley's death had not been revealed. She recalled how angry he'd been about it, and how it had seemed almost like he'd wanted to tell her something.

"You and Cordelia are working on a lost silver mine," he said.

Mr. Henderson had begun announcing which project topics he'd approved. She and Cordelia had gotten the go-ahead to work on theirs.

"Yes," she said slowly, "but what I'm looking for is

information about something else. I read about something really creepy that lurks in the woods. I know it's silly, but it's interesting."

He blinked. He studied her, then nervously licked his lips.

"Of course, you don't believe stuff like that, coming from the big city and all," he said slowly. "You probably think we're a bunch of hicks with our superstitions. . . ." He trailed off and averted his gaze. "Because we *are* hicks, I guess."

"Not at all," she said, inwardly wincing at how she and Kimi still made fun of Banjo Land. "The other day, you were going to say something about your grandmother," she said gently. "And . . . Haley."

He swallowed hard. "Haley," he whispered. *"God."*

"You didn't seem to agree with what people are saying happened to her." She was careful how she phrased her words. She didn't want to seem eager to talk about it. But she wanted to know.

She watched his face go gray. He sank slowly onto the edge of the abandoned librarian's desk. Then he shook his head.

"This stays between us," he said. "Deal?"

She nodded. "Sure," she said.

He managed a small smile. Then it fell. "My grandma says what happened . . . it wasn't just a random animal attack. She says that Haley was just the first. That it's starting again."

Katelyn waited, scared that if she broke the silence, he'd stop talking. Then finally, after a minute or so, she asked, *"What's* starting again?"

He cleared his throat and moved his shoulders. Time was slipping by. The bell was going to ring any second, and she knew it would kill his confessional mood.

"She said about forty years ago, there was a bunch of attacks around here. 'People tore up.' That's how she put it. Animals in the forest just went into a frenzy and killed anybody they crossed. And about fifty years before that, same thing." He looked hard at her.

"Why? What made them do it?" she asked.

"She didn't know. Nobody knew. Things were different back then. Wolf Springs was more cut off—if you can believe that—and folks kept to themselves. Mountain folks, superstitious and standoffish. They only talked about it in whispers. Everybody was scared. No one knew what to do—except go huntin'," he added. "Folks shot every wolf and bear they found. But it didn't help. People kept dying."

Ed must have heard about this, she realized, the thought of all that carnage—both human and animal—turning her stomach. Her dad would have been a little kid.

"Grandma says Wolf Springs is a banked fire. There's things here shouldn't be crossed. If something stokes the embers, flames are gonna burn this whole place down."

Katelyn shivered. "Something like what?"

He shrugged. "Don't know. Grandma doesn't know, either. I asked her. But she's scared to death. Good thing she lives with us." He gestured to the shelf she'd been dusting. "Maybe that's why your book is gone. Maybe it said something about all this."

"But why would someone want to hide it?" she asked carefully.

"So we won't panic? I dunno. The mayor and all them are trying to keep Wolf Springs from dying." He blinked, as if he'd just realized what he'd said. "I mean, dying as a town. We're so cut off. We don't have a lot of jobs and there's nothing for us teenagers to do. When that Bronson guy started that wolf retreat, folks started crossing their fingers that things would get better."

"It's a really cute town," she offered. "If it was easier to get to, I could see tourists coming here."

He nodded. "But my grandma says the fewer people come here, the better." He swallowed hard, and the stricken look came over his features again. "At least, until this is over."

The bell rang and he jerked as if waking from a trance. "Walk you to history?"

"Sure," she said. "Thanks."

As they left the library, he murmured, "You didn't hear any of this from me. My grandma made me promise to keep it to myself. She threatened to tan my hide when she found out I brought it up in class."

"Why?"

"She said she knows when to keep her mouth shut."

"Wow," Katelyn said, and he nodded.

As they walked down the hall, Mike Wright glared at them both.

"McBride!" he sneered. "Forgot your deodorant? I can smell you from here!"

Katelyn rolled her eyes and ignored him, focusing back on Beau.

"Why'd you tell me this?" Katelyn asked Beau quietly.

"'Cuz you're not from around here," he replied without hesitation. "And if I was you, I'd get out of Wolf Springs as fast as I could."

"Yeah," Katelyn murmured. "It's on my to-do list."

Mr. Henderson lectured the entire class time, so Katelyn never got the chance to tell Cordelia about her conversation with Beau. Then, on the way to gym and at lunch, they were surrounded by people. It seemed the new girl had been accepted, but Katelyn was dying to ditch the group and see what Cordelia thought about everything.

Cordelia had to go home before she went to Katelyn's, so when the final bell rang, Katelyn walked to Trick's car for her ride. He had a cardboard box, which he stowed in the back.

"Some art supplies," he explained. "For this thing I'm doing."

"Cool," she said, waiting to hear more. But mysterious Trick remained silent.

"Listen, I heard this weird story," she said, eager to tell *someone*. "Every forty or fifty years, there's a rash of animal attacks." She looked at him to see his reaction.

He eyed her askance. "Who told you that? Babette?"

"Who's Babette?" she asked.

"Who are you, Nancy Drew?" he asked with a guffaw. "I'm sorry, Kat. I don't mean to make fun—it's no weirder than half the other stories I've heard. But there's been one death by animal attack. *One.*"

"Things like that don't really happen in Santa Monica," she said quietly. "But we have other kinds of . . . I mean, people die." Her voice caught.

"I know, darlin'," he said gently. He peered at her. "Haley died because she crossed something in the forest."

She nodded, even though her pulse quickened when he called her "darlin'." "And about that 'something.' The priests who settled Wolf Springs said that something evil lived in the forest. They said they shunned the forest because of it."

"Big bad wolf. Big bad bear. Take your pick."

"You have no imagination," she said, chiding him.

"And you have too much," he retorted.

When Trick dropped her home, he offered to stay until Cordelia came. But despite being tempted—and a little freaked out by Beau's story—she passed. She hadn't been alone, truly alone, since her mom died, and she was looking forward to an hour just to *be* before Cordelia arrived.

And maybe, just maybe, she was a little shy about being alone with him. . . .

As soon as he'd gone, she closed the door, locked it, and stared at the cabin. Freedom, no one to watch or hear her. She had the urge to go crazy, jump on the furniture, scream her head off just because she could. Another part of her, though, felt like it was going to collapse. There was no one to put on a brave face for, no one to please or avoid or figure out. There was just her.

And the sound of a motorcycle coming through the woods.

The roar of the engine grew louder and louder, droning in from the left side of the cabin. Then finally it caromed around to the front and stopped. Curious, and a little trepidatious, she cracked open the door and looked outside.

With the engine throbbing in idle, Justin Fenner straddled his bike. His boots were on the ground, and the slanting sun caught the gold highlights in his hair.

Her heart stuttered. *What is he doing here?*

She opened the door and stepped out on the porch just as he turned off the engine, dropped his kickstand, and dismounted.

"Hey, Kat," he said. He made his way to the bottom of the steps and stopped.

She stared down at him, wondering if he could tell how fast her heart was beating.

"Hey, Justin," she managed to get out. It felt like she couldn't catch her breath, but she forced herself to take a beat before continuing. "Where's Cordelia?"

"Her daddy sprang something last-minute on her, and she's going to be late. She didn't know your home phone number, so I volunteered to come over and give you the message."

She felt an unreasonable disappointment that he was just a messenger. For one crazy moment she had thought he'd come to see her. "Thanks," she said, taking a deep breath. "That was a long way to come just to deliver a message."

"Not. Considering," he replied.

Her knees felt like they were turning to jelly. "Sorry?"

"I wanted to see you."

"Oh." It was all that she could think to say. She knew she should at least invite him onto the porch but was tongue tied. The silence was stretching on too long, and her mind raced, searching for words. Anything.

"Cool bike," she said, and immediately wanted to kick herself.

"Wanna ride?" Justin asked, eyes burning through her until she felt herself flush from head to toe.

She nodded silently, because her mouth had suddenly gone

dry. She closed the door and walked down the steps until she was next to him.

He peeled off his leather jacket and helped her put it on; then he pulled her hair out of the collar. She shivered as his fingertips brushed her neck and he turned her around slowly. The fabric of his T-shirt stretched tight across his chest and abs. She put a hand on his chest, stunned by her own boldness. He smiled down at her and she could feel the blood rushing through her body, until every part of her was pulsing in rhythm with the rise and fall of his chest, beneath her fingers. All she wanted was to kiss him.

He took her hand and pulled her to the bike, and she slid on behind him and thrilled as their legs touched. She wrapped her arms around his waist and leaned into his back. He smelled like the forest around them, and more—trees and earth, wild and untamed.

With a roar they were off, forsaking the road and racing through a narrowed clearing among the trees. Tears stung her eyes as he twisted and turned. Her blood sang as time and again, he saved them from crashing with his lightning reflexes. In California there was thousands of miles of roads, endless asphalt and concrete. Here there was none, just dirt and leaves that sprayed out from underneath the churning wheels.

She squeezed her eyes shut but then forced them open again because she didn't want to miss a single moment. The vibrations and roar of the bike, the feel of his shirt against her cheek became her whole world as they hurtled together through the lengthening shadows.

At last he spun to a stop in a circle of level ground ringed by giant trees. Piles of fallen leaves filled the space. He climbed off the bike and helped her down. Her legs were shaky as he led her to the nearest pile of leaves, their faces inches from each other.

"Did I scare you?" he asked as he reached over and pushed a strand of her hair away from her eyes.

She trembled. "Yes."

"Honest *and* brave," he whispered as he trailed his fingers down her jaw.

His touch sent chills through her and all thought slipped away. She heard a whimpering sound and realized she was making it. She should have been embarrassed, but she wasn't. She had to touch him, be closer to him. She locked her hands behind his head and a smile danced on his lips.

And she had to have more. Needed to be closer. He put his arms around her and pulled her hard against his chest. His lips were an inch away and then they were on hers, warm and soft. He slid his tongue into her mouth and she wanted more of him, wanted to taste and feel all of him. Everywhere their bodies touched she felt like she was on fire.

What's happening to me? she wondered dizzily. *This isn't me. I'm not this girl.*

She could hear so many things, the sound of Justin's breathing, the sighing of the wind in the trees, the chirping of insects, and something more, something that seemed to dance on the wind almost like a whisper.

Katelyn.

She opened her eyes, startled for a moment. But it had to have been in her mind. Justin was still kissing her. He pulled slightly away from her, as though sensing her sudden gaze, and she could see his beautiful face and nothing else.

She blinked and forced herself to turn her head, avoiding his next kiss. Then, as she felt panic creeping over her, she twisted around so she could look everywhere.

She couldn't make out anything else. It was dark there beneath the trees. Because it was night.

"What is it?" he asked.

"I'm not supposed to go in the woods after dark," she squeaked in a tiny voice. She wanted to hate her grandfather's rules for interrupting the moment, but as she gazed into the blackness, her fear grew, and all she wanted was to be home, safe and sound.

A twig snapped somewhere nearby and she jerked as her thoughts flew to the wolf . . . and then to Haley . . . and then Beau's story. "What was that?"

"An animal," he said with an amused smile. "Squirrel. Rabbit. Relax."

She shook her head fiercely. "I need to go home. Cordelia will wonder what happened to me. She might call my grandfather," she lied.

"Don't worry—I'll take you home right now. Even though I don't want to," he said with a sigh.

They both climbed back on the bike. She could barely feel the warmth radiating from him as they headed back, though. There was a creeping cold in the forest that was reaching out to her, penetrating her clothes and turning her very bones to ice.

They made it back to the cabin much faster than she expected. Once there, she slid off the bike and tried to stand on legs that suddenly felt weak and wobbly. Justin reached out a hand to steady her.

"Thank you," she murmured, feeling slightly awkward and embarrassed.

He smiled, slow and sexy, and it sent tingles up her spine. "Are you okay?"

She managed to nod, not trusting herself to answer. She turned and mounted the steps to the porch. With her hand on the doorknob, she looked over her shoulder, but he was only a shape in the darkness.

"I'll be seeing you, Kat," he said before riding away.

She opened the door and slammed it, locking it with shaking fingers. Fear skittered through her as she realized the house was pitch black. She tried to remember where the light switches were, and realized that she'd never used one. Her grandfather was always the last to go to bed and the first up in the morning. She groped for the wall and ran her hand along the surface, praying that she didn't touch anything dead.

Or alive.

Her fingers finally caught the switch and she heaved a sigh of relief as the lights came on. She ran quickly through the rest of the first floor, turning on every light she found. She did the same for the second floor, until the entire house was ablaze with light.

Calming down slightly, she walked to the kitchen and opened the refrigerator. She reached for the orange juice and poured herself a giant glass. By the time she'd drunk it, she heard a car engine outside. Cordelia. She exhaled another relieved sigh and flew to the door.

A couple of seconds later, there were footfalls on the porch.

Cordelia called out, "Hello?"

Katelyn opened the door and hugged her tight.

"I'm so glad to see you."

"You too," Cordelia said, clearly startled by Katelyn's eager welcome. "Justin came by, right?"

"Um, yes." Katelyn decided to stay mum on what had happened. She didn't really even *know* what had happened.

Cordelia dropped her duffel bag next to the front door and Katelyn shut and locked the door behind her.

"Are you okay?" Cordelia asked.

"Yes, fine. I just . . . heard some weird noises outside and it spooked me." Katelyn smiled. "I'm just happy you're here."

"Well, don't worry. We're locked in and this is a good, strong house. Besides, I think every critter on the planet knows to stay away from your grandfather." There was a mischievous glint in her eyes as she gestured to the row of animal heads.

"Thanks," Katelyn said, relaxing. "Sorry, I'm being a bad hostess." She grabbed Cordelia's hand and pulled her away from the front door. "Let's get dinner started."

They moved into the kitchen, where Katelyn found a note from her grandfather.

＊━◆━＊

I'll be back tomorrow morning. KEEP THE DOOR LOCKED. DON'T GO OUT IN THE DARK.

ED

＊━◆━＊

She put it in the drawer where she'd found the dog leash, and got out the makings for mini pizzas—veggie toppings for her and pepperoni for Cordelia. She turned to ask if Cordelia wanted something to drink and realized her friend looked exhausted. She was pale and was moving slowly.

"Are you okay?" Katelyn asked.

"Yeah, just tired, I guess," Cordelia said with a weak smile.

"More than tired. You look like you just ran a marathon."

Cordelia winced. "I kind of did. Footrace with my sisters."

"The two I met?" Katelyn was surprised. They didn't look like athletes.

"Call it the Fenner Family Games. Like the Olympics, only without the fame, glory, or product endorsements."

"That sounds fun," Katelyn quipped.

"Yeah, tons," Cordelia said wearily. "Sorry. Dad just sort of sprang it on us."

Cordelia apologized for a lot of things that weren't her fault, Katelyn noted.

"It's like the Kennedys," Cordelia went on. When Katelyn didn't respond, she said, "Like the president-of-the-United-States Kennedy and his brothers? Their father made them play touch football all the time."

Katelyn blinked. *Weird.*

"It's true."

"So are you running for public office?"

"No, just running to stay in place." Cordelia half smiled at her. "I shouldn't have said anything. Now you'll think I'm too strange for you."

Katelyn didn't know how to take that. Was Cordelia *really* worried or just trying to flatter the new girl with a bit of false modesty?

They finished making the pizzas and popped them into the

oven. As they sat down at the table to wait, Katelyn asked, "So who won? The Fenner-lympics?"

Cordelia muttered something under her breath that sounded like *No one,* and then she looked up with a smile. "I did. By a nose."

The image made Katelyn laugh. "Well, congratulations! That calls for a drink." Then she smiled at the memory of Trick carefully having a soda instead of a beer in front of her. "Soda or OJ? I'm fresh out of champagne."

Cordelia laughed. "Diet if you have it."

Katelyn grabbed her a Diet Coke from the fridge and, while she was there, poured herself another glass of orange juice.

"So Justin doesn't participate in these games, I take it?" she asked, shamelessly digging for a little more information about him.

Cordelia downed her soda before answering. "No. This is just between us girls. That's why he volunteered to come over here for me. Of course, any excuse to be out riding and he'll jump on it."

Katelyn flushed as she thought about their ride.

"He does seem very *Rebel Without a Cause.*"

Cordelia set down the empty can, then pushed on the top, as if to crush it. She drummed her fingers on it instead and leaned back in her chair.

"He's always been that way."

"Girls must love it," Katelyn said, trying to sound casual.

Cordelia gave her a careful look. "Justin's got what you'd call real animal magnetism. Girls have been throwing themselves at him for years. You don't like him, do you?"

"No, why?" It came out more sharply than she'd intended it to.

"He's taken. He's had the same girlfriend for five years. The perfect couple."

Katelyn felt as though she had just been punched. Impossible. If he was taken, then how could he have kissed her like that?

"Five years? He's old enough to have dated someone for that long?" It sounded lame, but it was the only thing she could think to say that wouldn't give away what had happened between them.

"He's nineteen."

"So he was *fourteen* when they started dating?"

"Lucy is really nice," Cordelia said. "She's like family at this point."

Katelyn thought of Justin's smoldering looks and figured Lucy was probably a lot more than just nice to land a guy like him. A stab of jealousy went through her, followed by anger. What kind of guy did that if he had a girlfriend?

Cordelia sighed and wrapped her arms around herself. "They'll be on me to choose someone next."

"What?" Katelyn asked. *What a weird thing to say.*

Cordelia jerked as though she hadn't realized she was talking out loud.

"Why?" Katelyn said, trying to smooth over the awkwardness.

Cordelia gave her another weak smile. "In my family we tend to fall in love young."

Katelyn wondered if you could actually fall in love when

you were only fourteen. "But are you even hanging out with anyone?" She thought of the boys who circled Cordelia's lunch table and surrounded them both on the way to gym.

She shrugged. "Well, there's a couple possibilities. I just haven't wanted to really think about it too much yet."

Katelyn could tell she wasn't telling her everything. She wanted to push but felt rude. If Cordelia didn't want to talk about it, she wasn't going to make her.

Cordelia slid a glance at her. "What about you? Do you have anyone back in California? Or maybe a crush here?" She smiled.

Katelyn bit her lip. Her gut still told her Cordelia wasn't the person to get into any of this with.

"No," she said finally.

"Right," Cordelia said, nodding slowly. "You had to think about that too long. If you don't want to talk about it, that's cool."

As if on cue, the timer went off, and they retrieved their pizzas from the oven. Katelyn was glad for something to do. Good smells filled the kitchen and she took comfort in how normal it all felt—having an overnight, making pizza, dishing on guys. It was nice, though she'd never admit to her grandfather she'd just thought that.

"So what about your possibilities?" Katelyn asked.

"Oh." Cordelia was flustered. "They're just . . . guys."

"Uh-huh," Katelyn drawled. "Captain of the football team, class president . . ."

"Well, there was Bobby Templeton, for a while," Cordelia said, and there was a catch in her voice. "He's on the football team. Running back. But my dad said no. Not good enough.

Maybe if he'd been the quarterback . . ." She wrinkled her nose as if to make light of what she was saying, but Katelyn saw the fleeting sadness in her eyes.

"There's still a couple more," Cordelia went on. "One of them's local. He already graduated, so you wouldn't know him. We've known each other since we were babies. He can be really fun. But I'm not entirely sure I trust him."

The cheese was bubbling like lava and Katelyn blew on her pizza. "Why not?"

Cordelia picked a piece of pepperoni off her own pizza and popped it into her mouth. "I'm just not sure he likes me for me."

"Oh, I'm sure he does," Katelyn concluded, picturing Justin in her mind. Feeling the touch of his lips on hers. Hot tingles skittered through her body and she had to wait a moment before she could make herself speak again. "And Bachelor Number Two?"

Cordelia's entire demeanor changed. She lifted her chin and squared her shoulders, as if she was proud of what she was going to say. Then a cloud passed over her face, and she exhaled long and hard. She tucked her hair behind her ears and studied the table.

"Complicated. His name is Dominic—Dom. It's a long-distance thing. He's twenty-two. His dad got killed in a car accident and Dom's, um, running the family business. He's doing *great*. But our families . . . don't get along." She was using her apology voice again.

So Dom was not approved of. Older man, plus Katelyn thought about what Paulette had said about country people holding grudges. She folded her hands and leaned on them.

"So a *Romeo and Juliet* kind of long-distance thing. That's romantic." She tried to sound hopeful.

"Yeah, I guess." Cordelia examined another piece of pepperoni at close range. Ate it. "Some days I hate him and I'm sure he feels the same. But there's something else there, too. He likes me and I know it's real, because he has too many reasons not to."

"Wow, that *is* complicated," Katelyn said. She had yet to have a relationship with a guy that was intense enough to generate mutual hatred. "So you've got one guy who might just want to jump your bones and one guy who is your grand and forbidden passion." She tried to sound lightly mocking, not insulting, but she didn't know Cordelia well enough to tell how the other girl was taking it.

Cordelia cleared her throat and smoothed her hair. "My dad would freak out if he knew, so *please* don't mention it."

"Your father?" Katelyn echoed. "Why would I?"

Cordelia shrugged. "What I mean is don't say anything about boys at all if you ever meet him." She made a face. "You know the type. No one's good enough for his little girl."

Katelyn grinned. Kimi's dad was like that.

"So who's hotter?" Katelyn asked.

"Dom, by miles." She slid Katelyn a sly glance. "I'll bet you thought all the boys around here would be missing a few teeth." Katelyn flushed and Cordelia brightened. "Oh, my God, you *are* crushing on someone!"

"I'll give you this. The guys around here are surprisingly good-looking." It was as confessional as Katelyn was going to get. Cordelia could think what she wanted to.

After they had finished eating and cleaning up, they moved to the living room.

"I didn't think this through too well," Katelyn admitted as she perused her grandfather's meager movie collection.

"That's cool. We could play a game or something," Cordelia said as she checked out his bookshelves.

"Or actually work on our history project," Katelyn suggested. "Guess what I . . . read," she finished awkwardly. "Forty years ago, a bunch of people died . . . um, violently, and then fifty years before *that,* the same thing happened."

Cordelia wrinkled her nose. "In Wolf Springs?"

"It was the wild animals in the forest. Like they went crazy all of a sudden," she went on.

"Wow." Cordelia looked from the shelves to Katelyn. "Where'd you read that?"

"In one of those books," she said faintly, hating to lie. "I was thinking we could switch to that. But maybe that's too close to what happened to Haley," she added, thinking of the confrontation in history class.

"Let's stick with the mine," Cordelia agreed. "Best to steer clear. Especially since you're the new girl, you know?"

"Okay." That made sense.

"I got a couple more books out of the town library," Cordelia said. "They're in my backpack. I haven't really looked at them, but they seemed like they might have some info on the mine."

"Cool." Katelyn hadn't expected Cordelia to go on a research trip. "Can I see them?"

"Later, okay? I never do homework on Friday night." She

gave Katelyn a look. "Let's just blow it off for a little while longer, you know what I mean?"

Katelyn smiled and nodded and wandered over to the paintings on the wall. An animal head broke up the sequence and she shivered at the image in her mind of the dead deer in the road. And at the thought that her own grandfather shot and killed living things and wanted her to learn how to, too.

"Hey, check this out," Cordelia said.

She was holding out a book with a stern-looking but attractive older man on the cover. He had silvery-gray hair and a trim gray beard, and he was wearing a polo shirt with a wolf head on it. The title of the book was huge and in a metallic red font.

"*Unleashing Your Inner Wolf*, by Jack Bronson? No way," Katelyn said, bursting out with a laugh. "My *grandfather* has a copy?"

Cordelia made a face. "I know, right? It doesn't look like it's ever been opened, no crack in the spine at all," she said. "Maybe he got it as a gift from someone."

"But who? If they know Ed, it had to be a practical joke."

Cordelia flipped it over. "Listen to what it says on the back. 'Within the heart of every man is a wolf waiting to spring forth. The wolf is there and if you let it, the wolf will give you strength, power, ambition, and fearlessness. These are gifts and one should learn to harness them by getting in touch with the wolf within.'"

Katelyn thought of the executive on the plane and started laughing harder. She took the book from Cordelia and flipped through it. There were tons of passages in italics and words in big capital letters, like *POWER! FEROCITY! AGGRESSION!*

"Yikers," she said.

"They should try getting in touch with their inner human," Cordelia said.

"I can hear them drumming from here," Katelyn said. "I'm keeping this. I'm going to read it."

"At my house, too. The drums must echo off the mountains. They make the animals freak out."

Katelyn put the book down on the coffee table. "That's what Trick said." Too late, she realized she'd spoken his name aloud.

Cordelia grimaced. "You know what the problem with Trick is?"

Katelyn opened her mouth, but in the distance a wolf howled and she froze.

A moment later a loud, shrill scream rang through the mountains.

7

"What's that?" Katelyn whispered.

"I don't know." Cordelia had turned white, scaring Katelyn even more. "A cat?"

"A *cat*? Are you kidding?" Katelyn said.

They both stared at the door. "They can sound human when they're fighting. Or scared," Cordelia said.

"I'm calling 911." Katelyn turned to bolt into the kitchen.

"Kat, this is the *country*," Cordelia said. "Not sure we need to."

"But that was a *scream*," Katelyn argued.

"Maybe," Cordelia said. Her voice was strained. "But it

would take anyone at least an hour to get here. And we only have two cops." Cordelia looked around. "Where's your grandpa's—there it is."

Cordelia crossed the living room and hefted the rifle out of the rack on the wall. She cracked it open, examined it, and said, "Good. Loaded." She snapped it shut.

"Oh, my God," Katelyn said. "Cordelia . . ."

"It's probably nothing." Cordelia carried the rifle pointed toward the ceiling as she walked toward the door. "For all we know, it's some drunk or one of those crazy businessmen trying to do a primal scream."

Katelyn stood beside her, staring at the door. "But you just said it was a *cat*."

"And I *stand* by cat," Cordelia insisted. "But it *could* be something else."

Someone in trouble. Someone like Haley, Katelyn thought. Then there were Beau's story and her grandfather's note: *Keep the door locked.*

And the wolf. Could it be attacking someone else? Who knew what would have happened to her if Trick hadn't shot at it?

"Get the door for me," Cordelia said.

Resolutely, Katelyn turned the knob and pushed the door open. It was unbelievably dark outside. She couldn't even make out the shapes of the trees.

"Hello?" Cordelia yelled. "Is anyone there?"

They stepped out on the porch. "We need a flashlight," Cordelia said. "I've got a little one in my overnight bag. I'll go get it. You take the gun."

Cordelia passed it to Katelyn. The weight of it startled her. She fitted it against her sore shoulder. For just an instant she wished she could actually shoot. She decided in this situation she was willing to try again if she had to.

And if it attacked . . . Too late, she realized that what she should have done was give the rifle to Cordelia and go to look for the flashlight herself.

"Okay, I found it," Cordelia said, returning.

A beam of light aimed past Katelyn and painted the trees. Cordelia handed her the flashlight and took the rifle.

Chills cascaded over her. She stared hard at the trees, imagining what might lurk there. There was another scream, high-pitched and scratchy. Thin and angry.

And familiar. It sounded just like one of the tomcats that had screeched in anger behind her house in California.

Her whole body sagged in relief.

"Oh, God," Cordelia whispered. She stopped and rooted her feet to the ground. She brought the rifle up to her shoulder.

"Wait," Katelyn said, surprised. "That *was* a cat."

Cordelia didn't respond. She kept the rifle planted against her shoulder, stock-still. Then she said, "Are you sure?"

"Pretty sure. We had a lot of feral cats around our neighborhood. Because of the beach. All the food." She took a breath and scanned a wider area with the flashlight. A low-lying tree limb shook, sending a scattering of autumn leaves to the ground.

"Is anyone out there? Are you okay?" Katelyn called, feeling a little braver.

Then a shape burst from the base of the tree and raced

away into the night. It moved too fast for her to focus on it, but it was the right size for a cat.

"There! Did you see that?" Katelyn pointed.

"No."

"It *was* a cat. Or a squirrel or something."

"Screeching squirrels. Cool." Cordelia lowered the rifle and wiped her forehead.

Somewhere far off the wolf howled again. At least, Katelyn was pretty sure it was a wolf and not a man pretending to be one.

They stared at each other, whirled around, and darted back inside the cabin. Katelyn slammed the door, locked it, and jumped away from it. As Cordelia began to put the rifle back, Katelyn waved the flashlight in protest, shaking her head.

"That was a wolf," she said. "A real, live wolf. Shouldn't we call about *that*?"

Cordelia looked amused. "We're safe, Kat. Wolves can't come in unless you invite them."

"*What?*"

"Oh, my God! I'm *teasing*." Cordelia laughed and then stopped and took a close look at Katelyn. "You *do* know about real live animals, right? Not just Hollywood cartoons and purse dogs?"

"Sure," Katelyn said, although she wasn't going to admit that the extent of her live-animal experience was with other people's pets and on a few trips to the L.A. Zoo.

Cordelia finished setting the rifle back on its rack and made a show of cleaning her hands of the whole business.

Katelyn clicked off the flashlight and sat down in the middle of the floor.

"Are you okay?" Cordelia asked, face filling with concern as she sat down, too.

Katelyn closed her eyes. She needed to talk about it. She didn't want to, but she needed to. "No. This huge wolf jumped on Trick's car the first day he brought me home from school," Katelyn said. "It tried to claw its way through the roof."

"Wow." Cordelia looked surprised. "I haven't seen a wolf in years."

"It was terrifying. Trick shot at it and scared it off. I could hear a second one growling, but I didn't see it."

"It's those lunatics at that seminar-thing. If I were a wolf, I'd go bite something, too." She mimicked Katelyn's toothy grimace and made a chomping noise.

Katelyn hadn't gotten to a place where she could joke about it. "There was a dead deer on the road. Trick dragged it away."

"So the wolf thought you were stealing its dinner. No wonder it growled at you."

"And there's a wolf out there now."

Cordelia sighed and moved Katelyn's hair out of her eyes. She gave her a quick hug. "This is the wilderness, Kat. You're going to have to get used to it."

She's right. Get a grip, she told herself. It was time to change the topic. "So, you really don't want to work on our history project."

Cordelia shook her head. "It's Friday night, live from Wolf Springs," she joked.

"Well, my grandfather has a pathetic movie selection, but why not watch one?"

"Okay." Cordelia grinned. "Let's pick the worst movie, make some popcorn, and laugh at it."

Let it go, Katelyn told herself. She forced some brightness into her voice.

"Sounds like a plan. I'll get the popcorn if you pick a movie."

"On it," Cordelia said cheerfully. She got to her feet and offered Katelyn a hand.

Katelyn took it. She made it into the kitchen, where she sagged against the counter and struggled to compose herself. She tried to shake the feeling that somewhere in the darkness something terrible was happening.

In the distance, the wolf howled again.

⌁⌁⌁

The next morning Katelyn woke up first and decided to let Cordelia sleep. Cordelia's overnight bag was open, and a thick book was poking out. Curious, Katelyn eased it out a little farther.

Lost Treasures of Arkansas, Oklahoma, and Missouri. Katelyn couldn't help herself; it looked interesting, so she took the book with her, went to the kitchen, and started a pot of coffee. Then she sat down and started flipping through the pages. The more she read, the more interested she got. Who wouldn't be excited at the prospect of discovering a treasure? Then she came to the section on a mine "located in the woods outside Wolf Springs." It was their mine, the Madre Vena.

Score, Cordelia, she thought as she continued to read eagerly. A passage jumped right out at her:

In one of the most unusual tales of the Madre Vena mine, it is said that the entrance is guarded by a supernatural creature called the Hellhound. Despite the name, this monster is not a dog but has been described as a huge, misshapen animal that vaguely resembles a wolf. According to an old diary written by one Xavier Cazador, it has wild, glowing eyes and elongated fangs "as sharp as knives," and it breathes fire. Cazador was a Spaniard who lived on the grounds of the old Catholic church that is now home to Wolf Springs High School.

"The Devil in Wolf Form chased me all night," he wrote in 1868. "Quite by accident, I stumbled upon the Lost Mine of Madre Vena. With only a torch to guide me, I espied the silvery riches in the rocks. I beheld a fortune, a king's ransom! I praised the Virgin, who had surely shown me this miracle.

"Then I heard a ferocious growling, and then another, much softer, as if farther away. Still, I was terrified, and I began to run. Little did I realize until later that the farther away the monster lurked, the louder its howl. The closer it slunk, the softer its voice. When it leaped at me, it made no sound at all! Then the Hellhound came after me! It would have caught me, too, except that I fell onto the holy ground of the churchyard, where it could not go."

Despite continued questioning, Xavier Cazador refused to reveal the location of the mine. Locals believed he had never actually been to it, and was spinning a tall tale in return for drinks at the local tavern. But notorious Arkansas outlaw Jubal DeAndrew, who lived with his family in the Wolf Springs Bog, kidnapped Cazador. One of the outlaw's daughters later reported that DeAndrew threatened Cazador at gunpoint to reveal the site of the mine or die. The daughter could not confirm if Cazador had disclosed it, but

DeAndrew set him free. Cazador died two days later, and Jubal DeAndrew was never seen again.

"Double score," Katelyn murmured as she turned the page. "Maybe this Hellhound is what the monks were scared of."

"What are you reading?" Cordelia asked from behind her.

Katelyn jumped. She'd been so engrossed in reading she'd almost forgotten the other girl was in the house. She turned and grinned, catching Cordelia in a yawn.

"I think I just found the monster in the forest."

"Sweet," Cordelia said. She still looked half-asleep; her red hair was puffed out in a halo of fire. She walked over to the table and leaned down, resting her head on her arms, then let out a soft little groan.

Katelyn snickered. "You have a hangover and we didn't even drink."

"Not a morning person," Cordelia muttered.

"Coffee? Diet Coke?"

"Coffee, if it's not too much trouble. Otherwise just give me a D.C." Cordelia unfolded herself and sleepily picked up the old book.

"I'm sorry. I snatched it," Katelyn confessed. "I saw it sticking out of your overnight bag."

"Jeesh. You *are* an eager beaver."

Katelyn went to the cupboard. "And guess what else. It has a monster. Is that not *mucho* cool?"

"*Sí,*" Cordelia said, turning the pages as she stifled another yawn. "*Mucho* cool."

Katelyn got out two coffee cups, then took them to the

sink and rinsed them out, to guard against rat "presents" and dust.

"There's also a lost map and a funny-shaped rock," Cordelia said, reading. "Where's the part about the monster?" She started flipping the pages back and forth.

"Go back one more," Katelyn told her, gazing across the kitchen at the pages. "A scary monster, a lost map, treasure." She turned off the water and picked the cups up. "It's Scooby-Doo perfection!"

She whirled around with a triumphant smile, but Cordelia was staring down at the open book, her lips parted, her face pale. Before Katelyn could get a peek at what had upset her, Cordelia closed the book and looped her red hair behind her ears.

"Are you okay?" Katelyn asked.

"Fine," Cordelia snapped, her tone suddenly almost nasty.

Katelyn was startled. She lifted the coffee cups defensively. "Am I too chirpy?"

"I'm sorry," Cordelia said, immediately backpedaling. "It's just . . . we're living on top of each other at my house. I'm getting kind of bummed thinking about going back."

"I understand. I don't like being here, either," Katelyn replied. They shared a grumpy smile, but she wasn't entirely sure that was all that was bothering Cordelia. She gestured to the book. "Did you see the monster part?"

"No," Cordelia murmured, stifling another yawn. "Sorry." She dragged herself to her feet. "I'll look at it later. As much as I don't want to, I should head home."

"Are you sure?" Katelyn asked.

Cordelia glanced at her watch and nodded. Her face was almost gray. And Katelyn wasn't positive, but she thought Cordelia's hands were shaking. "My dad . . . I think he has something planned for today." She ran her hands along her arms, as if she were cold.

"Is everything okay?" Katelyn pressed, still unsure about her friend.

"Oh, Kat, I'm so sorry," Cordelia said, reaching over and giving her a quick hug. "This was great. You're a perfect hostess and I had fun. I just really should get going."

Katelyn believed her, but she was still sad to see her go. As soon as she heard the crunch of Cordelia's truck wheels on the drive, she sat down at the table and opened the book again. There was a pen-and-ink illustration of an enormous, fierce animal half flying through the air at an old-time prospector. The Hellhound was not so much wolf-like as monster-like, a blur of black fur and glowing eyes. Its teeth were as long as its claws, and steaming saliva poured from its gaping maw as it closed in on the man.

"Haley," she murmured, then shook her head. Nothing like this had attacked her. It was just a legend.

The rest of the book was pretty dry, and as she read on, it got harder and harder to concentrate. Her mind kept drifting to Justin. She'd never been kissed like that. She'd hardly been kissed at all—just a few experiments at parties with boys who had barely touched her lips. She just couldn't believe that he was taken.

If she ever saw him again, she'd punch him out, she thought angrily.

Except she couldn't believe he hadn't meant those kisses. They'd been so passionate. Was it possible Cordelia had it wrong? Maybe he'd broken up with Lucy.

Or maybe he's just an ass and he's not the guy for you.

She decided to call Kimi to discuss it, but her call went straight to voice mail.

"I know it's way early there, but I've got something important," she said, hiding the disappointment in her voice.

She hung up and waited for a callback, but the phone remained stubbornly silent.

"Hellhound," she said aloud. Could that be the same thing the priests had been afraid of? Maybe it had been an extra-large wolf, or some kind of mutant or something. It would be long dead by now. Maybe it had descendants. Maybe every once in a while, one of those descendants started attacking people.

She went back to reading the book, but the rest was pretty boring—discussions of failed attempts to find the mine, with names, dates, and equipment lists. She started to doze off. The rest of her schoolwork still didn't sound fun, so Katelyn lounged around in her pajamas until her grandfather got home around noon. When she heard his truck pulling up to the cabin, she ran upstairs, threw on some clothes, and was back in the living room before he'd made it to the front door.

"Hi, Katie." She nodded at him. "Everything go okay?" he asked.

"Great," she said brightly. When he wasn't looking, she darted a glance at the rifle on the wall to make sure it had been replaced correctly.

"Good. Give me a hand?"

She followed him outside. The sun was out, but it was

still chilly. He pulled back the tarp from the bed of the truck. She was astonished to see rows and rows of canned food—pears, peaches, vegetarian-style baked beans, corn, tomatoes, pickled beets. Tuna. Beef stew. And other things: antifreeze and cartons of ammunition.

"Um, isn't Bentonville the world headquarters of Wal-mart?" Bentonville was where the airport was located. "Did you have to go all the way to Little Rock to get this stuff?" she asked him as she picked up a half-gallon container of antifreeze and held it against her chest. Her shoulder was still sore.

He led the way toward his detached garage. "I had other things to do in Little Rock. Saw a lawyer, for one."

Her eyebrows shot up, but as he was walking ahead of her, he didn't see.

"Your mama didn't leave you any money," he said bluntly. "But you'll get some social security and the city's sending you something because of your dad. I'm the guardian of your estate until you turn eighteen. For now, I'll give you cash every month, pay your phone, buy your clothes."

She hadn't even thought of any of that. "Thank you," she said softly.

"And I updated my will," he added. That startled her. She stumbled, found her footing, and hurried to catch up to him. He was a fast walker.

"Are you sick?" she asked him.

"No. Just careful," he replied.

He held the door to the garage open. It was dark inside. He flicked on a light switch. The small space was tidy, with tools and ropes hanging from pegboards, and a long tool bench holding tackle boxes and a row of screwdrivers and pliers.

There was a canoe in the center of the room and a metal fold-ing chair beside it.

"I hit a shoal during the summer," he said, gesturing to the canoe. "Scraped up the bottom. I'll be moving it so we can put the truck in here during the winter," he said. "The larder's over here."

He led her past the canoe, opened a door, and pulled on a chain. They entered a storage room. Wooden shelves held a few bottles of pasta sauce and some glass jars labeled J.D.'S PICKLES.

He looked at the way she was holding the antifreeze. "Is your shoulder bothering you too much to help me unload the truck?"

"No," she said; then she realized that back home, she would have said yes, because of her gymnastics and ballet. Here it al-most didn't matter if she got injured.

I can't think that way, she told herself, fretting. *This is all temporary.*

"We'll get snowed in. You can count on it," he told her.

"Yay," she said weakly. The idea of being trapped was a nightmare.

Once they were finished, he marched her into the forest for more rifle training. With the night's scare explained away, she was again reluctant to touch the weapon.

They practiced for more than half an hour, but it seemed to her that she was getting worse instead of better. She was tired and frustrated.

"How do you feel?" he asked after a particularly er-rant shot.

"Not good," she admitted. "My shoulder *is* still sore."

He nodded and took the rifle from her. "Let's end for the day." He turned and she fell into step beside him, relieved to be done.

"How do you think it went?" she asked tentatively, just to fill the silence.

He sighed. "I think it was a terrible waste of ammunition."

Her heart fell. She trudged back to the house beside him, staring at her feet. As much as she hated the rifle, she didn't want to disappoint Ed, and the realization surprised her. When had she started to care about pleasing him?

⊷ ▰◆▰ ⊷

That night, she dreamed about Justin. Red fog boiled around him as he rode his motorcycle; and surrounding that, blackest night. He was speeding toward her, but she was standing on the other side of an enormous chasm. As he reached the edge of the cliff, he gunned the engine and the motorcycle soared into the air, arcing like a comet, clouds of exhaust shooting out the back. She held out her arms, willing him to make it.

He flew, climbing higher and higher—but then something happened. He began to fall. And the red wasn't fog; it was smoke and flames, and he was diving into them.

"No!" she cried, bolting upright in bed.

Panting, she smoothed back her hair. *It was just a dream,* she assured herself.

Lying on her side, she curled into a ball. Her heart was racing. She considered getting up to call Kimi, but it was the middle of the night.

And Kimi still hadn't called her back from the morning.

She reached over and found her bear. Feeling foolish, she pulled it close and rested her chin on it. She wanted to go home. She wanted to go now.

⊷ ⊷ ⊷

On Monday afternoon, she was back in the forest next to her grandfather, who handed her the rifle. Just touching it made her stomach flip.

"Hold it steady," he urged her. "Pull the trigger."

Katelyn exhaled and let the rifle droop.

"I'm sorry," she said miserably. "I'm just not getting it."

He clicked his teeth and tipped the barrel of the rifle back up toward the sky. "You've got a birthday coming up."

She was a little surprised he remembered.

She nodded. "November sixth."

"What do you usually do to celebrate?"

"Oh, different things." For her sixteenth birthday, she and her mother had gone to a performance of the New York City Ballet when it was on tour in L.A. The Cirque performance of *Alegría* had been their last outing.

"Well, you mentioned something about that circus you like."

She bit her lip. She wanted to say more, but she didn't want to push her luck and risk his going on again about setting her sights on a career in the real world.

He reached into the pocket of his denim jacket and pulled out two tickets. "The Cirque du Soleil?" he said. "They're putting on a couple of shows in Little Rock. I saw the ads. I'll take you for your birthday. *If* you can learn to hit that target."

"What?" she asked, not sure she'd heard right. She reached out and touched the tickets. Her past and her future were colliding in her present, making her head spin.

"We can go?"

"If you can get a bull's-eye."

He stood aside. She steadied the gun and held her breath. Then she fired a shot. The shell casing made a chinging sound as it hit the ground.

They both looked. She was nowhere near the bull's-eye, but for the first time ever, she'd made it onto the paper.

"Ed," she said breathlessly. *"Look."*

"I am. And it makes me want to howl like a banshee," he replied.

Then she raised the rifle and pulled the trigger again.

8

The next morning Katelyn was in a great mood. She'd hit the target three more times, but her real target was the Cirque tickets. It meant so much that Ed had bought them. All was not lost after all. She'd been right when she'd told Kimi she was more likely to get her way if she was nice. As her grandfather hadn't shown in the kitchen yet, she made the coffee and smiled when she heard Trick's Mustang roll up outside.

She made sure she had all her school stuff, then poured him a cup of coffee and laid a piece of toast on top. Juggling everything, she opened the door. He'd already gotten out of the car and was heading up the steps leading to the porch. She went out into the chilly morning air and waited for him.

When he reached her, he didn't say a word. The dark brows, which furrowed above his deep green eyes, were nearly matched by the black circles underneath them. His mouth was pressed into a thin line, and there was a pallor to his usually warm bronze skin that made him look like a different person— someone related to Trick, but not Trick. There was something *nearer* about him, even though his seriousness made her step back.

She glanced down at the left sleeve of his dark gray hoodie. A black armband of duct tape was wound around his bicep.

"Trick?" she said. "What's wrong?"

He gave a strange kind of gasp and took a step toward her, then stopped, as if holding himself in check. Then he took the coffee and toast with one hand and closed his other hand over hers. His fingers were cold.

"Trick? You're scaring me."

He shook his head and walked her to the car. She slid in, and he walked around to the driver's side. Music started immediately. She recognized "Pavane for a Dead Princess" by Ravel. The music caught her off guard. Her mother had danced to this, dressed as a sixteenth-century Spanish princess. Katelyn had seen a video of her performance.

He was playing it loudly, driving slow, as if he wanted to drag out the time it would take to get to school.

"What happened?" she shouted over the music, but he couldn't hear her. She wanted to reach over and turn off the music but, at the same time, wanted just as badly for him to delay whatever bad news he had for her.

Just before they entered the tree tunnel, he put the car in idle, turned, and put his arms around her. He was shaking and he pressed her head into his chest. Katelyn felt the muscles against her cheek. His heart was pounding as the music swelled around them.

"Trick?" She choked on her own fear, but he let go and began to drive again.

When they finally arrived at school, Katelyn realized immediately that whatever was wrong wasn't affecting just Trick. She saw students clustered in small knots talking quietly. A blond girl was sitting in her car, sobbing with her head against the steering wheel, one foot on the ground outside and one inside. Katelyn's stomach tightened as she recognized the all-too-familiar signs of grief.

Trick turned off the car.

"Tell me *now*," she ordered him.

He exhaled, eyes fixed straight ahead through the windshield, not at her. "Becky Jensen wasn't at school yesterday. Turns out she went missing a couple of days ago. Her body was discovered early this morning." The muscle in his jaw worked as he shifted, locking his gaze on hers, fighting for calm. "Just like Haley."

Horror surged through her. Had Becky Jensen screamed? In the woods? On Friday night? And could Katelyn have done something to save her?

Her stomach twisted and she struggled not to be sick. She glanced up at Trick, who looked the same way she felt.

"Did you know her?" she whispered.

He nodded. "I told you. Everybody knows everybody out here. She was probably in a couple of your classes."

"Oh, God," Katelyn said, suddenly suspended in a strange

sort of languor. Part of her still felt the intense horror, the shock, but another part detached, as if she were hearing of it from a great distance in time and space.

"Trick, that story I told you. . . ," she began.

"Not now," he said, so quietly she almost didn't hear him.

Trick climbed out of the car and she caught up to him as he started to cross the lot. It was chilly, but as she passed the girl crying in her car, she began to sweat. She remembered the shock and pain she'd felt when she had heard her dad had been shot. Unlike with her mom, she hadn't been there to see it happen. Somehow that had made it even harder to believe.

I touched my mom's face just before she died. She died. My mom died.

Two girls are dead. Death followed me.

She walked into the building and everywhere she turned there were stunned, tear-streaked faces. Trick was right. In a town as small as this one, everyone did know everyone.

And her grandfather was right.

Going out into the woods at night *could* get you killed.

She shivered and wrapped her arms around herself.

That first scream . . .

Cordelia was in history, looking pale. Mr. Henderson attempted to review his grading system for their projects, but no one was listening. Throughout class Katelyn tried to get Cordelia's attention, but the other girl refused to look up, and when the bell rang, she bolted from the room.

Katelyn hurried to follow her and finally caught up to her in the hallway just before they reached the gym. She grabbed Cordelia's arm and spun her half around.

Cordelia looked up at her, eyes brimming with tears. Her mascara had run all over. "Oh, Kat!" she wailed. "First Haley and now Becky. We used to be so close."

Katelyn felt helpless; she didn't know what to say, but she reached out and hugged Cordelia. The other girl clung to her, sobbing as if her heart were breaking.

"Maybe you should go home," Katelyn said.

"I don't want to. There's no one there and then I'd have to think too much."

"Think?" Katelyn echoed. *About what we did and didn't do?*

"Please come with me," Cordelia begged. "I'll get you home before dark." She smeared her makeup even more. Then she looked hard at Katelyn. "What?"

Katelyn licked her lips. "Friday." Cordelia just stared at her blankly, which frustrated Katelyn, because she didn't want to have to say any more. "The scream."

Cordelia caught her breath. "*Oh.* Oh, no, Kat. She wasn't anywhere near the cabin. We for sure didn't hear her. Oh, I'm sorry you were worried about that."

Katelyn's intense, high-inducing relief that Becky's blood was not on their hands, combined with the way Cordelia kept smearing her makeup, made her reflexively smile.

"What? Do I look awful?" Cordelia asked, suddenly self-conscious.

"A little like the Joker." She bit her lip. It wasn't funny, but the relief was so great she couldn't help herself.

Cordelia burst out with a choked, crazy laugh. She glanced down at her hands, and her eyes widened at the streaks of mascara, eye shadow, and blush covering her fingers. "I did not just laugh," she said.

"It's just nerves," Katelyn said grimly, painfully familiar with the cycle of crazy emotions. "Laughing, crying, and in between . . . numb."

"Please come home with me," Cordelia pleaded again. "I need someone of my own there."

Her phrasing was odd, but Katelyn understood it.

"I need to be home by dark," she reminded her.

Cordelia nodded, then, wordlessly, stepped forward and kissed her cheek.

Katelyn texted Trick that she had a ride home, but he didn't reply. Luckily, on their way out, she bumped into a girl she'd seen sitting at Trick's lunch table and the girl promised to let him know.

When Katelyn and Cordelia stopped at the office to get permission to leave, Mrs. Walker said the principal told her to excuse anyone who asked to go.

The two girls headed for the parking lot. Once they were inside Cordelia's car and heading away from the school, Katelyn felt herself relax a little. Cordelia's grief was raw and fresh, but better to deal with one person feeling that way than five hundred.

For a long time they drove in silence and Cordelia cried off and on. Her makeup was completely gone by then and she looked much younger. A wave of protectiveness rushed over Katelyn. She wished she could say something to make Cordelia feel better, but knew there wasn't anything. People had tried that with her and it had only made her feel more alone.

When they finally pulled up around the back of the house, Katelyn noticed another black truck in the small gravel lot, this one bigger and shinier than Cordelia's. The other girl turned the engine off and sat for a moment, looking at it, without moving.

For a second Katelyn thought of Justin and a shiver went through her. She tried to remind herself that he was a lying, cheating jerk and she had no desire to see him ever again.

"Dad's home," Cordelia said. There was something odd in the way she said it, like she was catching her breath.

Katelyn was taken aback.

"Is everything okay?" she asked.

"What? No, it's good. You should meet. It's good for him to meet my friends."

And still Cordelia sat, hands wrapped around the steering wheel in a death grip.

"We can go somewhere else if you want," Katelyn said, her friend's trepidation communicating itself all too well.

But it was too late. The back door to the house opened, and out stepped a very tall man with a shock of white hair. His face was tan and leathery, like a cowboy's. He was older than she had expected, but looked strong. His amber eyes were flecked through with gold, and she felt as if he were staring right through her. A chill ran up her spine.

Then he moved his attention to Cordelia, breaking into a broad, welcoming smile. She got out of the car and headed toward him, and after a moment, Katelyn trailed behind.

"My youngest! So what brings you home so early in the day?" he asked, throwing open his arms to embrace her.

Cordelia's voice was muffled against his chest. "Kat and I got time off to work on our history project."

Katelyn blinked at the lie. Why not just tell her father the truth? It wasn't every day you found out a friend of yours had been killed. Surely he would understand that.

Cordelia turned and gestured to Katelyn.

"Kat, this is my father, Lee Fenner."

"Kat," he said, biting off her name. He wrapped his hand around hers and shook, then leaned forward as though he was going to kiss her cheek, and she jerked. He took note of her reaction and moved slightly back as well. She didn't know what to think of him.

"So, you and my little Cordelia have become pretty close," he said.

Behind him she saw Cordelia flush. Parental types. They would embarrass you. Some things didn't change no matter where you went.

"Yes, I'm lucky to have her as a friend," Katelyn replied, feeling awkward.

"And she you." He released her hand. "Always nice to welcome a new face into our home."

His tone was warm but the look he shot Cordelia was distinctly not happy. Cordelia dropped her head, and Katelyn felt sorry for her and even more awkward. Her entire family was weird. No wonder she'd hesitated about having Katelyn over.

"And you're working together on a history project?" he continued.

"Yes," she said, forcing herself to smile like nothing was wrong in the world.

"History is important. You know what they say: those who

don't learn from the past are doomed to repeat it. The Fenners have a proud history, goes back centuries."

Cordelia looked stricken. Katelyn didn't know what to do other than nod politely.

"The silver mine," he said.

"We're going to go study in my room," Cordelia cut in quickly.

"That's fine, good," he said.

Before Katelyn could get around Lee to the back door, it swung open and Arial and Regan appeared on the threshold. Arial was wearing yoga pants and a workout top, and Regan had on bike shorts and a red T-shirt that read WOLF SPRINGS, JEWEL OF THE OZARKS. Both of them held coffee cups that read FENNER CONSTRUCTION.

"Well, well, well. Look what the *cat* dragged in," Arial said.

"Dad?" Cordelia asked anxiously. "What's up?"

"Oh, the girls came by," he said offhandedly.

"While I was at school?" Cordelia sounded upset and Katelyn watched her carefully, wondering why. She knew Cordelia didn't enjoy being around them, so it should have been a good thing that they were there when she wasn't.

"It's no big deal, Cordelia." Regan fished in her pocket, found a hair band, and began gathering up her hair. "You'd never win this one, anyway."

"A little sibling rivalry going on," Mr. Fenner explained to Katelyn. "All in fun."

But Cordelia didn't look like she was having fun. She looked pissed off. Katelyn wondered if this had anything to do with the Fenner family's apparent obsession with sports competitions.

"We should do this later," Cordelia said, glancing at Katelyn.

Regan rolled her shoulders. "I'm all warmed up."

"Me too," Arial added. "You don't need to bother, Cor."

Cordelia rubbed her face again. Her hands were shaking. Katelyn was dumbfounded. The Fenners were insane.

"Hey," Katelyn said, sounding falsely cheery, but unable to completely hide her freak-out. "It's okay if you have stuff to do, Cordelia. I can get a ride." She pulled out her cell phone. "Really, it's not a problem."

Cordelia looked up at her father. "May I speak to you alone, Daddy?" She glanced at Katelyn. "I'll be just a minute. It'll be okay," she added, which seemed both random and untrue.

Mr. Fenner gave Katelyn a long look. Then he opened the door and said, "Ladies?"

Cordelia scooted inside—followed by her two sisters, who exchanged smug smiles. So Cordelia wasn't going to be allowed to speak to him alone. Katelyn kind of hated her two sisters for their scuzzy attitudes. Correction: she *totally* hated them.

Standing with his hand on the door latch, Mr. Fenner studied Katelyn. It was a look that made her feel itchy and creeped out.

"So, you're Mordecai McBride's granddaughter?" he stated more than asked.

Did they know each other? "So I'm told," she murmured, and he guffawed.

"How are you liking Wolf Springs?"

She thought of Becky Jensen. "Well, today, I . . . ," she began, then trailed off. Cordelia hadn't told her father about the death. "It's small," she said. "I'm from L.A."

"Oh, the big city." He sounded a bit contemptuous. "Big bad city."

"Big, anyway," she said, floundering. *What the heck?*

At that moment Katelyn's phone rang. She was so startled she nearly dropped it. A glance at the faceplate revealed that her caller was Trick.

"I'll let you get that," Mr. Fenner said grandly, then went into the house. She was grateful to get the privacy denied to Cordelia.

"Trick, hi," she said in a rush.

"Sam said you left with Cordelia." His voice was tense. "Are you okay?"

He'd been worried about her. And it made her feel good, she realized.

"She needed a friend pretty badly and—and right now *I* need one," she said, still shaking off the oddness of Mr. Fenner.

"What's wrong?" His voice changed as if he had switched to high alert.

She stepped off the porch, lowering her voice even though she didn't think the Fenners could hear her. The whole situation was so massively *weird*.

"I'm at her house and her family's being a little . . . intense with group time. Could you come pick me up?" she asked as sweetly as she could. Just trying to explain it made it even stranger.

"Sure." He didn't miss a beat or even ask for more explanation. "On my way."

"Do you know where it is?"

"Yup."

"Okay, thanks," she said, relief washing over her once more.

She ended her call, still feeling bad. She felt as if she were ditching Cordelia, but no one—not even Cordelia—had objected when she'd said she could find another ride home. At least someone could have invited her in. Or not.

The door opened, and Cordelia stood there in sweatpants and a Wolf Springs High Cheer sweatshirt. Tears were welling in her eyes. "Kat, I'm so sorry," she said in a rush. "I didn't realize my dad had left you out here. I'm—I was just . . ." She swallowed hard.

"It's okay," Katelyn said, although it was anything but. The Fenners just got more and more wacko. Cordelia really needed someone normal in her life, and Katelyn was startled to realize that thus far, she was the most likely candidate. "Trick's coming."

"Oh, *God*," Cordelia moaned. She covered her face with her hands. "*Please* don't let him see any of this."

"Any of what?" Katelyn asked gently.

Cordelia started to cry. "This is too much. It's too . . ."

Katelyn pulled her into a hug. Cordelia went slack, let loose with a couple of sobs, and then jerked and raised her head. She pulled away, wiping her face and smoothing back her hair.

"Could you wait up at the top of our drive for Trick?" she asked in a tight voice.

And it just kept getting weirder and weirder. "Sure." Overcompensating for her own nervousness, Katelyn nodded too hard. "Let me get my stuff out of the truck."

"Of course." Cordelia gave Katelyn a small troubled smile

and walked with her. She stopped at the passenger door and, as Katelyn grabbed her bag, added, "Can you please not tell him anything? It'd be just like him to lord it over me."

Katelyn frowned. That sounded more like Mike. It certainly wasn't how she saw Trick. But then, did she really know him? Did she know Cordelia, for that matter?

Before she could answer, the front door burst back open. "Okay, Cordelia!" Mr. Fenner boomed. Arial and Regan flanked him as he walked down the steps. Arial had her head on his shoulder and Regan's arm was looped through his. Their smugness was almost as nauseating as the strange family portrait they presented.

Mr. Fenner raised his brows at Cordelia, who looked one more time at Katelyn. She reminded Katelyn of a drowning person searching for a rope. But what could Katelyn do—offer her a ride out of there for, like, the rest of her life?

"I'll go wait for Trick," Katelyn said.

"Thanks. So much," Cordelia murmured, fresh tears welling. Then she ran after her family and disappeared among the trees.

Katelyn started up the steep driveway to wait for Trick. She was about to put in her earbuds when she heard Mr. Fenner shout, "Put your back into it!"

Katelyn was dying of curiosity to see what was going on, but she kept walking. Mr. Fenner yelled some more, but she couldn't make out the words.

"C'mon, Trick," she muttered to herself.

She didn't have to wait long. When his car appeared at the top of the road, he stopped a distance away, as if there were an invisible NO TRESPASSING sign and he was not fond of buckshot. She ran to the car, jumped in, and slammed the door shut behind her.

"Home, Jeeves," she said, sighing, expelling the Fenner air from her lungs.

"Very good, madam," he replied in his best snooty accent. Trouble was it mixed with his own Southern accent and came out so comical that she couldn't hide her faint smile. She'd assumed he would be downcast, but he was joking around.

"Does madam find something amusing?"

"It just feels good after the day I've had," she confessed as the shadows of the death crept up once more and the weirdness of Cordelia's family hit her fresh.

"Then I've done something right," he said, his voice soft as he dropped his lighthearted act.

"You're always doing stuff right." Her voice came out just as soft, and she was glad of it.

"I'm happy to end this day with you," he said.

That felt good to hear. "Thanks for picking me up. I— I didn't expect to need a ride."

He inclined his head. "Happy to come to the rescue. Got sick of their particular brand of freak?"

"They're not freaks," she said a bit defensively. "Just different." It wasn't true, but she felt bad for Cordelia and didn't want to make her life worse by gossiping about it—especially with Trick.

He gave her a look. "Whatever you say."

"You, however, are a freak," she said teasingly, desperate to change the subject.

His smile was private and triumphant. A little flurry of butterflies reminded her of how it had felt when he'd hugged her that morning. With Justin turning out to be such a creep, she could use a nice guy like Trick. She hoped there were more hugs in their future—maybe even full-on kisses. She blushed and looked out the window as Trick turned around. Her gaze went to a turret extending from the third story of Cordelia's house.

Framed by the wooden sill, Justin Fenner gazed down at her. Her heart lurched. He was too far away for her to read his expression. Had he been there the entire time? Was he too ashamed to show his face after cheating on his girlfriend? Or was he done with the new girl because he'd gotten what he wanted?

The car moved on, and so did Katelyn. Justin was left behind, where he belonged. Still, she brooded. And remembered how it had felt—all of it.

Including the voice that had called to her in the dark when he'd been kissing her.

It was just my imagination, she told herself.

But the screaming on Friday had not been. And now she was finding it hard to believe it had been a cat. She kept holding on to Cordelia's assurance that Becky had died too far away for them to have heard her scream.

"Are you okay?" Trick asked her.

She didn't answer but looked at him carefully. "What about you, Trick? You knew them both." Then, before she knew what she was doing, she squeezed his hand. She heard him catch his breath. A muscle danced in his cheek.

"I'm glad you answered your phone," he said quietly.

Then he focused on the road as the darkness slid over the Mustang.

When they reached home, her grandfather was sitting on the porch, waiting for them. School was still in, so she wasn't sure how he'd known they were coming.

"I gave him a heads-up," Trick said when she glanced questioningly at him.

She climbed onto the porch, feeling slightly guilty. "I'm sorry I didn't call. One of the girls at school died and Cordelia was friends with her. She needed to go home and didn't want to be alone. Her family was there, though, so I had Trick come get me. We told the office we were leaving school before we did. We didn't cut."

Ed nodded. "Why don't you go inside? Trick and I have things to talk over."

His eyes were hard as he turned to look at Trick. She glanced back and saw Trick standing next to his car, shoulders hunched, hands in his pockets. Like he was in trouble. She was confused. Was Ed mad at Trick for bringing her home?

"I'll see you in the morning, Kat," Trick said.

She gave him a little wave. Whatever talk they were about to have wasn't going to be nice and wasn't going to end with Trick staying for lunch, let alone dinner.

She heard raised voices outside as soon as she closed the door. She ran upstairs and tried to listen but had no luck. The thick cabin walls made it impossible to decipher any words, but the volume was loud enough she couldn't stop straining to hear. She wished for the hundredth time that she were back in California, where at least she understood the rules.

It was well past lunch by the time she heard the front door

open, then shut. She listened as Ed climbed the stairs. He came into her room and sat down on the edge of her bed. His face was lined, his shoulders hunched, as if he were tired.

"I heard what happened to that girl from school. Are you okay?"

She nodded, a little surprised that he'd asked. "Kind of. I'm really thrown. But I didn't know her. Or Haley." She frowned. "Is it wrong I'm not more upset?"

He patted her shoulder. "No, it's not wrong, honey. I'm just glad you're okay."

"Thank you." She took a deep breath. She realized this was her chance. "Someone at school told me that forty years ago, some animals went berserk and started attacking people. And that it wasn't the first time—it had happened before."

He listened, his forehead wrinkled, but she couldn't tell if he was mad, upset, or just mildly curious. "Who told you that?"

"He didn't want me to say."

He cocked his head. "Why not?"

"I-I'm not sure. Is it true? Did it really happen?"

"Forty years ago," he said, "I didn't live here full-time. This was just our summer cabin. I was busy teaching philosophy." His face softened. "And your dad was just a little guy." A wave of sorrow rushed over his features, and she remembered how grief-stricken he had been when he'd come out for the funeral. He had left the church during the service and hadn't made it to the graveside ceremony.

"You never dream that you'll bury your own child," he murmured, more to himself than to her; then he cleared his throat, seemed to snap back to the present. "I did hear rumblings about something going on out here, but you have to understand, Katie. It was different back then. Wolf Springs was very cut off from civilization. People liked it that way."

"And it's so different today," she said dryly.

"We didn't have a phone or electricity out here," he replied. "Drove your grandma crazy."

"My friend's really scared. He says Wolf Springs is like a"—Katelyn had to search for the words he'd used—"a banked fire. I mean, two girls have died."

He shook his head sadly. "Normally, wild animals avoid people. But if they're starving, or feeling threatened, or infected with rabies . . ."

Rabies. She thought of the wolf that had attacked her in Trick's car, the crazy light in its eyes and the blood on its mouth. Could it have been rabid? She shivered.

"Bad things happen." He looked at her sadly. "I don't have to tell *you* that."

"No," she murmured. "You don't."

They sat together quietly. Then he cleared his throat again. "So, Trick told me about this party he wants to take you to."

The topic change caught her off guard. She hesitated. "Yeah," she said carefully.

"I don't want you to go," he began, but as her lips parted in protest, he went on. "But I reckon you've got enough of your father in you that if I forbid you to go, you'll just find a way to do it anyway."

She held her breath.

"I don't know how it's done in Santa Monica, but around here the kids have these all-night, dusk-to-dawn parties.

Everyone's so spread out. Maybe it's a rural thing. In any case, seems as though this one's in town, so you should be safe and not out in the woods."

She nodded even though she hadn't known it was an all-night party. That was kind of amazing. She'd never been to anything like that back home, unless it was an all-girl overnight.

"I know you're his date, but I'm going to loan you the truck. I want you to meet him there, and if anything happens, you come straight home, make him or someone else follow you along the way if you can so you don't get lost or stranded."

That seemed odd. Didn't he trust Trick to get her to and from town, just like he always did? Was this what they had been arguing about?

"Okay," she said.

"Make him follow you if it's still dark out," he repeated.

"Yes. Got it," she assured him.

He exhaled sharply, as though what he was saying was costing him dearly. "This isn't a prison, Katelyn."

"I know, you just want to keep me safe," she said. It was the time for agreeing and encouraging, lest he change his mind.

And maybe if things went well, this was just the first step to freedom.

"Now, how about we take advantage of all this daylight and do some more sharpshooting?" he asked.

＊＊＊

Katelyn practiced for an hour, until there was a pile of shell casings beside her foot. The rings on the black-and-white bull's-eye targets were numbered, with one the farthest from the center and nine the bull's-eye itself. She was hitting the rings numbered one, two, and three fairly often.

When they finally trudged back to the house, she asked, "How am I coming on those birthday tickets?"

He raised a steel-colored brow. "I'd say you've just about earned 'em. You're not hitting dead center, but at least you're not closing your eyes anymore."

"You know what they say about proper motivation." Internally, she danced a jig.

"Maybe you inherited the McBride eye," he retorted.

Suddenly a chorus of howls burst out and Ed spun, assuming a shooting position with a rapid-fire reflex.

A moment later he lowered the rifle. "Dang fool, having another one of those retreats. I'll make *him* howl. In falsetto." He grunted. "A bunch of city boys think they can come out here for a few days and get in touch with their inner man."

"I believe it's their inner wolf."

"Their inner idjit is what it is," he said.

"I sat next to a guy on the plane out here. He was really into it," she said.

"That moron and his stupid book," Ed said. He looked like he wanted to spit in the dirt. "He's like the pied piper of lunatics."

She smiled. It was a funny way of looking at it. She just hoped it wasn't true.

"I'm reading your copy," she said.

He made a face. "I thought I threw it out."

"At first I thought we might be able to use it for our history project. It's about a mine," she added. "The Madre Vena. Have you heard of it? This creepy monster is supposed to live in it. The Hellhound."

He grunted again. "Hellhound. Sounds properly terrifying to scare off claim jumpers."

"The Spanish priests who built the church were scared of something that lived in the forest," she said. "What if it was this same Hellhound?"

"Or maybe they just said that to keep their parishioners from running away. Enslaved Indians and gullible Spanish soldiers. Now, as for what your friend told you, let me know if you hear anything else, okay? And I'll do the same. Could be useful for your history project."

"I will," she promised. She didn't tell him that it was way off topic for the project.

Katelyn tried to do homework the rest of the day, but her thoughts kept drifting. There was Trick and the party. There was the strangeness of Cordelia's family. And sitting there on her desk was the Jack Bronson book. She finally gave up and flipped it open.

No man knows what he is capable of until he is pushed. The wolf is a naturally elusive creature that melts into shadows. But let that wolf or his pack or cub be threatened and the beast is unleashed and is capable of great and terrible things. The key is to find a way to harness that power when there is no danger, even when you are alone in your room at night and the darkness comes and your own demons mock you.

"Nice," she drawled, but it scared her a little, and as she finally tried to go to sleep, her demons came to mock her: her thoughts turned to Becky and rabid wolves, and the things in the dark that could kill you. And with branches scratching at her skylight, she finally drifted to sleep. Her dreams chased her the whole night long.

⋅⋅ ▬✦▬ ⋅⋅

The wind. And the howls.
The wind. And the screams.
Fangs, and fur,
flashing in fury and madness,
charging through the forest.
Relentless, a killing machine, a demon.
It is screeching; it is raging; it is shrieking:
Vengeance is mine.
Click. Click. Click.
The sound of claws on hardwood echoed through it all.

9

The next morning, the sign mounted on the roof of Wolf Springs High read BECKY JENSEN IN MEMORY. Stuffed animals, bouquets of flowers, and pictures of Becky lay on the floor in front of a locker very close to Katelyn's. Katelyn recognized Becky from English class—brown hair cut in a bob, freckles, like her.

There were more tributes scattered in clusters throughout the building. Girls were hugging each other, crying. Teachers were grim-faced. A boy in a black knit cap was passing out flyers. Katelyn took one. *WHAT IS HAPPENING TO OUR CHILDREN? DEMAND ACTION! TOWN HALL MEETING TOMORROW NIGHT 7 PM.*

Cordelia cornered Katelyn on her way to history class. "Sorry again for everything," she said. Cordelia looked even more tired than she had before, and Katelyn felt closer to her, knowing that she had so much strangeness to deal with outside school.

Katelyn shrugged like it was no big deal. "Who won?" *And what did they win at?* she wanted to add.

"Arial," Cordelia said, sounding disgusted.

"Do you even care?" Katelyn asked, surprised.

"It's complicated." She bit her lip. "So, what did you tell Trick?"

"Just that you were involved in family time and I needed a ride home."

"I'd appreciate you not telling people how strange . . . well, anything about my family, actually," she said, looking relieved.

Yeah, no kidding, Katelyn thought. "Of course I won't."

There was an awkward pause. Katelyn wanted to make things better. She cleared her throat. "On an unrelated topic, I think Trick's taking me to this party. If they still have it. What should I wear?"

Cordelia brightened a little. "Oooh, party! Whose?"

Katelyn wanted to kick herself. Because obviously, Cordelia hadn't heard about the party and wasn't invited. Katelyn had just assumed she would be.

"I'm not sure."

"If you want, I can drive you home today and help you pick something out."

Her clothes had been destroyed in the fire and she didn't have much. But maybe that wasn't the real reason Cordelia wanted to come home with her. Maybe she just needed a place to go.

"Make you a deal," Katelyn said. "I don't have anything to wear. Maybe we could go shopping tomorrow afternoon, then after, you can come over for dinner. Then we'll do some work on our project."

A smile twisted Cordelia's lips. "Are you implying that I'm a slacker?"

"My lips are sealed," Katelyn said, smiling back.

Their lighthearted moment faded as they walked down the hall. The Timberwolves looked shell-shocked. When the two girls made it to gym class, Mike and his group seemed meaner than usual. Katelyn did her best to ignore them, chalking up the hostility to fear. He really rubbed her the wrong way, but she was afraid of what he'd do if she said anything, so she kept her mouth shut.

"Tomorrow I'm taking you to Babette's," Cordelia vowed.

Katelyn recalled Trick mentioning that name. "What's Babette's?"

"You'll see," Cordelia said enigmatically.

"Cool. Now let's talk about Xavier Cazador," Katelyn said.

"Oh." Cordelia's face fell. "I—I wanted to talk to you about that," she said. "The mine thing. I'm really just not loving it, you know? Maybe we could pick something else."

Katelyn was baffled. "But you told me you wanted to do it. And your dad knows about it. And you know, maybe this Hellhound *is* the same thing that the priests were talking about. And it could be linked to the attacks. We could really do some digging and . . ."

She trailed off, taken aback. Cordelia looked positively green. Katelyn cocked her head. Cordelia was afraid.

Of the Hellhound?

"It's just kind of bogus," Cordelia said unconvincingly. "Let's go to Mr. Henderson and ask if we can switch topics."

"Okay," Katelyn said. "Sure."

But Mr. Henderson said no at lunch. They were too far into their research to start over, he insisted.

Katelyn was secretly glad, and Cordelia seemed to take his refusal pretty well. She muttered something about how her father would be happy about it, and Katelyn wondered if Cordelia's original one-eighty about picking the mine had been an attempt to please her father in the first place. The twisted dynamics of the Fenner family had really done a job on poor Cordelia. But wanting to quit because there was a monster in the story? Katelyn was disbelieving. On the other hand, everyone in Wolf Springs was upset. Two girls were dead. But it wasn't as if a real, live Hellhound had done it.

She didn't share any of her thoughts with Cordelia, and the next afternoon as they were driving through town, Cordelia seemed pleased and more lighthearted as Katelyn took it all in. It was Katelyn's first trip to Wolf Springs proper, and she marveled at the gables, cupolas, and widow's walks on the beautifully preserved buildings.

The only downer was the flyers for the town meeting that night hung in every store window. Katelyn had forgotten to ask her grandfather if he was going.

They had to park a couple of blocks away from the store

and walk down the cobbled paths of the extremely quaint, old-timey town. They passed one structure with a small white metal sign on the wall that read WOLF SPRINGS TAVERN, EST. 1859, A HISTORIC SITE.

"That might be where Xavier Cazador got his free drinks," Katelyn said excitedly.

"I still say he never found the mine," Cordelia insisted. "I think he made it all up. After all, he was the town drunk."

"Then why did Jubal DeAndrew disappear two days later?"

"His daughter killed him."

"Nice," Katelyn drawled.

"No. *This* is nice," Cordelia announced, gesturing to Babette's.

The tiny storefront window of Babette's Vintage featured mannequins dressed in clothes from different time periods; one wore a cute Katy Perry 1950s dress, and a male figure stood in embroidered bell-bottom jeans and a baggy Indian-print top with wide sleeves. In the far right corner hung the flyer for the meeting, beside a poster that read WE LOVE YOU, HALEY AND BECKY. LOVE, BABETTE & CO.

A little bell tinkled over the door as they walked in. An attractive middle-aged woman seated behind a counter looked up from a book and gave them a wave.

"Hi, Babette," Cordelia said.

"Help yourselves, girls." The woman flashed a smile and went back to her book.

Katelyn walked slowly down one of the aisles, marveling at the variety of the clothes. It was almost as good as any place on Melrose Avenue.

And then she saw it—the perfect dress. It was a short floral print in creams and burnished golds with a faint sheen to the fabric. Cream lace cap sleeves fluttered on it. The neck was a rounded scoop. A cream belt complemented the sleeves.

"Ooh la la," Cordelia gushed as Katelyn modeled it for her. "Even *I* want you."

Katelyn fluttered her lashes with a pleased laugh.

Katelyn paid for the dress and took the bag from Babette.

"This must be for a special occasion," Babette said.

"Party," Cordelia said, winking.

"The one at Sam's?" Babette asked, and Cordelia nodded a little too brightly. Katelyn wished she could invite her along, but as the new girl, she didn't have the power to include other people. "Guess they're not canceling after all. There was talk about it."

Then Babette nodded at Katelyn. "You're the new girl. Kat McBride."

"Yes," Katelyn said, surprised.

"Babette is gossip central," Cordelia told Katelyn. "She knows *everything* that's going on."

Katelyn took a deep breath. "Do you know anything about . . . what happened to Haley and Becky?"

Babette exhaled slowly and let her smile fall, as if she no longer had to pretend that everything was all right.

"Oh, girls, I don't know *what* to think." She scanned the room, as if making sure no one else could hear her. "I was one of the people who really pushed to let Jack Bronson purchase the old hot springs. He's been buying my little wolf figurines for his gift shop." She gestured to a display of ceramic statues—a wolf standing on its hind legs, wearing a Superman costume; another one doing kung fu. "And I've got some of my nicer pieces on consignment in his gift shop."

She chewed her lower lip. "But I can't remember the last time an animal attacked a human being around here. And hunting season's right around the corner. The bears are going to be even more jittery."

"Is that what you think it was? A bear?" Cordelia asked.

Babette picked up the figurine of the wolf in the Superman uniform. "Well, I don't think it was a wolf. Wolves are shy."

"A wolf attacked me," Katelyn said, but Cordelia nudged her to be silent.

"What? When?" Babette's eyes widened.

"It was my first week here; there was a dead deer in the road," Katelyn said hastily.

The bell on the door tinkled, signaling the arrival of another customer.

"We should go," Cordelia announced.

"I'm going to be getting some pretty winter formals," Babette said in a stage whisper. "I'll set aside some dresses for the two of you." She eyed Katelyn. "I'm thinking something in an ice blue to set off that gorgeous hair of yours."

"Thanks," Katelyn said sincerely, warming to the woman.

"Enjoy the party," Babette replied, waving goodbye.

Katelyn and Cordelia turned to go, then nearly ran into an elderly woman walking with a cane. She wore a heavy black coat and a broad hat trimmed with black feathers.

"Terrible business, terrible," she said. She frowned at Katelyn and Cordelia. "You two girls shouldn't be out. You should be home, where it's safe."

"Yes, ma'am," Cordelia said sweetly, then pulled Katelyn past the woman.

"Listen, Kat," Cordelia said as soon as they were outside. "Don't tell Babette anything about *anything*. She'll broadcast it all over town."

"But why should I hide what happened?" Katelyn asked.

"Do you want Mike Wright shooting around your cabin?" Cordelia pressed. "Shooting out the windows?"

"You have a point," Katelyn said. "But is there some kind of investigation going on? Do you get the news?" It seemed like a luxury to be connected to the outside world.

"Satellite," Cordelia told her. "Maybe we can watch sometime." Her voice trailed off, as if simply having someone over to watch TV was a luxury to her.

"There's a sort of coffee house up the block that way," Cordelia said, changing the subject. "You want to get something to drink?"

"Sure," Katelyn said, eager to extend the afternoon excursion.

"Cool." Cordelia patted her jacket pockets. She looked stricken. "Oh, great. I forgot my cell in the car. My dad wants me to stay in contact. I'll be right back."

"Take my dress?" Katelyn asked.

"And such a dress." Cordelia smiled and trotted off with Katelyn's purchase.

The wind began to pick up. Katelyn wrapped her arms around herself. It was getting chilly. Leaves fluttered down, obscuring her line of vision as Cordelia disappeared around the corner.

"*Oooroooo!*"

Katelyn jumped. Someone—and it was definitely a some-*one,* not a some*thing*—was howling close behind her. She spun around and a man in a destroyed gray INNER WOLF sweatshirt leered at her. His hair was matted and both sleeves of his sweatshirt were torn off at the shoulders. The bottoms of his jeans hung in tatters.

She took a couple of hasty steps back. The guy looked crazy.

"What have we here?" he asked.

"My, my." A second man appeared behind the first. He was wearing a business suit that was in decent shape, tie loosened, and had leaves in his hair.

Sweatshirt flashed her a vicious smile. "Hi. You look . . . cold."

"We can warm you up," the suit guy said, staggering toward her.

"That's okay." She took a few steps backward, trying to understand what was going on. Had they been drinking?

Sweatshirt grinned at Suit Man. "Hear that? It's okay!"

They both threw back their heads and howled.

"Hey, back off!" she shouted, scared.

The suit guy staggered toward her. Katelyn tried to remember something, anything, from the one and only self-defense class she had taken in her entire life. But probably the best thing she could do was run. She turned . . . and came face to face with Cordelia. Her head was held high, and her hands were balled into fists.

"Hey, losers!" Cordelia bellowed.

A chill shot down Katelyn's spine.

Oh, my God, she's going to get us both killed!

Before anyone could move, a third man charged from around the corner, heading for the four of them. He looked familiar—silver hair, trim beard, a polo shirt, and Dockers. His movements were athletic, like those of a personal trainer or a bodyguard, and as he neared, she felt an odd kind of power about him.

"What's going on here?" he asked, his voice low but filled with authority.

Sweatshirt laughed uncertainly. "Jack, we were just..." He laughed again.

"Yes?" the man—Jack—demanded. "Just *what*?"

"Letting out our wolf," number two murmured, clearly embarrassed. His breath reeked of alcohol. Katelyn had been right: they had been drinking.

"Is that what this is?" Jack's eyes flashed as he stared down the two men.

And then Katelyn realized who he was—Jack *Bronson,* in the flesh. She watched openmouthed as the scene continued to play out.

"But we—we—" Sweatshirt stammered. "It's okay. Everything's all right."

Bronson looked hard at him. At both of them. The air was charged with tension so thick Katelyn could feel it.

She glanced at Cordelia, who blinked and looked back. Cordelia's free hand hovered inches above her cell phone, as if trying to decide if she should call someone.

"Go back to the center. *Now*," Bronson said.

"But, Jack," Sweatshirt protested, his shoulders rounding. Beside him, the Suit Man backed down, also lowering his head.

"You too," Bronson commanded the Suit Man; then he pulled out a cell phone. "The van will take you to the airport when you get back. Both of you."

"What?" Sweatshirt cried.

"My company paid for the training," Suit Man protested. "I didn't *do* anything!"

Bronson said nothing, only stared them down again. Abashed, the men silently withdrew, turning and shuffling away.

As soon as they were out of sight, Bronson turned to Katelyn. "I'm sorry. My students are not like that."

Katelyn was amazed at the way he'd handled them. All he'd had to do was speak and they backed down. She thought about Mike and wished she could handle him the same way. Still, she didn't like Jack Bronson. That she was sure of. He was scaring her, and she didn't understand why. She wanted to get away from him as fast as possible.

"You should think about keeping your animals in a cage," Cordelia said angrily. She grabbed Katelyn's hand. "Let's go."

Cordelia charged down the street, practically dragging Katelyn behind her.

"They should shut that guy down," she said.

"He *did* come to our rescue," Katelyn pointed out.

"Yeah, from *his* groupies," Cordelia retorted.

Katelyn was still trying to process Cordelia's bold reaction to the two drunk men. She'd been really pissed—and ready to take them on. It reminded Katelyn of the chin-up episode in the gym. Cordelia's temper had flared then, too. Maybe that was what Paulette had meant—not too deep down, Cordelia had a short fuse that ignited if she felt threatened.

They reached the coffee house. It was in the bottom floor of an old-fashioned wooden building. Katelyn could smell coffee and cinnamon before she even saw the big goofy cow face hanging over the entrance. It wore a cowbell that read COW-FFEINE. Cordelia opened the door, and warm air wafted toward them. Jazz music was playing.

And there was a display table containing a dozen or so copies of *Unleashing Your Inner Wolf.*

"No way," Katelyn blurted. She walked straight to the display, picked up one of the books, and showed it to Cordelia. "He's everywhere."

"Cordelia," said a thirty-something man behind the counter. He was wearing a white apron over a plaid shirt. "I was so sorry to hear about Becky."

Cordelia grabbed the book out of Katelyn's hand and shook it at him. "You shouldn't be selling this," she said. "This guy is psycho. For all we know, one of his groupies killed her. Or maybe *he* did!"

The man blinked. Then he glanced at Katelyn. She didn't know what to do or say. But after what had just happened outside, she had to admit that Cordelia had a point.

· ·· ⇥✦⇤ ·· ·

Friday came, and with it, the party.

With butterflies in her stomach, Katelyn pulled up around the corner from the house where the party was going to be, grateful that Trick's directions were easy to follow. Located on a rambling street not far from the high school, the little stone house had a chimney and was pressed on either side by broad trees whose leaves were beginning to erupt in purple, pumpkin, and egg-yolk yellow. It looked kind of like a hobbit dwelling, something from a storybook, and reminded her of one of the old stone houses in Hollywood, very few of which were left.

Trick had told her that the hostess, Sam, used to coedit a literary e-zine with him in middle school. It was the same girl she'd asked to relay the message to Trick that she was leaving early that Tuesday, and she was happy to meet her formally.

She'd picked the corner so she could approach without being seen right away. She needed a moment to compose herself and make sure her hair and makeup were still good. After she checked in the rearview mirror, she slid out of the truck and locked it, tossed the keys in her tiny shoulder-strap purse, then walked around the corner.

Trick was leaning against his Mustang in a tight pair of jeans, a white button-down shirt, and his cowboy boots. She couldn't help noticing that his eyes lit up when he saw her. He pushed away from the car and stood up straight.

"Whoa," he said, giving her a once-over.

Suddenly a bit shy, she twirled in a circle to show off her new dress. "You like?"

"I'm going to have to fight 'em off."

She beamed at him as he took her hand and they walked toward the house. When they reached it, Trick stopped and turned to her. His sea-green eyes seemed to darken, lending them mysterious depths. Or maybe it was just the angle of the light or the way he was holding her hand that made her stop and really look at him. She was aware that something was shifting between them again.

"It's okay," he said quietly, and she jerked, startled. It was as if he had read her mind. "We're here, at a party, and we're young, and it's all good." He tilted his head, his gaze never wavering, and then he took a step closer to her. She could feel the heat of his body, smell something good on his skin, like cinnamon. And all the need inside her rushed toward him. Sure and steady, but thrilling and death-defying, too.

Justin had crashed in on her, but Trick was different.

Then why am I thinking about that jerk right now?

Trick took a step back. Gave her a nod.

Then he opened the door and they walked into a much larger room than she would have expected, lit only by candles, and filled with a dozen people their age. A very tall, thin guy in a black duster and Doc Martens played an electric violin in time to the music.

Katelyn's gaze went immediately to a girl in a shapeless black dress. She had tattoos on her bare legs and was wearing ballerina flats. She also had multiple piercings and her hair was a shade of blue-black that came only out of a bottle. She would have stood out from the others even if her face wasn't blotched with tears.

"Trick," she said in a strangled voice. She pushed past two guys and put her arms around him. She started to cry harder. He held her quietly and Katelyn hung back awkwardly, aware that the party guests were looking from her to Trick.

"Tina, I'm so sorry," he said. The girl—Tina—kept crying and holding on to him, letting her head drop back almost as if she were inviting Trick to kiss her.

Sam walked over to Katelyn. She had short henna-tinted hair and was wearing a black velvet corset and leggings—not at all what anyone wore to school.

"Hi, Kat. How about something to drink?"

"Um, sure," she replied, grateful for the distraction.

"Okay. Come to the kitchen and we'll fix you up."

Katelyn followed Sam into a cramped kitchen laden with bottles of wine, a scattering of hard liquor, and a cooler of canned sodas. She looked at Katelyn carefully. "We have every kind of liquor known to man. Lots of country kids start young."

"Oh," Katelyn said, feeling uncomfortable. She was an athlete and had never been able to drink.

"And . . . I figure you for something diet," Sam went on tactfully.

At Katelyn's nod, she dug around in the cooler and handed her a red can. Katelyn popped it open.

"Tina is Becky's cousin," Sam explained. "Tina's family moved to Oklahoma during the summer. They came back to town for the service."

Katelyn tried not to let the room tilt. Of course there would be a funeral. Ms. Brandao had handled the details of her mother's funeral. For the "burial," a small urn had been placed in a wall at the cemetery. After the formal memorial service, held in the Unitarian church on Eighteenth Street, Kimi, Kimi's mom, and Katelyn had driven to Santa Monica Pier and thrown leis into the water, a custom many Southern Californians had adopted from Hawaii. She hadn't wanted to throw hers in, hadn't wanted to let go.

Sam grabbed a soda, too, opened it, and kept talking. "Are you going to the funeral? I know you just moved here."

Katelyn's arm froze midway to her mouth. "I—I don't know."

"Becky had this total thing for Trick. She used to tell people they were dating. Made up these stories about what he said, what they did. It was all one-sided. Trick had no idea what was going on. She finally came on to him and he tried to let her down easy. But she went ballistic and told all her friends that he'd used her and then dumped her."

Katelyn was stunned. Trick hadn't told her any of that. And he had been so shaken by her death. Cordelia's dislike of Trick suddenly made sense.

"Why was she in the forest?" she asked Sam.

"She wasn't in the forest," Sam said. Then she looked hard at Katelyn. "There's a lot more going on in Wolf Springs than most people want to admit."

"What do you mean? Like what?" she asked, practically holding her breath. Katelyn set the can on the counter, eager for Sam to say more.

"Hey," said a voice behind her. It was Trick. "Sorry about that."

Katelyn swallowed, disappointed. She was positive that Sam wouldn't finish what she was saying. The moment was gone.

"I filled her in on Tina," Sam told him, picking up both their soda cans. "We should introduce her around."

With Trick back at her side, she returned to the living room. Trance music was playing and Trick pulled her into the middle of the space where others were dancing. She went with the flow, moving her shoulders and hips, losing herself, until all she focused on was his face. Green eyes, bronze skin, angular features. She was holding her breath but couldn't let it out. What would it be like to kiss Trick the same way Justin had kissed her?

I think I'm going to find out, she realized. Every part of her felt tingly with anticipation.

He was looking at her looking at him. His face became serious, and he knit his brows. She blazed inside, excited and embarrassed at the same time, as if he could read her mind. She wished she could read *his*.

Suddenly he stumbled, losing the beat, then caught himself.

"Are you okay?" she asked.

His answer was a weak half smile—not the response she was looking for. He looked as if he was in pain.

"I'm okay," he said, but if he meant to reassure her, his strained tone of voice did anything but. After a couple more beats, he abruptly turned away and left her.

She faltered, watching him head for the kitchen. She danced a few more steps, then stopped, looked around, and scooted to the side of the room. She could almost, but not quite, see into the kitchen.

She waited a little bit, and when he didn't come back,

she finally went to look for him. No one remembered seeing him in the kitchen. She checked other rooms. No one knew where he was, and she started to get anxious. Had he seriously ditched her in the middle of the party? Uncertainty turned to anger. Finally she found Sam coming out of a room in the hallway.

"Have you seen Trick?"

Sam raised her brows. "No, I thought he was with you."

Katelyn shrugged but hesitated before moving on. "What was it you were about to tell me in the kitchen? About a lot more going on than people want to admit?"

A flush of red washed up Sam's neck. She slid a glance down the hall as though to see if anyone had heard.

Katelyn persisted. "And if she wasn't in the forest . . . when it happened, where—"

Sam hunched her shoulders. "Not now, okay?"

"But—"

"Tina's freaking out. I have to take care of her," Sam said.

Sam moved down the hall. Frustrated, Katelyn watched her go, then resumed her search for Trick. After another ten minutes, she decided to check outside and see if his car was still there. An autumn wind cut through her thin dress, lifting the hem, and she crossed her arms, shivering. The moon poured light down onto the top of his Mustang.

She blinked in surprise. He was sitting inside it.

As she walked toward it, she glanced at the passenger side. He was alone.

Gripping her arms to hold in a little warmth, she marched up to the driver's side and knocked. He jerked, then peered through the window at her. He looked a little glassy-eyed, and she tensed. Was something wrong with him?

She could hear Cordelia's voice: *Trick's kind of unpredictable.*

The lock clicked; he opened the door and climbed out. It was as if he was a different person from the one who had greeted her earlier. He didn't look glad to see her. If anything, he seemed angry. His eyes were narrowed, and his lips were pressed into a thin line, as if she was the last person he wanted to see. And that just enraged her more.

"Kat," he said tersely.

"What happened? Are you trying to bail on me?" she demanded.

There was silence. He blinked, long black lashes brushing downward. Then he opened his eyes wide and looked at her square in the eye.

"You need to go," he said flatly.

She felt as if he had slapped her. "Excuse me?"

"I-I'm sorry." He stuffed his hands into his pockets. "I'm not feeling well."

Humiliation swept through her. Utter mortification. And shock.

"Look, if this hasn't worked out for you . . ."

"*No,*" he said, exhaling, then running his hands through his hair. A vein in his neck was pulsing. A muscle jumped in his cheek. "Damn it, Kat, just go, okay?"

She wanted to die. She couldn't believe it. It wasn't his party; he had no say.

Without another word, she turned. Tears welled as she clenched her jaw and stomped back toward the house.

To her back, he yelled, "You don't even know what you're getting into!"

"Just shut up," she muttered, too low for him to hear. She heard the car door slam.

Furious, she realized she had just walked past the front door. *Fine.* She half ran around the corner to the truck, yanked open the door, and hoisted herself inside. Hands shaking, she finally got it going, shifted into drive, and pulled forward.

She blasted down the street, still clenching her jaw. *Jerk, jerk, jerk,* she thought.

Then she saw headlights approaching the rear of the truck. So he was coming after her. Fine. But no way was she stopping or going back. Because no way did she want him to see that tears were spilling down her cheeks.

The headlights followed her onto the narrow, steep road leading out of town. Next stop would be the inky tunnel of trees, then deeper into the forest, where the wolf had attacked the Mustang with her in it. She cranked up the music on her iPhone and forced herself to sing along in an effort to calm herself down.

She drove for quite a while, making the turns she needed. Then the headlights behind her were gone.

She blinked. Had she taken a wrong turn? Frowning, she stared into the rearview mirror, willing Trick to reappear.

Or . . . maybe that wasn't Trick. It was someone else, going somewhere else. . . .

Suddenly the truck lurched. She pulled her foot off the gas and could feel the sickening limping that signaled a flat tire.

Heart in her throat, she pulled as far to the side of the road as she could without hitting any trees.

She glanced around uneasily. The woods were dark and foreboding, as they always were. She might still have cell coverage, but her grandfather couldn't come get her. She had the only vehicle. She tried Ed's number, but the call failed. Tried Cordelia. Same thing—maybe because of her low battery.

As she turned off the engine, she realized she was going to have to get out of the truck to replace the tire. She stared into the darkness, hating the way the headlights seemed to penetrate only a small portion of it. She cursed herself for leaving the party, and for not making sure that Trick had been the driver behind her.

She checked the glove compartment and was relieved to find a flashlight, which worked, but still didn't want to get out. The thought of just sitting tight until the sun came up occurred to her, but she knew it was silly. There was no way she could sit there for hours. She needed to be home, safe. She took a deep breath and eased her door open. She sat for a moment, waiting, half sure that something would lunge at her from the shadows.

The night was full of the sounds of life, but none seemed threatening. In fact, most sounded welcoming, if not comforting—noises of crickets, frogs. She got out, leaving the truck door open so that she'd have more light and could climb in the cab quickly if she had to. She shined the flashlight around but didn't see anything out of place. No glowing eyes stared at her from the trees.

She moved around to the back, where it felt like the flat

was. Running her flashlight over the tire, she found a gash—like she'd run over a nail or a sharp rock. From the bed she retrieved the spare tire and a jack. She set about jacking up the left rear side. She'd learned to take care of her mom's old Volvo from Mr. Brandao. He was keeping it for her until she came back to California.

As soon as she had the tire up in the air, she set about loosening the lug nuts. The first one wouldn't yield and she finally stood on the bar, jumping up and down until it gave. She shook her head, wondering if her grandfather had been the last one to change the tire. Whoever it had been was incredibly strong. The next two loosened more easily, but the fourth required more hopping up and down until it finally gave with a groan.

And somewhere behind her, something *else* groaned.

She whirled, flashlight piercing the darkness. "Who's there?" she called.

She couldn't see anything, no matter how hard she strained. But she suddenly realized that around her everything else had gone quiet. Frogs, crickets, all silenced.

"This isn't funny!" she shouted, hoping against hope that whatever had groaned was human. She struggled to steady the flashlight in her shaking hand as the beam jittered over the trees.

Only that same empty silence greeted her and it terrified her more than any sound she'd ever heard. She twisted back, yanking the dead tire free and tossing it into the bed.

Sweat beaded on her forehead as she wrestled the new tire into its place. She moved to put on the first nut. A branch cracked right behind her and she jerked up, the nuts slipping from her hand into the piles of leaves that littered the road.

Her heart raced and she began to sweat even harder. Her heartbeat sounded thunderously loud in her ears and she panted out of fear and exertion.

"Who is it?" she asked, her voice a hoarse whisper.

She traced a line back and forth in front of her with the flashlight, as though she could make the light a physical barricade that could block the passage of all manner of monsters and creatures. Faster and faster she swept the light, but there was nothing. Only the wind, which seemed to pick up and howl a warning through the trees above.

She crouched down and, with her other hand, searched in the leaves for the lug nuts. Her fingers groped, finding and discarding small pebbles and what felt like an old bottle cap. Finally she grasped one of them, and she spun and feverishly worked to affix it, tightening it as far as she could without the others.

She plunged her hand back into the pile of leaves, shining her light down at them, hoping to catch the glimmer of metal. Her searching fingers found the second one but her hands were shaking so badly she almost couldn't put it on.

She kept looking, and as she grabbed the third one, hot breath touched her neck.

With a scream she fell forward, catching herself on the truck. The jack groaned as the extra pressure was put on it. She twisted around, swinging the flashlight like it was a weapon. It sliced through thin air. Nothing was there behind her now.

Wind, wind, she tried to tell herself. *But the wind is cold and the breath was hot.*

She swung back around, jamming the third nut, which she had miraculously held on to, into place. She tightened it down and groped around for the fourth and final one.

Come on, come on, come on! She searched frantically, bracing the flashlight between her knees so that she could use both hands.

There!

She snatched up the last nut and screwed it on, and then she seized the jack. She began twisting frantically and it went down slowly. She finally was able to yank the jack free with a sob of relief.

And something roared in her ear and then grabbed the back of her dress and pulled her off her feet. Pain erupted from her shoulder as a razor-sharp blade cut her flesh. She tried to scream, but her breath had been knocked out of her.

Before she knew what was happening, she was being dragged at incredible speed across the uneven dirt ground. She barely had time to register the pain as sticks and sharp stones tore at her clothes and skin. She flailed wildly, searching for something she could grab as she slid closer and closer to the trees. Her mind was racing, panicked, but she knew that she couldn't let whatever it was take her into the forest.

It was too late, she realized, as she was pulled over some gnarled tree roots with a bone-shaking thud. She hit the back of her head on a rock and struggled to push back the darkness that was closing in on the edges of her vision. She could see the light from the truck disappearing as she was dragged farther into the dense, dark forest. Now she screamed and screamed, sobbing and choking with fear, but she was in the woods at night and even if someone heard, they wouldn't come save her.

She was going to die.

Just like Haley.

Just like Becky.

10

Katelyn decided then and there that she was not going down without a fight. She lashed out, trying to grab whatever it was that had hold of her. Her right hand closed around a fistful of coarse hair and she yanked for all she was worth.

She heard a slight yelping sound and for a moment the creature slowed but didn't let go. She twisted her head around, trying to see what had her and where it was going, but the darkness of night wasn't even punctuated by the stars, their light obscured by the trees.

The trees!

Katelyn readied herself as her body jolted over more roots,

and then reached out and grabbed one as she hurtled past. Bracing for the impact, she still cried out when her shoulder was yanked hard. She gritted her teeth and forced herself to hold on.

Then suddenly whatever had her let go. She leaped to her feet and turned to face her assailant. The same monstrous silvery-gray wolf that had jumped on Trick's car stared at her, blue eyes glowing in the moonlight, and fangs dripping with saliva.

Katelyn screamed and tried to run, but her foot caught in a tangle of roots and she crashed to the ground. The creature leaped onto her back with a roar and she tried to roll, but it scrabbled and managed to stay on top. Massive paws pinned her shoulders to the ground as the wolf snarled down at her. She felt as if her heart was going to explode, and she could hear herself breathing in wheezing gasps. She thrashed, trying to throw it off. Then there was a sudden sharp pain in the back of her head, followed by blackness.

Katelyn came to with a gasp. She lay on the forest floor, alone. It was still dark out and she had no idea how long she'd been unconscious. She twisted her head to the side and couldn't see anything but the trees nearest her, their skeletal branches reaching out to her like arms. The back and side of her head were throbbing and it felt like her face was on fire. She struggled to turn in the opposite direction, moaning as she rolled over.

And she came face to face with bared fangs. She reached out and grabbed a medium-size stone and slammed it into the wolf's head, knocking it sideways. Then she staggered to her feet and ran again, picking her knees up high to avoid the roots this time.

Behind her, the creature howled and the sound made her stumble. She whimpered and ran faster. And then, as it dawned on her that nothing looked familiar, a terrible feeling swelled in her chest.

Am I running away from the road?

She was lost and turned around—possibly heading even farther into the heart of the forest. And now she could hear the wolf chasing her again. No time to worry about changing course. She didn't think wolves could climb trees, but none of them offered a branch low enough for her to leap up and grab. And then finally, through the pitch black, she could see light.

It was the truck. She sobbed and pushed herself to run. She burst out of the trees and careered toward the truck. She was almost there when the wolf hit her from behind, sending her flying, then skidding along the ground. Just as she slammed against the truck, she felt razor-sharp fangs sink into her leg.

An overwhelming wave of pain crashed over her. She tried to kick the creature off, but it held on tight. Then she saw the tire iron in the dirt where she'd dropped it. She reached out, grabbed it, and brought it down on the wolf's shoulder. It cried out in a high-pitched yelp, released her leg, and jumped away. She looked down at the blood swiftly oozing from her calf and pooling on the ground beneath her. She had to get in the truck and make it to the cabin. She was losing a lot of blood and the sight of it made her light-headed.

Suddenly in the distance she heard another wolf howl, this

one deeper and even more savage. It turned her blood to ice. The wolf beside her swiveled its head, clearly listening. Then, without another glance at her, it spun and ran back into the darkness.

And as it went, shadows seemed to rise and spread around it, and engulf it. Or were the shadows part of it? It had to be a trick of the light, and her terror, making her see things.

She forced her arm to move and she leaned on the tire iron to help her stand. She staggered to her feet, tossed the jack into the bed of the truck, and then pulled herself into the cab. Her shoulder burned where the creature had clawed her, but the pain was nothing compared to that in her leg. She slammed and locked the door, started the engine, put her foot on the gas, and bounced down the road, trying to get as much distance between her and the wolf as possible.

She swung around a tight turn in the road, nearly fish-tailing out of control and straightening just in time to miss hitting a tree. She sobbed as she felt the blood running down her leg and into her shoe. She should do something to staunch the bleeding, but she'd have to stop the car, and there was no way she was doing that. She screamed out loud in pain and terror, just trying to keep herself going.

The road twisted and wound, and half a dozen times she thought she had missed the turnoff, but finally there it was and she tore up the drive. She almost fell out of the truck and forced her shaking legs to carry her up the stairs.

She struggled to fit the key into the lock and finally got it open, threw herself inside, and slammed the door behind her.

"Grandpa!" She shouted for help.

There was no answer. Confused and scared, she limped into the kitchen, flipped on the light, and stared at a note on the counter.

She picked the note up with trembling fingers. *Katie, I had to take a sick friend to the hospital. Back later. Be safe. MM.*

Be safe.

She started to laugh uncontrollably, feeling her mind slipping away from her amid a torrent of pain and fear and relief. She laughed harder and wilder than she ever had in her entire life. She laughed until she began to sob again, and then she slid onto the floor of the kitchen and cried harder than she had when her father had died, harder than when her mom had died, harder than she had thought a person could. And then she cried some more.

And when she was done, she dragged herself to the bathroom, where she found alcohol, Neosporin, and bandages. The bleeding had stopped. She cleaned her leg up as best she could and gingerly touched the back of her head. It didn't seem to be bleeding, either.

She looked in the mirror and almost didn't recognize herself. Her dress was torn in at least three spots she could see and she was covered in dirt, leaves, and tiny twigs.

Changing out of her dress, she realized that she was going to have to throw it away. The shower was steamy and hot; she stood beneath it with her eyes closed, hiccupping with shock, trying to wash the dirt and the fear off her. But the wound on her leg burned and itched and wouldn't let her forget what had happened.

The water had long turned cold by the time she could

make herself leave the refuge of the shower. Reluctantly, she wrapped herself in a towel. Then she reapplied bandages to her leg. It looked horrible. There would definitely be a scar.

She checked her eyes in the mirror for signs of concussion. Her pupils were slightly dilated, but she couldn't tell if it was from injury or from the lingering effects of terror. Her gymnastics coach had told her it was okay to sleep with a concussion, but her mother had always insisted that if you did, it could kill you. She wished she'd taken the time to learn the truth. Better to stay up.

Kimi, she thought. She went back downstairs, still wrapped in her towel, and grabbed the kitchen phone. She dialed with shaking fingers, praying Kimi would pick up. It rang and then went to voice mail. Her heart sank. "I need to talk to you. I was . . ." She hesitated, mind racing ahead to Kimi calling back and saying something to Ed. She was supposed to have had backup on the way home. And she had just left.

Because she had been dissed by her date.

"The party, it sucked. Call me when you can, okay?" It was the lamest thing to say, but her voice was shaking and surely Kimi would realize something was very wrong and return her call as soon as she could.

Cordelia. Maybe she could come over and then . . . *Then when Ed gets back, he'll know for sure something awful happened.*

She needed to talk to someone, to tell them what had happened to her. But it dawned on her that there was no one. A strangled sob escaped her. *I was almost killed.*

The wound on her leg burned and itched and she thought she was going to completely lose it. She forced herself back upstairs, where she pulled on sweats with trembling hands, feeling every bruise and scratch as she did so, then returned to the living room. She paced back and forth, trying to pull herself together.

It had been the same wolf; she was sure of it. She remembered seeing those large blue eyes. But was that possible? It wasn't even the same part of the road as the first time it had attacked her. And she had been out of the car changing the tire for only a couple of minutes when it showed up. It couldn't have smelled her and reached her in that short amount of time from very far away.

Could it be a coincidence that it had approached the two times she was out of a car on the road? It didn't feel like coincidence, but she shuddered at the alternative.

Was it possible that the wolf knew she would be there at the side of the road?

She was getting hot even though she didn't have the fireplace lit. She was also getting sick to her stomach. That was one of the signs of a concussion. It was a good thing she had decided to stay up. If she still felt like that in the morning, she'd ask her grandfather to take her to the hospital.

Her grandfather. What was she going to tell him? Somehow, *Hey, guess what, I was running around in the forest by myself tonight* didn't seem like the best choice.

Her grandfather was going to be pissed that she'd driven home at night, and by herself. If she'd had someone follow her, she could have gotten help with the tire. So he'd be even more pissed. Any way she looked at it, this wasn't going to end well. She had too little freedom, and this party had been a big step. She couldn't confess to him that something had gone wrong or she'd be locked in this house the rest of the year.

At least I'd be safe, a voice deep inside whispered. She rejected the voice, as she had every other time she'd heard it.

No, she had to think of something else to tell Ed.

She got woozier and she rushed to the bathroom, where she proceeded to get sick. Crouched on the floor, she formulated her plan. She would tell him a dog had bitten her, a stray that had been hanging around the house. If it was a stray, he couldn't ask the owner about it. The dog had knocked her down and she'd hit her head. Concussion, maybe?

Grandpa, where are you?

It was eight in the morning when Ed came home. She was up, waiting for him in the kitchen. She'd finally stopped vomiting around three in the morning but still hadn't wanted to risk going to sleep.

"Morning," he said as he walked in and headed immediately for the coffeepot. "You're home early."

"How's your friend?" she asked without acknowledging his comment.

"He . . . died." He didn't look at her.

Her stomach twisted into knots. "Oh, my God. I'm so sorry. What happened?"

He filled the coffeepot with water. "We can talk about it later. First, tell me how the party went." She looked at him, startled that he'd even care in the face of his loss.

"Fine," she forced herself to say.

Her answer must not have sounded sincere, because he stopped measuring out coffee and turned to look at her, eyebrows raised.

She grimaced. "I mean, the party was okay. I got to meet a few more people, which was cool. But a dog, a stray, bit me when I was getting something out of the truck. Knocked me down and I hit my head."

His face registered concern and he moved swiftly, examining the back of her skull. She winced as he parted the hair.

"Did anyone look at it?" he asked. "The kid's mom?"

There had been no adults there—none she'd seen, anyway. She decided not to mention that.

"No, I think I had a slight concussion but I haven't slept at all and I'm feeling better now."

He stared at her. *"A slight concussion?"*

"I've had them before," she said quickly. Then, at his horrified expression, she said, *"One.* Before. Very slight." That was almost true. She'd had two others, both while training, but figured it wouldn't be wise to bring that up.

"We should have a doctor take a look at that. Show me where the dog bit you."

She rolled up her sweatpants leg and took off the bandage, wincing at the pain. She was grateful that while it did look bad, it didn't look as terrible as she remembered.

He glanced swiftly up at her. "That was a mighty pissed-off dog."

"I didn't do anything to antagonize him, either," she said, eager to deflect any suspicion, answer any questions he might have before he asked them.

"We should check you for rabies. And the dog will have to go into quarantine."

Uh-oh. Her lie was becoming a little too complicated.

"Uh, he ran off," she said nervously.

"And nobody caught it? Or volunteered to take you to the clinic?" he asked, eyes clouding over in anger.

"I didn't want to make a fuss, so I didn't let on how bad it was," she said.

He closed his eyes and shook his head, as if at the stupidity of it all. Another blow for emancipation.

"Next time, you holler your lungs out when you need a doctor."

"Okay," she promised.

"Let's go. We'll take you in and have you checked out good."

"Thank you," she said, hurrying to stand up. "I'll go change."

"Sweats are good enough for the hospital," he said.

She followed him outside, trying not to limp too much. There was a Subaru Forester parked beside the truck. His friend's, she decided.

His dead friend's.

He opened the cab of the truck and paused, a strange look on his face. Her heart skipped a beat as she wondered what she'd forgotten. Then he pulled the tire iron out of the cab, where she'd left it.

She sagged in relief. "I got a flat and had to change it before I . . . we drove home. I forgot to throw that in the back."

He put it away and then they both got in the truck and started down the mountain.

"Your daddy teach you to change your own tires?" he asked, looking pleased.

She didn't have the heart to remind him that her dad had died long before she would have wanted to know how.

"Yes," she said. It was the most innocuous lie she had told that morning.

"That's nice." His voice sounded far away. "Hold on just a little longer, Katie. We're almost there."

The "hospital" was a tiny clinic that was open 24/7. She wondered if it was where her grandfather's friend had died. Fortunately there wasn't a long wait. She was relieved, and embarrassed by herself for it, that the doctor who examined her had a Boston accent. In her less charitable moods she had imagined that the local doctors probably doubled as veterinarians.

"Well, you do have a mild concussion, but it looks like you'll be just fine," he said at last. "You can go to sleep when you get home."

"What about the bite?" Ed asked, voice tight.

The doctor frowned at it. "Definitely looks like some kind of canine dentition. Teeth," he added.

She stiffened. She hadn't thought the doctor would be examining the wound in that much detail. She'd said it was a dog. Why was he checking it out like that?

"I'm going to clean it up a bit more and it looks like you need some stitches. We can do the rabies treatment just to be on the safe side."

"Let's do it," Ed said.

The doctor nodded and got to work. He examined the wound again and Katelyn worked hard not to scream.

"Sorry," he said. "Let me numb it." He very gently injected something into the jagged skin. Once he was sure she couldn't feel anything, he sewed it up and covered it with a large bandage.

"Now for the rabies," he said. "One shot in the arm, and one in the tush. You'll have to come back three more times."

"Oh, joy," she grumbled. She hated shots.

"It's better than rabies," the doctor replied.

Katelyn was grateful when they were back in the truck and relieved that she'd been patched up. She experimentally touched her calf, but it was still numb. She'd sworn off painkillers, but she supposed they were okay as long as they didn't make her loopy.

"You okay?" Ed asked.

"Yes, thank you," she said. "I really appreciate you taking me." Exhaustion was setting in and it made her tear up a little.

"Of course. I wasn't about to risk the health of my grandchild, not for anything."

It was a nice thing to say and she believed he really meant it. It made her feel worse about lying to him, but she knew she couldn't tell him the truth.

"Why didn't Trick look out for you?" he asked suddenly.

"Oh, um." She flushed. She really didn't want to talk about it but couldn't figure a way out. "He wasn't there when it happened. He's mad at me at the moment."

"Why?"

I wish I knew, she thought, frustration building in her at the memory.

"It's guy stuff," she said, hoping that he would get the

clue to let it go. Apparently, though, that was the wrong thing to say.

"What did he do?" His voice was low and dead serious.

She didn't know how to explain his behavior, and even if she could, her grandfather wasn't the person she wanted to discuss it with. "He didn't do anything."

Her grandfather's voice rose. "Did he try to make *you* do something?"

She flushed, embarrassed at the implication. "No, it was nothing like that. He was just mad because I—I talked to Justin Fenner. He doesn't like him." She had no idea why she'd said that. It was the first thing that had come to mind.

Ed relaxed only slightly. "Trick's got pretty good instincts about people."

"I think he's just jealous." Great. Now she was dying of embarrassment in front of her grandfather on top of the deep mortification she felt every time she thought of Trick.

Ed chuckled. "Is this the point where you tell your grandpa to butt out?"

"Yes, actually," she said with relief.

They drove along. Halloween decorations were going up everywhere in the cute little town. She could almost imagine that they were in Sleepy Hollow, and the headless horseman was waiting at that metal bridge to carry off Ichabod Crane.

"Okay, I'll butt out, so long as you promise me that if any of those boys does anything out of line, you tell me so I can beat 'em within an inch of their life."

"O-okay," she said, not sure she wanted to see what that would look like.

He patted her shoulder. "Don't worry about it, honey. There's nothin' dumber on the face of this earth than a teenage boy. They do grow out of it, eventually. The ones who live long enough."

"Thanks," she said.

She couldn't help wondering what kind of advice her dad would have offered her about boys if he'd had the chance.

She leaned her head back and sneaked a peek at her grandfather. She had never known her grandmother and she began to wonder what she had been like. What was their story? She knew her mom and dad's—met at a ballet performance of *The Sleeping Beauty* one Christmas at the Paris Opera, got married, came back to California together. Giselle had stopped dancing when she'd found out she was pregnant with Katelyn.

"Can I ask you something?" she asked cautiously.

"Sure."

"What was Grandma like?"

His features softened and he smiled a little. "She was a kind, warm, generous woman. She laughed at everything, especially me. She always told me I took myself too seriously. Family was everything to her; fiercely loyal she was. You hurt one of hers and she was like a mama grizzly. Watch out."

"I wish I'd known her," Katelyn murmured.

"I'd give everything I own if you could have," he said, voice fierce.

"You know, I've never even met my other grandparents," she said. "The ones in France." It had always seemed weird to her.

"I guess family doesn't mean quite the same to your mom's folks as it does to us."

She glanced sharply at him, wondering if somewhere in there was a criticism of her mom. It was true, though. Her mom had liked small, intimate. Her father had always liked large and boisterous. Could that be why after Dad had died, they never saw Ed? Had her mom not wanted the contact because to her only her immediate family mattered?

Katelyn had always assumed it was Ed who was keeping his distance from them. Could it have been the other way around?

"How come you never came to see us after Dad died?" she asked before she could stop herself.

Ed swore and swerved, the brakes squealing.

11

It happened so fast.

Katelyn faced forward in alarm as her grandfather slammed on the brakes. A child—just a toddler—was running across the road with a red balloon in her fist, unaware of the oncoming truck. For a moment everything seemed to telescope, and she could see every freckle on the little girl's face.

"We're going to hit her!" she screamed.

There was a loud droning to her right; as the truck skidded, the droning became a roar. A motorcycle shot across the road in front of them. The rider leaped off, tackled the little girl, and rolled with her to the side.

"Oh, my God!" Katelyn shouted.

With the truck under his firm control, Ed stopped just as the bumper tapped the motorcycle. Katelyn pushed open the door and climbed down, limping to rider and child. The girl was screaming. She'd let go of the balloon in her hand and the rider was holding her up and checking her for injuries. The rider's helmet was still on, and he turned and looked up at Katelyn.

Though she couldn't see his face, she knew at once that it was Justin. Her heart stuttered. He'd just saved that little girl.

"Where the hell are her parents?" Justin growled as the girl batted at him.

People poked their heads out of the shops and Justin gave a wave to show everyone he was okay. Ed came up next to her and after a moment took the child from Justin.

"You need help?" Ed asked.

"I'm good, I'm good," Justin replied as he unbuckled his helmet and took it off.

"Maybe her mama's in the drugstore," Ed said, carrying the little girl across the street.

Still crouched on the ground, Justin gazed up at Katelyn. His eyes were even bluer than she remembered. His face, unshaven. She knew how soft his lips were, what they tasted like. What he felt like.

"Kat," he said huskily.

She stiffened, amazed by her reaction to him. He had a girlfriend, and yet she still wanted to bend down and kiss him.

"Help me up?" he asked, holding out a gloved hand.

She was afraid to touch him, afraid of what she would do,

but she stretched out her hand. He got up on his own and she dropped her arm to the side.

"Are you hurt?" she asked, aware of the people walking toward them.

He stood still, holding her wrist. "In a way. I should have told you." He flushed. "Not even. I shouldn't have touched you."

He was talking about kissing her.

She swallowed hard, pulse skittering at the memory. "What you did was wrong."

"I didn't mean to do it," he replied, gazing at her, taking in every inch of her face as if it were water and he had been dying of thirst. "Don't you feel it? A connection between us?"

Her mouth went dry and all she could do was stare at him. It wasn't just her. He felt it, too.

"Okay, got the girl taken care of," Ed announced, jogging over to them. "Her mama was in the store, didn't realize she was gone. She's coming out to thank you."

"I'm glad you have such great reflexes," Justin said to him as Ed helped him pick up his bike.

"Runs in the family. And Katie here thought she got her speed and grace from her mama," he joked.

She closed her eyes as her head suddenly began to pound. Maybe it was all the crazy drugs in her system. Maybe it was the exhaustion from not sleeping. Maybe it was the fear culminating in the latest near accident.

Or maybe it was being around Justin.

"A few scratches," Ed said, looking at the fender of the motorcycle.

"I can polish those out," Justin said.

Katelyn's head felt as if it were about to explode. She pressed her fingertips against her forehead.

"I have a headache," Katelyn said. "A bad one."

Ed frowned. "I'll take you back to the clinic."

"No. If you just have something I could take . . ." she said. "Something like aspirin."

He grunted. "I don't have anything in the truck. I'll go back into the store and get you something. How about you go sit down?"

"Okay."

As Ed walked away, Justin frowned anxiously at Katelyn.

"Clinic?" he said.

"Yeah, I had a little accident. Nothing big."

Then she walked back to the truck and climbed in. Justin stood there looking at her as people milled around. The throbbing in her head had a rhythm, like music. And even when she closed her eyes, she felt as if she could see the sun through her eyelids. A rap on her window startled her, and she opened her eyes to see Justin, peering in at her, looking troubled.

She rolled down the window.

"Hey," he said. "Are you okay? You're so pale."

"Killer headache," she said, her voice loud to her ears.

"Sorry." He cleared his throat. "We need to talk."

"No, we don't," she said icily.

"Kat, listen, please. I didn't come to your house to do . . . what I did." Color rose in his cheeks and he winced, then sighed. "I just wanted to see you. I swear it."

She looked down, angry and embarrassed. He reached in

and touched her hair, so gently and softly she wasn't certain he'd actually done it.

"Lucy and I . . . we've been together a long time."

She tried to speak but only succeeded in coughing. She didn't want to hear about Lucy.

"But if I had a choice," he said, "then I would . . ." He took a breath and looked at her straight on, all hesitation dropped. "I would do more of what I did. With you."

She wanted to say something snide. She wanted to douse the heat his words ignited. It frightened her, the passion he aroused in her.

"Kat," he whispered. "Please say something."

"You really don't have to explain this to me," she finally managed to croak out.

There was a long pause. She looked up at him. He was staring down at her with such longing that she had to catch her breath.

He seemed as if he was about to say something, but then he looked past her. His eyes widened and he muttered something she couldn't hear. Then he waved. "Hey, buddy. Hey, Jesse," he called.

Her head still throbbing, Katelyn looked in the direction of the store entrance, to see Justin's brother walking with a girl she didn't know. The girl had caramel-colored hair in a tight, thin ponytail and she was wearing a white tailored shirt and super-skinny jeans. Beaming, Jesse was carefully clutching an ice cream cone in his fist. The girl was looking at Justin, nervously touching her hair.

"Pretty lady!" Jesse shouted, jabbing his cone at Katelyn.

The girl cupped her hands around the scoop of ice cream

in case it fell. She said something to Jesse and he stared down at his treat, then carefully cupped his free hand around it. He looked back at her, beaming when she smiled and nodded at him.

Together they crossed to the truck, the girl eyeing Katelyn. Justin tensed, and Katelyn nearly did a forehead smack against the dash. She felt anger, jealousy, humiliation, and guilt all in the span of a moment as she realized that this was Lucy.

"Hey, we heard about the commotion," the girl said in a much twangier voice than Katelyn had heard so far. She gave Justin a kiss, and he kissed her back, but it was clear he was upset about something. "You're okay, right, sugar?"

"Right as rain," Justin said, voice wary. "I slid my bike, but nothing's broken."

"We were in the back of the pharmacy," she said, playing with her ponytail. "Didn't hear a thing."

"We saw LaRue," Jesse told Kat. "I have to pet LaRue softly, softly. Don't wanna squish him! This is Lucy. She's my sister."

Lucy smiled. "Not yet, honey. We're not *that* Southern."

Katelyn made herself smile at the pretty young woman. "Hi. I'm Kat."

"A pleasure, Kat," Lucy said.

"We don't kiss strangers," Jesse said, looking from Lucy to Katelyn. "Only family."

"That's right, baby." Lucy patted Jesse on the arm.

"I kissed Kat. Justin wanted to."

Katelyn felt herself blushing furiously and had no idea what to say.

"Oh?" A hard, appraising glint sparked in Lucy's hazel

eyes and she laced her arm through Justin's. "Jesse mentioned that someone new had come by the house."

"My pills were all gone," Jesse said, interrupting. "We need the pills or it's bad." He pushed past Lucy and Justin and stuck his head through the open window to kiss Katelyn on the cheek. "Not a stranger."

Katelyn smiled at him, but the way her head hurt, his kiss felt almost like a slap.

"Lucy got me ice cream," Jesse announced.

"I see," Katelyn said, massaging the back of her neck as Jesse's ice cream threatened to fall off the cone and splat against the side of the truck.

"Kat's pretty," he told Justin.

Justin smiled. "Yes, she is."

Katelyn bit her lip and looked away, not trusting herself at the moment.

"We didn't have my pills," Jesse said again.

"We should have had plenty," Justin replied edgily, looking at Lucy.

Lucy gave her head a little shake. "I looked everywhere. No one else was home. I had to come to town to get the prescription filled. So I brought him with me."

Jesse broke into a huge smile. "I got to see LaRue."

"Hey, buddy," Justin asked in a very friendly way, "did you hide your pills? So you could see LaRue?"

"I have to go home," Jesse announced. "I'm supposed to stay home. People might see—"

"I'll take him," Justin cut in.

"I've got a highlight in an hour and then I'm done. I'm a

hairstylist," Lucy added to Katelyn. "You should come by. I could do wonders with that hair."

No claws on this one, Katelyn thought sarcastically. "Thanks," she said.

Ed emerged from the store and Katelyn had never been so happy to see him. She was ready to go home and escape the awkwardness that was happening around her.

"Hi, man, hi," Jesse said.

"Hey, there," Ed said.

"I'm Jesse," Jesse told him. "This is Lucy. That is Justin. He's my little brother. You're a stranger."

"Mordecai McBride." Ed touched the brim of an imaginary hat. "And it seems you've already met my granddaughter, Katelyn."

"We call her Kat. Like LaRue," Jesse said. "LaRue is a cat. You pet him softly, softly. Justin is taking me home now."

"That's good, partner," Ed said warmly. "When you ride that bike, hold on tight."

"Lucy holds on tight, too," Jesse said. "Holds on tight to Justin."

Don't we all? Katelyn couldn't help thinking.

"Is that a fact?" Ed drawled.

"You can't pet LaRue too hard," Jesse said. "You don't want to break his neck."

"No one's broken anybody's neck," Lucy said quickly.

"Let's go home, buddy," Justin added, closing his eyes and shaking his head.

"Goodbye, Kat," Jesse said. "Softly, softly."

"See you later," Ed said as he opened the driver's-side door and handed Katelyn a small paper sack. She opened it and saw that he'd purchased six or seven different kinds of painkillers. Touched, she selected the Motrin and broke the seal.

"The little girl's mama come out to say thank you yet?" Ed asked Justin. He took the bottle from Katelyn and popped off the lid. As he handed it back to her, Katelyn and Justin shook their heads in unison.

"Maybe she's scared to show her face. I really gave her what for." Ed quirked his mouth into a smile. "I got a temper on me."

That surprised Katelyn. She'd seen no evidence of that. Yet.

"Well, I'll let you go," Justin said.

"It was nice to meet y'all," Lucy added.

"Nice to meet you, too," Katelyn replied, practically squirming in her seat.

"Come to our house. Come and play," Jesse said to Ed and Katelyn.

"I will," Katelyn told him with a smile. "Thanks for the invitation."

Ed started the truck and Katelyn gave the group a little wave as they pulled away, then leaned her aching head back against the seat. They drove off, leaving the drama behind them, and Katelyn was grateful.

"Seems Trick might be right to be jealous," Ed said.

"Did you get any water?" she asked, pretending she hadn't heard what he'd said.

"Damn," he said. "Clean forgot."

"Justin and Lucy are a couple." Her voice sounded strained even to her own ears.

"They're not married. And from what I just saw, it's clear as day that he likes you. Man who risks his life like that could be a fine man. Looks after his brother, too."

She closed her eyes against waves of pain. "I'm not into teen drama." She was done talking about Justin. She licked her lips, then changed the subject. "Your friend who died . . . It, um, wasn't at the clinic?"

The atmosphere in the truck shifted and Ed grew pensive. "His name was Mason Slater. I took him down to the medical center in Bentonville. It was his heart. He knew he was living on borrowed time."

His voice was strained, and she felt sad for him. She reached over and patted his hand. "I'm sorry, Grandpa." It was definitely starting to feel natural to call him that.

His face softened and he gave her hand a little squeeze. "Best name on earth," he said softly.

＊＊＊

When they got back to the cabin, she went up to her room to rest. She awoke several hours later to the most obnoxious odor she'd ever had the misfortune to smell. Bleary-eyed, she staggered down the stairs and into the kitchen.

"What is *that*?" she asked.

He was standing at the stove. "Artichokes. You said they were your favorites."

She wrinkled her nose. "Maybe they're a different kind."

"I've never made them before. All you do is boil them, right?"

"Right." She lifted the lid off the pot, releasing a cloud of steam. Two plump artichokes sat in the simmering water. "That's how you do it. I'm sure they'll be great."

She forced a smile but felt nauseated just thinking about it.

At dinner, she got down a few artichoke leaves and some steamed rice. Both she and Ed chalked up her nausea to the rabies shots. After dinner, they watched one of his old movies and she kept drifting off to sleep. Just as she was thinking of giving up and going to bed, there was a knock on the door. Her grandfather went to answer it. A shadow stood in the doorway and she squinted, trying to make out who it was.

Her grandfather stepped out onto the porch and shut the door behind him. He was out there for a long time and she couldn't hear his voice above the TV.

Then the door opened and Ed and Trick walked into the house. Trick was wearing a cowboy hat, a sheepherder's jacket, and jeans. Her heart stuttered, and she hardened it. He had deserted her. And look what had happened.

"Think I'll be out in the garage if you need me," Ed said quietly.

Katelyn pointedly looked back at the TV. Her palms were sweaty. Silence was her weapon of choice, and she used it.

"Kat, I'm sorry. I was an epic jerk. I . . . Something happened and I reacted badly and I'm sorry."

The silence grew. She tried to clear her throat or take a breath or do *something,* but she sat statue-still, barely able to think.

"Kat," he said.

"You should have come by to apologize this morning so you could have taken me to the hospital," she said icily.

His eyes widened and he moved to crouch next to her. *"Hospital?"*

She wondered what they'd discussed on the porch if not

that. She'd assumed her grandfather had lit into him for not taking her to the clinic the night before, or not catching the dog—thereby putting her cover story in jeopardy.

"I was attacked."

"What?" He sat down beside her and took her hand. She stiffened, trying to put some psychic distance between them, but Trick didn't seem to notice. He studied her face. "What happened? Kat, *tell me. Now."* His voice was rough, raw with concern. He swept his gaze over her body, which was completely covered by her sweats and a plaid blanket, then cupped her face with both his hands.

She jerked her head away and glared at him.

"Kat. It's *me,"* he said, as if that would make her feel better. "Who attacked you?"

His fear penetrated her defenses, softening her resolve. Maybe it was because he kept touching her. Or because he sounded so worried. She hesitated. She wanted to tell someone and she wanted to make Trick feel as guilty as possible, but Trick and her grandfather were close. What if he spilled the beans about what had *really* happened?

"Not who. *What.* It was a dog. When I was leaving the party."

Trick blanched. "How big of a dog?"

What a weird question. "Big enough to take a chunk out of my calf. My grandpa had to take me in for rabies shots just in case." She lifted her sweatpants leg and pointed to her bandaged calf. He leaned in to look at it, embarrassing her, and she pulled the pants leg back down.

"Kat, I am so sorry," Trick said, face crumpling. "I should

have been there for you. I fell asleep in my car. The sun woke me up. I saw that your truck was gone and Eric said he thought you'd left a while before."

"I left right after you yelled at me," she said. "Last night."

He looked stunned. "I had no idea."

She remained silent.

"This is my fault. I'll never let you out of my sight again."

"I don't need a keeper," she snapped. "I need a friend I can count on."

He hung his head. His profile seemed to be etched into the soft glow of the room, like frosted glass. He was so good-looking. "And that is one hundred percent me, except I don't want to be your friend. And I know you can translate that." He reached out as if to take her hand, but he didn't. "Whatever you need, I've got your back."

There was no teasing, no jokes, just complete sincerity from him. It was a bit unnerving, but it also made her feel better. Still, she found herself giving a little more credence to Cordelia's less-than-fuzzy opinion of him. Plus she needed closure.

"You *were* an epic jerk."

And to rub his nose in it.

He gazed off into the distance and hung his hands between his legs. "I know."

"What happened?" she asked him, wanting, deserving an explanation.

"Can we bookmark that? It had nothing to do with you or wanting to be with you."

She didn't reply; she just looked at him, waiting.

"Fair enough." He shrugged and continued. "I didn't expect a wake for Becky."

It didn't really answer her question or explain anything.

"I know I blew it. I wanted you to have some fun," he said, sounding regretful. "It's what you need."

"Oh. So you know what I need," she said.

"I do." He nodded as if to himself. "And it wasn't that."

"What I need is . . . a foot rub," she said, wiggling her feet. She couldn't help herself. Serious didn't sit well on him, and after the long, weird day, she wasn't up to staying mad.

He looked down at her feet and then back at her face. "I said I got your back. I never said anything about your stinky feet."

She laughed and after a moment, he joined in. But her headache was back, and she was unbelievably tired.

"I've got to get some sleep," she said.

"I'll see you Monday morning, though?" he asked.

She nodded. "You'll see me."

He made a show of crossing himself. "Thank you, God. I am forgiven."

"On probation," she said, correcting him. "Way on probation."

He mimicked flipping a switch. "All systems on alert."

"Okay." She couldn't even make herself smile.

"It's not funny, is it?" He sighed. "I'll see you."

And then he was gone. She stared at the door, jerking when it opened again. A little flare of hope was quashed when she saw her grandfather.

"Did you get him sorted out?" he asked.

"I think so."

"Good. How are you feeling?"

"I'm losing it," she admitted, yawning.

"Off to bed with you, then. We can finish the movie tomorrow."

Katelyn brushed her teeth and washed her face, then wearily lay down on her bed. As she stared up into the skylight, the room seemed to swirl and tilt. Her eyes began to flutter shut; then, at the last possible moment before falling asleep, she thought she saw two blue eyes staring down at her.

Green eyes.

Yellow ones.

Black.

·——◄◆►——·

Pad. Pad. Pad. Claws retracted.

Sprawled on the forest floor, Katelyn wore her beautiful dress.

The trees shook.

Moonlight shimmered.

Katelyn, a voice whispered. I'm coming for you.

Pad.

Claws.

She knew she was in bed in her room, dreaming, but she was covered in sweat, her muscles cramping, her bones aching. Her body felt like a suit she was wearing, like something artificial that was too small. Her skin was stretched taut.

She knew she was asleep.

And that something was in the room.

·——◄◆►——·

She was back in the clinic on Monday morning to get her second shot. Ed drove her himself; he had called Trick and told him about the change in schedule.

After a long wait in an icy examination room, a nurse appeared and gave Katelyn an injection in the arm, then was about to bustle away when Katelyn blurted out, "I've been having headaches. And feeling sick to my stomach." *And having crazy dreams.*

"That's all very normal," the woman said, sounding harried. "You're having a mild reaction to the vaccine. Do you have a headache now?"

"No, but—"

"You only have two more injections. Next one is Friday, and then the Friday after that. Then your discomfort will completely disappear."

Katelyn certainly hoped it would.

⊷ ⇥⬧⇤ ⊶

"I don't know what's normal about it," Katelyn told her grandfather as they sipped coffee in the truck. Or rather, he sipped and she held on to her cup with both hands. The smell alone was making her stomach roil.

"You want to go home?" he asked her. He was driving her to school. His voice boomed in the confined space, setting her on edge.

"Why are you shouting at me?"

He frowned. "I'm not." He gave her a worried look. "*Do* you want to go home?" he asked again, at a significantly lower volume.

She considered. It would be nice to go back to bed and get

over her "mild" symptoms. But she wanted to see Cordelia. If things got too bad, she could always go lie down in the health care office.

"I'm good," she told him.

They bounced along toward the back of the school with the seat springs twanging more loudly than Katelyn had noticed before. The jostling hurt her head.

She scanned the cars for Trick's Mustang and spotted it, and then the most bizarre thing happened: his license plate popped into her field of vision like a close-up in a movie. It was white with red letters and, below those, an image of a wolf, also in red. The words ARKANSAS STATE. GO RED WOLVES! were spelled out in black.

"Hey," she began, but then it was over. The back of Trick's car was the same as it always had been before, and the plate was too small for her to read it. She couldn't even make out the tiny wolf's head; it was just a blob.

Staring hard, she tried to will her eyes to do it again, with no luck.

She stole a glance at Ed. Her grandfather was busy negotiating the lot. Her mom used to have migraines, and she'd told Katelyn what they were like—flickering vision, disorientation, and then hideous, horrible pain. She said that sometimes she would stare down at her hands and they would look enormous. At the first symptom, Giselle took painkillers and drank coffee—something to do with the caffeine helping blood flow. Maybe that was what was happening to her. She fished in her purse for the Motrin and forced it down with the now-cold coffee before her body had a chance to rebel.

Her grandfather rolled to a stop. "If you don't feel good later on, call me and I'll come get you," he said.

"Thanks." Now she dithered a moment about going with him. Then she opened the door and climbed down.

As soon as she walked into history, Cordelia gestured impatiently for Katelyn to sit down beside her.

"Oh, my God, what happened to you this weekend?" Cordelia asked. "I heard you were attacked by Sasquatch."

"No such luck. It was a dog," Katelyn replied, continuing her lie.

"Sam's mom works at the clinic," Cordelia said. "She said your grandfather brought you in for something and you were really shaken up."

"Dog," she said again, but this time she felt her cheeks warm.

Cordelia stared at her intently. "You don't sound too sure."

Katelyn needed to talk to someone, tell someone about what had happened and all the other weirdness since. It couldn't be Trick. She didn't want him worrying her grandfather. And Kimi was getting more distant every time she talked to her—and she hadn't called her back all weekend. Cordelia was who was left.

"Okay, but if I tell you what really happened, will you promise not to tell anyone? Especially my grandfather?"

The other girl nodded.

"It wasn't a dog."

Cordelia stared at her. Then Mr. Henderson walked in.

"Happy Monday," he said. "Let's do a check-in on how the projects are going."

"What was it?" Cordelia whispered.

"Ladies, how's it going?" Mr. Henderson smiled pleasantly at Katelyn and Cordelia. "Care to bring us up to date?"

"*Kat?*" Cordelia whispered, obviously dying of curiosity.

Katelyn nodded. "Sure, Mr. Henderson," she said. "We're all about the silver mine. And the Hellhound," she added, uncertain why she did so.

"Hellhound, eh? Love it," Mr. Henderson replied. "Be sure to document your sources."

Katelyn nodded and then he turned to the next pair of students.

"Lunch," Katelyn whispered to Cordelia. "I'll tell you about it then."

Cordelia barely responded.

"Did something happen to *you* over the weekend?" Katelyn whispered.

Cordelia shook her head and looked away. "No," she said, but Katelyn knew a lie when she heard one.

<hr />

One look at her leg was enough to get Katelyn out of P.E. The coach sent her to study hall, where she spent the time with her head on her desk, praying the day would end.

When the bell rang, she decided to track down Sam and resume their conversation from Friday night. She couldn't shake the feeling that Sam had been about to tell her something important.

Yet after Katelyn had looked what felt like everywhere, Sam was still not to be found. Her headache got worse and she considered calling her grandfather, but wanted to make it to lunch so she could talk to Cordelia.

At lunchtime, Katelyn studied the stained-glass window of the saint with the wolf as she and Cordelia passed beneath it. Why would the priests put a wolf in a church window? There had to be another story there.

They left the main building and headed on dry brown grass to a scattering of old-fashioned picnic tables. It was chilly, but Cordelia had insisted they go outside to eat.

As Katelyn opened her lunch bag, she wondered if Ed's peanut butter had gone rancid. Her sandwich stank. More *mild* symptoms?

"Hey," Trick said, trotting up beside Katelyn. "How did it go at the clinic?"

"We're having a girl lunch." Cordelia's tone was flinty, unwelcoming.

Trick looked at Katelyn for confirmation. Embarrassed, she nodded, and he shrugged, his face a mask. "Sorry," Katelyn said. "It went fine."

"Good." He looked relieved, then gave Cordelia a cold glare before turning to leave. Katelyn watched him as he wandered over to a picnic table where a couple of the kids from Sam's party were sitting, but Sam was missing.

"What is it between Trick and—" Katelyn began, but Cordelia cut her off.

"You said it wasn't a dog." She was very tense. "So what was it?" Cordelia's knuckles were white where she clutched her lunch bag. She stared at Katelyn as if her life depended on the answer.

Katelyn let out a breath. "I got a flat tire and I was fixing it, and it . . . it dragged me. Oh, God, I thought it was going to kill me." Suddenly her head throbbed in pain and she had to stop. She clutched her temples and took a deep breath.

"What? *What* dragged you?" Cordelia demanded. She didn't seem to notice or care that Katelyn was in pain. Her eyes were wide, desperate-looking.

Katelyn looked back at her and didn't want to tell her. She didn't know why, but she struggled with herself.

"Tell me," Cordelia whispered.

"A wolf."

Cordelia stared at her. She blinked several times, and then she contracted her shoulders and stomach, as if she had been punched.

"What?" Cordelia whispered.

The secret was out and instead of feeling better, Katelyn felt worse. There was so much fear she'd been keeping to herself. She wanted—needed—Cordelia to believe her, to understand. "A wolf. I'm sure it was the same one that attacked Trick and me."

Cordelia covered her mouth with both her hands. "Oh, Kat," she said. Her voice was quiet and flat.

"Friday night it dragged me into the woods. I got away, but it came after me. And it bit me."

"It *bit* you?" Cordelia echoed. Something in her expression changed and she stopped and grabbed Katelyn's arm and looked her square in the eyes as she asked her next question. "Did it break the skin?"

Her voice was so intense it frightened Katelyn. "It's okay." Katelyn hastened to reassure them both. "I'm getting rabies shots."

Cordelia sat, frozen and silent. She stared at Katelyn as if her friend were speaking in a foreign language.

"I know." Katelyn scrambled to explain herself. "I'm too stupid to live. But I didn't *plan* to be out alone in the woods. I mean, if my grandfather found out—"

"*Kat,*" Cordelia said, her voice low.

Katelyn couldn't stop herself, spilling details, knowing she probably sounded insane. "I'm stuck. I don't want my grandfather to know I completely ignored what he told me to do, but what if this is the same animal that went after Haley and Becky? It went after me. I know this sounds crazy, but it was like it was *waiting* for me. Like it knew who I was. I mean, I was in two different parts of the forest, yet the same wolf shows up in both places? I should say something, right?"

"*Did it break the skin?*" Cordelia repeated herself, voice shrill.

Heads swiveled their way, and Cordelia slowly lowered her hands to her sides. Cordelia was staring at her as if she'd never seen her before in her life. It frightened Katelyn almost as much as the wolf had. *What is happening? Is she afraid of rabies?*

"Cordelia, the shots are just in case. You won't catch rabies from me or anything."

Cordelia just kept staring.

"I'm all messed up," Katelyn said. "My sense of smell is whacked and my eyesight sort of telescopes or something. My ears are so sensitive it sounds like people are yelling at me." Katelyn was speaking faster and faster, desperate to get her story out, desperate for someone to know she was scared. "I told them at the clinic, and they said it's the shots. But it's so extreme. I've been having these nightmares about the wolf. It's attacking me and laughing at me and its blue eyes are *glowing*."

"Blue eyes?" Cordelia echoed. "Are you sure they were blue?"

Katelyn took a deep breath and really looked at Cordelia. The other girl was chalk white and she was shaking.

"Are you okay?" Katelyn asked. Then it hit her. "You *do* think it's what attacked the other girls. You think I should tell my grandfather about it?"

"No!" Cordelia shouted.

People at the other picnic tables looked at the two of them. Katelyn's ears were ringing from the shout. "Cordelia, what's wrong?"

"Nothing." Cordelia lowered her voice and took a huge breath. She looked like she was about to throw up. "You—you were right. I'm just . . . freaked out for you and glad that you're okay."

Katelyn didn't believe her. Not a word.

"What happened to *you* over the weekend?" Katelyn asked her. "Because I know something did."

"Maybe you should go back to L.A." Cordelia was trembling now. "That's what you need to do. Go home."

Then, to Katelyn's amazement, Cordelia got up, ran across the grass, and disappeared inside the building.

12

Katelyn's head began to throb harder as she jumped to her feet and stared in the direction Cordelia had disappeared. She tried to call after her, but a sharp pain exploded in the back of her skull. Her knees buckled, and she might have fallen, except that Trick was there to catch her. His hands gripped her tightly as he helped her sit down on the bench.

"What's up?" he said.

"Head. Ache." She bit off the words in a strangled whisper.

"With you and Cordelia?"

"Girl stuff," she said, barely able to speak. The sun was too bright. The rays were practically stabbing her eyes. She was even more unnerved by Cordelia's reaction. "My head is killing me. Can you call my grandfather to come and get me?"

"Hell with that. I'm driving you home," he informed her.

—————————

They didn't speak much on the drive through the forest. Her head hurt too badly, and she was too freaked out. What was up with Cordelia? Why had she panicked? And told her to go back to California?

Finally she nodded off, waking up when she felt the car stop and heard the engine go off. They were at the cabin.

"Stay," Trick ordered her as he climbed out of the Mustang. He came around to her door and opened it as her grandfather was hurrying down off the porch.

Ed bent over her, studying her face.

"Katie?" he said. "How bad is it?"

"I should have taken her to the clinic," Trick said.

"No. It's the shots," she told them both. She needed to be alone. She had to think everything through.

"You should lie down," her grandfather told her. "You need help up the stairs?"

"No. I can do it. Thanks, Trick."

"Got your back," he assured her, walking behind her and her grandfather.

Exhausted, her head still pounding, she left the two downstairs as she went into her room and fell into a fitful but dreamless sleep. When she came down for dinner, Trick had gone. Katelyn was quiet, her mind swirling with everything that had happened—that was happening. What was wrong with her? And why had Cordelia lost it?

The smell of the food—vegetable soup and corn bread—made her queasy; outside, in the darkness, the drums pounded, echoing against the mountains, making her want to scream. She lingered at the table, trying to get something down, but it was no use.

"I'm going back upstairs," she finally announced.

"Rest up, honey," her grandfather said. "Come and get me if you need to."

She nodded and trudged back to her room.

＊ ＊ ＊

The woods are lovely, dark, and deep.
I shall do thee mischief in the woods.
Hot breath on her closed eyelids. Sharp claws on her leg, where the bite was. Where the sutures closed the torn skin back together.
Katelyn, you are marked.
You are mine.

＊ ＊ ＊

A horrible pain seared her leg, as if someone had placed a hot fireplace poker on it, and she woke up.

Bolting upright, she leaped out of her bed. She felt as if her bones were on fire.

She staggered into the bathroom, closed the door, and flipped on the light. She pulled up her pajama leg and looked at her wound. The sutures were coming undone, as though her skin was rejecting them. The pain was increasing, and in desperation she reached down and gave a tug, and within a few seconds, all of them had come free.

The pain instantly lessened. She grabbed her washcloth and dabbed at the bit of blood that welled to the surface. The wound looked like a nasty scratch, nothing more.

She stared at it in shock.

This is so not happening. It's not possible to heal that fast.

She pulled down her pajama top and stared at her shoulder. It was smooth and unblemished.

"Okay, so it wasn't as bad as I thought," she said. Then she gazed at her own reflection and shook her head. Who was she fooling?

I needed stitches. Something like that doesn't go away.

She went back to her room and sat on her bed with her hands around her knees. She kept checking, rechecking. It really was gone. She sat staring into the darkness, hearing the drums, and the wind, and her rapid heartbeat.

Eventually she fell back asleep and her dreams were filled with the drums, and the wind, and someone calling her name.

Katelyn.

———— ※ ————

By morning, all evidence of the bite had vanished. Like on her shoulder, the skin was completely smooth, as if nothing had ever touched her. Katelyn was bewildered . . . and scared.

She thought of the look on Cordelia's face when she'd described the attack and her symptoms. Cordelia had completely and totally lost it.

Because she was scared of me. She knows what's going on.

And Katelyn was going to make Cordelia tell her what it was.

———— ※ ————

"You're not okay," Trick said that morning on their way to school.

She shook her head. "No. I'm not."

"Wanna talk about it?"

Right then, in the car, Katelyn almost confided in him. She was about to tell him everything, about the attack, the wound's healing, everything.

Her phone pinged and she glanced down. It was a text message from Kimi.

Yo, babe. U dont call u dont text whazzup

Katelyn was taken aback. Kimi was the one who had been pulling away.

Trick turned on some music. "How Soon is Now?" by the Smiths blared as he tore through the forest like a wildfire. The moment for confidences was lost.

Better to wait and confront Cordelia, she decided. Make her explain.

She texted back. *Sorry—lots happnin.*

That was an understatement.

No excuse! Kimi texted back.

"Are you okay now?" Trick bellowed over the music.

No. Not even.

"Yeah," she yelled back.

He gave her a look but said nothing.

The rain came crashing down as they pulled up to the school. They were early, and as was her habit, she headed for the library, realizing that she could make use of the reference section to see if there was anything about weird wolf bites. As she walked, Katelyn looked for Cordelia, and Sam and Beau. The rain pelted the roof. Thunder and lightning accompanied the torrents, and wind whistled down the hall. Around her, students gossiped. Waving her gold fingernails, Dondi motioned her over.

"Sam's leaving," Dondi informed her. "Her family's moving to Little Rock. They're going at the end of the week."

"Oh?" Katelyn said, surprised. That seemed sudden.

"Yeah, it sucks," Dondi said. "We were working on a presentation for English together. Now she's just *bailing*. Argh." She made a face, then saw Maria. "Hey, did you hear? Sam's leaving," she called to the other girl.

Katelyn's phone chimed again and up popped Kimi's reply—a photo of Kimi and Jane in pigtails, posing with two saws with ARKAN written on them in black marker. They were blowing kisses at the camera. It was clear that Kimi had replaced her.

I can't confide in her, she thought glumly. *No, I can't confide in* anyone.

Cordelia got to class and sat down right as the bell rang. Katelyn waited for her to turn so she could get her attention, but her friend wouldn't look at her. When class ended, Cordelia walked on ahead with Dondi. Katelyn followed, her confusion growing. When they got to P.E., they discovered that they had a last-minute substitute, who decided to hold study hall. Everyone spread out around the gym in little clusters; then the sub announced she had to "get something" and left the gym.

Katelyn got up and grabbed Cordelia's arm and dragged her to the top of the bleachers. Cordelia sat reluctantly, rubbing her arm where Katelyn had gripped her. When Cordelia moved Katelyn's hand, she saw that she had left red fingerprints on Cordelia's skin.

"What's happening to me?" she asked fiercely. She was desperate.

Cordelia's eyes went huge. "I don't know what you're talking about."

Anger flashed through Katelyn.

"You ran away from me yesterday. You were scared of me."

"No," Cordelia insisted.

"Look. Look at this." She rolled up her pants leg. Cordelia looked at the unbroken skin, and her eyes widened. "You can't even tell I was ever bitten."

"It's a miracle," Cordelia said, clearly trying to sound excited. And failing.

"I'm pretty sure it's not. And I think you know what it is. You have to tell me."

Cordelia crossed her arms tightly and hunched forward, her face wan, guilt clear in her expression. "I have no idea what you're talking about."

"Stop lying to me," Katelyn demanded, angry and pleading at the same time. "You're supposed to be my friend."

"I *am* your friend," Cordelia said, but avoided her gaze. "That's why I'm telling you that you're fine. Your imagination is just running away with you and you need to calm down. Take a break. You've obviously been through a lot. First with your mother and then the attack—"

"Don't you dare try that on me," Katelyn said in a low, angry voice. "This has nothing to do with my mother. And I can't believe you would even go there. That night when we heard the screams and you refused to let me call the police, something weird was happening then, too, and you knew it, didn't you?"

Katelyn waited for her friend to answer. She watched as scarlet crept up Cordelia's neck and fanned out across her cheeks. "It was a cat. You said it was."

"But we *heard* a wolf. It was when Becky was being killed, wasn't it? We were outside when Becky was being killed, weren't we?"

Cordelia took a deep, shuddering breath. "Even if that's true, there was nothing we could have done."

"What?" Katelyn was shocked. As much as she'd feared it, that was not the answer she had been expecting. She reached out to grab Cordelia again but the other girl flinched, and Katelyn dropped her hand back to her lap.

"I mean, I don't know what happened to Becky." Cordelia's tone was steeped in misery.

"Well, what about me? You know something."

"No, I don't," Cordelia said.

"You *do.* I know you do. *Please,* tell me what's happening."

"No," Cordelia whispered, "I couldn't help Becky and I can't help you."

"But what does that mean?" Katelyn was going crazy. She was sure now that Cordelia could tell her why things had turned so strange, but the girl wouldn't budge.

Cordelia sat with her eyes downcast. The anger continued to build in Katelyn. Cordelia wouldn't even make eye contact, which made it impossible to connect with her.

"Look at me," Katelyn begged, desperate for an answer. *Any* answer.

But Cordelia didn't move.

"Cordelia, *please.*"

There was still no response. Deep inside, Katelyn's anger simmered, then boiled up and over; she couldn't contain it.

"Look at me!" Katelyn shouted, shaking with rage. Cordelia jumped and lifted her eyes as Katelyn's words echoed. People stopped talking and stared at them.

Tears welled up and ran down Cordelia's cheeks. She took a deep, ragged breath. "I don't know who—or what—did this to you," she murmured.

"But you know *something*," Katelyn said, forcing herself to speak quietly.

"Believe me, Kat, if I could tell you anything, I would. But it's not just me. . . . There's too much history, too much everything."

"What on earth does *that* mean?"

Katelyn watched her friend flounder. Cordelia was clearly frightened, but not by her. It was like something was holding her back, controlling her. She thought of the fairy tale–like house where Cordelia lived with the Arkansas equivalent of the Addams Family. She had tried to reach out to Cordelia, be a friend . . . and now that she needed one, Cordelia wasn't there for her.

"Fine, then," Katelyn said. She stood abruptly to show that she meant business. "I'll do what I should have done in the first place. Talk to my grandfather."

"No! You can't!" Cordelia cried as she leaped up and grabbed her arm, jerking her back down.

"Why not?" Katelyn pressed.

"Because." Cordelia's lips trembled as she stared in horror at Katelyn. "Because my father will kill you."

Katelyn stared at Cordelia in disbelief. "Your father will *kill me?*" she asked incredulously. "As in, literally?"

Cordelia looked as horrified as when Katelyn had told her the dog that had attacked her had actually been a wolf.

"Yes." Cordelia hung her head forward, draping her hands over her knees. "Yes. He will."

The sub appeared in the doorway and looked up at Katelyn as she walked briskly back into the gym. "This is study hall, girls," she called. "Do I need to separate you two?"

Katelyn shook her head. "No," she called back.

But as soon as the sub turned her attention elsewhere, Katelyn looked back at Cordelia. She was pale and shaking, but at least she was looking Katelyn in the eyes.

"You need to talk to me," Katelyn whispered.

Cordelia nodded. She looked utterly defeated. "I will. I promise. Just . . . not here. Not at school."

Relief flooded Katelyn. *Finally,* she thought. *Some answers.* But she wasn't going to let her friend avoid it. She wasn't ready to give in so quickly. "Right after," Katelyn insisted.

"I have to get something first."

Katelyn let out her breath. *What on earth could she possibly need to get in order to talk to me?*

"Don't dodge me." Katelyn stared straight into Cordelia's blue eyes.

"Kat, I'm not. Please. Trust me. This is hard enough."

Cordelia grabbed Katelyn's hand as Katelyn opened her mouth to protest. Her grip was so strong that Katelyn's bones felt as if they were rubbing together. She winced. Then she looked down at Cordelia's arm, where she herself had left red fingerprints earlier. Was a bruise blooming on her skin?

"I'll go home after school to get what I need," Cordelia said. "Tell your grandfather you invited me to your house for dinner. We'll talk after."

"And you'll tell me the truth," Katelyn said, allowing herself to hope.

"I will." Cordelia swallowed hard. "But you can't tell anyone what I tell you. You have to swear."

"I promise," Katelyn said firmly. It was the hardest lie she'd ever told, but she really needed to know what was going on.

Cordelia still looked uncertain. But finally she nodded. "Deal."

<hr>

Because of the rain, Katelyn ate lunch inside. The school had a huge, dreary cavern of a space that was used as a lunchroom—though no one ate there unless it was raining. She'd been there a few times but hadn't really noticed the murals painted on the walls. From floor to ceiling they were covered with faded images of wolves. She felt a sudden urge to destroy the art, attack it as she had been attacked.

She forced herself to look away. She didn't see Cordelia, but as she searched for an empty seat, Trick rose from a table of people and came over to her. He was carrying a cup of ramen, but something he was eating smelled like pine needles. Or maybe it was something he was wearing.

"Hi," she said wanly. She welcomed his company—he always had a way of making her smile—but she didn't want him to ask her anything.

"Come on," he said, guiding her past all the tables to a stairwell on the other side of the room. He sat down on the top step. "You've been staggering around all morning like you've lost your best friend."

She smiled, trying to brush off the comment. Then, as she looked at him, the strange telescoping thing happened again. Her field of vision was taken up with nothing but Trick's eyes, set widely apart on either side of his arched nose and fringed by heavy lashes. Green, with gold flecks, and tiny bits of deep blue she'd never noticed before.

Then the image vanished and she was looking at Trick's entire angular face again—taut with concern and . . . something else. Was he *angry*?

She swayed a little on the step. "What are you eating?" she asked as casually as possible to cover it. "It smells like a Christmas tree."

"Just ramen," he said. He regarded her closely. "What's going on with you?"

"I want to go over to Sam's after school today," she said suddenly. Cordelia wouldn't be over for at least a couple of hours. It would be the perfect time to find out exactly what Sam had been hinting at during her party. "To say goodbye. She's leaving, you know. Would you mind waiting half an hour to take me home afterwards?"

"I didn't know you two were close." He shrugged. "Sure. I can take you there if you need a ride."

"No," she said quickly. "I mean, I don't need a ride there. She's like what, three blocks from here?"

"Trickster," called a guy in emo clothes—black, black, and

more black, plus black-dyed hair. Kohl around the eyes, lots of piercings. "Your turn."

"We're playing Go," Trick told Katelyn. "You know it? Like Japanese chess."

"No. Go play Go." She was trying hard to sound nonchalant. "I'll come back over here and meet you in the lot after I say goodbye to Sam."

He nodded and stood to leave but looked at her for a moment as if he was going to say something else. Instead, he turned and made his way back to his table. Despite everything, her eyes followed him, fixing on his broad shoulders. She didn't want to sit at the table, but she sort of wished he'd stayed with her in the stairwell. Maybe he didn't want to be just her friend, but he was the closest thing she had to one.

Then she saw Beau standing at the doorway to the room. He was looking straight at her. She half stood, pointing to herself and then the door, and he gave her a little nod and disappeared.

She walked into the hallway, where he was waiting for her. His hands were in his pockets and his shoulders were hunched. They hadn't spoken since Becky had died.

"Hey," she said. "What's up?"

He made a face. "Well, as you may have expected, after Becky died, my grandma went pretty ballistic. 'It's happening. More will die,' that kind of stuff." He sounded as if he was trying to make light, but his voice was low and dead serious.

Katelyn nodded.

"Then about two this morning she just started screaming. She said there was a monster in her window."

"A *monster*?" Katelyn repeated. "Like what? Like a . . . an animal, maybe?" *A wolf?* She thought the words but didn't say them, waiting to see if Beau said them first.

"All she said was that it was huge. She just carried on something terrible. We couldn't get her to calm down. And then . . ." He cleared his throat and looked down. "Then she had a stroke. They took her down to Bentonville. She's in intensive care."

"Oh, my God." Shocked, she gave him a quick hug. "Beau. I'm so sorry."

"I think you met her in Babette's," he went on. "You were with Cordelia."

She remembered the old lady with the big black-feathered hat. She had warned Katelyn and Cordelia to go home, where it was safe. Katelyn should have listened to her.

"Is there anything I can do?" she asked him.

He exhaled. "I don't know. I just wanted to tell you."

She nodded. "I'm so sorry. Were you going to eat your lunch in there?" she asked, gesturing with her head to the lunchroom.

"No. I was just looking for you." His cheeks reddened. "So . . . I'll see you later."

"Okay. Thanks for letting me know," she said. She gave him another quick hug. He smiled shyly at her, then turned and trudged down the hall toward Mrs. Walker's office.

⊶ ⧓ ⊷

The rain had stopped, but the wind hadn't. It picked up the leaves and blew them across the road as Katelyn stood in front of Sam's house. She almost turned around and left. But she didn't really have that choice, did she? If Cordelia bailed on her, Sam might be the only person who could give her answers, and she'd be gone in another day or two. Her heart thumping, she pressed the doorbell, and it was Sam herself who answered. Her face was drawn, but when she saw Katelyn, she brightened up a little.

"Hey." She opened the door wide, to reveal stacks of brown cardboard cartons.

"I heard you were leaving," Katelyn said.

Sam nodded, and the warmth left her eyes. She turned around and padded into the house, indicating that Katelyn should follow her.

"My parents are splitting up," Sam said dully as she looked at all the cartons.

"Oh, I'm so sorry," Katelyn said, but found she was actually relieved. At least it was a normal reason.

Sam shrugged. "It wasn't a surprise. My mom has never liked it here. She got a job offer in Little Rock and decided to take it. My dad's moving back to Oklahoma. I'll see him over Christmas."

Katelyn nodded. She felt bad about wanting to bring up Becky's death, but it was now or never and she couldn't think of any subtle way to do it.

"Um, I'm really sorry about all of it, really. And I hope I don't sound cold. But you said something at the party about the way Becky died. . . ."

"Right." Sam nodded, then turned and walked into the kitchen. Katelyn trailed after her. "Want a soda?"

"Sure." Resting her hands on the white breakfast bar,

Katelyn spotted a big pile of newspaper clippings and something that looked like a weathered piece of parchment folded on top.

Sam got them both cans of soda and gestured for Katelyn to sit at the bar.

"My mom works at the clinic, you know? And she heard the doctor talking on the clinic phone—the police took Becky there first, before they went to Bentonville—and he was saying her injuries didn't add up and he had never seen anything like it in his life."

Katelyn swallowed hard. "Like how?"

"I don't know." Sam ran her fingers through her hair. "He also said she'd been moved. There was some kind of evidence that she was sneaking into the Inner Wolf Center. My mom couldn't make it out."

"So are the police investigating the Wolf Center?" Katelyn asked.

Sam puffed air out of her cheeks. "I don't know. Wolf Springs is such a bizarre place. People are so secretive about the weirdest stuff. Everything is about your family. If your great-grandparents didn't grow up here, forget about ever being accepted."

Katelyn remembered how Cordelia had told her she'd quit cheerleading because of her family.

"They'll act nice, right to your face," Sam said. "But if you weren't born here, you'll always be an outsider. I'm glad we're leaving. I just wish"—her voice trailed off—"my parents weren't getting divorced."

"That sucks," Katelyn said sincerely, and gave her a quick

hug, just as she had Beau. The bad news just kept coming in Wolf Springs.

"Thanks." Sam flashed her a weak smile. Then she pointed to the pile of clippings. "Those are old newspaper articles about Wolf Springs. My mom found them in this cool box. She wants to keep the box. She's going to see if the historical society wants the clippings."

Katelyn picked up the folded parchment and opened it. It was a pen-and-ink landscape. In the foreground was the rough sketch of a three-dimensional heart shape, very craggy. Maybe a boulder. Trees stood in the middle ground, and in the background, a waterfall cascaded down the face of a mountain. Something tugged at the back of her mind, but she couldn't put her finger on it.

"Could I take these home to look through them?" Katelyn asked. "They'd be great for my history project."

Sam slid off her bar stool. "Sure. If I know my mom, she'll wind up tossing them in the trash. She's got a little too much going on to worry about the historical society. Just promise me you'll give them back if she asks for them, okay?"

"Of course." Katelyn felt a surge of triumph as Sam put the papers into a plastic bag, and Katelyn loaded it into her backpack. She gave Sam her cell phone number and her grandfather's landline, in case Sam's mom wanted the papers back. Then Sam walked her to the door and gave her a quick hug.

"Be careful, okay?" Sam said. "This town has always given me the creeps. Don't trust anybody." She smiled faintly. "Except Trick. He's a good guy."

"You'll miss him," Katelyn said.

"Trick's made of awesome." Her smile turned sly. "And he likes you. If I had it going on with Trick, I might actually want to stay here. *You're* here. Go for it."

"Maybe I will," Katelyn said, forcing herself to smile back.

But she had far more on her mind than guys and history projects. As she walked back to the lot, her thoughts turned to Cordelia. Sam hadn't had much to tell her, but hopefully Cordelia would. Someone needed to start filling in the blanks.

Trick was leaning against his Mustang, waiting for her, but as she neared, she saw his upper lip was split, and there was a bruise on his cheekbone.

"Trick, what happened?" she cried, rushing up to him.

"Doesn't matter," he said. "The other guy's dead."

13

"Ha," she said mockingly. "How hysterically funny. Who was it? Was it Mike?"

He jerked slightly and she figured she had hit the mark. Her fear flared into anger and she hoped Mike looked worse than Trick by a mile.

"Did you get to say your goodbyes to Sam?" he asked.

"That's all you have to say about the fight?"

"The fight's not your business. How was Sam?"

Before she could respond, he opened the door to the Mustang and let her in. She could tell he was pissed off. Not at her, but at Mike, or whoever had done this. It helped her calm down even though she wasn't happy that he wasn't going to tell her about it.

Once inside, Trick cranked up "Sympathy for the Devil" and like some demonic charioteer, he drove through the town and up through the tunnel of trees. Everything was lost in a blur. His expression was clouded, guarded, and he barely said a word when he let her out at her grandfather's.

Then his Mustang blew back into the woods like a phantom jet, leaving her alone on the porch. She went inside and greeted Ed, asked him if Cordelia could come for dinner, left a message on Cordelia's cell to confirm, then went upstairs "to study." In reality, she checked her leg and her shoulder again, finding them still unblemished.

She thought of Becky Jensen. A murder, made to look like a mauling?

Cordelia's words echoed in her mind: *My father will kill you.*

A knock on her bedroom door interrupted her spiraling thoughts. She braced herself, expecting Cordelia, but when she opened the door, her grandfather stood there.

"Something's up," he said. "I could hear you pacing."

"Boy stuff," she said, giving him a little frown to help sell it. It seemed to be the easiest thing to say to shut him down.

He hovered on the threshold. "You know," he said, "I used to be a boy."

She wanted to scream, her patience gone. "Women have gotten the vote since then," she muttered, and the strangest look crossed his features. It was a mixture of expressions—surprise, amusement, grief, and something else. . . . Shame?

Her own shame hit her in the gut. Had she really just said something so mean?

"That sounds like something your father would say," he said. He sighed. "You look so much like him."

She blinked in surprise. No one had ever said that to her before. Everyone back in Santa Monica said she looked just like her mother. Of course, most of her friends had never met her father.

"You're right," he said softly. "I should have come for her funeral."

"You should have," she agreed. She wanted—needed—to talk to him about all this. But at the moment, she could barely string words together. All she wanted was to talk to Cordelia, to wring the truth out of *her*. She closed her eyes and struggled for composure, some sense of calm. Her grandfather had walked into a hornets' nest and he didn't deserve the attitude she was giving him. Worse, if it continued, he might suspect that there was something a lot bigger than boy trouble wrong with her.

A silence settled over them. Katelyn reached out to him and took his hand. Then she said gently, "Your friend who died. Is there going to be a service?"

His face softened and he smiled sadly. "Old men and hard earth. Tough combination."

"I missed you, you know," she said softly, old memories coming back to her. "I wanted to see you. I *needed* to see you."

"I know. I needed to see you, too." His eyes were shiny. He really meant it.

"Then why didn't you come?" she asked in a tiny voice.

He looked away and she felt her heart sink. More secrets,

more things people didn't want to tell her. But then he shocked her by speaking.

"I had something to take care of here. Please, Katie, trust me on this."

Katelyn was stunned. Before she could say anything, he cocked his head. "Was that the door?"

She followed him down the stairs, staring at the back of his shirt, his head of gray hair. As much as she had hoped it was Cordelia at the door, she was unspeakably grateful to have had that moment with her grandfather. It gave her hope for the future.

When Ed opened the front door, Cordelia was standing there, slightly out of breath, holding her backpack in her arms. She managed a smile at him, then shifted her attention to Katelyn. Her eyes were clear and bright. Katelyn saw fear there, but determination as well.

"So, um," Cordelia said. "Do we have time to work on our history project before dinner?"

Katelyn nodded, eager to get her alone, but forcing herself to seem casual. "Yeah. I got some cool stuff from Sam, too. Newspaper clippings." She motioned for Cordelia to follow her upstairs.

"I went over to her place after school. I wanted to say good-bye," she added as she climbed.

Both girls dropped their false smiles as soon as they turned down the hallway that led to Katelyn's bedroom, and she pulled Cordelia the last few steps into her room, then turned to face her.

But Cordelia looked around, then up at the skylight, and shook her head.

"We can't talk here."

Katelyn frowned. "Then, where? There really aren't a lot of options."

"We could take a walk," Cordelia suggested. "I just . . . If he comes in and sees what I'm showing you . . ." She licked her lips and stood waiting.

"You're scaring me," Katelyn said.

"Good. You should be scared."

Katelyn glanced up at the skylight. "It's getting too dark. He'll never let me go. Let's just lock the door. He's downstairs cooking—it'll be fine."

Cordelia had had ninety minutes to rehearse whatever she was going to say. Katelyn wasn't letting her leave until she got something out of her.

Cordelia sat down on the bed and tucked her knees under her chin. "My father," she began, her voice soft, "is losing his mind. It's a kind of dementia, like Alzheimer's."

"I'm sorry," Katelyn said, confused. It wasn't at all what she'd been expecting.

"So he's been behaving very oddly," Cordelia continued, as if she hadn't heard her. "As you've seen—the Fenner Family Olympics."

"Which explains why he'll kill me?" Katelyn pressed. It sounded as crazy out loud as it had when she'd thought it.

"Maybe," Cordelia murmured.

"Cordelia, that makes no sense. It doesn't explain anything." Katelyn had to struggle to keep her voice down, keep her frustration in check.

Cordelia was silent for a long time and then she abruptly raised her head and tilted back her chin, gazing up at the skylight again. She exhaled as if she were a million years old, and then she looked at Katelyn.

"Second: I told you the truth. I'm not sure what happened to you. I don't know who or what attacked you. And you have to believe me."

Katelyn nodded slowly, disappointment flooding her. She'd thought this would be the moment that all the pieces would fall into place. But life wasn't like that, was it?

"We both agree it was an animal, right?" Katelyn said. *Not a crazy person. Not a man with Alzheimer's.*

"We do," Cordelia said. Then added hesitantly, "Sort of." She cleared her throat and continued in a stronger voice. "Even if you subtract my dad's . . . condition, you might have noticed that my family is a little . . . odd."

"A little?" Katelyn said before she could stop herself.

Cordelia didn't smile. "Yes. And ours isn't the only one. There are a few other families who live around here who are also *odd*."

"I've been told this place is odd," Katelyn said, leaving it open for Cordelia to explain.

The other girl reached out and gripped Katelyn's hand tight. She leaned closer so that their foreheads were nearly touching. Then she opened her backpack and pulled out a framed color photograph. It was of a wolf—its fur a ruddy brown—with intelligent blue eyes that gazed directly at the camera. The image was eerie—as if somehow the photographer had captured its essence.

Its soul.

Katelyn went cold. What was it about wolves and this place?

Cordelia turned the frame over and pushed away the flanges

that held the black velvet backing in place. She lifted it off, revealing the other side of the photograph. There was strange writing in each corner, almost like some kind of ancient runes or something you'd see on tarot cards. Wordlessly, Cordelia held the picture out to Katelyn, who squinted, trying to make out the letters.

"'Cordelia, Hunter's Moon,'" Cordelia translated. "And my lineage. Mother's side, father's side. But it's all the same side."

It was as if Cordelia were speaking in a foreign language. Katelyn was lost. "I'm still not following," Katelyn said very slowly.

"But you *are* following," Cordelia said in a low voice. "You know. You just don't want to admit it."

"Know what?" Katelyn asked, but her mouth went dry, and the words cracked as she said them. Her mind was working and it felt as if things were changing from hazy to focused.

Cordelia tapped the photograph. "What I am. What my family is. And what you might be now, too."

Katelyn shook her head, suddenly feeling faint. "No. I don't understand."

She tried to pull away but Cordelia grasped her hand tight, crushing it. "It's why we live in the middle of the forest, why my sisters act so weird. My cousin Jesse kisses you because that's how . . . wolves . . . greet one another."

Katelyn's insides were quaking. "Are you trying to say that you—you're . . ."

She tried to stand, but Cordelia held her fast with an incredibly powerful grip. Using her free hand, Cordelia pulled out more framed photographs.

Of wolves.

"Arial. Regan. My father." The metal frames clanked against each other as Cordelia leaned in close, her breath brushing against Katelyn's ear. "Werewolves, Kat. That's what we are."

"No." Katelyn shook her head fiercely. "That's crazy."

"You know it's not. You *know*."

With a burst of adrenaline, Katelyn jerked away from Cordelia and jumped to her feet. Dizzy, she reached out and touched the wall. Katelyn fought back tears. Cordelia was crazy. She had to get away from her. Her grandfather would know what to do.

Cordelia threw her arms around her and Katelyn tried to push her away, but the other girl was too strong. "You know it's true," Cordelia whispered. "Wolves only have blue eyes when they're pups. There's no way that what you saw out in the woods and with Trick was just a regular wolf."

"But there must be *some* wolves—"

"Only hybrids, or maybe, once in a great while, a genetic mutation. Adult wolves just don't have blue eyes. But werewolves do. We keep the same eye color in both forms."

"What are you saying?" Katelyn asked, shuddering.

"The sight, the heightened senses. They're all part of it."

And then it struck Katelyn what Cordelia was saying. *Heightened senses, like I've been experiencing.* Her mind screamed in horror as she went back over the past few days for confirmation.

"So now I'm a . . . I'm like that?" Katelyn asked hoarsely.

"I don't know," Cordelia said, biting her lip.

"How do you not know?" Katelyn asked, wanting to shake her.

"I told you, I don't know what bit you!" Cordelia said. Anger laced with fear flared in her eyes. Katelyn jerked, hard, even more afraid as she tried to grasp what Cordelia was . . . and what she herself might be.

This can't be happening. This can't be real. Oh, my God. She was shaking so hard her bones began to ache.

"Katelyn, I . . . ," Cordelia murmured.

"But what happened to you?" Katelyn asked.

"What do you mean?"

"Who bit *you*?"

Cordelia blinked. "No one. I was born a werewolf."

Katelyn was silent as she took that in. Hope flared inside her, because she, Katelyn, had *not* been born a . . . thing like that . . . and then terror, just as intense, just as white-hot. Cordelia could change into a wolf. She could attack her.

"Werewolf parents have werewolf pups," she said. "Katelyn, there are no humans in my family."

There are no humans in my family.

"Justin," Katelyn said, her stomach turning. She'd let him kiss her.

"And Jesse, too," Cordelia confirmed.

Trembling as a chill ran down her spine, Katelyn covered her mouth. Cordelia wasn't human. "And if you bite someone?" Her voice broke. "If you *break the skin*?"

Cordelia let her go.

"They change," she said finally. "But *I* didn't bite you. I swear it. I couldn't have. I can't change except on the full moon. I'm not mature enough. And you weren't bitten on a full moon."

Katelyn went silent. She was shivering uncontrollably, from shock and disbelief. Then she forced herself to ask the next question.

"Who *have* you done this to?"

Cordelia shook her head. "Me personally? No one. But one of my pack mates *was* brought in with a bite. My brother-in-law Doug. He dated Regan all through high school. He was screened and tested and our alpha gave permission first."

"And who is the alpha?" Katelyn asked, hearing herself speaking, and feeling as if she'd totally lost her mind. It was insane.

Cordelia exhaled slowly and bit her lower lip. "My father runs the pack. He's served as alpha since the year before I was born."

"And he's . . . getting demented," Katelyn said, still struggling to grasp the reality.

"Yes," Cordelia said quietly.

"And I wasn't screened or tested, and he didn't give his permission."

"No."

Katelyn slumped down on the bed, because she didn't know what else to do. If she ran downstairs to tell her grandfather, he'd do what? Would he even believe her? And if it was true, what would Cordelia do to him? She leaned over for a moment, putting her head down as the room seemed to tilt and whirl around her.

She felt Cordelia sit down next to her. She didn't want to believe, but deep down she had to admit that she'd known something was very, very wrong. The way that wolf had tracked her. Her enhanced senses. Her nightmares, so vivid. The way her wound had healed practically overnight.

"You've known about me all along," Katelyn said. "When I told you about my symptoms, you already knew."

"No." Cordelia emphatically shook her head. "My dad bit Doug the night before the full moon. So there wasn't time to really notice any changes before it happened. Doug changed on the full moon. I mean, we all naturally change on the full moon, but older wolves can change at will."

Katelyn hugged herself. "That means you kill everyone you attack."

Cordelia's face transformed in shock. "No! We *never* attack people. It's forbidden. That's why this doesn't make any sense. *No one* would do this. It would be like expecting that little stuffed bear you like so much to come alive and bite you."

Katelyn was bewildered. "But it happened. What else could it have been?"

Cordelia took a deep breath. Then she mouthed a word with two syllables, one that Katelyn could not make out. Katelyn inched in closer, and Cordelia repeated herself.

"*Hellhound,*" she whispered.

Katelyn frowned. She sat back and looked at Cordelia. "Like in the story about the mine," Katelyn said.

Her friend's face went stark white. She nodded.

"But Cordelia, that's just a story," she began, then caught herself. Because until thirty seconds earlier, werewolves had just been stories, too.

"My sisters used to tell me stories about the . . . about *it* when I was little, to scare me," Cordelia said in a low, strained voice. "They tortured me with them. And it worked. I had horrible night terrors. There was one year that I hardly ever slept."

Katelyn just listened. Cordelia looked as if she might throw up. "When Haley was killed, I went to my dad and I asked him if he thought maybe that's what attacked her. Justin overheard. And they both laughed at me." She took a deep breath. "But I wasn't fooled, Kat. They were afraid, too. Then, after Becky died, I heard my dad patrolling around outside our house, night after night. But he denied it."

"What's going to happen to me?" Katelyn asked, disbelief passing and terror taking an even firmer grip on her. This could not be happening. But it *was*.

"If it was . . . *that*, I don't know. Change into one of his kind? Her kind?"

"What kind is that?" Katelyn asked.

Cordelia looked terrified. "A monster."

"What kind of monster?" *Worse than you?*

"No one really knows what it looks like. There's just stories, like the boogeyman, or the Candyman. Some folks say it can pass for one of us, but then it changes, and it's hideous. Deformed."

Like the monster at Beau's grandmother's window? The one that gave her a stroke?

Katelyn was going to lose it. She was on the verge of full-blown hysteria.

"But if it *was* one of us . . . you're going to change into a werewolf on the next full moon." Cordelia took a deep breath. "Or maybe nothing will happen. Maybe a husky bit you. Or a mutant wolf. Maybe that's why it attacked you. And that would explain the blue eyes."

"When is the next full moon?" Katelyn rasped.

"A week after Halloween," Cordelia said with hesitation.

Her birthday week. And then life as she knew it might end.

Cordelia took her hand again, more gently this time. "I'll help you, Kat. I'll stay with you—watch over you."

Katelyn's stomach contracted. This couldn't be happening. It was like some horrible joke.

"And your father ... ," Katelyn said.

"On the full moon, we all meet for a ritual, then go on a hunt. But I could make an excuse—say I don't feel good—and take you somewhere private. Watch you. It wouldn't be the first time someone's been too sick to go."

Katelyn closed her eyes. "But you're saying we need to hide it from your father?"

Cordelia hesitated, then nodded. "He's so unpredictable, and it's getting worse. Last night he woke me up to ask me questions about the Constitution. Then he called my sisters and tested them. It was about three a.m." She wiped tears from her eyes.

"Oh, Cordelia." Katelyn stared at her. "But you said you never kill people. So he wouldn't kill me. Right?"

"If you're ... one of us, all bets are off," Cordelia said, looking down. She stood and picked up the framed picture of her father. "He's got to pick a new alpha soon, or someone will challenge him." She let out a long, shaky breath.

"Challenge him?"

"Fight him. To the death, if necessary."

"Are you people *crazy*?" Katelyn swayed, and Cordelia ran back to the bed, supporting her, slipping an arm around her.

"I'm sorry that it's so scary. It's all I've ever known. Except for my dad losing his mind. That's why all the contests. He's trying to pick one of us to be the new alpha."

"You . . . you and your sisters?" Katelyn asked, astounded. "But you're only sixteen."

Cordelia didn't speak for some time. Then she said, "I'm seventeen. I'm his favorite, but I'm the youngest and I'm not mated. Some days he thinks that's great, because he can pick someone out for me, but other days, he tells me I'll be so distracted that I won't be a good leader."

She looked bereft. "And . . . some days he forgets who I am." She sighed. "Since you were bitten without his permission—*if* it was one of us—he'll be furious."

"Great," Katelyn said weakly. "Is that why you told me to go back to L.A.?"

Cordelia nodded. "I panicked. But you'd be all alone out there. That would be bad for you. And for L.A. A werewolf on the loose, alone . . ." She shook her head.

"Then come with me," Katelyn begged.

"I can't just pick up and leave," Cordelia said. "I need permission. My father has already put all of us on notice that we have to stay close. Not just because of the succession. There's been friction with other packs. It's so important for us to look strong. If they found out that someone attacked a human on our territory and we didn't know who it was, we'd look like huge fools."

"They?"

"Dom's pack. Our rivals." She flushed and shook her head. "You don't need to worry about all that right now. But it's why I can't leave."

"The guys you liked . . ." She caught her breath. "Your possibilities. They're werewolves, too?"

"Except for Bobby." Cordelia touched Katelyn's hair. "I asked to bring him in, but my dad said no. He wasn't good enough."

For some reason, Mike's face appeared in her mind. She had a terrible thought.

"Are any of the other kids at school . . . ?"

"Not the high school," Cordelia said. "But there are a couple in middle school, and in elementary school, and that's a problem." She sighed. "Our pack has gotten too big. Back in the old days, only the alpha pair would mate. That kept our population down. Then better birth control came along, and the alpha changed the rules, because we figured everyone would be careful. But people haven't been careful enough. We've got over thirty pack mates, and that's about twenty too many."

As Cordelia's words rushed over her, Katelyn stood slowly. She walked to her dresser and looked at herself in the mirror.

She hesitated. "Once we found out about the Hellhound, you didn't want to research the silver mine."

"I never wanted to do the silver mine," Cordelia said quietly. "Silver is toxic to us. It can kill us. So . . . say two packs weren't getting along, and the alpha's kid started looking for it for a school project." In the mirror, the reflection of Cordelia's features twisted, and Katelyn didn't know how to read it. "My dad ordered me to keep working on it with you. That's why I was all back and forth."

Katelyn gripped the top of the dresser, sensing there was more.

"And then when you found out that the Hell . . ." Cordelia's voice faltered. *"Hellhound,"* she said firmly. "That it lives in the Madre Vena, I begged him to let me stop working on it. He just laughed. Like he always has."

"He's your father," Katelyn said. "He wouldn't make you do anything risky."

"Maybe . . . before," Cordelia murmured. "But now, with his mind going . . ." She raised a shaking hand to her forehead. "The Hellhound goes after bad werewolves," Cordelia said.

"Bad?" Katelyn echoed uneasily.

"Those of us who don't follow the rules. Or"—she swallowed hard—"anyone who betrays our secret." She looked at Katelyn with wide, stricken eyes. "Like me."

Katelyn thought a moment. "Have you ever told anyone else?"

"No." She shook her head. "But when Jesse and Justin showed up, I was so scared that Jesse would tell, I stopped having friends over."

"But you can't control him."

"Exactly." Cordelia took a ragged breath and looped her hair over her ears. "Nobody can. In my grandparents' day, he wouldn't have survived. They would have . . . He wouldn't be here."

Katelyn stared at her. "Do you mean they would have killed him?" she whispered.

Cordelia glanced anxiously at the closed bedroom door.

"They would have left him in the forest when he was a new-born," she said.

Katelyn pursed her lips together; the idea of leaving Jesse in the woods to die was horrifying.

"But we don't do things like that anymore," Cordelia assured her. "Too many people. Someone might see."

"Plus it's *wrong*," Katelyn pointed out.

"Kat, you have to understand. We're *not human*."

Katelyn didn't know what to say. What to think.

"Maybe the Hellhound has come because we've lost our path," Cordelia said. "Justin says we're trying too hard to be like people. That we should go back to the older ways."

"Justin?" After everything, the idea of Justin wanting to be less human only made it feel worse.

"Now you know why I didn't want to talk about it. So . . . we don't need to talk about it now, right? Until we know." She gazed hard at Katelyn.

Until we know.

"But it seems obvious that one of you—that a werewolf—bit me," Katelyn insisted. "And that's something we do need to talk about."

"No. I just can't accept that," Cordelia insisted. "Tell me about it again. Start from the beginning."

Katelyn shut her eyes as the memories washed over her, chilling her to the bone. "It jumped on me and dragged me. It bit me." She couldn't stop holding her breath. "It had blue eyes. It was huge." She mimicked raising a tire iron. "I hit it and then it just kind of dissolved into the shadows. It was almost like it became the shadows."

Cordelia caught her breath. "Like how?"

Katelyn ran her hands through her hair. She didn't like remembering. But she needed to help herself, find out everything about what was happening to her. "I don't know how else to describe it. I wasn't sure what I was seeing. I thought I might be hallucinating."

"Hellhound," Cordelia whispered.

"Or . . . I was just really scared," Katelyn protested.

Cordelia shook her head and looked down.

The silence stretched between them as Katelyn struggled to process everything. When the wolf had attacked her, she had thought she'd be killed, like the other girls. She'd been so relieved when she escaped. Maybe they'd been the lucky ones.

"What about Becky and Haley?" Katelyn murmured.

Cordelia hesitated. "I don't know," she admitted. "I don't know about them, and I don't know about you. But you can't talk about this. Not with anybody. Your grandfather, Trick. No one." Her voice was stern and Katelyn knew she meant it.

"Okay," she whispered. She took a deep breath. "But how am I going to get through this?"

Cordelia exhaled. "It's going to be okay, Kat."

"You don't know that," Katelyn said angrily. "Forty years ago, a bunch of people were attacked. People are being attacked *now*. And I'm one of them. You can't tell me that I'm going to be okay. You don't even know what bit me!"

"Girls, dinner!" Her grandfather's voice made her start.

"I need help," Katelyn went on, ignoring his call.

"I said I'd help you," Cordelia snapped, looking up at her. Then her face crumpled. "And I'm really sorry, Kat, but I'm all the help you've got."

Dinner was spent in painful silence. After Cordelia left, Katelyn scoured all the books she had, looking for more information about the Hellhound, the silver mine, and the wolves of Wolf Springs. She had practically memorized the story about Xavier Cazador. But there was nothing new.

Later that night, Katelyn lay in bed and raised her hand to the skylight, a rectangle of black raindrops. Exhausted, she let her arm drop back down. But she didn't sleep. She stared into the dark and couldn't seem to stop herself from shaking.

She got up and took another hot shower. Her heart was pounding as if it were too big for her chest. And then, as she climbed into fresh fleece pajama bottoms and a tank top, she realized that what she was hearing was not her heart, but the pounding of drums. Howls wailed, blasting through the layers of black on black on black, weaving through the treetops. Jack Bronson's disciples.

She listened for a while, then went downstairs. A fire was burning in the fireplace, but the front room was empty. She flicked on the light switch and the howls rose, then poured down one on the other like a cascade of sound. The drums pulsed like blood through veins.

And something inside her urged her to go outside to join them.

No, she told herself firmly.

Leaving the light on, she turned to go back upstairs. Her gaze was drawn once again to the painting of the deer and the tree. And the boulder. The heart-shaped boulder, in the foreground.

She remembered where else she'd seen it: in the piece

of parchment on top of the stack of clippings Sam had given her.

"Katie?" her grandfather called from the top of the stairs.

"I can't sleep with all that drumming," she said.

He was silent a moment. Then he asked, "What drumming?"

14

It was hard to get through the days—and the nights—pretending that nothing was wrong. That Katelyn wasn't keeping track of every single hour. She had figured out there were 408 hours in seventeen days. She spent many of those precious hours searching for more information about werewolves and Hellhounds and what had happened forty years earlier in Wolf Springs. She told Cordelia to ask her sisters to tell her the Hellhound stories again, and to go through her house for anything else that might reveal what was going to happen to Katelyn on the full moon. Cordelia insisted that there was nothing new. But Cordelia was so afraid of the Hellhound that Katelyn had trouble believing her, and she realized her trust in the only person who knew her secret was getting shaky.

At night, she tossed and turned, listening to the drums, to her heart. Tortured by worry, tormented by strange dreams . . . and the realization that she might never make it back to Los Angeles.

She had her next rabies shot and didn't even bother to ask about side effects anymore. The last innoculation would be on Halloween. It seemed ironic to her. What she really wanted was to ask the nurse if she had a werewolf vaccine, but she didn't dare breathe the "w" word most days, not even to Cordelia.

Katelyn was beginning to understand what it was like to live in a small town. It was smothering, unnerving. She needed privacy with Cordelia if she was going to get her to talk, but it was difficult, if not impossible, to find any. Cordelia's house was out for obvious reasons, and Katelyn's grandfather's cabin was too small for them to be able to talk freely. And every building they entered seemed to contain someone who wanted to get to know the new girl.

One afternoon after school, Katelyn and Cordelia went driving. Katelyn had found a book in her grandfather's shelves called *Tall Tales of the Ozarks*. As they bumped along the dirt road in Cordelia's truck, brilliant autumn leaves fell like sparks into the bogs and floated down the river.

"Listen." Katelyn began to read from the book.

In early 1937, a man named Barry Cazman arrived in Wolf Springs. He claimed to be a descendant of Xavier Cazador, the man who had rediscovered the Lost Mine of Madre Vena in 1868. Cazman, described as a handsome man with blue-black hair, said that Cazador had left him a map.

Cazman hired local Wolf Springs men to help him locate the Madre Vena, but he ran out of money with nothing to show for it. He then tried his luck at the Wolf Springs Club, gambling at the illegal casino located at the mineral-rich hot springs that gave the town its name. For a time it seemed his luck had turned, and he amassed enough money to resume his search for the Madre Vena mine.

Then, on Christmas Eve, he staggered onto the grounds of the Wolf Springs Club, his clothes in tatters. His hair, once so dark, had turned completely white. He said that he and his men had finally found the distinctively shaped rock they had long sought. As they raced toward it, a wolf stepped from behind it. Cazman raised his rifle to shoot it. And in that moment, the wolf transformed into a "hideous beast" and attacked the party. Cazman alone survived, or so he said.

"That monster came from hell," he said. And then he died. The map was found inside his pocket.

Katelyn stopped reading. Neither spoke. She closed the book with shaking hands and looked at Cordelia, who clenched the wheel tighter.

"Another Hellhound sighting," Katelyn said, even though she was stating the obvious. The part about the rock tugged at something in her memory, but she couldn't place it.

"My dad asked me how we're doing on the mine project," Cordelia murmured in a low voice. "I told him we're stuck."

"We're probably lucky he hasn't asked your sisters to look for it," Katelyn said.

Cordelia swallowed. "I think he has. I think he just didn't tell me that he did."

"Have *they* said anything about it? Or about the Hellhound?"

"*Please* stop saying that word," Cordelia said angrily. She gazed in the rearview mirror, then out the side window.

"We need to talk about it," Katelyn insisted.

"No. We don't," Cordelia retorted. "It's going to get dark soon. You need to get home."

And that was the last they spoke of it that day.

The rough draft of their paper was due a week before the final paper was due. Katelyn and Cordelia turned it in, and the next day, Mr. Henderson asked to see them after school.

He was sitting at his desk, but when they came in, he rose and perched on the corner, casually holding their paper in his hand.

"I want to tell you this is really great stuff," he began, smiling at the two of them. "Your bibliography's a little skimpy. Is it complete? You didn't by chance come across a book by Theodore Switliski?"

"Sorry, no," Cordelia said. "Who's that?"

"An archaeologist. He studied this area in his seminal work: *Ozark Folklore*. I've never been able to locate a copy."

Katelyn recalled that Mr. Henderson had been an archeologist before he'd relocated to Wolf Springs.

He looked disappointed. "Well, okay. If this is all you could find, I can't fault you for it. Thanks for coming in."

They left the room and walked down the hall toward their lockers.

"Why do I not care what grade I get in history this semester?" Katelyn asked. "And that's a rhetorical question—you don't have to answer it. I can't concentrate. I can barely even think. I'm too scared."

"I know. I'm scared, too. But . . ." She gave her head a little shake.

"What?" Katelyn asked.

Cordelia didn't answer. They moved down the hall together. Katelyn was so numb that she could barely feel the floor beneath her feet. Then Cordelia tensed up beside her, and Katelyn raised her gaze.

Trick was coming toward them from the other end of the hall. Katelyn had been trying hard to act normal around him— like he was just a friend and her ride to and from school—but right then she wanted to run to him and throw her arms around him and tell him exactly what was going on. She took a deep breath and steadied herself.

Trick smiled at her, then slid his gaze warily toward Cordelia.

"Why don't you like him?" Katelyn whispered to Cordelia.

"He broke Becky's heart," Cordelia murmured.

"No," she said. "Sam told me—"

"Hey." Trick came straight up to Katelyn. "How you doing? You okay?"

"Yes," she said, too quickly.

He cocked his head. "Are you okay?" he repeated.

"Yes. I'm fine," she said more firmly.

He didn't even look Cordelia's way. "So, I wanted to make

sure you knew my Halloween party's on. I just hung up with my parents and they're good with it." When Katelyn just stared at him, he gave her a perplexed look. "The one we talked about this morning in the car?"

"Oh, um. Right," Katelyn said. She had obviously zoned out.

"You're coming, right, Cordelia?" Trick asked, lifting his chin as if daring her to say no.

"Everyone goes to Trick's Halloween parties," Cordelia said to Katelyn, as if Trick wasn't there. "Even people who don't like him."

"Because I don't really care who shows." He focused his green eyes on Katelyn. "Except, I want you to come."

"We are." Cordelia glared at Trick. "Kat, we can go over to Babette's to look for costumes. In fact, we can go right now."

"Cool. I'm headed that way," Trick said. "Kat, would you ride over with me? I want to talk to you for a second. Then you two can go shopping and I'll leave."

"Well," Katelyn said, hesitating. "I'm hanging out with Cordelia." She wanted to go with Trick so badly. She *needed* to. She needed him to tell her that everything was fine and her great, amazing life was going to happen, and she wanted him to put his arms around her, and—and—but she knew she couldn't tell him a thing about what was going on.

"Okay," Trick said, looking disappointed.

"Yes," Cordelia replied. "Let's go, Kat."

The three of them turned to go to the parking lot, Katelyn between Trick and Cordelia. She stumbled, too full of emotion, fighting to keep herself under control. Trick took her hand, his fingers warm around hers. Cordelia didn't seem to notice, or if she did, she didn't show it.

Cordelia's truck was closer than Trick's Mustang. The two girls climbed in. Trick stood at the passenger side, and Katelyn rolled down the window.

"Be careful," he said. He was very serious. The sunlight bronzed his cheeks and lips. So handsome. So *human*.

Katelyn smiled at him and nodded and Cordelia started up the truck. They pulled out of the lot and began down the road. Glancing in the rearview mirror, Cordelia huffed.

"Can you believe it? I think he's following us!" she said indignantly.

Katelyn said nothing; she only leaned her head against the window, staring at Trick's car in the side mirror. If she tried really hard, she could pretend that Trick was coming to her rescue from a great distance.

⋯⋯⋯

It wasn't far to the center of the quaint town, and almost as soon as they merged onto the town's main artery, Cordelia pulled over and turned off the truck.

"Ready?" she said brightly.

"Cordelia, I can't," Katelyn said. She'd made up her mind. "I'm not buying a Halloween costume. I'm not going to a party." She pressed her fingertips against her forehead. "Please, let's just go."

"C'mon, let's try," Cordelia insisted. She opened the truck door. "It'll be fun."

Katelyn got out on wobbly legs and caught up with Cordelia. The bell on the door tinkled as she opened it, and

Babette was seated behind the counter, her phone to her ear. She gave the girls a welcoming wave as Katelyn shut the door behind her.

"How about a sexy vampire?" Cordelia suggested, picking up a couple of pairs of fishnets. "Or a sexy witch?"

Katelyn passed her by and went straight into the dressing room. She sat down on the bench and crossed her arms over her chest.

"This is crazy," she said as Cordelia came in.

"No. It's life." Cordelia put the fishnets down beside her. "Here's what I'm thinking, Kat. We'll go to the party, both of us, even though, yes, Trick is a loathsome user, and then we'll spend the night at Trick's, like half the school is going to do."

Katelyn's lips parted in surprise. "At *Trick's*?"

"That's how we have parties out here," Cordelia reminded her.

"Girls, do you need anything?" Babette called, sounding perhaps a little too close to the French door.

"We're fine, Babette," Cordelia called back. Then to Katelyn she whispered, "Okay. You're not in the mood. We'll deal with the costumes later. Forgive?"

"Sure," Katelyn replied, but she was still upset.

The morning of Halloween, it was time for Katelyn's final rabies vaccine injection. It was also when Ed presented her with Mason Slater's Subaru Forester, an early birthday gift. He had bought it from the estate of his dead friend, swearing to her that the old man had not died in the car, which made it easier for her to accept the gift—although, in truth, it hadn't been hard in the first place. With a car came more freedom.

Her grandfather trailed behind her as she gripped the steering wheel of the Subaru, negotiating the two-lane road to the clinic. If she felt okay after the injection, she would drive on to school. If not, they'd leave the Subaru at the clinic and pick it up later. In a small town like Wolf Springs, no one thought twice about such a thing.

She was thinking twice, three, four times about what would happen after school. The plan was to drive to Cordelia's to get ready for the party and then go over to Trick's. She was still amazed that it was all right with the parents of the party-goers for everyone to spend the night—and that it was just as okay with her grandfather. He told her it used to be very common in spread-out areas like Wolf Springs to invite your guests to stay. Because of the bad roads and the forest, the custom just hadn't died out there as it had in other towns.

What will I do if Trick tries something? Her face tingled; her palms were damp. Chills tickled the small of her back. Her imagination conjured up all kinds of images as she waited in the exam room. Luckily she didn't have to wait long. As soon as she got the shot, she tried to talk to the nurse about possible side effects, but as before, it went nowhere. When the nurse said the doctor needed to check her sutures, Katelyn lied. She told her that he'd already taken them out. The woman believed her. Problem solved.

Katelyn and her grandfather waited awhile to see how she was feeling, then got some coffee from the doughnut shop next door. This time Katelyn drank it down with no problems. It didn't smell bad. Her grandfather's voice wasn't too loud. She had no headache.

She could barely breathe she was so hopeful. Was it possible that after all that worrying, she was okay?

"I can drive to school," Katelyn said. "And everything else."

"So off you go," Ed said. "Have a great time, Katie. And . . . be careful."

She climbed behind the wheel of the Subaru, and when she turned to say goodbye, she noticed that her grandfather's face was drawn, as if he hadn't slept. Fretting over her?

If only he knew the half of it, she thought. What would have happened to him if she had told him about the actual attack? Were there people in Wolf Springs who knew the Fenners' secret and helped them keep it? She shivered. She really didn't want to find out.

<hr />

After school, Katelyn drove over to Cordelia's. Cordelia had sworn to her that her father wouldn't be home. Justin and Jesse were also nowhere to be seen, and Katelyn was relieved, but a little disappointed.

The girls busied themselves getting ready immediately. Cordelia had ultimately decided to be a sexy vampire, but when they got to her house, they discovered that Jesse had smeared chocolate all over her costume.

"Now what?" Cordelia wailed.

Katelyn flipped through her friend's rather large closet and pulled out a long black sleeveless silk dress. It reminded her of what she herself had been wearing in her dream the night of the earthquake.

"How about we pull your hair into a severe bun and pin it with a flower?" Katelyn offered. "Dark eyes and red lips—you could be a Spanish senorita."

"I like it," Cordelia said, calming perceptibly.

Half an hour later they emerged from the bedroom and Katelyn had to admit that she was quite pleased with herself. Cordelia looked amazing. A dusting of shimmer on her cheeks and eyelids added to the mystique they had created with her hair and her dress. Katelyn also marveled at how the other girl carried herself, regally, like a queen.

I guess in a weird sort of way she is a princess.

Katelyn's outfit ended up contrasting nicely with Cordelia's. She had decided to wear a simple white toga with gold bands crisscrossed over her chest and a golden cord around her waist. The toga was actually a sheet she'd gotten from her grandfather, and he'd found the gold cord and some gold leaves in a box in his garage that had belonged to her grandmother. She put a coronet of the golden leaves on her head. She was bare-legged and wearing a pair of jeweled sandals she'd brought from home.

"You look too innocent," Cordelia decreed. "At least put these on." She handed Katelyn a pair of very high gold heels. "I think we're the same size."

Katelyn smiled faintly and bent down to put them on. As she did so, the slit in the side of her toga wafted open, and Cordelia nodded approvingly.

"Okay, maybe not so innocent," she said.

The heels fit perfectly, and they did look good with the rest of her costume. Katelyn found her mood lifting a little. "Maybe I should get a little sexier," she said, and ripped the other side of the toga up to above her knee.

"Love it," Cordelia said.

They put their sleeping bags and overnight duffels in the hatch of Katelyn's Forester. No one would wear pajamas at Trick's; when they changed out of their costumes, it would be into jeans and sweaters. Cordelia behaved as if sleeping over at a boy's house was perfectly normal. But it was a huge deal to Katelyn. She couldn't stop thinking about Trick. Where would *he* sleep? Where would she?

Cordelia navigated as Katelyn drove. They traveled down into a valley bisected by a stream. Branches bent over it, dropping their persimmon-hued leaves into the water. Headlight beams bounced back off oak and ash trees. As they got closer, they joined a parade of vehicles all headed in the same direction, and music echoed off the hills.

An ersatz parking lot had been created in a meadow beside a white wood fence and a matching double gate that hung wide open. A wrought iron plaque that bore signs of rust and age read SOKOLOV DAIRIES.

"His family owns a dairy?" Katelyn asked in surprise.

Cordelia snickered. "That shut down ages ago. But the Sokolovs are probably the richest family around. His dad is some kind of design guy. He flies all over the country and Trick's mom usually goes with him. Trick has his own *building* on their property."

Katelyn blinked, stunned. She would never have pegged Trick as having money. What else did she not know about him?

"I thought *you* were the richest family," Katelyn said somewhat shyly. "I mean . . . because of your house and . . . who you are."

"Not really. My grandparents built our house," Cordelia said. "We have status, but we don't have all that much money."

Katelyn gathered her coat and her little shoulder-strap purse and the two climbed out of the Subaru. The sun was nearly down and it was cold. Katelyn was glad of her coat.

"Got my cell," Cordelia said, half to herself. "If I forgot it, I'd be in such huge trouble." She pulled it out and looked at it. "No coverage. My dad won't be able to call me every five minutes."

Suddenly huge plumes of fog wafted over the ground. They gathered around Katelyn's and Cordelia's shins, then rapidly billowed into rolling clouds that obscured the two girls first from the waist down, and then to the shoulders. Other partiers started laughing and cheering as zombies appeared on either side of the path, their faces gray and white, arms dangling, hair dirty. They lurched along, shepherding everyone toward a huge dilapidated barn alive with bursts of strobe lights.

"It's a zombie walk!" Cordelia cried, applauding.

Then Cordelia grabbed Katelyn's hand and they ran toward the barn. Both of them paused to yank off their heels, and Katelyn wished she'd brought her sandals. She'd had no idea she'd be dashing through a corn maze on the bottom floor of the barn, then climbing a wooden ladder to the top of the barn, large portions of which were stacked with fresh bales of hay. Trick and his friends had created a ghoulish chamber of horrors, complete with hanging "bodies"; a witch brewing up a potion; a guy pretending to be electrocuted; and a fake surgery scene, in which the patient, strapped to the operating table, screamed while the doctor operated. Fake blood sprayed everywhere. When Katelyn and Cordelia stopped to watch, the electrocution victim jumped out of his chair and started chasing them.

They both shrieked as the guy flew after them, herding them to a long aluminum slide and Cordelia shouted, "Hay chute!"

She grabbed a burlap sack from a pile beside the chute, flung it onto the steeply angled slide, and plopped onto it, then zoomed away. Laughing, Katelyn did the same. She screamed as she careered toward the wall of hay bales draped in orange and black lights at the end of the chute. From her vantage point, she saw strings of black lights draping trees and bushes. Strobe lights flashed.

The angle of the slide straightened so that she wasn't going very fast by the time her bare feet tapped the hay bales. Then Cordelia helped her up. Katelyn staggered with laughter, clutching her borrowed shoes, and she nearly slammed into Trick, who was dressed as he had been the first time she'd met him—black long-sleeved T-shirt pushed up to his elbows, jeans, and cowboy boots. He was wearing a black cowboy hat with a black feather tucked into the hatband, and he was chewing on a piece of straw. The backs of his hands looked strong; they reminded her of Alec, the boy who'd been her trapeze catcher at her gymnastics studio. He was holding two plastic cups containing something tinted red, with flashing plastic ice cubes bobbing in the liquid. She felt her pulse spike and she couldn't stop the big smile that spread across her face. He looked her up and down and let out a slow, appreciative whistle.

"Evening, ladies," he said, holding out the two drinks. "Have a little blood-lite."

"Thank you, Vlad," Katelyn said in her best Bela Lugosi voice.

"You have been varned about speaking the accursed name," he replied, also in thick Hungarian-vampirese.

As if on cue, "Bela Lugosi's Dead" by Bauhaus began to play. A live band was covering the song, and the lead singer had a smoky, seductive voice.

"Well, since the buzzkill has arrived, I think I'll go find somewhere else to be," Cordelia said hostilely, ignoring Trick's offer of the second cup.

The "buzzkill" is your host, Katelyn wanted to remind her. But before she could say anything, Cordelia kissed her on the cheek.

"I'll find you later," she told Katelyn, then wandered away without another word.

Katelyn turned back to Trick and her heart skipped a beat. He was staring at her. He reached out and took her free hand, and before she could say anything to break the tension, a couple of people Katelyn recognized from Trick's lunch table had walked over. The guy wore a devil costume, complete with a red face, horns, a cape, and a tail, and there were two girls. One, in a black ruffled Victorian dress, had her hair in a bun and her face coated wearing glow-in-the-dark makeup; the other was dressed as a Victorian man wearing a goatee and a bloody suit.

"Eric's edited another scene. Come with us to check it out," the girl in the suit said to Trick. She took the drink he'd offered Cordelia and sipped it, then handed it to the girl in the Victorian dress. The girl finished it and set the cup on a picnic table.

"Oh, God." Trick rolled his eyes. "*Please* not now."

"A scene from what?" Katelyn asked, intrigued.

"C'mon, Trick." The two girls tugged on his arms as they giggled. Katelyn felt a sudden swift pang of jealousy.

The guy—Eric?—came up to Katelyn. "We're doing *Dark of the Moon* in Russian. I've got the new footage ready to roll in Trick's house."

"Count Trickula!" the girl in the glow-in-the-dark makeup squealed. Then she let go of Trick and turned to Katelyn. "Hi, Kat! Guess who we are."

The girl in the suit fluttered her lashes. "The Curies. Marie and Pierre. We both died horribly."

"It's a Halloween natural," the girl in the dress—Marie Curie—concurred.

Then the two broke away and ran ahead, past the barn to a small white building with a sloping green roof. They pushed open the door and disappeared. Eric followed them, leaving Trick and Katelyn alone again.

"It's our own nouveau theater thing. It's kind of obnoxious," Trick said, glancing down at her. She was trying to take it all in—Trick, rich and arty, and his quirky friends. She liked him. So much.

"I'd love to see it. Plus I'm freezing," she added so she didn't sound *too* eager.

He raised his brows; then he put his arm around her and

pulled her against him. Chills and tingles skittered all through her, and suddenly she felt very, very warm. She didn't want him to stop—not ever.

They walked to the building together. It was Trick's very own house. That was amazing.

Trick stood back and let her go in first. She walked into a living room furnished with two worn couches and an overstuffed chair abutting a black theater curtain and facing a coffee table piled with books and a laptop. Across the room, a TV screen indicated that the laptop was ready to play. The wall flush with the door and the one opposite were covered with bookshelves crammed with books, cans of brushes, and tubes of oil paint.

"Wow. This is all yours?"

"Casa Trick," he confirmed. "Velcome. I invite you in, my Grecian goddess."

Eric and the girls had dogpiled on the sofas with three other kids in costume.

"Okay, roll it," Eric called out.

"Do you know the story of *Dark of the Moon*?" Trick asked Katelyn. "And I don't mean the third Transformers movie. I'm talking about the play. John is a witch boy and he's in love with a mortal girl."

"A Transformers movie in Russian would have so much more depth," Katelyn quipped, and he grinned at her.

"Oh, I *like* you, Kat McBride," he murmured in her ear. "I like you beyond liking."

She felt his breath on her ear and joy rushed through her. Then he moved away, holding her hand, leading her toward the laptop.

"We're the two witches who want him for their own, of course," Marie Curie told her. "And Eric is the Conjur Man."

Katelyn grinned. It reminded her of some of the things that kids at her old high school had done. Maybe she should be hanging with the drama kids.

An image came on the screen. It was Trick, barefoot, wearing a pair of jeans and a white wife beater, with his hair slicked back away from his forehead. An eagle feather dangled from his ear. He looked older. She loved the deep tan color of his skin, the length of his neck, and his broad chest. He was so hot that she felt a little embarrassed and looked away.

In the video, the Curies were wearing leotards and tights—one all in white, one in black—and big wigs that made them look like Kabuki dancers. They were singing and Trick was speaking, all in Russian.

"My character is asking the Conjur Man to turn him into a human," Trick explained. "So he can marry the girl he loves."

She listened to the Russian and found it beautiful. He was so breathtaking she couldn't stop smiling.

The frame expanded to show Eric dressed in a leather robe with feathers in his hair. The witches coiled themselves sensuously around Trick's body, singing louder, as if to drown out his voice. He took a step toward Eric, and the witches clung to him.

Katelyn felt her cheeks grow pink, and the jealousy from earlier roared back.

Then the screen went black.

"What?" Marie Curie cried.

"Huh. How did that happen?" Eric said.

"Let me look." Trick gave Katelyn a squeeze and bent over the laptop. The kids on the couch made room for him as he sat down and typed on the keyboard.

Flushed, Katelyn was swaying, dizzy with happiness. This night was unbelievable. Maybe if she splashed some water on her face, it would help. "Where's the bathroom?" Katelyn asked one of the guys. She put her shoes on the floor and followed as he gestured toward the black curtain.

Katelyn hesitantly drew back the edge of the curtain nearest the door. She didn't know what to expect, but the room extended into what looked like an open loft—one large undefined space. She realized that this was Trick's bedroom. There were a large cherrywood canopy bed covered with a simple white bedspread and two pillows, and a nightstand piled with a crook-neck lamp and more books.

And sitting on a pedestal was something that made Katelyn freeze, her breath catching in her throat: a clay bust of her mother, Giselle Chevalier.

It was perfect. The sculptor had captured Giselle's classical features, her small turned-up nose, her cupid-bow lips, her huge expressive eyes. She was wearing the Spanish comb she'd had on in the photo taken of her dancing "Pavane for a Dead Princess"—the photo Katelyn knew had burned in the fire that had killed her mother.

Tears welled in her eyes, and her chest tightened as she walked over to it, extending her hand, pressing her fingers against the cheek. She closed her eyes as a tide of emotions crashed over her. Grief, sorrow, guilt, longing, love, joy: her mother.

Where on earth had Trick found it? And why?

"I didn't want you to see it yet," Trick said, coming up behind her. His breath was warm on her shoulder. "It's not finished."

"Oh, my God, did *you* make this?" she asked him, taking in her mother's young, hopeful expression, her eyes, her mouth. The memories.

"I found the picture on the net," he said. "It's for your birthday."

"How did you know . . . ?"

"Give me some credit, Kat."

He put his arms around her, leaning her back against his chest. His warmth penetrated, spread out. Then he bent his head and kissed her cheek, a gesture so tender, so loving . . . and it broke the dam inside her. She began to weep.

"I miss her so much. Oh, I miss her."

He moved around in front of her, careful not to block her view of the bust, and held her. She bundled herself against his chest, crying softly. He put his hand on the back of her head and cradled it.

"I'm sorry," she murmured, muffled against his chest. "At your party . . ."

"Shhh, it's all right." He stopped her. "It's what you need."

After a while, she quieted. Then she lifted her head and looked up at him, at the blue flecks in his green eyes, and her mouth parted. He kissed her, gently. She gathered up handfuls of his black shirt in her fists and raised herself on tiptoe, meeting him. He caught his breath and tightened his arms around her.

"Invite me in," he said.

"Trick," she replied, then, "Vladimir."

He kissed her again, testing. She put one hand around his neck; the other clutched his T-shirt. He groaned, low and deep. Then his mouth came down hard on hers. Warmth flash-fired into heat; comfort burst into passion. She put her other arm around his neck and they kept kissing, catching breath, exhaling through each other. He held her, cradled her, wanted her.

"Katelyn," he said, using her full name. No one in Wolf Springs called her that.

"Yes," she whispered, covering his face with kisses.

"Katelyn, oh," Trick whispered, and her heart began to pump so loudly that she couldn't hear his words. It was like the drumming in the woods; it was her pulse, racing. She kissed his cheek, then covered his face with more kisses. She wanted him closer. She wanted to do things she had never done. She wanted to do them with him.

Now.

"Whoa," Trick murmured. His forehead was beaded with sweat, and his breath came in hitches. "We need to slow down, Katelyn."

Mortified, she pulled away. What was *wrong* with her?

And then, as if they were in a movie she was watching, she saw the framed pictures of her mother jittering on the walls of their house as it collapsed. They morphed and blended into the photos Cordelia had shown her of her family.

And Cordelia's words: *I asked to bring him in, but my dad said no.*

Trick closed up the space between them, putting his arms

around her. She could smell her own scent on his T-shirt. The vein in his neck was throbbing. His pupils were dilated.

"I said slow down, not stop," he said, kissing her forehead, each eyelid, her right temple. He kissed the tears on her cheeks. "I promised your grandfather I would treat you with respect."

My grandfather. My life. If it's happened, what will happen to us? What would Mr. Fenner do to him?

She pushed Trick away. But she'd pushed harder than she'd realized, and he staggered backward, arms windmilling. His eyes were wide with surprise and hurt.

"Katelyn," he began.

"I'm Kat," she said in a hoarse, agonized voice. "That's who I am now."

Fresh tears obscured her vision as she ran for the door.

"Katelyn!" he shouted after her.

＊＊＊＊＊＊

She ran.

Into the crazy lights and noise and music, Katelyn ran in her bare feet. Frosty dew sparkled on the grass. She smelled the night; the moon, not yet full, hung overhead like a luminous fist ready to crush her. Her body was on fire. Surges of adrenaline made her shiver and gasp. She felt as if she needed to throw herself into ice water to cool down.

Across the pasture she stumbled, weaving around startled, costumed partygoers. A jagged parade of maples beckoned her with their shadows. Without thinking twice, she ran in among them, sending showers of leaves bursting around her like fireworks.

Then she bolted into the safety of the darkness, falling

against a tree, gasping for air. Shaking from head to toe, she couldn't seem to clear her vision; everything was blurry, and her heart was beating so hard she was afraid it would tear out of her chest.

"Hey, girl," said a familiar voice.

From the inky darkness, dark blue eyes blazed at her.

Justin.

Before she realized what was happening, he stepped directly into her path. He was wearing a dark suit with a white shirt unbuttoned at the neck. It set off the chiseled angles of his face and accentuated the deep blue sapphire of his eyes.

"I'm looking for Cordelia," he said. "Her father called her a bunch of times. Have you seen her?"

She should move away. She knew it. But it seemed all she could do was stand stock-still, as if she were waiting for him to come to her.

And then he did.

She saw his lips, close up. They were parted; they looked warm and moist.

Without warning, he kissed her.

And she kissed him back. As if Trick didn't exist . . .

As if Lucy didn't exist.

He pressed his body closer to hers and all thought fled.

He picked her up in his arms and carried her into the brush, the way he had come, kissing her all the while. And she kissed him back.

She kissed him back.

"Did I scare you just now?" he asked, his lips against hers. "Oh, Kat, Kat, I can't *not* do this. . . ."

And those words made her heart beat faster with new fear. This was wrong. It was a bad dream. But he bent down and kissed her and she poured her soul into kissing him back. And before she knew how it happened, she was lying on the forest floor and he was on top of her, his body pinning hers down, and his kisses had become harder, more intense, and she knew what he wanted, because she wanted it too.

I don't want to want it. I don't want this. I want Trick.

"Justin, stop," she managed to gasp.

And then a shadow darkened her vision. "What do you think you're doing?" a voice thundered.

15

Katelyn looked up and saw Cordelia standing over the two of them, her features twisted in fury. Katelyn had never seen her so angry.

"You have a girlfriend!" Cordelia shouted at Justin, who was already on his feet, his arms out, as if to plead his innocence. Then she turned her wrath on Katelyn. "And you know it!"

"Cordelia, please, something's happening to me," Katelyn said in a rush as she sat up. Her words felt slurry, but her senses were on high alert. "Please, help me!"

"You called Bobby to tell me to meet you here," Cordelia

said, flinging the words at Justin. "Why? So you could cheat on Lucy with a witness?"

"Your dad sent me," Justin said. "He needs you home. We've been calling you, but you didn't answer your phone."

Without a word, Cordelia whirled on her heel and stomped away.

"Cor, wait," Justin called, running after her.

Katelyn pushed herself to her feet to go after the two of them. Tingling, numb, ashamed, and confused, she lurched forward. Her right foot came down on a sharp twig; it pierced her instep like a knife and she gasped and stumbled, falling sideways and catching herself with a branch. Leaves scattered.

"Cordelia," she called. The branch snapped and she fell on her butt. She pulled the twig out of her foot and wrapped her hands around her instep to ease the pain, then shut her eyes against the images of Justin and her that strobed in her mind.

She adjusted her purse, got to her feet, and took an experimental step forward. It hurt, but she limped out of the forest, back into the pasture, grimacing as her foot throbbed.

Heavy metal horror music swelled and soared around her as she neared the barn, scanning the crowd of kids for Cordelia. She'd seen her angry before, but never so enraged. What would Cordelia do? Would she lose her temper and say something, do something?

Katelyn had to get to her; she had to explain.

She spotted Dondi sitting on a picnic table and limped over to her.

"Have you seen Cordelia and her cousin?" Katelyn yelled over the music.

"Yeah. They went to the parking lot," Dondi shouted back. "What happened to *you?*"

But Katelyn didn't answer; she just gave her a wave of thanks and kept going. Past the barn, down the walkway. Her foot throbbed and her mind raced. She felt like she was careening out of control, like all her emotions were colliding together.

How could she be kissing Trick one minute and then Justin the next? What was happening to her?

She hurried toward the path that led to the parking lot. A single taillight winked in the blackness—a motorcycle's—and she made out two figures riding tandem as it pulled out onto the main road. Justin and Cordelia.

The night swallowed them up, and Katelyn stood shell-shocked, with no idea what to do next. Go home? Go back to the party? Go to Cordelia's and try to talk it out? She clenched her hands, feeling sick and scared and frustrated. There was no way she was going back to the party now. Performing her own zombie walk, she crossed the parking lot and made her way to her car. She was about to climb in behind the wheel when she noticed a small glowing rectangle lying on the ground by the front tire. She threw her purse into the car and went to pick it up.

It was Cordelia's cell phone. Katelyn pressed the home button.

No service.

She got in her car and turned on the engine. Her feet were sore and icy. She looked down at the phone again, trying to decide what to do. Cordelia was always careful to have her phone with her. Though if she'd gone home to have it out with Justin in front of her dad, what would she need her phone for?

The realization of the situation hit Katelyn with all its force then. *What if Cordelia decides she has to tell her father about me now? What if she's so mad she tells him on purpose to get rid of me?*

Katelyn could only hope that maybe when Cordelia got home, she would call either her own phone or Katelyn's. She got her cell out of her purse and set the two side by side on the passenger seat. Then she backed out of her spot, took one last look at the illuminated barn, and drove out of the parking lot.

She couldn't figure out why Cordelia had been as pissed as she was. Lucy wasn't her sister or best friend. Tearing off her crown of gold leaves, she bit her lip to keep from crying as she doggedly retraced the route they had taken to get there. After about ten minutes, she realized that she wasn't sure how to go from the Sokolovs' property to her grandfather's cabin without going to Cordelia's house first. So maybe she was meant to go to Cordelia now and try to talk to her.

Except Justin will be there.

Despite everything, just thinking of him enflamed her again. She kept going, trying to decide what to do when she got closer to Cordelia's, crossing her fingers that Cordelia would have called her from the Fenners' landline by then—or already had, and had left a message. She wouldn't be able to tell until she had cell phone coverage.

As she drove, she began to recognize landmarks and little by little was able to calm down. Just when she was sure she knew where she was, a call came in on her phone. Trick. Sucking in her breath, she answered.

"Katelyn. Where are you?" he asked, worry threading his voice.

"I'm okay. I'm—I left," she said, her voice cracking.

"Where are you?"

"In my car, driving," she said. She wanted to tell him everything but couldn't.

"I didn't mean to come on so strong," he said.

Her cheeks burned. She'd been the one who'd kicked it up.

"Your shoes are here," he continued.

"Can you bring them to school?" It was all she could say before her voice gave out.

"So you're not coming back?"

She let her silence be her answer.

"Is Cordelia with you?"

She hesitated. "She's on a motorcycle ahead of me," she said carefully.

There was a pause. "Her cousin's motorcycle?"

"Trick, let's talk later. Please."

Another pause. "Are you going home alone in the dark?"

"We'll talk later," she repeated. "I'm driving. I have to go."

"Not loving that," he said. "But I . . ."

She sucked in her breath. Cordelia's house was ahead, and it was all lit up.

"Gotta go," she repeated, and hung up.

She drove up the crest of the hill in front of Cordelia's house. But when she got to the top, she saw that the side of the road was lined with trucks and cars, which was strange. There hadn't been anyone there when they'd left. Were the Fenners having a party?

She pulled over to the side of the road the first chance she got, squeezed both phones into her purse, and opened the door. She got out and hobbled toward the drive, where she noticed that Justin's motorcycle was parked in the grass among other cars and trucks.

About halfway down, Katelyn spotted Cordelia's truck and considered what to do. Maybe she could put the phone on the hood or, better yet, drop it beside Justin's motorcycle so it would seem as if Cordelia had had it with her when she'd left Trick's, and dropped it when she got home.

Or maybe she should just leave.

Uncertain, she took a few tentative steps toward Justin's motorcycle. Then she spotted two guys at the top of the drive—one older, one younger, unaware of her, it seemed—unintentionally blocking the path of her retreat. One was wearing a suit, and the other had on a dark long-sleeved shirt and jeans. She ducked between cars, clenching her teeth at the pain that shot through her foot.

These people could be werewolves. Her heart skipped beats. *Maybe one of them is the werewolf who attacked me.*

"He must be planning to announce the succession," said the older man. He had honey wheat–colored hair and a white-flecked beard. "Why else would he call everyone so last minute?" He glared at the younger man. "You should have worn a suit."

"Are you kidding, Dad? Cordelia would just laugh at me."

Katelyn felt dizzy. These men seemed so normal. But they weren't even human. She had to get out of there. Now—before she was discovered.

The older man exhaled in frustration. "It's not Cordelia I'm thinking of, Steve. Lee's given you cause to hope." His teeth gleamed in the moonlight as he smiled. "That gal is our ticket to pack royalty."

"Only if the alpha picks her to lead," the younger man—Steve—replied. "And, like, no offense, but Cordelia isn't my type."

"Don't be an idiot!" Steve's father hit him on the side of the head. "You don't have the luxury of *types*."

Even from her vantage point, Katelyn heard the force of the blow and winced, hard. What would happen if they found her there?

"Dad," Steve protested. "Being mated to the alpha would suck."

"Are you *insane*? Our lives would be set."

"Unless someone decided to challenge me for her," Steve retorted.

"You young people are so pampered," his father said, sighing. "In my day, we fought for every position in the hierarchy we achieved."

"But don't you think that's kind of barbaric?" Steve asked.

His father hit him again, harder.

"Stop that," his father said. "Stop it or next hunt I'll take skin."

Katelyn shivered; the implication was clear. She was afraid she was going to be sick to her stomach. She would give anything to be back in her car, or at the party. It had been insanity to follow them here.

Steve straightened. Without another word, the two began walking along the side of the drive opposite Justin's motorcycle. Katelyn's stomach flipped as she crouched as low as she could and hurried farther down the drive, holding on to a dark blue truck for balance at one point, praying she didn't set off anyone's car alarm. Then she noticed the stand of trees beside the house and considered just making a run for it. She was so frightened she wondered if she'd be able to move at all. She thought of Haley and Becky, mauled to death, and pursed her lips to hold her fear in.

"Daniel. Steve," said a third voice. It was a woman's. "What on earth is going on? Everyone's here. I had to park practically a mile away."

"Too bad it's not a full moon," the man—Daniel—replied. "We wouldn't have needed cars."

Her fear making her awkward, Katelyn continued to creep forward until she was only a couple of feet from a thickly limbed pine tree located about midway along the exterior wall of the house. She hazarded a glance in the direction of the newcomers. The woman had on a short ruffled dress and heels, and more people were coming down the walk. There was no way she could go back up the drive.

Taking a deep breath, she made for the shield of the pine, careful not to shake the branches as she maneuvered her way behind it.

"Well, Steve, what do you think?" the woman said conversationally. "Time to declare for Cordelia?"

"She'd be a fool not to leap at the chance," Daniel said, his voice considerably lighter. "Look at him. He took down a deer all by himself last moon." He cleared his throat. "*You* don't have any theories about what's going on, do you, Myrna?"

"Hi, people, hi," interrupted a cheery voice Katelyn knew well. It was Jesse.

With trembling hands, Katelyn parted the branches so she could get a good look at him. He was dressed in a suit with his hair carefully combed, and he greeted the trio each with a kiss on the cheek, which they returned.

"Happy Halloween," Jesse said.

"Same to you, Jesse," the woman answered.

"Mr. Gaudin is here. You can't call him Dominic. Don't kiss him," Jesse informed them.

Katelyn sucked in her breath. Dominic? As in *Dom*? Cordelia's crush? The rival pack leader?

"What?" Daniel sounded as shocked as Katelyn was.

Steve looked as if he wanted to throw up. "He won't challenge me over Cordelia, will he, Dad?"

"The Gaudins are savages. Invaders," the woman— Myrna—said. Her voice had risen to a shrill pitch. "I'm leaving."

Savages? Katelyn was about to burst apart in a frenzy of panic. She felt like a caged bird with cats slinking around her, about to spring.

"Our alpha summoned us," Daniel reminded her. "You need to be here. And Steve, calm down. Dominic Gaudin has as much chance of marrying Cordelia as Jesse."

"I don't want to marry Cordelia. I want to marry Lucy," Jesse said very seriously.

"Jesse?" Katelyn heard Lucy before she saw her. Lucy, whose boyfriend she wanted. She was dressed in a frilly white blouse and a black velvet skirt. Her hair was pulled back in a complicated braid, and a black feather perched on the side of her head. "Oh, hello," Lucy said nervously as she saw the rest of the group. "Dominic Gaudin's here."

Katelyn stared at Lucy, and an unreasoning hatred toward

the other girl broke over her like a wave. She bit her lip, trying to control the anger that raged through her. *What's wrong with me?* she wondered. *Justin is her boyfriend, not mine. If anybody should be angry, it should be her.* Katelyn wanted to take a deep breath but she was terrified of making even the tiniest sound.

"We just heard," Steve said.

"*Why* is he here?" Myrna asked in a hushed voice. "What do they want?"

"To see every one of us dead," Daniel muttered.

"He came under a white flag. So let's be pleasant, shall we?" Lucy was smiling, but she looked worried. Then she turned and led the way around to the back of the house. Everyone followed her except for Jesse.

"Is someone hiding?" he asked excitedly. He started walking toward where Katelyn was crouched behind the tree. "Here I come, trick or treat!"

Chills rushed down Katelyn's spine. Her scalp prickled and her face went numb. Moving as quietly as she could, she limped over to the next tree. It took her toward the back of the house—farther away from escape—but Jesse kept coming, and more waves of fear rippled through her. She crept along, trying not to make any noise, moving from tree to tree, terrified of discovery. Then she reached the side of the house, near the back door. She tucked herself close to the building, beneath one of the boxes with purple flowers. The smell of pine wafted over her and she sniffed the planter. It was the *flowers* that smelled like Christmas trees.

"Jesse!" Lucy called. "C'mon, baby!"

"Smell my feet!" Jesse bellowed. "Give me something good to eat!"

He was getting closer. Fighting to keep control, Katelyn continued along behind the trees, focusing only on staying hidden and being as quiet as she could manage. Her lungs were bursting. Other voices grew louder, and there were many of them. She had worked her way around to the back of the house, where everyone was congregating.

"Jesse James Fenner!" Lucy shouted. "You come here *now*!"

"Don't yell, don't yell," Jesse said.

Abandoning his game, Jesse trotted away. And Katelyn exhaled, leaning against a tree trunk. Tears slid down her cheeks as her knees began to give way.

A howl pierced the chatter and she jerked hard. A second howl answered it. A third, fourth, fifth. Human voices raised in a mournful, fierce chorus, like Jack Bronson and his Inner Wolf executives. Trembling, Katelyn covered her ears and ordered herself not to scream. She was more afraid than she'd been in the forest, when the wolf had attacked her. Were these the howls she had heard night after night—the cries of a werewolf pack?

Then the howls abruptly stopped, almost as if someone had signaled for it.

Katelyn gingerly moved a branch, then another, so that she could peer through the pine needles to see. There were probably twenty people—*werewolves*—seated on haphazardly arranged folding chairs. Some were formally dressed in suits and sophisticated black dresses. Others wore jeans.

One of them is the one. Coldness settled in the pit of her stomach, a fury that couldn't be denied. *If it was a werewolf,* she reminded herself, trying to regain some semblance of control. She looked, working to memorize the faces so she'd know them if she saw them again.

On a small wooden platform, at a black metal patio table and some matching black chairs, Cordelia sat with her father, Justin, Lucy, Jesse, Arial, Al, Regan, and the man who had to be the only bitten member of the pack—Regan's husband, Doug. Doug had dark hair and piercing brown eyes, very much like Regan herself. The five men, including Justin, wore suits. Moonlight gleamed down on Justin's hair, frosting it with silvery highlights.

Arial wore a gold halter dress, and Regan was slinky in black satin. Beside Lucy, Cordelia was wearing the same black dress that she'd worn to Trick's Halloween party, with the flower in her hair. It fit the occasion perfectly.

"I'd like to welcome y'all and thank y'all for coming out on such short notice," Lee Fenner said, standing. "We're here to welcome the Gaudin alpha, Dominic, to our mountains."

Polite applause greeted him. Clearly the guests were waiting to see exactly what kind of occasion this was.

Katelyn shifted her line of sight to get a better look and saw that someone else was sitting at the head table. He was seated between Cordelia and her father, and he was muscular, young, and very, very hot. His reddish-gold hair tumbled to his broad shoulders like a setting sun. His forehead was high, his eyebrows brown, and although Katelyn couldn't tell what color his eyes were, she could tell that they were light. He wore a white open-necked silk shirt and black trousers that together looked almost 1930s, and a brass cuff glinted on his right wrist.

"Greetings from the Gaudin pack," he said, getting to his feet. There was a lilt to his voice, sounding almost French. "I lead the pack in the name of my late father, Jean-Marc Gaudin."

"Your daddy was a fine alpha," Lee Fenner said, but his voice was strained. "A legend." There was more polite applause, and the two men sat down.

"The Son of Gévaudan has come to discuss pack business with me," Mr. Fenner said to the group. "But first, we have our own pack business. Don't we, girls?"

Arial and Regan looked at each other, both smiling like smug Siamese cats. They looked back at their father with gleaming eyes, and Katelyn shuddered at the sight.

It looked as if all the blood had left Cordelia's cheeks. She squirmed in her chair, and Justin reached across the table and squeezed her hand. Without realizing what she was doing, Katelyn touched her lips, still bruised from Justin's kisses. A hot flare of desire shot through her and she shivered, shocked at the effect he had on her.

"My daughters have grown into fine women," Mr. Fenner said, smiling at all three of them. "And one of them will become the Fenris alpha. As you know, loyalty is our highest virtue. And here's one more test for my daughters. Exactly that. A test of loyalty."

"Daddy," Cordelia blurted out, turning scarlet. "Um, maybe we shouldn't—"

A gasp went through the group. Dominic's brows rose, and he grinned.

"Are you challenging me?" Lee Fenner thundered.

"No, Daddy, no!" Cordelia cried, and visibly cringed in her chair. Justin half rose and extended his arms as if to shield her, then dropped his hands to his sides and submissively lowered his head.

"Who is alpha here?" Mr. Fenner shouted at her.

But before she could answer, he spun on his heel and marched away, opened up the back door, and stormed into the house. The door slammed hard behind him and no one spoke. No one moved.

Oh, my God. Katelyn shivered. *What if he hurts her?*

As Katelyn watched him go, she realized that the trees she was crouched behind were clustered in front of the sliding glass door that led to Cordelia's room. When Cordelia had first brought her home, Katelyn had thought the door led out into the woods, but she'd been wrong. If she remained where she was, she would be visible through the glass. But if she went inside, quickly, and hid, she might be safe—at least temporarily.

Cordelia got to her feet, and Katelyn watched as she started toward the house.

As the guests murmured among themselves, Katelyn made her move. She crawled through the trees, pushed open the glass door, and slipped into Cordelia's darkened room. The cool, bare floor was a blessing for her injured foot.

"You've got some nerve," Mr. Fenner's voice bellowed from down the hall. Katelyn ducked. The door that connected Cordelia's room to the hall was ajar.

"Don't try your intimidation tactics on me." It was a male voice with an accent. It was Dominic, and he sounded calm. "I came with a white flag."

"You came to stir up trouble," Mr. Fenner yelled. "Last-minute safe passage. Any fool with manners knows the way these things are done."

"Your pack has snuck onto my land repeatedly to dump silver in our streams. This time I brought evidence," Dominic shouted back.

"You're a liar. You'd poison your own people and say we did it."

"Daddy," Cordelia pleaded. *"Please."*

Katelyn heard the sound of a slap.

"One more sound out of you and I will take your throat. Do you understand me?" Mr. Fenner raged.

Katelyn bit back a gasp. The thought of being slapped by her father—or her grandfather, even—was beyond her.

"Leave her alone!" Dominic bellowed. "Or so help me—"

"Are you challenging me, boy? This is *my* daughter and *my* pack."

"*And* one of your pack attacked a human," Dominic said steadily. "That is expressly forbidden by both our packs. *All* the packs."

Katelyn's heart stuttered. *He knows about me. How could he know about me? Cordelia couldn't have told him, could she?*

"Another lie," Lee Fenner said angrily. "That's all you got? Lies?"

"With all due respect," Dominic replied, "we have proof that the sons of the Fenris Wolf have trespassed on our property. And that a human girl named Becky Jensen was mauled to death by one of you."

Katelyn sagged in relief. *Not me. They're not talking about me.* She closed her eyes for a moment. *But what about Haley?*

"Another lie! You're just like your father!" Mr. Fenner was nearly screaming.

"And I thank the Beast for that," Dominic replied. "Face it, Fenner. You've lost control. To humiliate your daughters like that—"

"*I* wasn't humiliated," Regan said.

Katelyn was startled. She hadn't realized others had come inside.

"Cordelia was right to stop you," Dominic insisted.

"She doesn't love me. She's never loved me!" Mr. Fenner bellowed.

"Daddy," Cordelia pleaded.

"If you opened your eyes, you'd see she's the only one who really cares about you," Dominic said. "Listen, alpha, I won't put up with attacks on my people. But it's not too late to take another tack. If Cordelia and I got married—"

"Never! I'd kill her before I'd let you have anything of mine! Cordelia, go to your room," he shouted. *"Now."*

Katelyn jerked. She couldn't let Cordelia know she'd heard all that. She needed to hide.

Clutching her purse to her chest, she lurched forward and ran into the edge of Cordelia's desk. A book wobbled and she grabbed it, tucked it under her bag.

Light footsteps sounded in the hall. They grew louder, echoing in her ears like drums until the sound was unbearable. She lowered herself to the floor, lay on her back, then scooted beneath the bed seconds before Cordelia stormed in and flicked on the light.

Katelyn held her breath as the other girl flopped onto the

bed. Down the hallway, the two men were still arguing. Katelyn barely breathed, hugging the book and her purse. She could hear her friend crying above her and wished she could offer some kind of words of comfort. But she knew there was nothing she could do.

· — ·≡·◆·≡· — ·

Katelyn listened to Cordelia's gentle breathing for what seemed like hours before she dared to scoot out from beneath her bed. She left Cordelia's phone for her on top of the book, which she very quietly put back on the corner of the desk. Moonlight shone in through the large glass doors and hit the gold letters that spelled out the title on the book's cover, illuminating them: *Ozark Folklore. Theodore Switliski.*

It was the book Mr. Henderson had asked them about. Cordelia had had it and hadn't told Katelyn.

She snuck out through the sliding glass door, pulling it as closed as she dared, and raced to her car. Once inside the Subaru, she opened her overnight bag, found her Mary Janes, and slipped them on; then she drove the long way home through the dense black forest, her mind whirling with everything that had happened. Dom had thanked the "beast" that he wasn't like Mr. Fenner. Did he mean the Hellhound?

Shivering, tears sliding down her face, Katelyn made it home and grabbed her bag as she went inside. Her grandfather's door was shut, and she heard gentle breathing. She went back downstairs and picked up the phone, trying to decide if she should call Cordelia. Exhaling, she put it back. Then she checked the back door to make sure it was locked.

An hour went by. Another. She paced, her attention caught

by the rows of paintings in the front room. Something tugged at her memory as she glanced at the one with the deer and the strangely shaped boulder. Then she went back to the kitchen and looked at the dog leash in the drawer.

Then the phone rang and she grabbed it.

"Kat, are you okay?" Cordelia whispered over the line.

Relief flooded through her and words tumbled out of her mouth. "Yes, I'm so sorry, Cordelia. I don't know what happened with Justi—"

"Oh, God, oh, my God," Cordelia said in a rush. "I was so scared for you. I saw my phone and I smelled your blood—"

"*You smelled my blood?*" Katelyn said, shocked.

"And then I saw it, in the window."

"Saw what?" Katelyn asked her, suddenly even more afraid.

"It was here. It was here *at our house*. I thought it had gotten you."

"What? What was it?"

But the line went dead.

16

Katelyn tried to call Cordelia back, but all her calls went straight to voice mail. She didn't sleep the rest of the night; she only paced. Her thoughts bounced from Trick, to the bust of her mother, to their kisses; then to Justin in the woods, and then the scene at the Fenner house. The way Dom and Mr. Fenner had spoken, in that strange, formal way. Threatening each other. Mr. Fenner slapping Cordelia.

In the morning, her grandfather came into the kitchen, holding her overnight bag.

"I'm surprised to see you home so early," he said.

"Yeah, I just got back a little while ago," she said quickly, so he wouldn't ask her if she'd driven through the woods at night by herself.

"Didn't go so well?"

"No," she said, shaking her head. She would act out his assumptions, let him think she'd come home defeated. Avoiding his gaze, she added, "It's hard to fit in at a new school." It was certainly the truth.

"Yeah, I know," he said, putting down her bag. He clucked against his teeth sympathetically. Then he gestured to her to follow him. "Come with me."

Outside on the porch, she spotted the hated rifle. Then she saw that he had hacked some of the branches from the tree directly facing the house. Against the bare trunk, he had pinned up a paper target.

"Okay. Final exam," he said. "You hit that any way you can."

It seemed weird that they would do this first thing in the morning, before coffee. He'd obviously put it all together for when she returned home. Strangely, though, she realized she was ready; she really did need to be able to do this. Trying to hide how shaky she was, she picked up the weapon and took aim.

The landline rang, and she jerked hard. She moved her gaze to her grandfather, who smiled indulgently.

"Must be a friend of yours," he said. "I don't get a lot of calls."

She handed the rifle to him and raced into the house.

"I'm sorry about last night." Cordelia's voice was low and strained, but it sent relief flooding through Katelyn. "I had to go."

"Oh, my God, Cordelia. What's happening?" Katelyn asked.

"I'll tell you later. I just wanted you to know I'm okay." Cordelia hung up before Katelyn could say anything else.

Katelyn let out a breath she hadn't realized she'd been holding. She hung the phone on the cradle, then placed the flat of her hand on her chest, willing her heart to stop slamming against her rib cage. Then she smoothed back her hair and rejoined her grandfather on the porch.

Ed raised a questioning brow, to which Katelyn shrugged lightly.

"Cordelia," she told him. "Girl stuff."

"On top of boy stuff?" he asked.

"Yeah."

"That's too bad," he said, sounding genuinely sympathetic.

She knew he was still wondering what had happened at Trick's. He handed her the rifle and she took aim. The shot went wide. She tried again. She hit the lower right corner of the target. Frustrated, she set down the weapon—business end well out of the dirt—then suddenly raised it to shooting position, aimed, held her breath, and fired.

She hit the bull's-eye.

For a moment, neither of them moved. Then Ed let out a whoop, fished in the pocket of his plaid shirt, and held up two paper tickets.

"Cirque du Soleil, Little Rock, three weeks. We'll make a weekend of it."

She threw her arms around his neck in a rush of gratitude. Getting away from this place was just what she needed. "Thank you, Grandpa. So much."

He held her tightly. "You're welcome, honey."

Once breakfast was done, she tried to nap, but she was too wired. Trick called and wanted to come over, but she put him off. After what had happened with Justin in the woods, she couldn't handle seeing him—but more than that, she had to keep her distance until she knew one way or the other if she was going to become one of *them*.

"No," she whispered as Justin's face flared in her mind. It wasn't a question of Trick *or* Justin. Trick was honorable, and good. *And not androgynous.* She smiled wanly at the old joke between them. She wanted to be with Trick; it felt like she'd known him forever. But if this thing happened to her, she couldn't be. She'd have a secret life, and he could have no part in it.

And Justin? Why didn't she have the power just to push him away? Why didn't she hate him because he was a cheating jerk? There was something about him that pulled her to him. She didn't know how to explain how she felt.

Then Cordelia called again.

"I can't talk long. I have to be careful," she whispered.

"Tell me about what you saw," Katelyn insisted. *"Now."*

"It—I thought it was just one of us," Cordelia said. "At first. I was asleep, and I jerked awake. I smelled your blood and I freaked out. I sat up in my bed . . . and I saw two blue eyes staring through the window. I thought it might be Dom, and I started to get up. There was a wolf shape. And then . . . it all changed. It was like all I saw were the eyes, and it was surrounded by shadows, like you said. *Exactly* like you said, Kat. And all of a sudden, I was more terrified than I had ever been in my entire life. And I screamed bloody murder."

Katelyn's eyes widened as she gripped the phone. "What happened next?"

"It vanished. Just like that. Then my father and my sisters came into my room. My father went outside to look and my sisters started yelling at me, saying I was making it up to get attention so Dad would forgive me."

"Do you think it was the Hellhound?" Katelyn whispered.

She exhaled. "I'm not even sure what I saw. Just talking about it scares me all over again."

"But, Cordelia," Katelyn said. "What if it—"

"When were you in my room?" Cordelia interrupted her.

Katelyn licked her lips. "After you saw . . . us, and you left, I came after you. You dropped your cell phone in the parking lot. I—I was so scared you were going to say something. . . ."

"Katelyn, oh, my God, of course I wouldn't have. Justin came to get me because Dom was coming to our house. My father and Justin had been calling me, but of course I didn't get the calls. So Justin called Bobby, and Bobby found me. That was when I realized my phone was missing."

"I was going to leave it near Justin's motorcycle. So it would look like it had fallen out of your purse," Katelyn said. "Then all those"—she didn't know what to call Cordelia's pack mates—"people started showing up, and I had to hide." Her throat tightened, and she tried to discreetly clear it. "I heard what your father said to Dominic."

"He's losing his mind," Cordelia whispered. "I'm not sure Dom should have said what he did." She started to cry. "Everything's horrible. I'm so scared."

"I'm so sorry about Justin," Katelyn said in a rush. "I didn't mean for it to happen. He started kissing me and I just couldn't stop."

"No, I'm sorry I freaked," Cordelia said, sniffling. "We have strict rules in our pack for everything, including loyalty to a mate. Disloyalty is the biggest crime. You can get the death penalty for it."

"Oh, my God." Katelyn was horrified. She shut her eyes. This was way more than she was prepared to deal with. She changed the subject.

"When I was in your room, I saw the Switliski book Mr. Henderson mentioned."

Cordelia didn't answer right away. "Yeah. Um, I found it in my dad's library when I came home from Trick's last night," she said. "Before the party started. I went in there to ask my dad what was going on. Dom was in our bathroom and the pack was gathering. The name on the spine just jumped out at me. Switliski. So I took it."

Katelyn didn't believe it. How would Cordelia have had enough time to do all that between arriving home and being outside where Katelyn saw her with her family? But at the same time, why would Cordelia lie?

"Does your father know you took it?" she asked, fishing for more information.

"I don't think so. I've never seen him like this, Kat. He's never been this bad."

"Oh, Cordelia." Katelyn's heart broke for her friend again. They were both in such a terrible place.

"I'm sorry, Kat," she added, her voice wavering. "Sorry you've been dragged into all this."

"I know," Katelyn said sincerely. "And I'm sorry for you, too."

"Thank you," Cordelia murmured. "I've never had a friend like you before."

Katelyn smiled, but it was a sad smile. "Me neither, Cordelia." Which was the truth. She didn't think it was possible, but she hung up feeling even worse for Cordelia than for herself.

Since Katelyn had a car now, Trick didn't need to chauffeur her to school on Monday. And she was relieved beyond the telling that she didn't have to face him first thing in the morning.

He met her in the parking lot, though, regarding her cautiously as he handed her the shoes she'd left at the party. She took them with a nod and dropped them into her car. She was quiet, guarded. And he didn't push, but strangely, she almost wished he would.

To her intense relief, Cordelia was there and turning in their final paper when she got to history. They gave each other a tight hug, and after class, they walked toward the gym.

"Are you okay?" Katelyn asked.

Cordelia grimaced. "Things are . . . tense . . . at home. How about you?"

"I'm—"

Before Katelyn could answer, someone crashed into her from behind, sending her careering into Cordelia. As Katelyn regained her balance, she saw Mike barreling ahead of her, shoving others out of the way as well. Anger exploded within her. She jumped forward, ready to chase him down and deck him. She was going to grind her heel into his face, but Cordelia grabbed her shoulders and yanked her back before she could take off.

"Let me go." Katelyn struggled to break out of her friend's tight grip.

"Even if you do manage to hurt him, the war will never end."

Katelyn turned to glare at Cordelia, a retort on her lips, but it was choked off when she saw the naked fear in her friend's eyes.

"What?" she asked.

Cordelia swallowed hard. "Increased aggression . . . that's not a good sign."

Katelyn pressed her trembling hands to her face, feeling her smooth skin, her jaw and cheekbones. "I'm turning, aren't I?" She felt human to her touch but was sick to her soul. What was happening to her?

"I don't know, but it would make sense."

"You *sure* Mike's not . . . one? What if he's just by himself, not in your pack?"

"That'd be nice," Cordelia replied with a sour smile. "Lone werewolves don't last long." Her voice was strained, and Katelyn picked up on it.

"What's wrong?"

"That would be like a nightmare. I can't even imagine being without a pack." Cordelia swallowed hard. "If my father picks someone else to be our new alpha . . . like Justin . . . I don't know what will happen to me."

That surprised Katelyn. "Justin wouldn't make you go away, would he?"

"We shouldn't talk about this here," Cordelia murmured.

Katelyn took a deep breath. It seemed there was nowhere they *could* talk.

＊＊＊

Each passing day, each hour, each minute, Katelyn examined herself for more signs of impending transformation. She dreamed about Justin and Trick and silver and wolves and Kimi. She dreamed about her father and mother and woke up in tears. She asked Cordelia a couple of times to bring her the Switliski book, but she kept "forgetting."

Katelyn and Trick managed to avoid discussing Halloween—or much of anything, for that matter. He was always there, though, always looking concerned about her. And he was right to be concerned. The dreams continued, stranger, and more violent. As the days ticked by to the full moon, she realized just how much her life was on hold until she knew.

One way or the other.

＊＊＊

Her birthday came. Seventeen. It should have felt as if her whole life was before her instead of behind her. When she went downstairs that morning, she was surprised to find her grandfather had made strawberry pancakes in the shape of hearts. He looked proud and a little embarrassed at the same time and it made her smile.

"Thank you," she said, throwing her arms around his neck.

"Happy birthday, honey."

She shut her eyes against her tears. She had dreamed of a big, amazing life—performing and traveling the world. When she'd been dragged to Arkansas, she'd felt as if her life was over.

And at seventeen, she was now afraid that it really was.

At school, Trick wished her a happy birthday and said he'd drop her present by sometime over the weekend. The thought of the bust he was sculpting of her mother just made her want to cry more for all she had lost and all that she might be about to lose.

Days before the full moon had become hours; in a blur of fear and frustration, she counted them down as the moment of truth came rushing up at her.

When the sun rose Friday morning, Katelyn cursed it. It was the last sunrise she might see as a normal girl. She tried going back to sleep, but she could hear the sound of her grandfather's boots on the stairs. She flipped over and put her pillow over her ears. Minutes later, though, the smell of breakfast cooking drove her to her feet.

She quickly padded downstairs and entered the kitchen.

"Morning," she murmured.

"Morning," her grandfather said. "Your oatmeal will be done in a moment." He handed her a cup of coffee.

"What are you having?" she asked, sipping it.

"Scrambled eggs and bacon."

"That sounds good," she said, still tired.

He gave her a look. "The eggs?"

She shrugged. "No, the bacon."

"Are you feeling all right?" he asked her.

"Yeah," she said, then stopped. Fear skittered through her. Meat smelled good. She had just about asked him for some.

"Well, I suppose that's progress," he said with a grin. "By the way, the Subaru's got a flat, and I don't trust the spare—not for you. It looks soft. So I called Trick and he's coming to pick you up."

Her heart skipped in her chest. "What?"

"I figured it'll work out fine, since you're spending the night at Cordelia's."

She'd told him a couple of days earlier that Cordelia had invited her for an overnight. It was sort of true. She didn't know where she was actually going to be, just that Cordelia had promised to take her far away from the pack's hunting grounds.

She began to panic. "Is he already on his way? Maybe *you* could take me—"

"I reckon he is." He frowned. "You still got boy problems?"

There was no way she wanted to talk about it. She'd worked hard not to spend too much alone time together with her grandfather so they wouldn't have to talk about what was going on with her. She didn't trust herself not to break down around either him or Trick.

When she'd finished pretending to eat, she went back upstairs and slowly got dressed. She looked at herself in the mirror and saw the fear and uncertainty in her eyes. Anyone who looked at her for more than a second wouldn't be able to help seeing them, too. She vowed not to let Trick or her grandfather really look at her as she left the house.

Trick was quiet on the drive. He didn't play music. He

didn't talk to her. She squinted against the light of the new day streaming through the windshield. It seemed brighter to her, more garish, and she wished she'd brought sunglasses.

As they neared the school, her hearing went into overdrive. Even inside the Mustang, the voices and engines and radios overwhelmed her. She clenched her hands together and tried to get a grip.

"You okay?" Trick asked with a raised eyebrow.

"Just not feelin' school today, I guess," she answered, grinning weakly.

He pulled into the lot and parked, and before he could say anything else, she pushed open the door and climbed out. Without looking back at him, she began to walk. Noise bombarded her. But Trick's voice was absent from the tumult.

It was insane to her that she was in school on this day. She just had to hope that the act of going through her daily routine like everything was normal would help it feel normal, *be* normal. She knew it was crazy, but crazy was the only game in town.

She walked into her history class and froze just inside the door. Cordelia wasn't there. Someone shoved past her and she forced herself to move, take her seat. She turned and stared at the door. *It's okay, sometimes I get here before her,* she thought, trying to calm herself. But she could feel the panic winning. She needed Cordelia that day more than ever. *She wouldn't blow me off now, would she?*

She could hardly stay in her seat. Pulling out her cell phone, she texted her. There was no reply.

The bell rang. No Cordelia.

"Good morning, people," Mr. Henderson said. "I'm still going over your projects, so don't ask about your grades."

She turned around, realizing Cordelia wasn't coming to class. Beau caught her eye, nodded at her. Her vision telescoped. In extreme close-up, she saw Beau's jaw and ear—the individual pores and hairs of soft stubble. A wave of panic washed over her.

It's happening. It's happening.

Beau looked at her strangely, as if he thought she was trying to tell him something.

"Mr. Henderson," she said, turning back around, shooting her hand into the air. "I'm not feeling well. Maybe I should see Mrs. Walker."

He looked concerned. "Okay, sure."

She grabbed her bag and ran to the bathroom, where she splashed cold water on her face. Her heart was hammering away in her chest and she felt like her throat was closing. She could barely breathe. And yet she could smell the cleanser that the janitor used on the mirror, the minerals in the water.

I can't do this. I can't go through school today, not like this! She closed her eyes. She didn't have a car, which meant getting either Trick or her grandfather to take her home. And either way, she'd have questions to answer, and she'd have to come up with some fake illness that would still allow her to leave the house that night.

There was no use denying what was happening. She could feel every square inch of her skin where the air molecules touched it, and it terrified her.

When she had no more tears left, she washed her face.

After a moment's hesitation, she trudged toward the gym, hoping to find a quiet place in the bleachers to sit until class started. There was no way she was going to go see Mrs. Walker. What would she say? *I'm going to turn into a werewolf in a few hours. Do you have a pill for that?*

Halfway to the gym, her phone vibrated. She felt a wave of tremendous relief as she saw Cordelia's name in the caller ID plate. She accepted the call and, turning toward the wall, whispered fiercely, "Where are you?"

"I'm making sure everything is ready. How are you feeling?"

"It's happening. I know it. I can feel it. And I'm so scared."

Cordelia caught her breath. "I'll help you get through this. I'll be with you every step of the way, no matter what this is."

"Okay," Katelyn said, trying to choke down her fear.

"That's what friends do. They back you up, no matter what. Right?"

Katelyn was grateful for her words, but something seemed off. Cordelia's voice was tense. "Is there something wrong?"

"I'm trying to make sure I'm excused from the hunt," Cordelia said. "That's why I stayed home. I told my dad I'm sick, but he said he knows I'm afraid to hunt, because of . . ." Her voice trailed off.

"The Hellhound." Katelyn paced. She suddenly couldn't stop moving. If it had been the Hellhound that had bitten Katelyn, what would she become?

"Kat, even if it didn't attack you, what if it comes for *me* while we're alone? I've crossed all kinds of lines. I'm in the wrong."

Or me? Katelyn thought. Her throat went dry, and she found she couldn't make a sound. *I'm not supposed to have happened. I'm the thing that's wrong.*

Katelyn licked her lips. "Do you think we should just tell your father?"

"No!" Cordelia shouted into the phone. "No. He's—he's so bad today, Kat. He's just raging. Listen, let me tell you where to meet me. That'll be less sneaking around—"

"I don't have my car." She heard the panic in her own voice.

Cordelia pondered. "Okay. I'll pick you up after school." She lowered her voice and added hurriedly, "I have to go."

She hung up.

The day dragged on until finally it was lunch. Katelyn carried her sandwich and apple into the lunchroom. Immediately, Trick rose from his table of friends and took her hand. She resisted, but he pulled hard, and rather than make a scene, she finally went with him. They left the room and Trick led her to a private corner under the stained-glass window. The saint gazed down at them; beside him, the blue-eyed wolf looked on, too.

"Hey," Trick said. "So let's do it."

She blinked. "Excuse me?" She tried to focus on what he was saying.

"Talk about what happened. You liked it. And then you ran off. And ever since then, you've been looking like you're going to be hung by the neck until dead."

"Trick," she began, relieved that that was all he wanted to talk about. How she wished she could tell him what was happening to her. Cordelia had been a werewolf her entire life. How could she possibly understand what Katelyn was about to lose?

"We need to talk," he said, trying to look in her eyes.

She dropped her gaze to the floor. "I know, just not . . . now."

"Listen to me. I don't know what's wrong, but I'm here for you. *Katelyn.*"

She believed him. Maybe because when she glanced up, he looked so sincere or maybe because she needed to badly. She didn't know. But she couldn't stop herself from reaching out and touching his cheek. Something flickered in his eyes and then she leaned forward and kissed him.

She pulled back immediately.

I shouldn't have done that.

But then he was pulling her toward him, kissing her. And it felt good and right. She wrapped her arms around his neck and pressed her body close to his. It was what she wanted, and she needed him, needed this.

He pulled away, holding her at arm's length. His skin was flushed.

"You know how much I want you. But not like this. There's something wrong. And I know you're not telling me what it is. I care about you too much to let you do something you're going to regret later. When you're ready to trust me . . . when you're ready to let me help you . . . then I won't stop kissing you. Not ever."

He touched her cheek, looked deeply into her eyes. "Do you understand?" he asked her.

Her mind shot ahead to a dozen mini-scenarios of the two of them together—in school, at his house, at prom. Impossibilities collided with daydreams, ignoring the present. For a moment she felt safe.

Then the bell rang, signaling the end of lunch, and the moment ended.

"Trick," she whispered, "I have to go."

"You can be late for class," he insisted. "*Talk* to me."

"I can't be late," she replied as reality came crashing in on her.

She turned and walked away as fast as she could, not daring to look back.

She didn't know how she made it through the rest of her classes. She didn't even remember having been in them by the time she headed to the parking lot after the last one.

Cordelia's truck was idling at the curb; Katelyn walked to it, wanting to collapse with every step she took. The anguish of the past weeks, months, beating down on her.

She climbed in, and as they headed away from the school, Katelyn began to sob hysterically, the fear washing over her anew.

"I know, baby," Cordelia said. "I'm sorry. So sorry."

—◆◆◆—

She didn't know how long they drove; she just sort of came to when Cordelia stopped the car and turned off the engine.

"We're here," she said somberly.

They were deep in the forest. At least, Katelyn thought they were.

"My father lost his temper and ordered me *not* to come

with the pack tonight," Cordelia said. "Which works out great for us *now*, but . . ." Her voice trailed off as she gathered up her hair. "Oh, Kat, he's so mad at me." She sounded despondent, and Katelyn became even more afraid.

"I hate how dark it is," Katelyn said, staring out through the windshield.

"The moon will rise," Cordelia murmured as she collected a green duffel bag from behind the seat. Then they got out and the smells of the forest assaulted Katelyn. The burgundy-velvet and crimson leaves piled beneath the trees looked so soft and inviting she wanted to lie down in them and go to sleep, waking when the nightmare was over.

She followed Cordelia around a couple of dense thickets of trees and came to a clearing. Sunlight filtered through the canopy of leaves. Yellow flowers that looked like lilies and hot pink blossoms grew around the edges; and the grass was still lush and green. Overhead she could see the indigo sky and she marveled at the peace and the silence. She breathed in deeply, wishing she could make it a part of herself.

"Why here?" Katelyn asked.

"It's far from the pack's hunting grounds. We never come here, so I figured we would be safe." She jerked. "Safe from *them*, anyway."

"Thank you. No matter what happens, thank you." Katelyn was still terrified, but she was also intensely grateful to have Cordelia with her, looking out for her.

"You're welcome. Hey, I brought you something to eat," Cordelia said with a bit of cheer. She pulled some foil-wrapped packages and two bottles of sports water from the duffel bag.

"And a blanket. It's going to get cold." The blanket was blue-and-white plaid fringed with darker blue.

"I can't eat anything," Katelyn said, her stomach churning at the thought.

They watched as the sky darkened, and the air began to chill. Night was coming, and with it the moon.

"Now what?" Katelyn asked.

"Now we strip down to our undies."

"Are you kidding me?"

Cordelia smiled faintly. "Whatever clothes you're wearing when it starts, *if* it starts, are going to get shredded. Trust me. I've lost more than one pair of awesome jeans just because I cut it too close."

Reluctantly, Katelyn undressed down to her underwear, feeling terribly cold and exposed. Her teeth chattered together and she hugged herself tight. Cordelia tossed her the blanket to wrap up in, then folded both sets of clothes and put them in the duffel and wrapped herself in a blanket as well.

Call Trick, Katelyn thought. *Tell him to come get you.*

But she couldn't. This was not his battle. This had nothing to do with him.

"What now?" Katelyn asked, shivering harder. Part of her couldn't accept what they were doing, and why. It was like some crazy prank, like being on a silly TV show.

"Now we wait. The sun will set, and the moon will rise. And then we'll know if it's going to happen."

"*How* will I know?" Katelyn said, struggling not to panic.

Cordelia grunted. "If you're going to become like me, trust me, you'll know. You'll think your entire body is on fire. And new werewolves change faster. I can hold my transformation off for a few seconds to verify yours."

Katelyn felt funny. Her skin tingled, but she couldn't tell whether it was from the cold or something else. Her nails seemed longer. She thought of the pictures of Cordelia, her father, and her sisters. They didn't look like monsters. They looked like ordinary wolves.

Katelyn could feel the minutes ticking by.

Cordelia spoke, almost conversationally. "We follow the old Norse ways. We're the descendants of the Fenris Wolf. But Dom's pack follows the Beast." She took a deep breath. "If I ever *did* marry him, I'd have to change my loyalty."

Katelyn had to force herself to pay attention to her—to hear her over the sudden rush of blood in her own ears.

"Maybe it's okay," Cordelia said. Then suddenly her face changed and Katelyn saw panic there.

"Cordelia—" Katelyn blurted as her entire body began to tingle.

"If you're not going to turn, then maybe you should go." She averted her eyes. "If you're not one of us, then . . . then you shouldn't see me change."

"Cordelia—"

"Take my keys to the truck and get the heck out of here."

"Cordelia!" Katelyn shrieked as she fell to her knees. Pain seared through her, unlike anything she'd ever known.

"Something's happening!"

17

"No," Cordelia whispered, sounding heartbroken, and the word echoed through Katelyn's own heart. "I'm so sorry, Kat. I'm sorry."

Katelyn opened her mouth and no words came. White-hot pain seared through her, tracing every nerve in her body. She screamed in agony, but the cry that came out didn't sound like her. It was something else, and she could hear it echoing in her head. Over and over. Louder and louder.

She looked at Cordelia, jaw open, eyes wide in horror, and her face seemed to fragment until all Katelyn saw was a blur of color where her friend had been.

Her vision swam with silver. The light of the moon.

She felt a sharp prick on her lip and realized it was her own teeth growing. She felt her face shifting, elongating. And then the bones in her legs broke and she crashed to the ground. Instantly, the bones knit, but the structure of her legs was horribly wrong, backward, deformed. Her vision cleared suddenly as she tried to push herself up off the dirt, and she saw her fingernails turn into thick yellow-white claws as her hands twisted and grew into paws.

And now the screaming was howling—a raw fury that tore, aching, from her throat.

Cordelia was also changing—her auburn hair darkening to reddish brown. Her face stretched horribly. Her body made terrible cracking noises and a tail sprouted from the small of her back.

And then Katelyn saw movement flashing through the trees. Wolves bounded toward her.

But it didn't matter, because . . . She couldn't remember why. All that mattered . . .

And Katelyn was gone and only the wolf remained.

Pain. Fear. Mind-numbing cold. Katelyn slowly became aware of all these things, followed swiftly by a scratchy sensation under her cheek. She opened her eyes slowly and saw grass and, beyond the grass, a line of pine trees.

There was a blanket on top of her and she realized that beneath it she was naked.

She sat up quickly, pulling the blanket around her. As she blinked in the dim sunlight, her eyes swept the clearing. It looked familiar, like the one they had been in the night before, except this one was filled with people. Naked people, in various stages of waking up. The guys from the driveway. Jesse, curled up like a baby. Arial and Regan, beside their husbands. Lucy, lying on her stomach.

"Hey," Cordelia whispered. She sat nearby, already dressed. There was blood on the sleeve of her sweater. "Kat, you're okay. You're a regular werewolf, like us."

Not a hellhound, Katelyn translated. She stared at Cordelia mutely. At the moment, the difference between hellhound and "regular werewolf" didn't matter to her. She was no longer human.

Katelyn licked her lips and tried to speak. Cordelia put her finger to her mouth to shush her and held out the clothes Katelyn had been wearing the night before. Numb, Katelyn took them. She stared down at her hand. She didn't remember anything past the horrible pain that had wracked her body. Maybe it hadn't happened. Maybe it had been a dream.

"This is the pack," Cordelia whispered.

"They know." And if they knew, Katelyn realized, so did Cordelia's father. "You said it would be just us. You *promised*."

"Someone must have known," Cordelia said. "And brought the others."

Her voice sounded leaden. There was fear and worry in her eyes and it gave Katelyn a horrible, sick feeling in the pit of her stomach.

The others were getting up now, retrieving their clothes from the forest. And there, in the middle of the clearing, a mutilated carcass glistened in the sun.

"Is that a deer?" Katelyn asked, fresh horror creeping through her. Had she helped kill it? Had she eaten it?

"What's left of it," Justin said.

Wearing jeans and a white T-shirt, he stood over her, his expression filled with confusion. She pulled the blanket closer and looked down at her hands again. There was blood under her fingernails.

Katelyn leaned sideways and retched. She was a werewolf. She killed animals. Her body convulsed as she continued to throw up.

She was aware that others were moving, drifting closer. Booted feet planted themselves in front of her face and she looked straight up, into the eyes of Lee Fenner. They were blazing with fury.

She had never been more afraid in her life.

He's going to kill me.

"What did you do?" he whispered, leaning down toward her. He stared at her, hard, every muscle in his body rigid, as if he was preparing to spring. It was so terrifying she couldn't move.

"Daddy, I can explain," Cordelia pleaded, rushing to him.

He ignored Cordelia completely and kept staring down at Katelyn. She tucked her legs up close to her chest and wrapped her arms around them. This was the end, just as Cordelia had warned.

"Hi, Kat, hi!" Jesse cried shrilly from across the meadow. "Kat came to play! We can play tag!"

"Looks like little sis wanted a playmate," Arial purred, leaning her head on her husband's shoulder. The man patted her absently, never tearing his eyes from the unfolding drama.

"No, that's not what happened! I didn't bite her," Cordelia cried.

"If not you, then who? It's forbidden to bite a human. Everyone knows that," Regan said, touching her chest in what was clearly feigned dismay. "Unless the alpha gives you permission. And I don't think he did."

Katelyn's mind raced. *They're going to kill me, and when they find my body, no one will ever know what happened to me.* She thought of Trick and her grandfather, and she began to cry. She tried to push herself up but her muscles had gone slack. All she could do was lie beneath the furious glare of the alpha werewolf of the Fenner pack.

"I don't know who did it," Cordelia said, crossing her arms and keeping her distance from her father. "But there's a wolf who tried to attack her when she first got here. Then it bit her three weeks ago."

Katelyn glanced at Justin and saw raw horror in his eyes when he looked at her.

"Keep talking," Mr. Fenner ordered Cordelia. "Fast."

"I was hoping it was just a normal wolf that did it. But Kat says it—it had blue eyes," she stammered.

That caused a stir throughout the group. Faces turned from Katelyn to each other. They were checking eye color and they looked scared.

"Guess what! Guess what! I have blue eyes," Jesse said. "Justin has blue eyes."

"Yes," Mr. Fenner said, his full attention focused on Cordelia.

Cordelia has blue eyes. Katelyn looked around. How many of them did?

"Daddy, I couldn't believe that anybody would break the

law," Cordelia said. "I wanted to be sure she was a werewolf before I came to you."

Cordelia took a deep breath. "She had a few signs. And I—I was afraid that if I didn't tell her, she'd go to an outsider. But we didn't know if they were the right signs—she had rabies shots after the bite."

"And you didn't come to *me* about it?" Mr. Fenner asked in a low, dangerous voice.

Someone coughed nervously and the wind blew through the trees, causing the branches to dip and bend. Things weren't going well. Katelyn wanted to say something, wanted to defend them both, but instinctively she knew that if she did anything, it would make things worse.

"Daddy, I'm sorry."

"Sorry for doing it, or sorry that you got caught?" Arial said.

Katelyn couldn't hold back any longer. She forced herself to sit upright, holding the blanket around her.

"I could tell that Cordelia knew something about what was happening to me. I made her tell me," Katelyn told Mr. Fenner. "I threatened her—"

"You don't speak unless I tell you to," Mr. Fenner said without even bothering to look at her.

"But—" she protested. Her life was on the line; she had a right to speak.

Without a word, Mr. Fenner charged at her. He grabbed her by the hair and yanked back her head. Fiery pain shot through her scalp and she gasped. A bone in her neck made a cracking sound.

Then he flung her away. She went sprawling. With a roar, he whirled on Cordelia, who covered her mouth with her hands and shook her head.

Mr. Fenner's eyes bulged. "You went behind my back? Told an outsider about us? Thought to hide her possible condition from *me*?" Spittle flew from his mouth.

Shaking, Katelyn looked over at Justin. He was watching everything. He locked gazes with her and gave her a slow, nearly imperceptible nod.

I'm here for you.

Close beside him, Lucy was holding on to Jesse, who had taken her hand and looked scared. Her face was white. Justin put an arm around her.

"I was trying to protect all of us, including her, including you," Cordelia rasped, looking down, her head bowed in submission.

"I do not need protection from you!" he roared.

"Daddy, I'm so sorry. I *am*. I'm so sorry," she pleaded, her voice faltering. "I—you . . . Daddy, I didn't know what to do!"

He stomped toward her. Balling his fists, he pounded the air between Cordelia and him. He shouted like a madman— no words, just shouts. Whirling in a circle, he threw back his head and screamed her name.

"*Cordelia!*"

Everyone drew back, cringing. He was working himself into a rage.

"I didn't want to believe them," he said. "They told me, and I came out here to prove them wrong." He looked over at Arial and Regan, who both pulled sad faces. Regan nodded as if to herself and Arial sighed heavily. Katelyn stared at them in horror. How had they known? She and Cordelia had been so careful. Unless one of them had been the wolf that bit her?

"My girl," he said. "My little girl." He spat on the grass. "You are a *traitor*!"

"Daddy, please! I'm sorry. I—I didn't know what to do, because you've been acting—"

"Cordelia, no," Justin said sharply. Beside him, Lucy began to cry. Something shifted in the group, which had gone utterly silent.

"I expected better of you," Mr. Fenner murmured.

For the first time, Katelyn heard more than anger from him. She heard despair. "I can't look away from something like this. You were my little girl," he said. He hiccupped a sob. "My little girl."

Justin took his arm from around Lucy and stepped forward. Hope flared in Katelyn. Maybe he could make it better.

"Uncle Lee, Cordelia loves you. She's a kid. Kids make mistakes."

"A mistake like this could destroy us," Arial chimed in.

Justin ignored her. "Forgive her. Can't we accept Kat into the pack, regardless of how she came to be?"

"I can marry Lucy," Jesse called out. "Justin can marry Kat."

Lee Fenner's face softened slightly. Jesse bobbed his head, murmuring, "Yeah, yeah. Kat is not a stranger."

"You've got a pair, boy," Mr. Fenner told Justin. "Maybe I should pick *you* to lead this pack when I'm gone."

Justin dipped his head. "You'll be my alpha for a long time yet, Uncle Lee."

Justin walked slowly over to Katelyn and put a hand on her shoulder. "Kat, did you tell anyone else what was happening? Your grandfather? That . . . boy?"

"No," she said. Her voice sounded strange to her own ears. "Cordelia told me not to, and I didn't. I swear it."

Guarded expressions of approval traveled around the group, but Arial's and Regan's faces were stony and unforgiving. Justin gave Katelyn's shoulder a furtive squeeze, and she wanted to grab his hand and beg him to get her out of there, *now*.

Mr. Fenner turned back to Cordelia. "Your cousin makes a good argument for mercy. For *his* sake, I'll show some."

"Oh, Daddy, thank you, thank you," Cordelia said in a rush. "I—"

His face hardened as he cut her off. "Cordelia Lynn Fenner. You were always my choice to succeed me. But you've proven yourself unworthy of the trust I placed in you. I'll spare your life if you leave this pack. If you leave my home and leave my sight and never return, I'll let you live."

Gasps and a few soft cries of protest rose. Cordelia staggered, shock on her face. Katelyn remembered how afraid she'd been when she told her that nothing would be worse than being without a pack.

"What is happening?" Jesse asked, bursting into tears.

Katelyn's heart pounded as she stared at her friend. There had to be something she could do. She glanced back at Arial and Regan. They both looked happy, as if they were finally getting what they wanted. It could easily have been one of them who'd bitten her. If she could only prove that, uncover the guilty—

"Better take off," Mr. Fenner said, his voice flinty.

"But where am I supposed to go?" Cordelia asked in a trembling voice.

"You can go to hell for all I care," he said.

"What about Kat?" she asked. "Please, Daddy, she was *attacked*—"

"Kat's not going anywhere," he said. "Certainly not with *you*."

Cordelia was gray-faced. Her mouth was working but no sound was coming out as she swayed on her feet.

"Kat, you have to come with me!" Cordelia cried. "He'll kill you!"

Justin put a hand on Katelyn's shoulder and she could tell it was a warning. She bit her lower lip to keep herself from screaming. This wasn't right. Someone had *attacked* her and killed Haley and Becky. Cordelia hadn't done anything wrong.

"You say you care about this girl and then you ask her to leave her pack? She'd be dead inside of a year. Is that what you want for her?" Mr. Fenner demanded. "She stays." He glared at Kat. "If you try to go with her, I'll take you both down. Have no doubts. You're one of us now, and she's not."

"Please, Mr. Fenner," Katelyn said, tears streaming down her cheeks. "Please."

"No," he said firmly.

She looked at Cordelia, willing her to understand. *I will find a way to help you.*

"Get out," Mr. Fenner ordered Cordelia.

Wordlessly, she picked up her duffel bag and started in the direction of her truck.

"Oh, Cordelia?" Arial called out.

Cordelia stopped. "What?" she asked without turning.

"You can walk," Regan answered.

"Better yet, run," Mr. Fenner said. "As fast as you can."

Cordelia turned and stared at her father and then at Katelyn.

"You did this to me," Cordelia said. "You went home alone. You got out of your truck. And all I tried to do was help you."

Katelyn opened her mouth to speak, to plead with her friend, but was cut off.

"You did it to yourself," Regan said.

Cordelia held her hands out to her father. "I didn't tell you because you're losing your mi—"

"*Cordelia!*" Justin bellowed. "No!"

"Better go. Better run!" Mr. Fenner shouted at her.

"*You,*" Cordelia said to Katelyn.

And then she ran.

* * *

Katelyn wept as each person, male and female, kissed her cheek in greeting. They told her their names. Myrna, the woman from the driveway. Steve and Daniel Berglund, who told her he had graduated from Wolf Springs High the year before.

"Drive her to the house, Justin," Mr. Fenner said at last. "Her grandfather's not expecting her back until later today. There's a lot we need to hash out."

Justin looked at Lucy, who nodded, then took Jesse's hand. "Come on, darlin'," Lucy said. "We'll drive back together."

"I want to go with Justin," he said, pouting. "I want Cordelia."

"It's going to be okay, Jesse," Lucy said, giving Katelyn a sharp look.

Katelyn followed Justin to Cordelia's truck in a fog. She climbed in as he got behind the wheel, pushing back the seat to give his long legs room. He put the key in the ignition but he didn't start the engine. Katelyn sat in the passenger seat, practically catatonic.

"It would have made things easier if you'd told me," he said finally.

"How?" she managed to say.

His expression was a mixture of shame and amusement. He looked in the rearview mirror and all she saw reflected were his blue eyes. It seemed that everywhere she looked, the werewolves' blue eyes looked back at her—that everyone could have been the one who'd attacked her.

"I couldn't stop myself from kissing you," he said. His voice was low and deep. "I kept thinking about you. Even when I'd think about Lucy, it was you who I'd come back to. And now that I know, it makes sense. You're an unclaimed female."

That might be true now, but it hadn't been that first time, when he'd come to the cabin and they'd gone riding in the woods. She hadn't been attacked yet.

He turned on the truck and slowly guided it out of the clearing. She bit her lower lip and studied the passing trees. So many, closing in on her. Where was Cordelia? Was she running? Would they go after her?

"Someone did this to me," she said quietly. "Cordelia told me—"

"Rule number one. You can't mention her name when you're with the pack, ever," he said. "She's dead to you."

Katelyn looked at him. This was all so crazy, so medieval. This was the real Banjo Land and she hated them.

"But she's not," Katelyn whispered. "You have to help me find her. Because she—"

"Of course I will," he replied.

She stopped and stared at him. That had not been the response she'd expected.

"Kat. Here's something you should know about me. I believe in pack harmony. I believe in honoring our customs and traditions. Lee Fenner is my alpha, and what he says goes. But it was a different world, a different time, when my pack first came to these hills. There weren't cell phones and GPS and public schools and truant officers. For all we know, if Cordelia gets desperate enough, she'll tell our secret."

"She wouldn't," Katelyn insisted.

His face was somber. "She tried to oversee your transformation all by herself. What if something had gone wrong? Good thing her sisters found out and told their father."

"But *how* did they find out?"

"I don't know," he replied. "Cordelia must have slipped up. Maybe they overheard a phone call. What I'm saying is that she could expose all of us, and we'll have to run, too."

Katelyn's pulse quickened. There was so much she didn't know.

"What about what happened to those two girls? What if Cordelia is attacked?" She tried to breathe. Couldn't.

He pulled the truck over. Sunlight washed his face with gold. His body heat radiated toward her. Her heart pounded and she hitched a breath.

"I won't let anything happen to Cordelia," he said.

He leaned toward her and she breathed in. Her senses filled with him.

"Thank you," she whispered.

He lowered his voice. "Like I said, Lee is my alpha. But this is a bad call. Not only is it bad for Cordelia, it's bad for the pack. And I think he'll see that and regret his decision. The pack needs to stick together." He said the last part ominously.

"She was afraid of the Hellhound," she said, wanting to gauge Justin's reaction. "Afraid it would come after us."

He didn't reply, but she saw his expression change.

"There's a lot of scary things in this world," he said, his face so close to hers their noses were practically touching. All she saw were his eyes. She wanted him to kiss her and tell her he would keep her safe. But he did neither. He just . . . looked.

"I can't imagine anything scarier than what just happened to me."

"Give yourself time. You'll be able to think of plenty of things that are scarier."

"Like the Hellhound?" she asked, pushing.

"I don't believe in it," he replied bluntly. "Now I'm going to drive you to our house, and Lee's going to lay down the law. Agree to everything, no matter what. You're on trial, and if he can cast out his own daughter . . ." He left the rest unsaid. "I need to do some damage control. And we need to find out who attacked you."

"Yes. Yes, thank you," she said in a rush. She hadn't expected any of this from him. Had never thought the kind of guy who cheated on his girlfriend would turn out to be so generous. He was putting himself at risk by helping her.

They drove for a few minutes without speaking. She was exhausted but her body was on overdrive. Every fiber of her being urged her to get closer to Justin.

To tempt him.

Then she noticed a speck of blood on his cheek, and while part of her recoiled, another part wanted just as badly to kiss it away.

As they came to the rise above the Fenner house, Justin cleared his throat. His features went rock hard, and the tension in the cab went sky high. Bad tension. Like anger. No, not just anger.

Fury.

"Now here's one more rule," he said coldly, his eyes narrowing. "You need to keep the hell away from me."

18

Katelyn was stunned by what Justin had just said. Keep away from him? It was the last thing she thought he'd say to her.

Her face blazing with humiliation and shock, she ducked her head, looking at her hands, and nodded.

Justin got out of the truck and didn't come around to open the door. He stomped toward the front door, completely ignoring her. She trailed after him, trying to catch up.

He slammed open the door and went inside, not holding that door for her, either.

Katelyn entered the Fenner house, feeling conspicuous and alone. Justin had stood up for her in the meadow, but here? He crossed the room without looking back at her.

Only the family was there, Mr. Fenner seated on a leather sofa and the others in chairs. They'd been waiting for her. The mood was somber and Katelyn wrapped her arms around herself. It was horrible being there without Cordelia. She didn't like these people.

"Jesse, how about you, Albert, and I go for a walk, maybe play some football?" Doug suggested.

Jesse nodded, looking relieved to be leaving. "Justin, do you want to come?"

"No, but you have fun," Justin told his brother.

The three men left the room—quickly, as if they were happy to be going. Arial and Regan sat up a little straighter, bending forward, as if eager to watch the unfolding drama.

Katelyn swallowed hard and tried to pull herself together. Justin took the chair Jesse had vacated and gazed at Katelyn with the cold, expressionless eyes of a stranger. She didn't understand the complete change in his behavior toward her.

Mr. Fenner beckoned her forward.

"There is nothing to be gained now by lying," Mr. Fenner said. His voice was kinder, but he was in command, and she responded to it. At that moment, he was her leader, with all his faculties intact. "Tell me who bit you. Was it *her*?"

Regan and Arial waited breathlessly. She could see how much they wanted it to be Cordelia, and realized that they didn't know. It wasn't them.

"No. I don't know who it was," she said. "Cordelia had so much trouble believing it could be one of yo—"

"Don't mention that name in this house again," Regan snapped.

"It had blue eyes," Justin reminded Mr. Fenner. A bold gesture, since he did, too.

Mr. Fenner crossed his leg at the knee, head tilted forward, as if he were gazing down on her from a great height.

"Run it down for me," he ordered her.

Katelyn recounted the whole story and the others listened intently. Fear and adrenaline rushed through her as she relived it, leaving her shaken at the end.

"There was no full moon that night," Mr. Fenner said.

That caused a stir.

"I assume *she* told you only older, stronger wolves can shift at will without the aid of the full moon. Wolves like me." Mr. Fenner raised his head in a gesture of pride.

"I can't do it yet, and neither can Jesse," Justin explained.

"And neither could *she,*" Mr. Fenner mused. He looked at Arial and Regan.

"Or me," Arial chimed in, obviously eager to clear her name. "I've been trying for months, but nothing yet."

"I've been able to shift at will for about a year," Regan told Katelyn, "but I didn't attack you."

Mr. Fenner's face hardened. "If this was a Fenner, I'll find out who it was and punish him . . . or her . . . according to our laws." He sighed and suddenly looked very old and tired as he leaned back against the sofa. Arial bent over and kissed his cheek.

"There's only been one human we've taken in since I became alpha," he said.

Katelyn said nothing, not wanting him to know Cordelia had told her that, too.

"Regan's husband. We spent a year teaching him what he needed to know before we changed him. Now that the cart's before the horse, we'll have to do the best we can."

"I'll do my best, too," she said. "I promise."

Regan snickered. Arial rolled her eyes.

"We come from a proud bloodline," Mr. Fenner went on. "Several families make up this pack. But our family, the Fenners, are the direct descendants of the Fenris wolf. We have always been the leaders, both in the Old Country and here. We have a history that goes back centuries."

"And enemies we've had just as long," Regan said.

Katelyn ducked her head, but she was listening carefully.

"There are a few rules we follow to maintain order and ensure our survival," Mr. Fenner said. He looked expectantly at the other three werewolves in the room.

"First, we never harm humans," Justin said.

"Second, we never hunt alone," Regan added.

"Third, we always obey our alpha," Arial said.

"Finally, we never reveal our existence to outsiders," Mr. Fenner added. *"Ever."*

And yet whoever had attacked her had broken at least two of those rules.

"What is it?" Justin asked, seeing the expression on her face. She tried to find concern in his voice, but it was unnervingly neutral.

"The night I was bitten wasn't the first time I saw that werewolf. The first time, it didn't hurt me because Tr—a friend chased him off. But that time I could have sworn I heard two wolves growling."

"Did you ever see a second wolf?" Mr. Fenner asked.

"No, though I'm almost positive there were two." She swallowed. "But that's all that happened. That night."

"What about the night you were bitten?" Mr. Fenner asked. "Tell me again."

"I had a flat tire." She stopped. Now her Subaru had a flat. There were an awful lot of flat tires in Wolf Springs. "It charged me and then it chased me. I hit it with a tire iron. On the shoulder."

Mr. Fenner considered. "Have we seen any of our pack with injuries like that?"

Arial and Regan shook their heads.

"Where did it bite you?" Mr. Fenner asked.

"On my calf. I had stitches and everything. But now you can't even tell I was bitten." She touched her shoulder, remembering the claw marks there.

"That's what turned you, for certain," Mr. Fenner said. "Is that when you told *her* about it?"

"Yes. And she thought maybe it was something else, because she just couldn't believe that anybody in your pack would attack a human."

"Something else," Regan said. "What else is there?"

Katelyn cleared her throat. "The Hellhound."

The two sisters began to laugh. Mr. Fenner just shook his head. But Justin looked away.

He lied to me, she realized. *He* is *afraid of it.* That frightened her even more.

Then Mr. Fenner stood.

"If you breathe a word of this, you are dead, and I mean

that. So is your grandfather. We can make it look like an accident, and we will."

She felt as though he had just thrown her into a frozen river. Chills rushed down her spine, and her heart thudded.

"I won't say anything," she assured him. She took a deep breath. "But my grandfather is expecting me soon."

He scowled. "Damned inconvenient."

She swallowed hard. "I-I'll call him if you want. I can say Cordelia invited me to stay another night—"

"Don't say that name!" Mr. Fenner roared.

"How are we ever going to make this work?" Arial moaned.

"That's not your business. That's my business," Mr. Fenner snapped. He looked at Katelyn. "Can you behave yourself if I let you go?"

Regan made a face. "Daddy, are you sure—"

"What did I just say to your sister?" he yelled at her. She held up her hands in a gesture of innocence and cleared her throat.

"Sorry, Daddy."

"Take her home," Mr. Fenner said to Justin.

Justin pulled a ring of keys out of his pocket and headed for the door. Afraid to look at Mr. Fenner, in case she did or said something to make him change his mind, Katelyn turned and followed him without a word. She couldn't wait to be out of there.

"I'll be sure to let Lucy know you'll be missing . . . dinner," Arial called after him.

"Bitch," Justin muttered. But they were far enough out the door that only Katelyn heard it.

Outside, the air was crisp; pines swayed in the gusty wind. "We'll take the truck," Justin said, opening the passenger door of Cordelia's truck. She was hyperaware of him, tensing when, this time, he wrapped his hand around her forearm to help her climb inside.

"Thank you," she said, easing onto the seat and dropping her hands to her lap to break contact. "I feel like I've been up all night."

"You have," he said shortly.

She flushed. "That's right. My new double life."

"Don't worry. You'll get used to it." He slammed the door.

What if I don't want to get used to it? she thought.

He went around to the driver's side and slid behind the wheel, shutting the door and putting the keys in the ignition. He started the engine and backed the truck up the driveway, then eased out onto the road.

She tried to look past him to catch a glimpse of the house, wondering what was going on in there—if they were talking about her, if Mr. Fenner was having second thoughts about kicking Cordelia out of the pack. She swallowed. Cordelia blamed her, probably hated her.

The truck picked up speed, leaving the Fenner house behind. Katelyn reached out a hand toward Justin, then quickly pulled it back. She was bewildered by the change in him. More than that, she was afraid of him. But she had to put that fear aside. She had to try to help her friend.

"Justin, don't take me straight home," she said. "Let's look for Cordelia. While she's still close."

He didn't answer.

She leaned away from him as the truck bounced along the unpaved road. Peering into the darkness, she searched the trees for her friend, not really expecting to find her this close to the house. She imagined her fighting her way through dense forest, lost, alone. The tears came, and she cried softly. Justin remained silent.

Then her cell phone rang. She caught her breath and slid it out of her pocket. Disappointment rushed through her when she saw that the call was from her grandfather. She shook her head at Justin, who had glanced at her and raised a brow.

"It's my grandfather."

"Kat, your and your grandfather's lives depend on how convincingly you can lie to him, and keep lying," Justin reminded her. He sounded as if he was going to be the judge of her performance, and she wondered if he was supposed to report back to Mr. Fenner about how well she did.

She licked her lips and nodded, then took the call.

"Hi, Grandpa," she began. "I'm on my way home."

"Okay, honey. But listen, we've had a little trouble here."

Her heart skipped a beat. "What? What happened?" she asked, looking over at Justin. He raised a brow again.

"I'm fine. But we've had a break-in. Someone jimmied the back door while I was in town last night. I got Officer Patrick here. And Trick."

"Trick?" she said. Her stomach did a flip. Justin cocked his head, looking curious and a little impatient. She cupped the phone. "Someone broke into our cabin," she murmured to him. Then, into the phone, she said, "Why is Trick there?"

"He came by with a late birthday present for you. Something he made. Looks like only a couple of things were taken. Grandma's sterling silver carving set and a couple of pictures off the wall. Patrick thinks it was kids." He huffed. "I had the silver out to polish it up for Thanksgiving dinner. Hold on."

There was silence for a moment.

"Hey, Kat." It was Trick. "Your grandpa's okay."

She exhaled deeply, her body beginning to tremble from the intensity of her pent-up emotion. "Thank you, Trick." Her voice caught on his name.

"I'm sure it was the same clowns who got me in trouble in the first place," Trick went on. "This time I'm in the clear."

"That's good." She could hear how strained and odd she sounded. Justin was glaring at her. She had to do better.

"I just thought you'd like to know," Trick said, clearly puzzled by her muted response.

"Yeah. I'm glad." She tried to clear her throat. Failed.

"See you soon," he added.

Katelyn disconnected and stared at the phone. Justin turned his attention to her.

"They think some kids did it," she said, aware that she was babbling. "They took some pictures and a silver carving set."

"Silver." He made a face. "Did Cordelia at least warn you about that?"

She nodded. "Justin, please," she began, then pressed her fingertips against her forehead as she fought for composure. "Please, don't be so hard on her. Everybody seems to be forgetting that a werewolf attacked me and bit me. And that two girls are dead."

"You're wrong." His face hardened, and he clenched his jaw. "No one's forgotten. And when we find out who did it . . ." His voice was low and dangerous, and it unnerved her. She would never want Justin to be angry with her.

Justin pulled off the paved road and drove into the dark forest, where all this had begun. Katelyn glanced over at Justin as she recognized the route Cordelia had taken the night before, to the meadow. She rolled down the window. And as if on cue, drumming and howls echoed off the trees. Justin groaned aloud.

"That moron," he said, rolling his eyes. "We need him gone."

Then they reached the meadow, and Justin turned off the engine. Sunlight streamed into the clearing. The deer carcass was gone.

He got out; Katelyn did, too, and she joined him as he raised his chin, sniffing the air. She smelled dirt and tree bark, the coppery tang of blood, human sweat, soaps, and shampoos.

"Come on," he told her. They moved together from the meadow to the trees, deep into the underbrush. Katelyn breathed in a thousand more odors. The drumming and the howls grew louder, more impassioned. They matched her thundering heartbeat.

Heat washed over her face as she sniffed the area, and the drums and the howls echoed off the darkness of the deep woods, giving voice to her fears. She strained her eyes, staring into the shadows, searching for her friend.

They pushed deeper into the woods. Fear fell over her like

a shroud, and she looked around anxiously. A leaf jittered, then broke from a branch and sailed downward like a tiny bat. Below the drumming, she heard something moving along the forest floor. The trees swayed. Goose bumps rose along her arms. She was suddenly cold. She kept going, kept straining her eyes to make out something, anything, that would tell her where Cordelia had gone. Smells rose, still too many to be helpful.

From a distance away, Justin said, "Time's up. Lee will be expecting me back."

"No. We can't give up yet," she begged, raising her voice so he would be able to hear her. She couldn't see him anywhere. "Please, Justin."

"As long as you're in the pack, you have to do what he wants."

"No," she whispered, heartbroken, turning in a tiny circle. "Cordelia, please, if you can hear me, *please* answer me."

Then the forest seemed to whirl around her, spinning. Dizzy, she balled her hands against her chest and stopped moving. The forest blurred around her and the voice overwhelmed her.

Katelyn.

I shall do thee mischief in the woods.

"Justin?" she whispered, barely able to get the word out. She was rooted to the spot in fear. Something was in the woods with her. With them. It was creeping toward her. She felt it, knew it with every fiber of her being. And she knew it was dangerous.

"Justin!" Her voice tore out of her, raw and terrified.

You are marked.

You are mine.

"There's something, there's . . . Justin!" she cried. "Justin, help!"

It was coming from the left. She sensed it. She bolted to the right, pushing through a net of tree branches. Then she ran into something hard, and the impact made her stagger backward a few steps. Her ankle twisted and she lost her balance, swaying left, right, as if she were drunk. Her legs gave way and she fell onto something jagged and sharp. It cut into her right forearm, and she screamed.

"Kat!" Justin shouted.

There was crashing through the underbrush. It was Justin, bursting from among the branches. There was a scratch on his forehead and she smelled his blood.

She clutched her arm. "Something cut me," she said.

"Get away!" he bellowed. "Silver!"

Then she looked down at what had cut her. It was a black thing that looked like a huge open mouth, with large pointed teeth. She'd never seen an animal trap in her life, but she had seen pictures. It was open and she had fallen onto some of the teeth.

"Kat, that thing's made out of silver," Justin said in a careful, flat voice. He looked sick. "I can smell it."

She whimpered. "It—it broke the skin."

She tried to get up, but her ankle seized. Justin darted forward and took her other arm, then wrapped his free hand around her waist. Her ankle gave way and he caught her, holding her against his chest tightly.

"No," he murmured. "No." Then he bent down and scooped her up in his arms. She put her arms around his neck, clinging to him, tears welling.

"Am I . . . am I going to die?" she asked.

He didn't say anything. With her in his arms, he pushed through the forest like a madman, then exploded into the clearing. He kept going, grim-faced, single-minded, racing for his truck. Katelyn saw the deep cut in her arm. Her blood was soaking into his white T-shirt.

Then he tripped on something and fell. She tumbled out of his arms, landing hard. With a cry, he scrambled over to her, gathered her up. There were streaks of sweat and blood on his cheeks.

"Damn it," he grunted. "Damn it to hell."

"How long does it take?" she asked in a tiny voice.

He froze. Then he looked at her. "Not this long," he said slowly. "You should be unconscious by now. At least."

Struggling to catch her breath, she returned his gaze. "But . . . I'm not. The cuts hurt, but . . . I feel okay." At his bewildered expression, she added, "Are you sure it was silver? Who would put out an animal trap made of silver?"

"Someone who wants to catch werewolves," he answered, staring wide-eyed at her. "But . . . I saw you change, Kat. I *know* you're a werewolf. So you can't be immune to silver."

He got up and opened the truck door, then helped her to her feet and into the cab.

"I think I might be," she replied shakily. "I might be immune."

He stared at her in amazement, then examined her arm.

He grimaced and looked back up at her. "What *are* you?" he breathed.

They locked gazes, and she trembled from head to toe.

"Don't tell anybody about this until I figure it out." He wiped his face with his bloody T-shirt. "It changes everything."

ACKNOWLEDGMENTS

First and foremost, thank you, Debbie, for seeing the big picture and planting the seed, and for all the love and care you lavish not only on our books but on me and mine. You're my pack mate, Deb, and always will be. To our wonderful editor, Krista Marino, we are so grateful for your excellent editorial vision and continued support of our work. As always, thank you to our fabulous agent, Howard Morhaim, and the unbeatable home team at Morhaim Literary— Kate McKean and Katie Menick—as well as to our international agents, Caspian Dennis and Danny and Heather Baror. Thank you to my sweet Chumash Woman, aka Belle, my coauthor, author tour escort extraordinaire, and all-around best daughter. My gratitude to Debbie's husband, Dr. Scott Viguié, whose unfailing patience and good humor served us so well. And a shout-out to the California Wolf Center for your amazing work with gray wolves. Congratulations on the two new pups!   —Nancy

Thank you to my wonderful coauthor, Nancy, for her support and friendship and amazing research skills! Thank you to her beautiful daughter, Belle, for all her enthusiasm and support. Thank you to my amazing agent, Howard Morhaim, and the equally amazing Kate McKean and Katie Menick, who work tirelessly on our behalf. I'd like to thank those friends and family who always offer me their undying support. And I would also like to thank all the volunteers the world over who work with wolves, ensuring their health and safety in the wild and in captivity. Your efforts on behalf of those magnificent animals are greatly appreciated.   —Debbie

About the Authors

NANCY HOLDER has published more than seventy-eight books and more than two hundred short stories. She has received four Bram Stoker Awards for her supernatural fiction and is the co-author of the *New York Times* bestselling Wicked series. She lives in San Diego with her daughter. You can visit her at nancyholder.com.

DEBBIE VIGUIÉ is the coauthor of the *New York Times* best-selling Wicked series and several other books, including the Once Upon a Time novels *Violet Eyes* and *Midnight Pearls*. She lives in Florida with her husband. You can visit her at debbieviguie.com.